READ HER ONCE
AND FALL IN LOVE.

lock & key

dreamland

what happened
to goodbye

that summer

along for the ride

this lullaby

just listen

keeping the moon

the truth
about forever

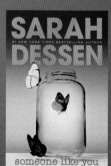

someone like you

Best friends

"Scarlett?" I said, there in the dark, and as she turned to me I saw her face was streaked with tears. For a minute, I didn't know what to do. I thought again of that picture tucked in her mirror, of her and Michael just weeks ago, the water so bright and shiny behind them. And I thought of what she had done all the millions of times I'd cried to her, collapsing at even the slightest wounding of my heart or pride.

So I reached over and pulled her to me, wrapping my arms around her, and held my best friend close, returning so many favors all at once. . . .

Novels by
SARAH DESSEN

SARAH DESSEN

someone like you

speak
An Imprint of Penguin Group (USA) Inc.

I would like to gratefully acknowledge my agent, Leigh Feldman, and my editor, Sharyn November, for their help, humor, and determination in seeing this book to publication. Thank you.

SPEAK
Published by the Penguin Group
Penguin Group (USA) Inc., 345 Hudson Street, New York, New York 10014, U.S.A.
Penguin Group (Canada), 90 Eglinton Avenue East, Suite 700,
Toronto, Ontario, Canada M4P 2Y3 (a division of Pearson Penguin Canada Inc.)
Penguin Books Ltd, 80 Strand, London WC2R 0RL, England
Penguin Ireland, 25 St Stephen's Green, Dublin 2, Ireland (a division of Penguin Books Ltd)
Penguin Group (Australia), 250 Camberwell Road, Camberwell, Victoria 3124, Australia
(a division of Pearson Australia Group Pty Ltd)
Penguin Books India Pvt Ltd, 11 Community Centre,
Panchsheel Park, New Delhi - 110 017, India
Penguin Group (NZ), 67 Apollo Drive, Rosedale, Auckland 0632, New Zealand
(a division of Pearson New Zealand Ltd)
Penguin Books (South Africa) (Pty) Ltd, 24 Sturdee Avenue,
Rosebank, Johannesburg 2196, South Africa

Penguin Books Ltd, Registered Offices: 80 Strand, London WC2R 0RL, England

First published in the United States of America by Viking,
a member of Penguin Putnam Inc., 1998
Published by Puffin Books, a division of Penguin Putnam Books for Young Readers, 2000
Published by Speak, an imprint of Penguin Group (USA) Inc., 2004, 2012

28 30 29

THE LIBRARY OF CONGRESS HAS CATALOGED THE VIKING EDITION AS FOLLOWS:
Dessen, Sarah.
Someone like you / by Sarah Dessen.
p. cm.
Summary: Halley's junior year of high school includes the death of her
best friend Scarlett's boyfriend, the discovery that Scarlett is pregnant,
and Halley's own first serious relationship.
ISBN 0-670-87778-6
[1. Pregnancy—Fiction. 2. Unmarried mothers—Fiction. 3. Friendship—Fiction.] I. Title.
PZ7.D455 So 1998 [Fic]—dc21 97-36437 CIP AC

Speak ISBN 978-0-14-240177-4

Set in Meridien

Printed in the United States of America

this one is for Bianca

Part I

THE GRAND CANYON

Chapter One

Scarlett Thomas has been my best friend for as long as I can remember. That's why I knew when she called me at Sisterhood Camp, during the worst week of my life, that something was wrong even before she said it. Just by her voice on the other end of the line. I knew.

"It's Michael," she said quietly. Her words crackled over distance. "Michael Sherwood."

"What about him?" The camp director, a woman named Ruth with short hair and Birkenstocks, shifted impatiently beside me. At Sisterhood Camp, we were supposed to be Isolated from the Pressures of Society in order to Improve Ourselves as Women. We weren't supposed to get phone calls. Especially not at midnight on a Tuesday, rousing you out of your creaky camp bed and through the woods to a room too bright and a phone that weighed heavily in your hand.

Scarlett sighed. Something was up. "What about him?" I repeated. The camp director rolled her eyes this time, thinking, I was sure, that this was no emergency.

"He's dead." Scarlett's voice was flat, even, as if she were

3

reciting multiplication tables. I could hear clinking and splashing in the background.

"Dead?" I said. The camp director looked up, suddenly concerned, and I turned away. "How?"

"A motorcycle accident. This afternoon. He got hit by a car on Shortcrest." More splashing, and suddenly I realized she was washing dishes. Scarlett, always capable, would do housework during a nuclear holocaust.

"He's dead," I repeated, and the room seemed very small suddenly, cramped, and as the camp director put her arm around me I shook her off, stepping away. I pictured Scarlett at the sink in cutoffs and a T-shirt, her hair pulled back in a ponytail, phone cocked between her ear and shoulder. "Oh, my God."

"I know," Scarlett said, and there was a great gurgling noise as water whooshed down her sink. She wasn't crying. "I know."

We sat there on the line for what seemed like the longest time, the buzzing in the background the only sound. I wanted to crawl through the phone right then, popping out on the other side in her kitchen, beside her. Michael Sherwood, a boy we'd grown up with, a boy one of us had loved. Gone.

"Halley?" she said softly, suddenly.

"Yeah?"

"Can you come home?"

I looked out the window at the dark and the lake beyond, the moon shimmering off of it. It was the end of August, the end of summer. School started in one week; we'd be juniors this year.

"Halley?" she said again, and I knew it was hard for her to even ask. She'd never been the one who needed me.

"Hold on," I said to her in that bright room, the night it all began. "I'm on my way."

Michael Alex Sherwood died at 8:55 P.M. on August thirteenth. He was turning left onto Morrisville Avenue from Shortcrest Drive when a businessman in a BMW hit him dead on, knocking him off the motorcycle he'd only had since June and sending him flying twenty feet. The paper said he died on impact, the bike a total loss. It wasn't his fault. Michael Sherwood was sixteen years old.

He was also the only boy Scarlett had ever truly loved. We'd known him since we were kids, almost as long as we'd known each other. Lakeview, our neighborhood, sprawled across several streets and cul-de-sacs, bracketed only by wooden posts and hand-carved signs, lined in yellow paint: *Welcome to Lakeview—A Neighborhood of Friends.* One year some high-school students had gone around and crossed out the *r*s in *Friends,* leaving us a *Neighborhood of Fiends,* something my father found absolutely hysterical. It tickled him so much, my mother often wondered aloud if he'd done it himself.

The other distinguishing characteristic of Lakeview was the new airport three miles away, which meant a constant stream of airplanes taking off and landing. My father loved this, too; he spent most evenings out on the back porch, looking up excitedly at the sky as the distant rumblings got louder and louder, closer and closer, until the white nose of a plane would burst out overhead, lights blinking, seeming powerful and loud enough to sweep us all along with it. It drove our neighbor Mr. Kramer to high blood pressure, but my father reveled in it. To me, it was something normal. I hardly stirred, even when I slept, as the glass in my windows shook with the house.

The first time I saw Scarlett was the day she and her mother, Marion, moved in. I was eleven. I was sitting by my window, watching the movers, when I saw a girl just my age, with red hair and blue tennis shoes. She was sitting on the front steps of her new house, watching them cart furniture in, her elbows propped on her knees, chin in her hands, wearing heart-shaped sunglasses with white plastic frames. And she completely ignored me as I came up her front walk, stood in the thrown shade of the awning, and waited for her to say something. I'd never been good at friendships; I was too quiet, too mousy, and tended to choose bossy, mean girls who pushed me around and sent me home crying to my mother. Lakeview, *A Neighborhood of Fiends*, was full of little fiendettes on pink bicycles with Barbie carrying cases in their white, flower-appliquéd baskets. I'd never had a best friend.

So I walked up to this new girl, her sunglasses sending my own reflection back at me: white T-shirt, blue shorts, scuffed Keds with pink socks. And I waited for her to laugh at me or send me away or maybe just ignore me like all the bigger girls did.

"Scarlett?" a woman's voice came from inside the screen door, sounding tired and flustered. "What did I do with my checkbook?"

The girl on the steps turned her head. "On the kitchen counter," she called out in a clear voice. "In the box with the realtor's stuff."

"The box with—" The voice came back, uneven, as if its owner was moving around. "—the realtor's stuff, hmmm, honey I don't think it's here. Oh, wait. Yes. Here it is!" The woman sounded triumphant, as if she'd discovered the Northwest Passage, which we'd just learned about at the end of the school year.

The girl turned back and looked at me, kind of shaking her head. I remember thinking for the first time how she seemed old for her age, older than me. And I got that familiar fiendette pink-bicycle feeling.

"Hey," she said to me suddenly, just as I was planning to turn back and head home. "My name's Scarlett."

"I'm Halley," I said, trying to sound as bold as she had. I'd never had a friend with an unusual name; all the girls in my classes were Lisas and Tammys, Carolines and Kimberlys. "I live over there." I pointed across the street, right to my bedroom window.

She nodded, then picked up her purse and scooted down a bit on the step, brushing it off with her hand and leaving just enough space for someone else about the same size. And then she looked at me and smiled, and I crossed that short expanse of summer grass and sat beside her, facing my house. We didn't talk right away, but that was okay; we had a whole lifetime of talking ahead of us. I just sat there with her, staring across the street at my house, my garage, my father pushing the mower past the rosebushes. All the things I'd spent my life learning by heart. But now, I had Scarlett. And from that day on, nothing ever looked the same.

The minute I hung up with Scarlett, I called my mother. She was a therapist, an expert on adolescent behavior. But even with her two books, dozens of seminars, and appearances on local talk shows advising parents on how to handle The Difficult Years, my mother hadn't quite found the solution for dealing with me.

It was 1:15 A.M. when I called.

"Hello?" Strangely, my mother sounded wide awake. It was all part of that professional manner she cultivated: *I'm capable. I'm strong. I'm awake.*

"Mom?"

"Halley? What's wrong?" There was some mumbling in the background; my father, rousing himself.

"It's Michael Sherwood, Mom."

"Who?"

"He's dead."

"Who's dead?" More mumbling, this time louder. My father saying *Who's dead? Who?*

"Michael Sherwood," I said. "My friend."

"Oh, goodness." She sighed, and I heard her telling my father to go back to sleep, her hand cupping the receiver. "Honey, I know, it's horrible. It's awfully late—where are you calling from?"

"The camp office," I said. "I need you to come get me."

"Get you?" she said. She sounded surprised. "You've still got another week, Halley."

"I know, but I want to come home."

"Honey, you're tired, it's late—" and now she was lapsing into her therapist voice, a change I could recognize after all these years—"why don't you call me back tomorrow, when you've had a chance to calm down. You don't want to leave camp early."

"Mom, he's *dead*," I said again. Each time I said the word Ruth, the camp director who was still standing beside me, put on her soothing face.

"I know, sweetie. It's awful. But coming home isn't going to change that. It will just disrupt your summer, and there's no point—"

"I want to come home," I said, talking over her. "I need to come home. Scarlett called to tell me. She needs me." My throat was swelling up now, hurting with its ache. She didn't understand. She never understood.

9

"Scarlett has her mother, Halley. She'll be fine. Honey, it's so late. Are you with someone? Is your counselor there?"

I took a deep breath, and all I could see in my mind was Michael, a boy I hardly knew, whose death now seemed to mean everything. I thought of Scarlett in her bright kitchen, waiting for me. This was crucial.

"Please," I whispered over the line, hiding my face from Ruth, not wanting this strange woman to feel any sorrier for me. "Please come get me."

"Halley." She sounded tired now, almost irritated. "Go to sleep and I'll call you tomorrow. We can discuss it then."

"Say you'll come," I said, not wanting her to hang up. "Just say you'll come. He was our *friend*, Mom."

She was quiet then, and I could picture her sitting in bed next to the sleeping form of my father, probably in her blue nightgown, the light from Scarlett's kitchen visible from the window over her shoulder. "Oh, Halley," she said as if I always caused these kinds of problems; as if my friends died every day. "All right. I'll come."

"You will?"

"I just said I would," she told me, and I knew this would strain us even further, a battle hard-won. "Let me talk to your counselor."

"Okay." I looked over at Ruth, who was close to dozing off. "Mom?"

"Yes."

"Thanks."

Silence. I would pay for this one for a while, I could tell. "It's all right. Let me talk to her."

So I handed the phone over to Ruth, then stood outside the door listening as she reassured my mother that it was fine, I'd be packed and ready, and what a shame, how awful, so young. Then I went back to my cabin, creeping onto my cot in the dark, and closed my eyes.

I couldn't sleep for a long time. I thought only of Michael Sherwood's face, the one I'd cast sideways glances at through middle school, the one Scarlett and I had studied in yearbook after yearbook. And later, the one in the picture that was tucked in the mirror in her bedroom, of Scarlett and Michael at the lake just weeks earlier, water glittering behind them. The way her head rested on his shoulder, his hand on her knee. The way he looked at her, and not at the camera, when I pushed the red button, the flash lighting them up in front of me.

My mother didn't look very happy when she pulled up at the front office the next afternoon. It was clear by this point that my experience at Sisterhood Camp had been a complete and utter disaster. Which was just what I'd predicted when I was dragged off against my will to spend the last two weeks of summer in the middle of the mountains with a bunch of other girls who had no say in the matter either. Sisterhood Camp, which was really called Camp Believe (my father coined the nickname), was something my mother had heard about at one of her seminars. She had come home with a brochure she tucked under my breakfast plate one morning, a yellow sticky note on

11

it saying *What do you think?* My first reaction was *Not much, thank you,* as I stared down at the picture of two girls about my age running through a field together hand in hand. The basic gist was this: a camp with the usual swimming and horseback riding and lanyard making, but in the afternoons seminars and self-help groups on "Like Mother, Like Me" and "Peer Pressure: Where Do I Fit In?" There was a whole paragraph on self-esteem and values maintenance and other words I recognized only from the blurbs on the back of my mother's own books. All I knew was that at fifteen, with my driver's license less than three months away, I was too old for camp or values mainte-nance, not to mention lanyards.

"It will be such a valuable experience," she said to me that evening over dinner. "Much more so than sitting around the pool at Scarlett's getting a tan and talking about boys."

"Mom, it's summer," I said. "And anyway it's almost over. School starts in two weeks."

"You'll be back just in time for school," she said, flipping through the brochure again.

"I have a job," I told her, my last-ditch attempt at an excuse. Scarlett and I were both cashiers at Milton's Market, the gro-cery store at the mall down the street from our neighborhood. "I can't just take two weeks off."

"Mr. Averby says it's slow enough that he can get your shifts covered," she said simply.

"You called Mr. Averby?" I put down my fork. My father, who up until this point had been eating quietly and staying out of it, shot her a look. Even he knew how uncool it was for your mother to call your boss. "*God*, Mom."

"I just wanted to know if it was possible," she said, more to my father than me, but he just shook his head mildly and kept eating. "I knew she'd think of every reason not to go."

"Why should I go waste the last two weeks of summer with a bunch of people I don't know?" I said. "Scarlett and I have plans, Mom. We're working extra shifts to make money for the beach, and we—"

"Halley." She was getting irritated now. "Scarlett will be here when you get back. And I don't ask very much of you, right? This is something I really want you to do. For me, and also, I think you'll find, for yourself. It's only for two weeks."

"I don't want to go," I said, looking at my father for some kind of support, but he just smiled at me apologetically and said nothing, helping himself to more bread. He never got involved anymore; his job was to placate, to smooth, once it was all over. My father was always the one who crept to my doorway after I'd been grounded, sneaking me one of his special Brain Freeze Chocolate Milkshakes, which he believed could solve any problem. After the yelling and slamming of doors, after my mother and I stalked to our separate corners, I could always count on hearing the whirring of the blender in the kitchen, and then him appearing at my doorway presenting me with the thickest, coldest milkshake as a peace offering. But all the milkshakes in the world weren't going to get me out of this.

So, just like that, I lost the end of my summer. By that Sunday I was packed and riding three hours into the mountains with my mother, who spend the entire ride reminiscing about her own golden camp years and promising me I'd thank her when it was over. She dropped me at the registration desk, kissed me on the forehead and told me she loved me, then drove off waving into the sunset. I stood there with my duffel bag and glowered after her, surrounded by a bunch of other girls who clearly didn't want to spend two weeks "bonding" either.

I was on what they called "scholarship" at Sisterhood Camp, which meant I had my way paid free, just like the four other girls I met whose parents just happened to be therapists. I made friends with my cabinmates, and we complained to each other, mocked all the seminar leaders, and worked on our tans, talking about boys.

But now I was leaving early, drawn home by the loss of a boy I'd hardly known. I put my stuff in the trunk of the car and climbed in beside my mother, who said hello and then not much else for the first fifteen minutes of the drive. As far as I was concerned, we'd come to a draw: I hadn't wanted to come, and she didn't want me to leave. We were even. But I knew my mother wouldn't see it that way. Lately, we didn't seem to see anything the same.

"So how was it?" she asked me once we got on the highway. She'd set the cruise control, adjusted the air-conditioning, and now seemed ready to make peace. "Or what you saw of it, that is."

"It was okay," I said. "The seminars were kind of boring."

"Hmm," she said, and I figured that I was pushing it. I knew my mother, though. She'd push back. "Well, maybe if you'd stayed the whole time you might have gotten more out of it."

"Maybe," I said. In the side mirror, I could see the mountains retreating behind us, bit by bit.

I knew there were a lot of things she probably wanted to say to me. Maybe she wanted to ask me why I cared about Michael Sherwood, since she'd hardly heard me mention him. Or why I'd hated the idea of camp right from the start, without even giving it a chance. Or maybe it was more, like why in just the last few months even the sight of her coming toward me was enough to get my guard up. Why we'd gone from best friends to something neither of us could rightly define. But she didn't say anything.

"Mom?"

She turned to look at me, and I could almost hear her take a breath, readying herself for whatever I might try next. "Yes?"

"Thanks for letting me come home."

She turned back to the road. "It's all right, Halley," she said to me softly as I leaned back in my seat. "It's all right."

My mother and I had always been close. She knew everything about me, from the boys I liked to the girls I envied; after school I always sat in the kitchen eating my snack and doing homework while I listened for her car to pull up. I always had something to tell her. After my first school dance she sat with me eating ice cream out of the carton while I detailed every single thing that had happened from first song to last. On Saturdays, when my dad pulled morning shift at the radio station, we had Girls' Lunch Out so we could keep up with each other. She loved fancy pasta places, and I only liked fast food and pizza, so we alternated. She made me eat snails, and I watched her gulp down (enjoying it more than she ever would admit) countless Big Macs. We had one rule: we always ordered two desserts and shared. Afterwards we'd hit the mall looking for sales, competing to see who could find the best bargain. She usually won.

She wrote articles in journals and magazines about our successful relationship and how we'd weathered my first year of high school together, and spoke at schools and parents' meetings about Staying in Touch with Your Teen. Whenever her friends came over for coffee and complained about their kids running wild or doing drugs, she'd just shake her head when they asked how she and I did so well.

"I don't know," she'd say. "Halley and I are just so close. We talk about *everything*."

But suddenly, at the beginning of that summer, something changed. I can't say when it started exactly. But it happened after the Grand Canyon.

Each summer, my parents and I took a vacation. It was our big splurge of the year, and we always went someplace cool like Mexico or Europe. This year, we took a cross-country road trip to California and then the Grand Canyon, stopping here and there, sucking up scenery and visiting relatives. My mother and I had a great time; my father did most of the driving, and the two of us hung out, talking and listening to the radio, sharing clothes, making up songs and jokes as state lines and landmarks passed by. My father and I forced her to eat fast food almost every day as payback for a year's worth of arugula salad and prosciutto tortellini. We spent two weeks together, bickering sometimes but mostly just having fun, me and my parents, on the road.

As soon as I got home, though, three very big things happened. First, I started my job at Milton's. Scarlett and I had spent the end of the school year going around filling out applications, and it was the only place with enough positions to hire us both. By the time I got home from the trip, Scarlett had already been there two weeks, so she taught me the ropes. Second, she introduced me to Ginny Tabor, whom she'd met at the pool while I'd been gone. Ginny was a cheerleader with a wild streak a mile wide and a reputation among the football team for more than her cheers and famous midair splits. She lived a few miles away in the Arbors, a fancy development of Tudor houses with a country club, pool, and golf course. Ginny Tabor's father was a dentist, and her mother weighed about eighty pounds, chain-smoked Benson and Hedges 100's, and had skin that was as leathery as the ottoman in our living room. She threw money at Ginny and left us alone to prowl the streets of the Arbors on our way to the pool, or sneak out across the golf course at night to meet boys.

17

Which, in turn, led to the third big event that summer, when two weeks after coming home I broke off my dull, one-year romance with Noah Vaughn.

Noah was my first "boyfriend," which meant we called each other on the phone and kissed sometimes. He was tall and skinny, with thick black hair and a bit of acne. His parents were best friends with mine, and we'd spent Friday night together, at our house or theirs, for most of my lifetime. He'd been all right for a start. But when I was inducted into the new crazy world of Ginny Tabor, he had to go.

He didn't take it well. He sulked around, glowered at me, and still came over every Friday with his little sister and his parents, sitting stony-faced on the couch as I slipped out the door, yelling good-bye. I always said I was going to Scarlett's, but instead we were usually meeting boys at the pool or hanging out with Ginny. My mother was more sad about our breakup than anyone; I think she'd half expected I'd marry him. But this was the New Me, someone I was evolving into with every hot and humid long summer day. I learned to smoke cigarettes, drank my first beer, got a deep tan, and double-pierced my ears as I began to drift, almost imperceptibly at first, from my mother.

There's a picture on our mantel that always reminds me of what my mother and I were then. We're at the Grand Canyon, at one of those overlook sites, with it spread out huge and gaping behind us. We have on matching T-shirts, sunglasses, and big smiles as we pose, arms around each other. We have never, in any picture before or since, looked more alike. We have the same small nose, the same stance, the same goofy smile. We look happy, standing there in the sunshine, the sky spread out blue and forever in the distance. My mother framed that picture when we got home, sticking it front and center on the mantel where you couldn't help but see it. It was like she knew, somehow, that it would be a relic just months later, proof of another time and place neither of us could imagine had existed: my mother and I, best friends, posing at the Grand Canyon.

Scarlett was sitting on her front steps when we pulled up. It was early evening, just getting dark, and all up and down our street, lights were on in the houses, people out walking their dogs or children. Someone a few streets over was barbecuing, the smell mingling in the air with cut grass and recent rain.

I got out of the car and put my bag on the front walk, looking across the street at Scarlett's house, the only light coming from her kitchen and spilling out into the empty carport. She lifted one hand and waved at me from the stoop.

"Mom, I'm going to Scarlett's," I said.

"Fine." I still wasn't totally forgiven for this, not yet. But it was late, she was tired, and these days, we had to pick our battles.

I knew the way across the street and up Scarlett's walk by heart; I could have done it with every sense lost. The dip in the street halfway across, the two prickly bushes on either end of her walk that left tiny scratches on your skin when you brushed against them. It was eighteen steps from the beginning of the walk to the front stoop; we'd measured it when we were in sixth grade and obsessed with facts and details. We'd spent months calculating distances and counting steps, trying to organize the world into manageable bits and pieces.

Now I just walked toward her in the half-darkness, aware only of the sound of my own footfalls and the air conditioner humming softly under the side window.

"Hey," I said, and she scooted over to make room for me. "How's it going?"

It seemed like the stupidest thing to ask once I'd said it, but there really weren't any right words. I looked over at her as she sat beside me, barefoot, her hair pulled away from her face in a loose ponytail. She'd been crying.

I wasn't used to seeing her this way. Scarlett had always been the stronger, the livelier, the braver. The girl who punched out Missy Lassiter, the meanest, most fiendish of the pink-bike girls that first summer she moved in, on a day when they surrounded us and tried to make us cry. The girl who kept a house, and her mother, up and running since she was five, now playing mother to a thirty-five-year-old child. The girl who had kept the world from swallowing me whole, or so I'd always believed.

"Scarlett?" I said, there in the dark, and as she turned to me I saw her face was streaked with tears. For a minute, I didn't know what to do. I thought again of that picture tucked in her mirror, of her and Michael just weeks ago, the water so bright

20

and shiny behind them. And I thought of what she had done all the millions of times I'd cried to her, collapsing at even the slightest wounding of my heart or pride.

So I reached over and pulled her to me, wrapping my arms around her, and held my best friend close, returning so many favors all at once. We sat there for a long time, Scarlett and me, with her house looming over us and mine right across the street staring back with its bright windows. It was the end of summer; it was the end of a lot of things. I sat there with her, feeling her shoulders shake under my hands. I had no idea what to do or what came next. All I knew was that she needed me and I was here. And for now, that was about the best we could do.

Chapter Two

Scarlett was a redhead, but not in an orangey, carrot-top kind of way. Her color was more auburn, deep and red mixed with browns that made her green eyes seem almost luminous. Her skin was pale, with masses of freckles for the first few years I knew her; as we grew older, they faded into a sprinkling across her nose, as if they'd been scattered there by hand. She was an inch and three-quarters shorter than me, her feet a size larger, and she had a scar on her stomach that looked like a mouth smiling from when she'd gotten her appendix out. She was beautiful in all the unconscious, accidental ways that I wasn't, and I was jealous more than I'd ever have admitted. To me, Scarlett was foreign and exotic. But she said she would have given anything for my long hair and tan in summer, for my thick eyelashes and eyebrows. Not to mention my father, my conventional family, away from Marion with her whims and fancies. It was an even trade, our envy of each other; it made everything fair.

We always believed we lived perfectly parallel lives. We went through the same phases at the same times; we both liked gory movies and sappy stuff, and we knew every word to every song

22

on the old musical soundtracks my parents had. Scarlett was more confident, able to make friends fast, where I was shy and quiet, hanging back from the crowd. I was forever known as "Scarlett's friend Halley." But I didn't mind. Without her I knew I'd be hanging out in the bus parking lot with the nerds and Noah Vaughn. That was, I was sure, the destiny in store for me until the day Scarlett looked up from behind those white sunglasses and made a spot for me next to her for the rest of my life. And I was grateful. Because life is an ugly, awful place to not have a best friend.

When I pictured myself, it was always like just an outline in a coloring book, with the inside not yet completed. All the standard features were there. But the colors, the zigzags and plaids, the bits and pieces that made up me, Halley, weren't yet in place. Scarlett's vibrant reds and golds helped some, but I was still waiting.

For most of high school, we hadn't known Michael Sherwood that well, even though we'd grown up in the same neighborhood. He'd gone away the summer after middle school to California and returned transformed: tan, taller, and suddenly gorgeous. He was immediately *the boy* to date.

He went out with Ginny Tabor for about fifteen minutes, then Elizabeth Gunderson, the head cheerleader, for a few months. But he never seemed to fit in with that crowd of soccer-team captains and varsity jackets. He went back to his buddies from Lakeview, like his best friend Macon Faulkner.

Sometimes we'd see them walking down our street, between our two houses, in the middle of the night, smoking cigarettes and laughing. They were different, and they fascinated us.

By leaving the popular crowd, Michael Sherwood became an enigma. No one was sure where he fit in, and he was friendly with everyone, sort of the great equalizer of our high school. He was famous for his pranks on substitute teachers and was always asking to borrow a dollar in exchange for a good story; he told outlandish tales, half true at best, but they were so funny you got your dollar's worth. The one I remember he told me had to do with psychotic Girl Scouts who were stalking him. I didn't believe him, but I gave him two dollars and skipped lunch that day. It was worth it.

Each of us had our own story about Michael, something he'd done or said or passed down. More than anything, it was the things he *didn't* do that made Michael Sherwood so intriguing; he seemed so far from the rest of us and yet implicitly he belonged to everyone.

At the end of every school year there was the annual slide show, full of candid shots that hadn't made the yearbook. We all piled into the auditorium and watched as our classmates' faces filled the huge screen, everyone cheering for their friends and booing people they didn't like. There was only one picture of Michael Sherwood, but it was a good one: he was sitting on the wall by himself, wearing this black baseball hat he always wore, laughing at something out of the frame, something we couldn't see. The grass was so green behind him, and above

SOMEONE LIKE YOU

that a clear stretch of blue sky. When the slide came up, the entire crowd in that auditorium cheered, clapping and hooting and craning their necks to look for Michael, who was sitting up in the balcony with Macon Faulkner, looking embarrassed. But that was what he was to us, always: the one thing that we all had in common.

The funeral was the next day, Thursday. I went across the street to Scarlett's after breakfast, in bare feet and cutoffs, carrying two black dresses I couldn't decide between. I'd only been to one funeral before, my grandfather's in Buffalo, and I'd been so little someone had dressed me. This was different.

"Come in," I heard Marion call out before I even had a chance to knock at the side door. She was sitting at the kitchen table, coffee cup in front of her, flipping through *Vogue*.

"Hey," I said to her as she smiled at me. "Is she awake?"

"Practically all night," she said quietly, turning the page and taking a sip of coffee. "She was on the couch when I got up. She really needs some rest, or she's just gonna crash."

I had to keep from smiling. These were the same words I heard from Scarlett about Marion on a regular basis; for as long as I'd known them their roles had been reversed. When Marion had been depressed and drinking heavily a few years back, it was Scarlett who came knocking at our front door in her nightgown at two A.M. because she'd found Marion passed out cold halfway up the front walk, her cheek imprinted with the ripples and cracks in the concrete. My father carried Marion

25

into the house while my mother tried her best therapy schtick on Scarlett, who said nothing and curled up in the chair beside Marion's bed, watching over her until morning. My father called Scarlett "solemn"; my mother said she was "in denial."

"Hey." I looked over to see Scarlett standing in the doorway in a red shirt and cutoff long johns, her hair still mussed up from sleeping. She nodded at the dresses in my hand. "Which one you gonna wear?"

"I don't know," I said.

She came closer, taking them from my hands, then held each up against me, squinting. "The short one," she said quietly, laying the other on the counter next to the fruit bowl. "The one with the scoop neck always makes you look like you're twelve."

I looked down at the scoop-necked dress, trying to remember where I'd worn it before. It was always Scarlett who kept track of such things: dates, memories, lessons learned. I forgot everything, barely able to keep my head from one week to the next. But Scarlett knew it all, from what she was wearing when she got her first kiss to the name of the sister of the boy I'd met at the beach the summer before; she was our oracle, our common memory.

She opened the fridge and took out the milk, then crossed the room with a box of Rice Krispies under her arm, grabbing a bowl from the open dishwasher on her way. She sat at the head of the table, with Marion to her left, and I took my seat on the right. Even in their tiny family, with me as an honorary member, there were traditions.

Scarlett poured herself some cereal, adding sugar from the bowl between us. "Do you want some?"

"No," I said. "I ate already." My mother had made me French toast, after spending most of the early morning gossiping over the back fence with her best friend, Irma Trilby, who was known for her amazing azaleas and her mouth, the latter of which I'd heard all morning through my window. Apparently Mrs. Trilby had known Mrs. Sherwood well from PTA and had already been over with a chicken casserole to relay her regrets. Mrs. Trilby had also seen me and Michael and Scarlett more than once walking home from work together, and late one night she'd even caught a glimpse of Scarlett and Michael kissing under a streetlight. He was a sweet boy, she'd said in her nasal voice. He mowed their lawn after Arthur's coronary and always got her the best bananas at Milton's, even if he had to sneak some from the back. A nice boy.

So my mother came inside newly informed and sympathetic and made me a huge breakfast that I picked at while she sat across the table, coffee mug in hand, smiling as if waiting for me to say something. As if all it took was Michael Sherwood mowing a lawn, or finding the perfect banana, to make him worth mourning.

"So what time's the service?" Marion asked me, picking up her Marlboro Lights from the lazy Susan in the middle of the table.

"Eleven o'clock."

She lit a cigarette. "We're packed with appointments today, but I'll try to make it. Okay?"

"Okay," Scarlett said.

Marion worked at the Lakeview Mall at Fabulous You, a glamour photography store where they had makeup and clothes and got you all gussied up, then took photographs that you could give to your husband or boyfriend. Marion spent forty hours a week making up housewives and teenagers in too much lipstick and the same evening gowns, posing them with an empty champagne glass as they gazed into the camera with their best come-hither look. It was a hard job, considering some of the raw material she had to work with; not everyone is cut out to be glamorous. She often said there was only so much of a miracle to be worked with concealer and creative lighting.

Marion pushed her chair back, running a hand through her hair; she had Scarlett's face, round with deep green eyes, and thick blond hair she bleached every few months. She had bright red fingernails, smoked constantly, and owned more lingerie than Victoria's Secret. The first time I'd met her, the day they moved in, Marion had been flirting with the movers, dressed in hip-huggers, a macramé halter top that showed her stomach, and heels at least four inches high. She wasn't like my mother; she wasn't like *anyone's* mother. To me, she looked just like Barbie, and she'd fascinated me ever since.

"Well," Marion drawled, standing up and ruffling Scarlett's

hair with her hand as she passed. "Got to get ready for the salt mines. You girls call if you need me. Okay?"

"Okay," Scarlett said, taking another mouthful of cereal.

"Bye, Marion," I said.

"She won't come," Scarlett said once Marion was safely upstairs, her footsteps creaking above us.

"Why not?"

"Funerals freak her out." She dropped her spoon in her bowl, finished. "Marion has a convenient excuse for everything."

When we went upstairs to get ready I flopped on the edge of her bed, which was covered in clothes and magazines and mismatched blankets and sheets. Scarlett opened her closet and stood in front of it with her hands on her hips, contemplating. Marion yelled good-bye from downstairs and the front door slammed, followed by the sound of her car starting and backing out of the driveway. Through the window over Scarlett's bed, I could see my own mother sitting in the swing on our front porch, drinking coffee and reading the paper. As Marion drove past she waved, her "neighbor smile" on, and went back to reading.

"I hate this," Scarlett said suddenly, reaching into the closet and pulling out a navy blue dress with a white collar. "I don't have a single thing that's appropriate."

"You can wear my twelve-year-old dress," I offered, and she made a face.

"I bet Marion's got something," she said suddenly, leaving

the room. Marion's closet was legend; she was a fashion plate and a pack rat, the most dangerous of pairings.

I reached over and turned on the radio next to the bed, leaning back and closing my eyes. I'd spent half my life in Scarlett's room, sprawled across the bed with a stack of *Seventeen* magazines between us, picking out future prom dresses and reading up on pimple prevention and boyfriend problems. Right next to her window was the shelf with her pictures: me and her at the beach two years ago, in matching sailor hats, doing a mock salute at my father's camera. Marion at eighteen, an old school picture, faded and creased. And finally, at the end and unframed, that same picture of her and Michael at the lake. Since I left for Sisterhood Camp, she'd moved it so it was in easy reach.

I felt something pressing into my back, hard, and I reached under to move it; it was a boot with a thick sole that resisted when I pulled on it. I shifted my position and gave it another yank, wondering when Scarlett had bought hiking boots. I was just about to yell out and ask her, when it suddenly yanked back, hard, and there was an explosion of movement on the bed, arms and legs flailing, things falling off the sides as someone rose out of the mess around me, shaking off magazines and blankets and pillows in all directions. And suddenly, I found myself face to face with Macon Faulkner.

He glanced around the room as if he wasn't quite sure where he was. His blond hair, cut short over his ears, stuck up in tiny cowlicks. In one ear was a row of three silver hoops.

"Wha—?" he managed, sitting up straighter and blinking. He was all tangled up, one sheet wrapped around his arm. "Where's Scarlett?"

"She's down there," I said automatically, pointing toward the door, as if that was down, which it wasn't.

He shook his head, trying to wake up. I would have been just as shocked to see Mahatma Gandhi or Elvis in Scarlett's bed; I had no idea she even knew Macon Faulkner. We all knew *who* he was, of course. As a Boy with a Reputation, his neighborhood legend preceded him.

And what was he doing in her bed, anyway? It couldn't mean—no. She would have told me; she told me everything. And Marion *had* said Scarlett slept on the couch.

"Well, I think I can wear this," I heard Scarlett say as she came back down the hallway, a black dress over her arm. She looked at Macon, then at me, and walked to the closet as if it was the most normal thing in the world to have a strange boy in your bed at ten in the morning on a Thursday.

Macon lay back, letting one hand flop over his eyes. His boot, and his foot in it, had somehow landed in my lap, where it remained. Macon Faulkner's *foot* was in my *lap*.

"Did you meet Halley?" Scarlett asked him, hanging the dress on her closet door. "Halley, this is Macon. Macon, Halley."

"Hi," I said, immediately aware of how high my voice was.

"Hey." He nodded at me, moving his foot off my lap as if that was nothing special, then got off the bed and stood up, stretching his arms. "Man, I feel awful."

31

"Well, you should," Scarlett said in the same scolding voice she used with me when I was especially spineless. "You were incredibly wasted."

Macon leaned over and rooted around under the sheets, looking for something, while I sat there and stared at him. He was in a white T-shirt ripped along the hem and dark blue shorts, those clunky boots on his feet. He was tall and wiry, and tan from a summer working landscaping around the neighborhood, which was the only place I ever saw him, and even then from a distance.

"Have you seen—?" he began, but Scarlett was already reaching to the bedside table and the baseball cap lying there. Macon leaned over and took it from her, then put it on with a sheepish look. "Thanks."

"You're welcome." Scarlett pulled her hair back behind her head, gathering it in her hands, which meant she was thinking. "So, you need a ride to the service?"

"Nah," he said, walking to the bedroom door with his hands in his pockets, stepping over my feet as if I was invisible. "I'll see you there."

"Okay." Scarlett stood by the doorway.

"Is it cool? To go out this way?" he was whispering, gesturing down the hall to Marion's empty room.

"It's fine."

He nodded, then stepped toward her awkwardly, leaning down to kiss her cheek. "Thanks," he said quietly, in a voice I probably was not supposed to hear. "I mean it."

"It's no big deal," Scarlett said, smiling up at him, and we both watched him as he loped off, his boots clunking down the stairs and out the door. When I heard it swing shut, I walked to the window and leaned against the glass, waiting until he came out on the walk, squinting, and began those eighteen steps to the street. Across the street my mother looked up, folding her paper in her lap, watching too.

"I cannot believe you," I said out loud, as Macon Faulkner passed the prickly bushes and turned left, headed out of *Lakeview—Neighborhood of Friends*.

"He was upset," Scarlett said simply. "Michael was his best friend."

"But you never even told me you knew him. And then I come up here and he's in your *bed*."

"I just knew him through Michael. He's messed up, Halley. He's got a lot of problems."

"It's so weird, though," I said. "I mean, that he was here."

"He just needed someone," she said. "That's all."

I still had my eye on Macon Faulkner as he moved past the perfect houses of our neighborhood, seeming out of place among hissing sprinklers and thrown newspapers on a bright and shiny late summer morning. I couldn't say then what it was about him that kept me there. But just as he was rounding the corner, disappearing from sight, he turned around and lifted his hand, waving at me, as if he knew even without turning back that I'd still be there in the window, watching him go.

33

*   *   *

When we got to the church, there was already a line out the door. Scarlett hadn't said much the entire trip, and as we walked over, she was wringing her hands.

"Are you okay?" I asked her.

"It's just weird," she said, and her voice was low and hollow. She had her eyes on something straight ahead. "All of it."

As I looked up I could see what she meant. Elizabeth Gunderson, head cheerleader, was surrounded by a group of her friends on the church steps. She was sobbing hysterically, a red T-shirt in her hands.

Scarlett stopped when we got within a few feet of the crowd, so suddenly that I kept walking and then had to go back for her. She was standing by herself, her arms folded tightly across her chest.

"Scarlett?" I said.

"This was a bad idea," she said. "We shouldn't have come."

"But—"

And that was as far as I got before Ginny Tabor came up behind me, throwing her arms around both of us at once and collapsing into tears. She smelled like hairspray and cigarette smoke and was wearing a blue dress that showed too much leg.

"Oh, my God," she said, lifting her head to take in me and then Scarlett as we pulled away from her as delicately as possible. "It's so awful, so terrible. I haven't been able to eat since I heard. I'm a wreck."

Neither of us said anything; we just kept walking, while

Ginny fumbled for a cigarette, lighting it and then fanning the smoke with one hand. "I mean, the time that we were together wasn't all that great, but I loved him *so* much. It was just circumstances—" and now she sobbed, shaking her head—"that kept us apart. But he was, like, everything to me for those two months. Everything."

I looked over at Scarlett, who was studying the pavement, and I said, "I'm so sorry, Ginny."

"Well," she said in a tight voice, exhaling a long stream of smoke, "it's so different when you knew him well. You know?"

"I know," I said. We hadn't seen much of Ginny since midsummer. After spending a few wild weeks with us, she'd gotten sent off to a combination cheerleading/Bible camp while her parents went to Europe. It was just as well, we figured. There was only so much of ongoing Ginny you could take. A few days later Scarlett had met Michael, and the second half of our summer began.

We kept following the line into the church, now coming up on Elizabeth. Ginny, of course, made a big show of running over to her and bursting into fresh tears, and they stood and hugged each other, crying together.

"It's so awful," a girl said from behind me. "He loved Elizabeth so much. That's his shirt she's holding, you know. She hasn't put it down since she heard."

"I thought they broke up," said another girl, and cracked her gum.

"At the beginning of the summer. But he still loved her. Anyway, that Ginny Tabor is so damn shallow," said the first girl. "She only dated him for about two days."

Once inside, we sat toward the back, next to two older women who pulled their knees aside primly as we slid past them. Up at the front of the church there were two posters with pictures of Michael taped to them: baby snapshots, school pictures, candids I recognized from the yearbook. And in the middle, biggest of all, was the picture from the slide show, the one that had brought cheers in that darkened auditorium in June. I wanted to point it out to Scarlett, but when I turned to tell her, she was just staring at the back of the pew in front of us, her face pale, and I kept quiet.

The service started late, with people filing in and lining the walls, shuffling and fanning themselves with the little paper programs we'd been handed at the door. Elizabeth Gunderson came in, still crying, and was led to a seat with Ginny Tabor sobbing right behind her. It was strange to see my classmates in this setting; some were dressed up nicely, obviously used to wearing church clothes. Others looked out of place, awkward, tugging at their ties or dress shirts. I wondered what Michael was thinking, looking down at all these people with red faces shifting in their seats, at the wailing girls he left behind, at his parents in the front pew with his little sister, quietly stoic and sad. And I looked over at Scarlett, who had loved him so much in such a short time, and slipped my hand around hers, squeezing it. She squeezed back, still staring ahead.

The service was formal and short; the heat was stifling with all the people packed in so tightly, and we could barely hear the minister over the fanning and the creaking of the pews. He talked about Michael, and what he meant to so many people; he said something about God having his reasons. Elizabeth Gunderson got up and left ten minutes into it, her hand pressed against her mouth as she walked quickly down the aisle of the church, a gaggle of friends running behind her. The older women next to us shook their heads, disapproving, and Scarlett squeezed my hand harder, her fingernails digging into my skin.

When the service was over, there was an awkward murmur of voices as everyone filed outside. It had suddenly gotten very dark, with a strange breeze blowing that smelled like rain. Overhead the clouds had piled up big and black behind the trees.

I almost lost Scarlett in the crowd of voices and faces and color in front of the church. Ginny was leaning on Brett Hershey, the captain of the football team, as he led her out. Elizabeth was sitting in the front seat of a car in the parking lot, the door open, her head in her hands. Everyone else stood around uncertainly as if they needed permission to leave, holding their programs and looking up at the sky.

"Poor Elizabeth," Scarlett said softly as we stood by her car.

"They broke up a while ago," I said.

"Yeah. They did." She kicked a pebble, and it rattled off of something under the car. "But he really loved her."

I looked over at her, the wind blowing her hair around her

face, her fair skin so white against the black of Marion's dress. The times I caught her unaware, accidentally, were when she was the most beautiful. "He loved you, too," I told her.

She looked up at the sky, black with clouds, the smell of rain stronger and stronger. "I know," she said softly. "I know."

The first drop was big, sloshy and wet, falling on my shoulder and leaving a round, dark circle. Then, suddenly, it was pouring. The rain came in sheets, sending people running toward their cars, shielding themselves with their flimsy paper programs. Scarlett and I dove into her car and watched the water stream down the windshield. I couldn't remember the last time I'd seen it rain so hard.

We pulled out onto Main Street in Scarlett's Ford Aspire. Her grandmother had given it to her for her birthday in April. It was about the size of a shoe box; it looked like a larger car that had been cut in half with a big bread knife. As we crossed a river of water spilling into the road, I wondered briefly if we'd get pulled into the current and carried away like Wynken, Blynken, and Nod in their big shoe, out to sea.

Scarlett saw him first, walking alone up the street, his white dress shirt soaked and sticking to his back. His head was ducked and he had his hands in his pockets, staring down at the pavement as people ran past with umbrellas. Scarlett beeped the horn, slowing beside him.

"Macon!" she called out, leaning into the rain. "Hey!" He didn't hear her, and she poked me. "Yell out to him, Halley."

"What?"

"Roll down your window and ask him if he wants a ride."

"Scarlett," I said, suddenly nervous, "I don't even know him."

"So what?" She gave me a look. "It's pouring. Hurry up."

I rolled my window down and stuck my head out, feeling the rain pelting the back of my neck. "Excuse me," I said.

He didn't hear me. I cleared my throat, stalling. "Excuse me."

"Halley," Scarlett said, glancing into the rearview mirror, "we're holding up traffic here. Come on."

"He can't hear me," I said defensively.

"You're practically whispering."

"I am not," I snapped. "I am speaking in a perfectly audible tone of voice."

"Just yell it." Cars were going around us now as a fresh wave of rain poured in my window, soaking my lap. Scarlett exhaled loudly, which meant she was losing patience. "Come on, Halley, don't be such a wuss."

"I am not a wuss," I said. "God."

She just looked at me. I stuck my head back out the window.

"Macon." I said it a little louder this time, just because I was angry. "Macon."

Another loud exhalation from Scarlett. I was getting completely soaked.

"Macon," I said a bit louder, stretching my head completely out of the car. *"Macon!!"*

He jerked suddenly on the sidewalk, turning around and looking at me as if he expected us to come flying up the curb in

39

our tiny car to squash him completely. Then he just stared, his shirt soaked and sticking to his skin, his hair dripping onto his face, stood and stared at me as if I was completely and utterly nuts.

"What?" he screamed back, just as loudly. *"What* is *it?"*

Beside me, Scarlett burst out laughing, the first time I'd heard her laugh since I'd come home. She leaned back in her seat, hand over her mouth, giggling uncontrollably. I wanted to die.

"Um," I said, and he was still staring at me. "Do you want a ride?"

"I'm okay," he said across me, to Scarlett. "But thanks."

"Macon, it's pouring." She had her Mom voice on, one I recognized. As he looked across me, I could see how red his eyes were, swollen from crying. "Come on."

"I'm okay," he said again, backing off from the car. He wiped his hand over his face and hair, water spraying everywhere. "I'll see you later."

"Macon," she called out again, but he was already gone, walking back into the rain. As we sat at the stoplight, he cut around a corner and disappeared; the last thing I saw was his shirt, a flash of white against the brick of the alley. Then he was gone, vanishing so easily it seemed almost like magic—there was no trace. Scarlett sighed as I rolled up my window, saying something about everybody having their ways. I was only watching the alleyway, the last place I'd seen him, wondering if he'd ever even been there at all.

40

Chapter Three

When I think of Michael Sherwood, what really comes to mind is produce. Deep yellow bananas, bright green kiwis, cool purple plums smooth to the touch. Our friendship with Michael Sherwood, popular boy and legend, began simply with fruits and vegetables.

Scarlett and I were cashiers at Milton's Market, wearing our little green smocks and plastic name tags: *Hello, I'm Halley! Welcome to Milton's!* She worked register eight, which was the No Candy register, and I worked Express Fifteen Items and Under right next to her, close enough to roll my eyes or yell over the beeping of my price scanner when it all got to be too much. It wasn't the greatest job by a long stretch. But at least we were together.

We'd seen Michael Sherwood come in to interview at the end of June. He'd been wearing a tie. He looked nervous and waved at me like we were friends as he waited for an application at the Customer Service Desk. He got placed in Fruits and Vegetables, his official title being Junior Assistant to Produce Day Manager, which meant that he stacked oranges, repacked fruit in those little green trays and sealed them with cling wrap, and watered the vegetables with a big hose twice a day. Mostly he laughed and had a good time, quickly making friends with everyone from Meat to Health and Beauty Aids. But it was me and Scarlett he was drawn to. Well, it was Scarlett, really. As usual, I was just along for the ride.

It started with kiwis. During his first week, Michael Sherwood ate four kiwi fruit for lunch each day. Just kiwis. Nothing else. He'd stick them on Scarlett's little scale in their plastic bag, smiling, then take them outside to the one little patch of grass in the parking lot and cut and eat them, one by one, by himself. We wondered about this. We never ate kiwis.

"He likes fruit," Scarlett said simply one day after he was gone, having smiled his big smile at her and made her blush. He came to my register once, but by the third day he was standing in line at Scarlett's, even when my overhead light was flashing OPEN NO WAITING.

I looked out at Michael, in his green produce apron, sitting in the sun with those tiny fuzzy fruits, and shook my head. It would always take at least fifteen minutes for Scarlett to stop blushing.

The next day, when he got to the front of the line with his kiwis and Scarlett was ringing him up, she said, "You must really like these things."

"They're awesome," he said, leaning over her little check and credit-card station. "Haven't you ever tried one?"

"Only in fruit salad," Scarlett said, and I was so distracted listening I rang up some rigatoni at two hundred dollars, screwing up my register altogether and scaring the hell out of the poor woman in my line, who was only buying that, some pineapple spears, and a box of tampons. Between voiding and ringing everything back out, I missed half of their conversation, and when I turned back Michael was walking outside with his lunch and Scarlett was holding one fuzzy kiwi in her hand, examining it from every angle.

"He gave it to me," she whispered. Her face was blazing red. "Can you believe it?"

"Excuse me, miss," someone in my line shouted, "are you open?"

"Yes," I shouted back. To Scarlett I said, "What else did he say?"

"I have these," said a tall, hairy man in a polka-dot shirt as he pushed his cart up, thrusting a pile of sticky coupons in my hand. He was buying four cans of potted meat, some air freshener, and two cans of lighter fluid. Sometimes you don't even want to think about what people are doing with their groceries.

"I think I'm going to take my break," Scarlett called to me, pulling the drawer from her register. "Since I'm slow and all."

"Wait, I'll be done here in a sec." But of course my line was long now, full of people with fifteen items, or eighteen items, or even twenty with a little creative counting, all staring blankly at me.

"Do you mind?" Scarlett said, already heading to the offices to drop off her drawer, that one kiwi in her free hand. "I mean . . ."

She glanced outside quickly, and I could see Michael on the curb with his lunch.

"It's okay," I said, turning back to Scarlett as I ran Hairy Man's check through the confirming slot. "I'll just take my break later, or something. . . ."

But she didn't hear me, was already gone, outside to the curb and the sunshine, sitting next to Michael Sherwood. My best friend Scarlett had traded a kiwi fruit for her heart.

I didn't get many breaks with her after that. Michael Sherwood wooed her with strange, foreign fruits and vegetables, dropping slivers of green melon and dark red blood oranges off at her register when she was busy. Later, when she looked up, there'd be something poised above her on her NO CANDY REGISTER sign; a single pear, perfectly balanced, three little radishes all in a row. I never saw him do it, and I watched her station like a hawk. But there was something magical about Michael Sherwood, and of course Scarlett loved it. I would have too, if it had ever happened to me.

That was the first summer when it wasn't just me and Scarlett. Michael was always there making us laugh, doing belly flops into the pool or sliding his arms around Scarlett's waist as she stood at the kitchen counter, stirring brownie mix. It was the first summer we didn't spend practically every night together, either; sometimes, I'd look across the street in early evening and see her shades drawn, Michael's car in the driveway, and know I had to stay away. Late at night I'd hear them outside saying good-bye, and I'd pull my curtain aside and watch as he kissed her in the dim yellow of the streetlight. I'd never had to fight for her attention before. Now, all it took was a look from Michael and she was off and running, with me left behind again to eat lunch alone or watch TV with my father, who always fell asleep on the couch by eight-thirty and snored to boot. I missed her.

But Scarlett was so happy, there was no way I could hold anything against her. She practically glowed twenty-four hours a day, always laughing, sitting out on the curb in front of Milton's with Michael, catching the grapes he tossed in her mouth. They hid out in her house for entire weekends, cooking spaghetti for Marion and renting movies. Scarlett said that after his breakup with Elizabeth at the end of the school year, Michael just didn't want to deal with the gossip. The day we went to the lake was the first time they'd risked exposure to our classmates, but it had been empty on the beaches, quiet, as we tossed the Frisbee and ate the picnic Scarlett packed. I sat with my *Mademoiselle* magazine, watching them swim together, dunking each other and laughing. It was later, just as we were leaving and the sun was setting in oranges and reds behind them, that I snapped the picture, the only one Scarlett had of them together. She'd grabbed it out of my hand the day I got them, taking my double copy, too, and giving it to Michael, who stuck it over the speedometer in his car, where it stayed until he traded the car a few weeks later for the motorcycle.

By the beginning of August, he'd told her he loved her. She said they'd been sitting at the side of her pool, legs dangling, when he just leaned over, kissed her ear, and said it. She'd whispered it as she told me, as if it was some kind of spell that could easily be broken by loud voices or common knowledge. *I love you.*

Which made it so much worse when he was gone so quickly, just two weeks later. The only boy who had ever said it to her and meant it. The rest of the world didn't know how much Scarlett loved Michael Sherwood. Even I couldn't truly have understood, much as I might have wanted to.

On the first day of school, Scarlett and I pulled into the parking lot, found a space facing the back of the vocational building, and parked. She turned off the engine of the Aspire, dropping her keychain in her lap. Then we sat.

"I don't want to do it," she said decisively.

"I know," I said.

"I mean it this year," she said, sighing. "I just don't think I have it in me. Under the circumstances."

"I know," I said again. Since the funeral, Scarlett had seemed to fold into herself; she hardly ever mentioned Michael, and I didn't either. We'd spent the entire first part of the summer talking about nothing but him, it seemed, and now he was out of bounds, forbidden. They'd planted a tree for him at school, with a special plaque, and the Sherwoods had put up their house for sale; I'd heard they were moving to Florida. Life was going on without him. But when he *was* mentioned, I hated the look that crossed her face, a mix of hurt and overwhelming sadness.

Now people were streaming by in new clothes, down the concrete path that led to the main building. I could hear voices and cars rumbling past. Sitting there in the Aspire, we held on to our last bit of freedom.

I sat and waited, shifting my new backpack, which sat between my feet, a stack of new shiny spiral notebooks and unsharpened pencils zipped away in its clean, neat compartments. It was always Scarlett who decided when it was time.

"Well," she said deliberately, folding her arms over her chest. "I guess we don't have much of a choice."

"Scarlett Thomas!" someone shrieked from beside the car, and we looked up to see Ginny Tabor, in a new short haircut and red lipstick, running past us holding hands with Brett Hershey, the football captain. Only Ginny could hook up with someone at a funeral. "School is this way!" she pointed with one red fingernail, then laughed, throwing her head back while Brett looked on as if waiting for someone to throw him something. She waggled her fingers at us and ran on ahead, dragging him behind her. I couldn't believe we'd spent so much time with her early that summer. It seemed like years ago now.

"God," Scarlett said, "I really hate her."

"I know." This was my line.

She took a deep breath, reached into the backseat for her

backpack, and pulled it into her lap. "Okay. There's really no avoiding it."

"I agree," I said, unlocking my door.

"Let's go then," she said grudgingly, getting out of the car and slamming the door behind her, hitching her backpack over one shoulder. I followed, merging into the crowd that carried us down through the teachers' parking lot to the courtyard in front of the main building. The first bell rang and everyone moved inside, suddenly thrown together in front of the doors and causing a major traffic jam of bodies and backpacks, elbows and feet, a tide I let carry me down the hallway to my homeroom, keeping my eye on the back of Scarlett's red head.

"This is it," I said as we came up on Mr. Alexander's door, which was decorated with cardboard cutout frogs.

"Good luck," Scarlett called out, pulling open the door of her own homeroom and rolling her eyes one last time as she disappeared inside.

Mr. Alexander's room already smelled of formaldehyde and he smiled at me, mustache wriggling, as I took my seat. The first day was always the same: they took roll, handed out schedules, and sent home about ten million different memos to your parents about busing and cafeteria rates and school rules. Beside me Ben Cruzak was already stoned and sleeping, head on his desk, with Missy Cavenaugh behind him doing her fingernails. Even the snake on Mr. Alexander's counter looked bored, after eating a mouse for the audience of science geeks who always hung out before first bell.

After about fifteen minutes of continuous droning over the intercom and a stack of memos an inch high on my desk, Alexander finally handed out our schedules. I could tell right away something was wrong with mine; I was signed up for Pre-calculus (when I hadn't even taken Algebra Two), French Three (when I took Spanish), and, worst of all, Band.

"Have a good day!" Alexander yelled above the bell as everyone headed toward the door. I went up to his desk. "Halley. Yes?"

"My schedule is wrong," I said. "I'm signed up for Band."

"Band?"

"Yes. And Pre-cal and French Three, and none of those are my classes."

"Hmmm," he said, and he was already looking over my head at the people streaming in, his first class. "Better go to your first class and get a pass to Guidance."

"But . . ."

He stood up, his mustache already moving. "Okay, people, take a seat and I'll be sending around a chart for you to fill in your chosen spot. This will be the seating chart for the rest of the semester, so I suggest you choose carefully. Don't tap on that glass, it makes the snake crazy. Now, this is Intro to Biology, so if you don't belong here . . ."

I walked out into the hallway, where Scarlett was leaning against the fire extinguisher waiting for me. "Hey. What's your first class?"

"Pre-cal."

49

"What? You haven't taken Algebra Two yet."

"I know." I switched my backpack to my other shoulder, already sick of school. "My schedule is so messed up. I'm signed up for Band."

"Band?"

"Yes." I stepped aside to let a pack of football players pass. "I have to go to Guidance."

"Oh, that sucks," she said. "I've got English and then Commercial Design, so I'll meet you after, okay? In the courtyard by the soda machines."

"I'm supposed to be in Band then," I said glumly.

"They can't force you to take Band," she said, laughing. I just looked at her. "They can't. Go to Guidance and I'll see you later."

The Guidance office was packed with people leaning against the walls and sitting on the floor, all waiting for the three available counselors. The receptionist, whose phone was ringing shrilly, nonstop, looked up at me with the crazed eyes of a rabid animal.

"What?" She had the kind of glasses that made her eyes seem wider than platters, magnified hundreds of times. "What do you need?"

"My schedule's all wrong," I said as the phone rang again, the row of red lights across it blinking. "I need to see a counselor."

"Right, okay," she said, grabbing the phone and holding one

finger up at me, like she was pushing a pause button. "Hello, Guidance office. No, he's not available now. Okay. Right, sure. Fine." She hung the phone up, the cord wrapped around her wrist. "Now, what? You need a counselor?"

"I got the wrong schedule. I'm signed up for Band."

"Band?" she blinked at me. "What's wrong with Band?"

"Nothing," I said as a kid carrying a clarinet case passed me, scowling. I lowered my voice. "Except I don't play an instrument. I mean, I've never been in Band."

"Well," she said slowly as the phone rang again, "maybe it's Introduction to Band. That's the beginning level."

"I never signed up for Band," I said a little bit louder, just to be heard over the phone. "I don't want to take it."

"Fine, well, then write your name on this sheet," she snapped, losing all patience whatsoever with debating the merits of musical training and grabbing the phone again in midring. "We'll get to you as soon as we can."

I took a seat against the wall, under a shelf with a row of teenager-related books on it, with titles like *Sharing Our Differences: Understanding Your Adolescent* and *Peer Pressure: Finding Your Own Way*. My mother's second book, *Mixed Emotions: Mothers, Daughters, and the High School Years*, was there too, which just put me in a worse mood. If I'd really felt like torturing myself, I could have picked it up and read again how good and strong our relationship was.

It was hot in the room, and everyone was talking too loud,

crammed in together. A girl next to me was busy writing *Die Die Die* in all different colors on the cover of her notebook, a stack of Magic Markers beside her. I closed my eyes, thinking back to summer and cool pool water and long days with nothing to do except go swimming and sleep late.

I felt someone sit down beside me, leaning back against the wall close enough that their shoulder bumped mine. I pulled my arms across my chest, folding my knees against me. Then I felt a finger against my shoulder, *poke poke poke.* I opened my eyes, bracing myself for hours in Guidance Hell with Ginny Tabor.

But it wasn't Ginny. It was Macon Faulkner, and he was grinning at me. "What'd you do?" he asked.

"What?" The *Die Die Die* girl had switched to the back cover, methodically filling letter after letter with green ink.

"What'd you do?" he said again, then gestured toward the front desk. "It's only the first day and you're already in trouble."

"I am not," I said. "My schedule's messed up."

"Oh, sure," he said slowly, faking suspicion. He had on a baseball cap, his blond hair sticking out beneath, and a red T-shirt and jeans. He didn't have a backpack, just one plain spiral notebook with a pen stuck in the binding. Macon Faulkner was definitely not the school type. "You've probably already gotten into a fight and been suspended."

"No," I said, and I don't know if it was just the day I'd had or a sudden wave of Scarlett-like boldness, but I wasn't nervous talking to him. "I got signed up for all the wrong classes."

"Sure you did," he said easily. He settled back against the wall. "Now, you know how to handle yourself in there, right?"

I looked at him. "What?"

"How to handle yourself," He blinked at me. "Oh, please. You need big help. Okay, listen up. First, admit nothing. That's the most important rule."

"I'm not in trouble," I told him.

"Second," he said loudly, ignoring me, "try to divert them by mentioning anything about your therapist. For instance, say, 'My therapist always says I have a problem with authority.' Act real serious about it. Just the word 'therapist' will usually cut you some slack."

I laughed. "Yeah, right."

"It's true. And if that doesn't work, use the Jedi Mind Trick. But only if you really have to."

"The what?"

"The Jedi Mind Trick." He looked at me. "Didn't you ever see *Star Wars*?"

I thought back. "Sure I did."

"The Jedi Mind Trick is when you tell someone what you want them to think, and then they think it. Like, say I'm Mr. Mathers. And I say, 'Macon, you're already pushing the limits and it's only the first day of school. Is this any kind of way to start the year?' And you're me. What do you say?"

I shook my head. "I have no idea."

He rolled his eyes. "You say, 'Mr. Mathers, you're going to let this slide, because it's only the first day, it was an honest mistake, and the fire got put out as quickly as it was started.'"

"The fire?" I said. "What fire?"

"The point is," he said easily, flipping his hand, "that you just say that right back to him, very confidently. And then what does he say?"

"That you're crazy?"

"No. He says, 'Well, Macon, I'm going to let this slide because it's only the first day, it was an honest mistake, and the fire got put out as quickly as it started.'"

I laughed. "He will not."

"He will," he said, nodding his head. "It's the Jedi Mind Trick. Trust me." And when he smiled at me, I almost did.

"I'm really not in trouble." I handed him my schedule. "Unless that trick works on getting out of this stuff, I don't think I can use it."

He squinted at it. "Pre-calculus." He looked up at me, raising his eyebrows. "Really?"

"No. I barely got through Algebra."

He nodded at this; obviously we now had common ground. "French, P.E. . . . Hey, we're in the same P.E. period."

"Really?" Macon Faulkner and me, playing badminton. Learning golf strokes. Watching each other across a gymful of bouncing basketballs.

"Yep. Third period." He kept reading, then reached up to take off his hat, shake his hair free, and put it back on backwards. "Science, English, blah, blah. . . . Oh! Looky *here*."

I already knew what was coming.

"Band," he said, smiling big. "You're in Band."

"I am *not* in Band," I said loudly, and that same kid with the clarinet looked over at me again. "It's a big mistake and no one believes me."

"What do you play?" he asked me.

"I don't," I said. I was trying to be indignant but he was so cute. I had no idea why he was even talking to me.

"You look like the flute type," he said thoughtfully, stroking his chin. "Or maybe the piccolo."

"Shut up," I said, surprising myself with my boldness.

He was laughing, shaking his head. "Maybe the triangle?" He held up his hand, pretending to hold one, and struck it wistfully with an imaginary wand.

"Leave me alone," I moaned, putting my head in my hands and secretly hoping more than anything that he wouldn't.

"Oh, now," he said, and I felt his hand come around my shoulder, squeezing it, and I wanted to die right there. "I'm just razzing you."

"This has been the worst day," I said as he took his arm back, sliding it across my shoulders. "The worst."

"Faulkner." The voice was loud, quieting down the entire room, and as I looked up I saw Mr. Mathers, the junior class head counselor, standing by the front desk, a folder in his hands. He didn't look happy. "Come on."

"That's me," Macon said cheerfully, standing up and grabbing his notebook. He tapped the side of his head with a finger, winking at me. "Remember. Jedi Mind Trick."

"Right," I said, nodding.

"See ya later, Halley," he said. He took his time walking over to Mr. Mathers, who clamped a hand on his shoulder and led him down the hallway. I couldn't believe he'd even remembered my name. The *Die Die Die* girl was staring at me now, as if by my short encounter with Macon Faulkner I was suddenly more important or worth noticing. I definitely *felt* different. Macon Faulkner, who before had said less than seven words to me total in my entire lifetime, had just appeared and talked to me for, like, minutes. As if we were friends, buddies, after only one day of knowing each other formally. It gave me a weird, jumpy feeling in my stomach and I thought suddenly of Scarlett, standing at register eight at Milton's, blushing down at a kiwi fruit.

"Hal—Hal Cooke. Is there a Hal Cooke here?" someone was saying in a bored voice from the front desk, and whatever elation I was experiencing screeched to a halt. It is times like the first day of school that I curse my parents for not naming me Jane or Lisa.

I stood up, grabbing my backpack. The counselor by the front desk, a huge African-American woman in a bright pink suit, was still trying to make out my name. "Halley," I said as I got closer. "It's Halley."

"Umm-hmmm." She turned around and gestured for me

to follow her down the hall past two offices to door number three. As I passed the middle door I thought I heard Macon's voice from behind the half-shut door, the low rumbling of Mr. Mathers mixing in. I wondered if his trick was working.

I had almost forgotten him altogether when I finally emerged, bruised and tired, with my new schedule in my hand, standing dazed outside the Guidance office as the bell ending second period rang and people suddenly began pouring out of classrooms and hallways. I went to the Coke machine to find Scarlett.

"Hey," she called out to me over the crowd of people pushing forward with their quarters and dollar bills, mad for soda. She waved two Cokes over her head, and I followed them until I found her against the far wall, the same one Michael Sherwood had his picture snapped against for the slide show.

She handed me a Coke. "How's Band?"

"Great," I said, opening my can and taking a long drink. "They say I'm a prodigy already at the oboe."

"Like hell," she said.

I smiled. "I got out of it, thank God. But you won't believe who I talked to in the Guidance office."

"Who?"

A loud booing noise went up at the Coke machine, drowning us out, and someone was sent to find the janitor. It always broke at least once each day, causing a minor mutiny. I waited until the crowd had calmed down, walking off jangling their change, before I said, "Macon Faulkner."

"Really?" She opened her backpack, rummaging through to find something. "How's he doing?"

"He was already in trouble, I think."

"Not surprising." She put her drink down. "God, I feel so rotten all of a sudden. Like just bad."

"Sick?"

"Kind of." She pulled out a bottle of Advil, popped the top, and took two. "It's probably just my well-documented aversion to school."

"Probably." I watched her as she leaned back against the brick wall, closing her eyes. In the sun her hair was a deep red, almost unreal, with brighter streaks running through it.

"But anyway," I said, "it was so weird. He just sat right next to me, just like that, and started talking my ear off. Like he knew me."

"He does know you."

"Yeah, but only from that one day of the funeral. Before then we'd never even been introduced."

"So? This is a small town, Halley. Everyone knows everyone."

"It was just weird," I said again, replaying it in my head, from the poking on my shoulder to him saying my name as he walked away, grinning. "I don't know."

"Well," she said slowly, reaching behind her head to pull her hair up in a ponytail, "maybe he likes you."

"Oh, stop it." My face started burning again.

"You never know. You shouldn't always assume it's so impossible."

The bell rang and I finished off my Coke, tossing it in the recycling bin beside me. "On to third period."

"Ugh. Oceanography." She put on her backpack. "What about you?"

"I have—" I started, but someone tapped my shoulder, then was gone as I turned around, the classic fake-out. I turned back to Scarlett and saw Macon over her shoulder, on his way to the gym.

"Come on," he yelled across the now-empty courtyard to me. "Don't want to be late for P.E."

"—P.E.," I finished sheepishly, feeling the burn of a new blush on my face. "I better go."

Scarlett just looked at me, shaking her head, like she already knew something I didn't. "Watch out," she said quietly, pulling her backpack over her shoulders.

"For what?" I said.

"You know," she said, and her face was so sad, watching me. Then she shook her head, smiling, and started to walk away. "Just be careful. Of P.E. and all that."

"Okay," I said, wondering if she had visions of me being nailed by errant Wiffle balls or blinded by flying badminton birdies, or if it was only just Macon, and everything he reminded her of, that made her so sad. "I will," I said.

She waved and walked off, up the hill to the Sciences building, and I turned and went the other way, pushing open the gym doors to that smell of mildew and Ben-Gay and sweaty mats, where Macon Faulkner was waiting for me.

P.E. became the most important fifty minutes of my life. Regardless of illness, national disaster, or even death, I would have shown up for third period, in my white socks and blue shorts, ready at the bell. Macon missed occasionally, and those days I was miserable, swatting around my volleyball halfheartedly and watching the clock. But the days he was there, P.E. was the best thing I had going.

Of course I acted like I hated it completely, because it was worse than being a Band geek to actually like P.E. But I was the only one in the girls' locker room who didn't complain loudly as we dressed out at 10:30 A.M. for another day of volleyball basics. All I had to do was walk out of the dressing room, nonchalant, acting like I was still half-asleep and too out of it to notice Macon, who was usually over by the water fountain in nonregulation tennis shoes and no socks (for which he got a minus-five each day of class). I'd sit a few feet over from him, wave, and pretend I wasn't expecting him to slide the few feet across the floor to sit beside me, which he always did. Always. Usually those few minutes before Coach Van Leek got organized with his clipboard were the best part of my day, every day. With a few variations, they went something like this:

Macon: What's up?
Me: I'm so beat.

Macon: Yeah, I was out late last night.

Me: (like I was ever allowed out past eight on school nights) Me, too. I see you're not wearing socks today, again.

Macon: I just forget.

Me: You're gonna fail P.E., you know.

Macon: Not if you buy me some socks.

Me: (laughing sarcastically) Yeah, right.

Macon: Okay. Then it's on your head.

Me: Shut up.

Macon: You ready for volleyball?

Me: (like I'm so tough) Of course. I'm going to beat your butt.

Macon: (laughing) Okay. Sure. We'll see.

Me: Okay. We'll see.

I lived for this.

Macon was not in school to Get an Education or Prepare for College. It was just a necessary evil, tempered by junk food and perpetual tardies. Half the time he showed up looking like he'd just rolled out of bed, and he was forever getting yelled at by Coach for sneaking food into P.E.: Cokes slipped in his backpack, Atomic Fireballs and Twinkies stuffed in his pockets. He was the master of the forged excuse.

"Faulkner," Coach would bark when Macon showed up, ten minutes late, with no socks and half a Zinger sticking out of his mouth, "you'd best have a note."

"Right here," Macon would say cheerfully, drawing one out

61

of his pocket. We'd all watch attentively as Coach scrutinized it. Macon never looked worried. He failed all of P.E.'s notoriously easy quizzes, but he could copy any signature perfectly on the first try. It was a gift.

"It's all in the wrist," he'd tell me as he excused himself for another funeral or doctor's appointment with a flourish of his mother's name. I kept waiting for him to get caught. But it never happened.

He didn't seem to have a curfew; all I knew about his mom was that she didn't dot her *i*s. I didn't even know where he lived. Macon was wild, different, and when I was with him, caught up in it all, I could play along like I was, too. He told me about parties where the cops always came, or road trips he up and took in the middle of the night, no planning, to the beach or D.C., just because he felt like it. He showed up on Mondays with wild stories, T-shirts of bands I'd never heard of, smeared entry stamps from one club or another on the back of his hands. He dropped names and places I'd never heard, but I nodded, committing them to memory and repeating them back to Scarlett as if I knew them all myself, had been there or seen that. Something in him, about him, with his easy loping walk and sly smile, his past secret and mysterious while mine was all laid out and clear, actually documented, intrigued me beyond belief.

Scarlett, of course, just shook her head and smiled as she listened to me prattle on, detailing every word and gesture of our inane sock-and-volleyball conversations. And she sat by without saying anything whenever he didn't show up and I sulked at lunch, picking at my sandwich and saying it wasn't like I liked him anyway. And sometimes, I'd look up at her and see that same sad look on her face, as if Michael Sherwood had suddenly reared up from wherever she'd carefully placed him, reminding her of the beginning of summer when she was the one with all the stories to tell.

Meanwhile, all through September, things were happening. My father's radio show on T104 had gotten an overhaul and format change over the summer and was suddenly The Station to Listen To. In the morning I heard his voice coming from cars in the parking lot or at traffic lights or even at the Zip Mart where Scarlett and I stopped before school for Cokes and gas. My father, making jokes and razzing callers and playing all the music I listened to, the soundtrack to every move I made. *Brian in the Morning!* the billboard out by the mall said; *He's better than Wheaties!* My father thought this was hysterical, even better than *A Neighborhood of Fiends*, and my mother accused him of always taking the long way home just to look at it. His was the voice I heard no matter where I went, inseparable from my life away from our house. It was somewhat unsettling that listening to my *father* was suddenly cool.

The worst was when he talked about me. I was in the Zip Mart before school one day, and of course they had T104 on; people were calling in sharing their most embarrassing moments. About half my school was buying cigarettes and cookies and candy bars, that early morning sugar and nicotine rush. I was at the head of the line when I heard my name.

"Yeah, I remember when my daughter Halley was about five," my father said. "Man, this is like the funniest thing I ever saw. We were at this neighborhood cookout, and my wife and I . . ."

Already my face was turning red. I could feel my temperature jump about ten degrees with each word he said. The clerk, of course, picked this moment to change the register tape. I was stuck.

"So we're standing there talking to some neighbors, right next to this huge mud puddle; it had been raining for a few days and everything was still kind of squishy, you know? Anyway, Halley yells out to me, 'Hey, Dad, look!' So my wife and I look over and here she comes, running like little kids do, all crooked and sideways, you know?"

"Damn," the clerk said, hitting the register tape with his fist. It wasn't going in. I was in hell.

"And I swear," my father went on, now chuckling, "I was thinking as she got closer and closer to that mud puddle, *Man, she's going in.* I could see it coming."

Behind me somebody tittered. My stomach turned in on itself.

"And she hits the edge of that puddle, still running, and her feet just—they just flew out from under her." Now my father dissolved in laughter, along with, oh, about a thousand commuters and office workers all over the tri-county area. "I mean, she skidded on her butt, all the way across that puddle, bumping along with this completely shocked look on her face, until she, like, landed right at out feet. Covered in mud. And we're all trying not to laugh, God help us. It was the funniest thing I think I have ever seen. *Ever.*"

"That'll be one-oh-nine," the clerk said to me suddenly. I threw my dollar and some change at him, pushing past all the grinning faces out to the car, where Scarlett was waiting.

"Oh, man," she said as I slid in. "How embarrassed are *you* right now?"

"Shut up," I said. All day I had to listen to the mud jokes and have people nudge me and giggle. Macon christened me Muddy Britches. It was the worst.

"I'm sorry," my father said to me, first thing that night. I ignored him, walking up the stairs. "I really, really am. It just kind of came out, Halley. Really."

"Brian," my mother said. "I think you should just keep Halley's life off limits. Okay?"

This from the woman who wrote about me in two books. My parents both made their livings humiliating me.

"I know, I know," he said, but he was smiling. "It was just so *funny*, though. Wasn't it?" He giggled, then tried to straighten up. "Right?"

"Real funny," I said. "Hysterical."

This was just one example of how my parents were suddenly, that fall, making me crazy. It wasn't just the statewide shame on the radio, either. It was something I couldn't put my finger on or define clearly, but a whole mishmash of words and incidents, all rolling quickly and building, like a snowball down a hill, to gather strength and bulk to flatten me. It wasn't what they said, or even just the looks they exchanged when they asked me how school was that day and I just mumbled *fine* with my mouth full, glancing wistfully over at Scarlett's, where I was sure she was eating alone, in front of the TV, without having to answer to anyone. There had been a time, once, when my mother would have been the first I'd tell about Macon Faulkner, and what P.E. had become to me. But now I only saw her rigid neck, the tight, thin line of her lips as she sat across from me, reminding me to do my homework, no I couldn't go to Scarlett's it was a school night, don't forget to do the dishes and take the trash out. All things she'd said to me for years. Only now they all seemed loaded with something else, something that fell between us on the table, blocking any further conversation.

I knew my mother wouldn't understand about Macon Faulkner. He was the furthest I could get from her, Noah Vaughn, and the perfect daughter I'd been in that Grand Canyon picture. This world I was in now, of high school and my love affair with P.E., with Michael Sherwood gone, had no place for my mother or what she represented. It was like one of those tests where they ask what thing doesn't belong in this group: an apple, a banana, a pear, a tractor. There wasn't anything she could do about it. My mother, for all her efforts, was that tractor.

Chapter Four

Macon finally asked me out on October 18 at 11:27 A.M. It was a monumental moment, a flashbulb memory. I hadn't had a lot of incredible events in my life, and I intended to remember every detail of this one.

It was a Friday, the day of our badminton quiz. After I handed in my paper, I pulled out my English notebook and started to do my vocabulary, at the same time keeping a close eye on Macon as he chewed his pencil, stared at the ceiling and struggled with the five short questions of the same test Coach had been giving out for the last fifteen years.

A few minutes later he got up to hand in his test, sticking his pencil behind his ear as he passed me. I braced myself, reading the same vocab word, *feuilleton*, over and over again, like a spell, trying to draw him over to talk to me. *Feuilleton, feuilleton,* as he handed his test to Coach, then stretched his arms over his head and started back toward me, taking his time. *Feuilleton, feuilleton,* as he got closer and closer, then grinned as he passed me, heading back to where he'd been sitting. *Feuilleton, feuilleton,* I kept thinking hopelessly, the word swimming in front of my eyes. And then finally, on the last *feuilleton,* the sound of his notebook sliding up next to me, and him plopping down beside it. And just like that, I felt that goofy third-period P.E. rush, like the planets had suddenly aligned and everything was okay for the next fifteen minutes while I had him all to myself.

"So," he said, lying back on the shiny gym floor, his head right next to my leg, "who invented the game of badminton?"

I looked at him. "You don't know?"

"I'm not saying that. I'm just asking what you said."

"I said the right answer."

"Which is?"

I just shrugged. "You know. That guy."

"Oh, yeah." He nodded, grinning, running a hand through his damp hair. "Right. Well, that's what I said too, Muddy Britches."

"Well, good for you." I turned the page of my English notebook, pretending I was concentrating on it.

"What are you doing this weekend?" he said.

"I don't know yet." We had this conversation every Friday; he always had big plans, and I always acted like I did.

"Big date with old Noah?"

"No," I said. Noah's P.E. class had come in for a volleyball tournament with ours, and of course when he grunted hello to me I had to explain who he was. Why I said he'd been my boyfriend I had no idea; I'd been trying to live it down ever since.

"What about you?" I asked him.

"There's this party, I don't know," he said. "Over in the Arbors."

"Really."

"Yeah. It might be lame, though."

I nodded, because that was always safest, then lied, which was second best. "Oh, yeah. I think Scarlett might have mentioned it."

"Yeah, I'm sure she knows about it." Scarlett was our middle ground. "You guys should come, you know?"

"Maybe we will," I said, having already made up my mind we would be there even if God himself tried to stop us. "If she wants to. I don't know."

"Well," he said, looking up at me with a shock of blond hair falling across his forehead, "even if she can't make it, you should come."

"I can't come by myself," I said without thinking.

"You won't be by yourself," he said. "I'll be there."

"Oh." That was when I looked at the clock, over his head, marking this moment forever. The culmination of all those badminton matches and volleyball serves, of laps run around the gym in circles. This was what I'd been waiting for. "Okay. I'll be there."

"Good." He was smiling at me, and right then I would have agreed to anything he asked, as dangerous as that was. "I'll see you there."

The bell rang then, loud and jarring and bounding off the walls of the huge, hollow gym as everyone stood up. Coach Van Leek was yelling about bowling starting on Monday and how we should all come ready to learn the five-step approach, but I wasn't hearing him, or anyone, as Macon grabbed his notebook and stood up, sticking out a hand to me to pull me to my feet. I just looked up at him, wondering what I could be getting myself into, but it didn't matter. I put my hand in Macon's, feeling his fingers close over mine. I let him pull me toward him, to my feet, and my eyes were wide open.

After school Scarlett and I went to her house, where Marion was busy getting ready for a big date with an accountant she'd met named Steve Michaelson. She was painting her fingernails and chain-smoking while Scarlett and I ate potato chips and watched.

"So," I said, "what's this Steve guy like anyway?"

"He's very nice," Marion said in her gravelly voice, exhaling a stream of smoke. "Very serious, but in a sweet way. He's the friend of a friend of a friend."

"Tell her the other thing," Scarlett said, popping another chip in her mouth.

"What thing?" Marion shook the bottle of polish.

"You know."

"What?" I said.

Marion held up one hand, examining it. "Oh, it's just this thing he does. It's a hobby."

"Tell her," Scarlett said again, then raised her eyebrows at me so I knew something good was coming.

Marion looked at her, sighed, and said, "He's in this group. It's like a history club, where they study the medieval period together, on weekends."

"That's interesting," I said as Scarlett pushed her chair out and went to the sink. "A history club."

"Marion." Scarlett ran her hands under the faucet. "Tell her what he *does* in this club."

"What? What does he do?" I couldn't stand it.

"He dresses up," Scarlett said before Marion even opened her mouth. "He has this, like, medieval alter-ego, and on the weekends he and all his friends dress up in medieval clothes and become these characters. They joust and have festivals and sing ballads."

"They don't joust," Marion grumbled, starting on her other hand.

"Yes, they do," Scarlett said. "I talked to him the other night. He told me everything."

"Well, so what?" Marion said. "Big deal. I think it's kind of sweet, actually. It's like a whole other world."

"It's, like, crazy," Scarlett said, coming back to the table and sitting down beside me. "He's a nut."

"He is not."

"You know what his alter-ego name is?" she asked me. "Just guess."

I looked at her. "I cannot imagine."

Marion was acting like she couldn't hear us, engrossed in buffing a pinky nail.

"Vlad," Scarlett said dramatically. "Vlad the Impaler."

"It's not the Impaler," Marion said snippily, "it's the Warrior. There's a difference."

71

"Whatever." Scarlett was never happy with anyone Marion dated; mostly they were men who stared at her uncomfortably as they passed out the door on weekend mornings.

"Well," I said slowly as Marion finished her left hand and waved it in the air, "I'm sure he's very nice."

"He is," she said simply, getting up from the table and walking to the stairs, fingers outstretched and wiggling in front of her. "And Scarlett would know it too, if she ever gave anyone a fair chance."

We heard her go upstairs, the floor creaking over our heads as she walked down the hall to her room. Scarlett picked up the dirty cotton balls, tossing them out, and collected the polish and the remover, putting them back in the basket by the bathroom where they belonged.

"I've given lots of people chances," she said suddenly, as if Marion was still in the room to hear her. "But there's only so much faith you can have in people."

We sat in her bedroom and watched as Steve arrived, in his Hyundai hatchback, with flowers. He didn't look much like a warrior or an impaler as he walked Marion to the car, holding her door open and shutting it neatly behind her. Scarlett didn't look as they drove off, turning her back on the window, but I pressed my palm against the glass, waving back at Marion as they pulled away.

When I went home later, my mother was in the kitchen reading the paper. "Hi there," she said. "How was school?"

"Fine." I stood in the open kitchen doorway, my eyes on the stairs.

"How was that math test? Think you did okay?"

"Sure," I said. "I guess."

"Well, the Vaughns are coming over tonight for a movie, if you want to hang around. They haven't seen you in a while."

Noah Vaughn was in eleventh grade and he still spent his Friday nights watching movies with his parents and mine. I couldn't believe he'd ever been my boyfriend. "I'm going over to Scarlett's."

"Oh." She was nodding. "Okay. What are you two doing?"

I thought of Macon, of that clock in the gym, of the momentous day I'd had, and held back everything. "Nothing much. Just hanging out. I think we're going out for pizza."

A pause. Then, "Well, be in by eleven. And don't forget you're mowing the lawn tomorrow. Right?"

My mother, deep into writing a book about teens and responsibility, had decided I needed to do more chores around the house. *It enhances the sense of family,* she'd said to me. *We're all working toward a common goal.*

"The lawn," I said. "Right."

I was halfway up the stairs when she said, "Halley? If you and Scarlett get bored, come on over. The more the merrier."

"Okay," I said, and I thought again how she always had to have her hands in whatever I did, keeping me with her or herself, somehow, with me, even when I fought hard against it. If

I'd told her about Macon, I could hear her voice already, asking questions: *Whose party was it? Would the parents be there? Would there be drinking?* I imagined her calling the house, demanding to speak to the parents like she had at the first boy-girl party I'd ever gone to. I knew I had to keep him to myself, as I'd slowly begun to keep everything. We had secrets now, truths and half-truths, that kept her always at arm's length, behind a closed door, miles away.

Scarlett and I pulled up at the party at nine-thirty, which we figured was fashionably late since there were already lines of cars up and down the street, parked haphazardly on the curbs and against mailboxes. It was Ginny Tabor's house, Ginny Tabor's party, and the first thing we saw when we walked up the driveway was Ginny Tabor, already drunk and sitting on the back of her mother's BMW with a wine cooler in one hand and a cigarette in the other.

"Scarlett!" she screamed at us as we came up on the front porch, which was white and chocolate brown like the rest of the house. The Tabors lived in what looked like a big gingerbread house, all Tudor and eaves and flower boxes.

Ginny was still yelling at Scarlett as she jumped off the back of the car, dragging Brett Hershey by the hand.

"Hey, girl!" Ginny said as she came closer, stumbling a bit, past a big fountain that was in the middle of the circular driveway. She was in a red dress and heels, too fancy for just a Friday night beer bash. "You're just the person I want to talk to."

Beside me I heard Scarlett sigh. She had a cold and hadn't wanted to come out anyway. It was only because I'd begged her, not wanting to make an entrance by myself, that she'd gotten up off the couch where she'd been comfortable with her tissue box and the television. And that was only after I'd had to dodge Noah Vaughn, who sat sulking in our kitchen as I said good-bye, glaring at me, as if he'd expected me to suddenly decide to be his girlfriend again. His little sister, Clara, clung to my legs and begged me to stay, and my mother reminded me again to bring Scarlett over if I wanted. I half expected them to tie me down and force me to be with them, keeping me from what I was sure would be the most important night of my life.

I only hoped that Macon could appreciate what I'd been through to meet him.

I kept trying to look for him without being obvious, while Ginny threw her arms around Scarlett. Brett stood by looking uncomfortable. He was a steely kind of guy, an All-American jock, with broad shoulders and a crew cut.

"This has been the *best* night. You would not believe the stuff that has happened," Ginny said into Scarlett's face, and I could smell her breath from where I was standing. "Laurie Miller and Kent Hutchinson have been in the guest bedroom like all night, and the neighbors already called the police once. But our housekeeper is chaperoning, so they couldn't do anything but tell us to keep it down."

"Really." Scarlett sniffled, reaching in her pocket for a tissue.

"And Elizabeth Gunderson is here, with all those girls she's been hanging out with since Michael died. They're all up in the attic drinking wine and crying. I heard they had some shrine set up to him, but I'm not sure if that's just a rumor." She took another swig of her wine cooler. "Isn't that weird? Like they're trying to bring him back or something."

"We should go in," I said, grabbing the back of Scarlett's shirt and pulling her behind me. Inside, the music had stopped suddenly, and I could hear a girl laughing. "We're looking for someone."

"Who?" Ginny shouted after us, as Brett wrapped his arms around her waist, holding her back. The music came back on inside, bass thumping, as we got closer. She yelled something I couldn't make out, words half slurred and unfinished, as we went inside.

I pushed the half-open door with my hand, then stepped in and promptly bumped right into Caleb Mitchell and Sasha Benedict, who were lip-locked next to the grandfather clock. In the living room, I could see some people dancing, others lying across the couch in front of the TV, an MTV VJ talking soundlessly on the wide screen. Further back, in the den, a group of girls were playing quarters, bouncing a coin across the coffee table. I didn't see Macon anywhere.

"Come on," Scarlett said, and I followed her down the hall into the kitchen, where a bunch of people were perched on the bright white counters and sitting at the table, smoking cigarettes and drinking. Liza Corbin, who had been the biggest geek before a summer of modeling school and a nose job, was perched on some linebacker's lap, head thrown back against his shoulder, laughing. Another girl from my homeroom was sitting on the floor, knees pulled up to her chest, holding a wine cooler and looking kind of green. Scarlett walked down a side hallway and pushed open a door, surprising a Hispanic woman inside who was sitting on a twin bed watching a *Falcon Crest* rerun and doing needlepoint.

"Sorry," Scarlett said as the woman looked up at us, eyes wide, and we closed the door again. She shook her head, smiling. "That must be the chaperone."

"Must be," I said. I was beginning to think this whole night had been a mistake; we'd seen just about every member of the football team, all the cheerleaders, about half the school tramps, and no Macon anywhere. I felt stupid in the clothes I'd so carefully picked out to seem thrown on at random, as if I went to parties to meet boys all the time.

We went upstairs, still looking, but he wasn't there. I felt like a fool, searching for him when he was probably miles away, on the way to the beach or D.C., just because he felt like it.

I could tell something big was happening before we even got back downstairs; it was too quiet, and I could hear someone screaming. As I peered around the corner, I saw Ginny in the living room, standing over a pile of broken glass on the carpet. A red stain that matched her dress was seeping into the thick, white pile. She was unsteady, her face flushed, one finger pointed at the door.

"That's it, get *out!*" she screamed at the group of people

huddled around her, who all stepped back a couple of feet and kept staring. "I *mean* it. *Now!!!*"

"Uh-oh," Scarlett said from behind me. "I wonder what happened."

"Someone broke some precious heirloom," a girl in front of us, who I recognized from P.E., said in a low voice. "Wedgwood or crystal or something, and spilled red wine all over the carpet."

Ginny was down on her hands and knees now, blotting the carpet with a T-shirt, while a few of her friends stood around uncertainly, offering cleaning tips. The crowd around the living room started to shift toward the door.

"This is lame," some girl in a halter top said over her shoulder as she passed us. "And there's no beer left anyway."

Her friend, a redhead with a pierced nose, nodded, flipping her long hair back with one hand. "I heard there's a frat party uptown tonight. Let's go up there. It's gotta be better than all these high-school boys."

One by one Ginny's friends drifted off, gathering their cigarettes and purses and backing out of the room. Brett Hershey, ever the gentleman, had found a brush and dustpan and was cleaning up the glass while Ginny sat down on the carpet, crying, as the house got quieter and quieter.

I just looked at Scarlett, wondering what we should do, and she glanced into the living room and called out in a cheerful voice, "Bye, Ginny. See you Monday."

Ginny looked up at us. Her mascara had run, leaving black

smudges under her eyes. "My parents are going to kill me," she wailed, patting at the stained carpet helplessly. "That glass was a wedding gift. And there's no way I can cover this."

"Soda water," Scarlett said as I inched open the door, hoping for a clean getaway. Ginny just looked up at us, confused. "And a little Clorox. It'll take it right out."

"Soda water," Ginny repeated slowly. "Thanks."

We slipped out the door, letting it fall shut behind us. Someone had left an empty six-pack container on the fountain, and a bottle was floating in its sparkling water and knocking against its sides, clinking, as we passed.

"What a drag," Scarlett said as we came up on her car. She was being quietly respectful of my sulking. "Really."

"I should have known better," I said. "Like he was really asking me to meet him."

"It sounded like he was."

"Whatever," I said, getting in the car as she started the engine. "I'm probably better off."

"I know *I* am," she said cheerfully, pulling out onto the street, the big houses of the Arbors looming on either side of us. "Now I don't have to hear the sordid details of P.E. every day."

"Leave me alone." I leaned my head against the cool glass of the window. "This sucks."

"I know," she said softly, reaching over and patting my leg. "I know."

When we got home we sat out on the front steps, drinking

79

Cokes and not talking much. Scarlett blew her nose a lot and I tried to salvage what was left of my pride, making lame excuses neither one of us believed.

"I never really liked him," I said. "He's too wild anyway."

"Yeah," she said, but I could feel her smiling in the dark. "He's not your type."

"He isn't," I went on, ignoring her. "He needs to be dating Ginny Tabor. Or Elizabeth Gunderson. Someone with a reputation to match his. I was so stupid for even thinking he'd look twice at someone like me."

She leaned back against the door, stretching out her legs. "Why do you say stuff like that?"

"Stuff like what?" Across the street I could see Noah Vaughn pass in front of our window.

"*Someone like you.* Any guy would be damn lucky to have you, Halley, and you know it. You're beautiful and smart and loyal and funny. Elizabeth Gunderson and Ginny are just stupid girls with loud voices. That's it. You're special."

"Scarlett," I said. "Please."

"You don't have to believe me," she said, waving me off. "But it's true, and I know you better than anyone. Macon Faulkner would be damn lucky if *you* chose *him*." She sneezed again, fumbling around for a Kleenex. "Shoot, I'll be right back. Hold on."

She went inside, the door creaking slowly shut behind her, and I sat back against the steps, staring up at my brightly lit house and the dark sky above it. Inside, my father was probably popping popcorn and drinking a beer, while my mother and Mrs. Vaughn talked too much during the movie so you couldn't hear anything. Noah was still sulking, for sure, and Clara was probably already curled up asleep on my bed, to be carried to the car later. I knew those Friday nights by heart. But my mother didn't understand why I couldn't spend the rest of my life on that couch with Noah, a bowl of popcorn in my lap, with her on my other side. Why just the thought of it was enough to make me feel like I couldn't breathe, or too sad to even look her in the eye.

Then, suddenly, I noticed someone walking up the street toward my house, dodging through the McDowells' yard and through their hedge, then darting across the sidewalk and down the far end of my front yard. I sat up straighter, watching the shadow slip past the row of trees my mother was trying to nudge into growing against the fence, stepping smoothly over the hole where my father had sprained his ankle mowing the lawn the summer before. I got up off the steps and crept across the street, coming up on the side of my house.

Whoever it was finally came to a stop under my side bedroom window, then stood looking up at it for a good long while before bending down, picking up something, and tossing it. I heard a *ping* as it bounced off the glass and I moved closer, close enough to see the person more clearly as he tossed up another rock, missing altogether and hitting the gutter, which was loose and rattled loudly. I was also close enough to hear the voice now, a hushed whisper.

81

"Halley!" Then a pause, and another ping of a rock hitting the glass. "Halley!"

I moved behind the tree that shaded my bedroom in summer, a mere two feet away from Macon Faulkner, who seemed determined to break my window or at least weaken it to the point of spontaneous collapse.

"Halley!" He stepped closer to the house, craning his neck.

I crept up behind him, silent, and tapped him on the shoulder just as he was launching another rock; he jerked to face me, not quite completing the throw, so it rained back down on him, bouncing off his head and landing between us on the ground.

"Shoot," he said, all flustered. He'd almost jumped out of his skin. "Where did you come from?"

"Why are you trying to break my window?"

"I'm not. I was trying to get your attention."

"But I wasn't home." I said.

"I didn't know that," he said. "You scared the crap out of me."

"Sorry," I said, and I couldn't believe he was here, in my yard, like some kind of ghost I'd conjured up with wishful thinking. "How'd you know this was my window anyway?"

"Just did," he said simply. I was noticing that he didn't usually explain what he didn't have to. He was still a little shaken but now he grinned at me, his teeth white, like this was not unusual or amazing. "Where were you?"

"When?"

"Earlier. I thought you were coming to that party."

"I was there," I said, trying to sound casual. "I didn't see you."

"Oh," he said confidently, "that's a lie."

"I was," I said. "We just got home."

"I have been there since seven o'clock," he said loudly, talking over me, "and I was looking for you, and waiting, and you stood me up—"

"No, you stood *me* up," I said in a louder voice, "and I have Scarlett to vouch for it."

"Scarlett? She wasn't there either."

"Yes, she was. She was with me." I looked back across the street, where she was standing on the steps, one hand shielding her eyes, looking over at us. I waved, and she waved back, then sat down and blew her nose.

"I was upstairs," he said. "I never saw you."

"Where upstairs?"

"In the attic."

"Oh," I said. "We didn't go there."

"Why not?"

I just looked at him. "Why would we?"

"I don't know," he said, out of arguments. "I did."

A light came on upstairs in my room, and I heard the window sliding open. My father stuck his head out, looking around, and I pushed Macon into the shadow of the house, then stepped back into the brightness of the side porch light.

"Hi," I called out, startling my father, who jerked back and slammed his head on the window. "It's just me."

"Halley?" He turned around, rubbing his head, and said into the house, "It's just Halley, Clara, go back to sleep. It's fine."

Macon was looking up at my father; if he had glanced down, he could have made him out easily.

"I was looking for something," I said suddenly. I hadn't lied to my father very much, so I was grateful for the dark. "I dropped a bracelet of Scarlett's out here and we were looking for it."

My father craned his neck, looking around. "A bracelet? Is Scarlett down there?"

"Yes," I said, and the lies just rolled out of me, on and on, "I mean, no, she was but we found it and she went back to her house. Because she's got this cold and all. So I was just, um, getting ready to follow her. When you opened the window."

In front of me, Macon was quietly snickering.

"Isn't it about time for you to be in?" my father said. "It's almost ten-thirty."

"I'll be home by eleven."

"You two should come over now. We've got this great movie on that Noah brought and I just made popcorn."

"That sounds great, but I better get back across the street," I said quickly, stepping back under the shield of the tree behind me. "I'll see you in the morning."

He snapped his fingers. "That's right! Don't you have a morning date with—" and here he paused, dramatically—"the Beast?"

I was about to die.

"The Beast?" Macon whispered, grinning. Above us, my father was making growling noises.

The Beast, of course, was my father's pet name for his mower, his most prized possession. He was so embarrassing.

"Yeah," I said, willing him with all my power to go away. "I guess."

"Okay, then," he said, starting to pull the window shut and having to bank it with the side of his hand at the point where it always stuck. "Don't creep around out there, okay? You scared Clara to death."

"Right," I said as the window clicked shut, and I could see my room behind him until the light cut off. I stood there, breathing heavily, until I was sure he was gone.

"You," Macon said, stepping out where I could see him, "are such a liar."

"I am not," I said. "Well, not usually. But he would have freaked if he'd seen you."

"You want me to leave?" He stepped closer to me, and even in the dark I knew every inch of his face from all those hours of P.E., studying him across a badminton net.

"Yes," I said loudly, and he pretended to walk off but I grabbed his arm, pulling him back. "I'm kidding."

"You sure?"

"Yes." And for a minute it was like I wasn't even myself anymore; I could have been any girl, someone bold and reckless. There was something about Macon that made me act different, giving that black outline some inside color, at last. I was still holding his arm, my face hot, and in the dark I might have been Elizabeth Gunderson or Ginny Tabor or even Scarlett, any girl that things happen to. And as he leaned in to kiss me, I thought of nothing but how unbelievable it was that this was all happening, in my side yard, the most familiar of places.

Just then a car came screeching around the corner, music blaring. It passed my house, horn beeping, and then turned onto Honeysuckle, where it sat idling.

"I gotta go," Macon said, kissing me again. "I'll call you tomorrow."

"Wait—" I said as he pulled away, holding my hand until he had to let go of it. "Where are you going?"

"Faulkner!" I heard a voice yell from down the street. "Where are you?"

"Bye, Halley," he whispered, smiling at me as he slipped easily around the side of the house, disappearing into the darkness of my backyard. I leaned around the corner, watching him as he ducked beneath the kitchen window, where Noah Vaughn was standing. His face was stony, solemn, as he stared at me, holding a Coke in his hand. He couldn't see what I saw: Macon, my last glimpse, vanishing into thin air.

The next morning my father was grinning when I came outside. He loved this. "Well, hey there, lawn girl. Ready to take on the Beast?" Then he made the growling noise again.

"You're not funny," I said.

"Sure I am." He chuckled. "Better get started before it gets any warmer. It'll take you a good two hours, at least."

"Shut *up*," I said, which just made him laugh harder. My father believes our lawn is impossible; over the years it had sent yard services and neighborhood mowing boys running for their lives. My father, the only one who could navigate it safely, saw himself as a warrior, victorious among the grass clippings.

"Okay, here's the thing," he said, now suddenly serious. "There's the Hole between the junipers that got me last summer, as well as a row of tree roots by the fence that were made specifically to pull you to the side and cut your motor. Not to mention the ruts in the backyard and the series of hidden tree stumps. But you'll do fine."

"Just let me get it over with." I leaned down and started the mower, pushing it to the front curb, with him still behind me chuckling.

It was hot, loud, and too bright out in that yard. I got sleepy, then careless, and hit the Hole, which of course I'd forgotten; my ankle twisted in it and I fell forward, the mower flying out from under me and sputtering to a stop. By this time my father had gone to the fence by the driveway and was busy talking lawns or golf or whatever with Mr. Perkins, our neighbor. Neither one of them noticed me do a faceplant in the grass, then kick the mower a few feet out of pure vengeance.

I heard a horn beep and turned to see a red pickup truck sliding to a stop by the curb, a green tarp thrown over something in the truck bed. It was Macon.

"Hey," he said, getting out of the truck and slamming the door. "How's it going?"

"Fine," I said. "Actually, it's not. I just fell down." I looked over at my father, who was staring right back at us.

"That your dad?" Macon said.

"Yep," I said. "That's him."

Macon looked around the yard, at the small patch I'd done so far and the high grass that lay ahead all around us, spurred on by a straight week of rain. "So," he said confidently, "you want some help?"

"Oh, you don't want to . . ." I said, but he was already walking back to the truck, pulling the tarp aside to reveal a mower twice the size of mine, which he wheeled off a ramp on the back. He had on his BROADSIDE HOME AND GARDEN baseball hat, which he flipped around backwards, readying for action.

"You don't understand," I said to him as he started checking the gas, examining the wheels, "this lawn is, like, impossible. You practically need a map to keep from killing yourself."

"Are you underestimating my ability as a lawn-service provider?" he asked, looking up at me. "I sincerely *hope* that you are not."

"I'm not," I said quickly, "but it's just . . . I mean, it's really hard."

"Psssh," he said, fanning me off with one hand. "Just stand back, okay?" And then he stood up, pulled the cord, and the mower roared to life and started across the lawn with Macon guiding it. It sucked up the grass, marking a swath twice as wide as I'd been managing with the Beast. I turned around to look at my father, who was staring at Macon as he glided over the tree roots and past the Hole, and edged the fence perfectly.

"Halley," my father said from behind me, yelling over the roar of the mower, "this is supposed to be *your* job."

"I'm working," I said quickly, starting up my own mower, which puttered quietly like a kid's toy as I pushed it along between the juniper bushes. "See?"

I didn't hear what he said as Macon passed us again, the mower annihilating the grass and leaving a smooth, green trail behind him. He nodded at my father, all business, as he turned the corner and disappeared around the side of the house, the roar scaring all the birds at the feeder on the back porch into sudden flight.

"Who is that kid?" my father said, craning his neck around the side of the house.

"What?" I was still pushing my mower, circling the trees by the fence. The smell of cut grass filled the air, sweet and pungent.

"Who is he?"

I cut off the mower. In the backyard I could see Macon mowing around the hidden tree stumps. My father saw it too, his face shocked. "He's my friend," I said.

There must have been some giveaway in how I said it because suddenly his face changed and I could tell he wasn't thinking about the lawn anymore.

My mother came out the front door, holding her coffee

cup. "Brian? There's some strange boy mowing the lawn."

"I know," my father said. "I'm handling it."

"I thought that was Halley's job," she said like I wasn't even there. "Right?"

"Right," he said in a tired voice. "It's under control."

"Fine." She went back inside, but I could see her standing in the glass door, watching us.

"This was supposed to be your job," he said, as if reading off a script she'd written.

"I didn't *ask* him to do it," I said as the mower roared around the corner of the house, edging the garage. "We were talking about it last night and I guess he just remembered. He works mowing lawns, Dad. He just wanted to help me out."

"Well, that doesn't change the fact that it was your responsibility." It was an effort, but he was fading.

The mower was roaring toward us now as Macon finished off the patch by the front walk. Then he came closer, until the noise was deafening, before finally cutting it off. We all stood there in the sudden silence, looking at each other. My ears were ringing.

"Macon," I said slowly, "this is my dad. Dad, this is Macon Faulkner."

Macon stuck his hand out and shook my father's, then leaned back against the mower, taking off his hat. "Man, that is one tough yard you have there," he said. "Those tree stumps out back almost killed me."

My father, hesitant, couldn't help but smile. He wasn't sure how my mother would want him to react to this. "Well," he said, easing back and sticking his hands in his pockets, "they've brought down a few in their time, let me tell you."

"I can believe it," Macon said. I looked over his head, back toward the house, and saw my mother standing in the doorway, still watching. I couldn't make out her expression. "This thing is equipped with sensors and stuff, so it makes it easier."

"Sensors?" my father stepped a little closer, peering down at the mower's control console. He was clearly torn between doing the Right Thing and his complete love of garden tools and accessories. "Really."

"This thing here," Macon explained, pointing, "shows how far you've gone. And then anything over a height the blade can handle pops up here, on the Terrain Scope, so you can work around it."

"Terrain Scope," my father repeated dreamily.

Then we all heard it; the front door opening and my mother's voice, shattering the lawn reverie with a shrillness she had never been able to control. "Brian? Could you come here a moment, please?"

My father started to back away from Macon, toward the house, his eyes still on the mower. "Coming," he called out, then turned to face her, climbing the steps. I could see her mouth moving, angrily, before he even got to the porch.

"Thanks," I said to Macon. "You saved me."

"No problem." He started pushing the mower back to the curb. "I gotta get this thing back, though. I'll see you later, right?"

"Yeah," I said, watching him climb back into the truck. He took his hat off and tossed it onto the seat. "I'll see you later."

He drove off, beeping the horn twice as he rounded the corner. I walked as slowly as I could up the driveway and front walk to the porch, where my mother was waiting.

"Halley," she said before I even hit the first step, "I thought we had an understanding that it was your job to mow the lawn."

"I know," I said, and my father was studying some spot over my head, avoiding making eye contact, "he just wanted to help me out."

"Who is he?"

"He's just this guy," I said.

"How do you know him?"

"We have P.E. together," I said, opening the door and slipping inside, making my getaway. "It's no big deal."

"He seems nice enough," my father offered, his eyes on the lawn.

"I don't know," she said slowly. I started up the stairs, pretending not to hear her, turning away to keep my secrets to myself. "I just don't know."

Part II

SOMEONE LIKE YOU

Chapter Five

"I need you," Scarlett said to me as I was busy weighing produce for a woman with two screaming babies in her cart. "Meet me in the ladies' room."

"What?" I said, distracted by the noise and confusion, oranges and plums rolling down my conveyer belt.

"Hurry," she hissed, disappearing down the cereal aisle and leaving me no chance to argue. My line was long, snaking around the Halloween display and back into Feminine Products. It took me a good fifteen minutes to get to the bathroom, where she was standing in front of the sinks, arms crossed over her chest.

"What's wrong?" I said.

She just shook her head.

"What?" I said. "What is it?"

She reached behind the paper towel dispenser and pulled out a small white stick-shaped object with a little circle on the end of it. As she held it out, I saw that in the little circle was a bright pink cross. Then, all at once, it hit me.

"No," I said. "No way."

She nodded, biting her lip. "I'm pregnant."

"You can't be."

"I am." She shook the stick in front of me, the plus sign blurring. "Look."

"Those things are always wrong," I said, like I knew.

"It's the third one I've taken."

"So?" I said.

"So what? So nothing is wrong three times, Halley. And I've been sick every morning for the last three weeks, I can't stop peeing, it's all there. I'm pregnant."

"No," I said. I could see my mother in my head, lips forming the word: *denial.* "No way."

"What am I going to do?" she said, pacing nervously. "I only had sex one time."

"You had *sex?*" I said.

She stopped. "Of *course* I had sex. God, Halley, try to stay with me here."

"You never told me," I said. "Why didn't you tell me?"

She sighed, loudly. "Gosh, Halley, I don't know. Maybe it was because he *died* the next day. Go figure."

"Oh, my God," I said. "Didn't you use protection?"

"Of course we did. But something happened, I don't know. It came off. I didn't realize it until it was over. And then," she said, her voice rising, "I thought there was no way it could happen the first time. It couldn't."

"It came off?" I didn't understand, exactly; I wasn't very clear on the logistics of sex. "Oh, my God."

"This is nuts." She pressed her fingers to her temples, hard, something I'd never seen her do before. "I can't have a baby, Halley."

"Of course you can't," I said.

"So, what, I have to get an abortion?" She shook her head. "I can't do that. Maybe I should keep it."

"Oh, my God," I said again.

"Please." She sat down against the wall, pulling her legs up against her chest. "Please stop saying that."

I went over and sat beside her, putting my arm around her shoulders. We sat there together on the cold floor of Milton's, hearing the muffled Muzak playing "Fernando" overhead.

"It'll be okay," I said in my most confident voice. "We can handle this."

"Oh, Halley," she said softly, leaning against me, the pregnancy stick lying in front of us, plus sign up. "I miss him. I miss him so much."

"I know," I said, and I knew now it was my job to hold us together, my turn to see us through. "It'll be okay, Scarlett. Everything is going to be fine."

But even as I said it, I was scared.

That evening, we had a meeting at Scarlett's kitchen table. Me, Scarlett, and Marion, who didn't know anything yet and ate her dinner incredibly slowly as we edged around her. She had a date with Steve/Vlad at eight, so we were working with a time frame.

"So," I said, looking right at Scarlett, who was overstuffing the napkin holder with napkins, "it's almost eight."

"Is it?" Marion turned around and looked at the kitchen clock. She reached for her cigarettes, pushed her chair out from the table, and said, "I better start getting ready."

She started to leave, and I shot Scarlett a look. She looked right back. We battled it out silently for a few seconds before she said, very quietly, in a voice flat enough to ensure anyone wouldn't, "Wait."

Marion didn't hear her. Scarlett shrugged her shoulders, like she'd tried, and I stood up and got ready to call after her. I could hear Marion heading up the stairs, past the creaky third one, when Scarlett sighed and said, louder, "Marion. Wait."

Marion came back down and stuck her head into the kitchen. She'd had to get two two-hundred-and-fifty-pound women glamorous that day at Fabulous You, one of whom wanted lingerie shots, so she was worn out. "What?"

"I have to talk to you."

Marion stood in the doorway. "What's going on?"

Scarlett looked at me, as if this was some kind of relay race and I could carry the baton from here. Marion was starting to look nervous.

"What?" she asked, looking from Scarlett to me, then back to Scarlett. "What is it?"

"It's bad," Scarlett said, and started crying. "It's really bad."

"Bad?" Now Marion looked scared. "Scarlett, tell me. Now."

"I can't," Scarlett managed, still crying.

"Now." Marion put one hand on her hip. It was my mother's classic stance but it looked out of place on Marion, as if she was wearing a funny hat. "I mean it."

Then Scarlett just spit it out. "I'm pregnant."

Everything was really quiet all of a sudden, and I suddenly noticed that the faucet was leaking, *drip drip drip*.

Then Marion spoke. "Since when?"

Scarlett fumbled for a minute, getting her bearings. She'd been expecting something else. "When?"

"Yes." Marion still wasn't looking at either of us.

"Ummm . . ." Scarlett looked at me helplessly. "August?"

"August," Marion repeated, like it was the clue that solved the puzzle. She sighed, very loudly. "Well, then."

The doorbell rang, all cheerful, and as I glanced out the front window I could see Steve/Vlad on the front porch carrying a bunch of flowers. He waved at us and rang the bell again.

"Oh, God," Marion said. "That's Steve."

"Marion," Scarlett began, stepping closer to her, "I didn't mean for it to happen—I used something, but . . ."

"We'll have to talk about this later," Marion told her, running her hands through her hair nervously, straightening her dress as she headed for the door. "I can't—I can't talk about this now."

Scarlett wiped her eyes, started to say something, and then turned and ran out of the room, up the stairs. I heard her bedroom door slam, hard.

Marion took a deep breath, composed herself, and went to

the front door. Steve was standing there, smiling in his sports jacket and Weejuns. He handed her the flowers.

"Hi," he said. "Are you ready?"

"Not quite," Marion said quickly, smiling as best she could. "I have to get something—I'll be right down, okay?"

"Fine."

Marion went upstairs and I heard her knocking on Scarlett's door, her voice muffled. Steve came in the kitchen. He looked even blander under bright light. "Hello there," he said. "I'm Steve."

"Halley," I said, still trying to listen to what was happening upstairs. "It's nice to meet you."

"Are you a friend of Scarlett's?" he asked.

"Yes," I said, and now I could hear Scarlett's voice, raised, through the ceiling overhead. I thought I could make out the word *hypocrite*. "I am."

"She seems like a nice girl," he said. "Halley. That's an un-usual name."

"I was named for my grandmother," I told him. Now I could hear Marion's voice, stern, and I babbled on to cover it. "She was named for the comet."

"Really?"

"Yes," I said, "she was born in May of 1910, when the comet was coming through. Her father watched it from the hospital lawn while her mom was in the delivery room. And in 1986, when I was six, we watched it together."

"That's fascinating," Steve said, like he really meant it.

SOMEONE LIKE YOU

"Well, I don't remember it that well," I said. "They say it wasn't very clear that year."

"I see," Steve said. He seemed relieved to hear Marion coming down the stairs.

"Ready?" she called out, all composure, but she still wouldn't look at me.

"Ready," Steve said cheerfully. "Nice to meet you, Halley."

"Nice to meet you, too."

He slipped his arm around Marion as they left, his hand on the small of her back as they headed down the front walk. She was nodding, listening as he spoke, holding her car door open. As they pulled away she let herself look back and up, to Scarlett's bedroom window.

When I went upstairs, Scarlett was on the bed, her legs pulled up against her chest. The flowers Steve had brought Marion were abandoned on the dresser, still in their crinkly cellophane wrapper.

"So," I said. "I think that went really well, don't you?"

She smiled, barely. "You should have heard her. All this stuff about the mistakes she'd made and how I should have known better. Like doing this was some way of proving her the worst mother ever."

"No," I said, "I think my mother's got that one pegged."

"Your mother would sit you down and discuss this, rationally, and then counsel you to the best decision. Not run out the door with some warrior."

"My mother," I said, "would drop dead on the spot."

101

She got up and went to the dresser mirror, leaning in to look at herself. "She says we'll go to the clinic on Monday and make an appointment. For an abortion."

I could see myself behind her in the mirror. "Is that what you decided to do?"

"There wasn't much of a discussion." She ran her hands over her stomach, along the waist of her jeans. "She said she had one, a long time ago. When I was six or seven. She said it's no big deal."

"It'd be so hard to have a baby," I said, trying to help. "I mean, you're only sixteen. You've got your whole life ahead of you."

"She did, too. When she had me."

"That was different," I said, but I knew it really wasn't. Marion had been a senior in high school, about to go off to some women's college out west. Scarlett's father was a football player, student council president. He left for a Big East school and Marion never saw or contacted him again.

"Keeping me was probably the only unselfish thing Marion's ever done in her life," Scarlett said. "I've always wondered why she did."

"Stop it," I said. "Don't talk like that."

"It's true," she said. "I've always wondered." She stepped back from the mirror, letting her hands drop to her sides. We'd spent our lifetimes in this room, but there had never been anything, ever, like this. This was bigger than us.

"It'll be all right," I told her.

"I know," she said quietly, looking into the mirror at herself and me beyond it. "I know."

It was going to be done that Friday. We never talked about it openly; it was whispered, never called by name, as a silence settled over Scarlett's house, filling the rooms to the ceiling. To Marion, it was already a Done Deal. She went to the clinic counseling sessions with Scarlett, handling all the details. As the week wound down, Scarlett grew more and more quiet.

On Friday, my mother drove me to school. I'd told her Scarlett had something to do and couldn't take me; then, we pulled up behind her and Marion at a stoplight near Lakeview. They didn't see us. Scarlett was looking out the window, and Marion was smoking, her elbow jutting out the driver's side window. It still didn't seem real that Scarlett was even pregnant, and now the next time I saw her it would be wiped clean, forgotten.

"Well, there's Scarlett right there," my mother said. "I thought you said she wasn't going to school today."

"She isn't," I said. "She has an appointment."

"Oh. Is she sick?"

"No." I turned up the radio, my father's voice filling the car. *It's eight-oh-four A.M., I'm Brian, and you're listening to T104, the only good thing about getting up in the morning. . . .*

"Well, there must be something wrong if she's going to the doctor," my mother said as the light finally changed and Scarlett and Marion turned left, toward downtown.

"I don't think it's a doctor's appointment," I said. "I don't know what it is."

"Maybe it's the dentist," she said thoughtfully. "Which reminds me, you're due for a cleaning and checkup."

"I don't know," I said again.

"Is she missing the whole day or just coming in late?"

"She didn't say." I was squirming in my seat, keeping my eye on the yellow school bus in front of us.

"I thought you two told each other everything," she said with a laugh, glancing at me. "Right?"

I was wondering exactly what that was supposed to mean. Everything she said seemed to have double meanings, like a secret language that needed decoding with a special ring or chart I didn't have. I wanted to shout, *She's having an abortion, Mom! Are you happy now?* just to see her face. I imagined her exploding on the spot, disappearing with a puff of smoke, or melting into a puddle like the Wicked Witch of the West. When we pulled into the parking lot, I was never so glad to see school in my life.

"Thanks," I said, kissing her on the cheek quickly and sliding out of the car.

"Come home right after school," she called after me. "I'm making dinner and we need to talk about your birthday, right?"

Tomorrow was my sixteenth birthday. I hadn't even had much time to think about it. A few months ago, it had been the only thing I had to look forward to: my driver's license, free-dom, all the things I'd been waiting for.

"Right. I'll see you tonight," I said to her, backing up, losing myself in the crowd pushing through the front doors. I was walking through the main building, headed outside, when Ma-con fell into step beside me. He always seemed to appear out of nowhere, magic; I never saw him coming.

"Hey," he said, sliding his arm over my shoulders. He smelled like strawberry Jolly Ranchers, smoke, and aftershave, a strange mix I had grown to love. "What's up?"

"My mother is driving me nuts," I said as we walked outside. "I almost killed her on the way to school today."

"She drove you?" he said, glancing around. "Where is Scar-lett, anyway?"

"She had an appointment or something," I said. I felt worse, much worse, lying to him than I had to my mother.

"So," he said, "don't make plans for tomorrow night."

"Why?"

"I'm taking you somewhere for your birthday."

"Where?"

He grinned. "You'll see."

"Okay," I said, pushing away the thought of the party my mother was planning, complete with ice-cream cake and the Vaughns and dinner at Alfredo's, my favorite restaurant. "I'm all yours."

The bell rang, and he walked with me toward homeroom

until someone called his name. A group of guys I'd met uptown with him a few days before, with longer hair and sleepy eyes, were waving him over toward the parking lot. No matter how well I thought I was getting to know him, there was always some part of himself he kept hidden: people and places, activities in which I wasn't included. I got a phone call each evening, early, just him checking in to say hello. What he did after that, I had no idea.

"I gotta go," he said, kissing me quickly. I felt him slide something in the back pocket of my jeans as he started to walk away, already blending with the packs of people. I already knew what it was, before I even pulled it out: a Jolly Rancher. I had a slowly growing collection of candy at home, in a dish on my desk. I saved every one.

"What about homeroom?" I said. For all my pretend rebellion I'd never missed homeroom or skipped school in my life. Macon had a scattered attendance rate at best, and I didn't even ask him about his grades. All the women's magazines said you couldn't change a man, but I was learning this the hard way.

"I'll see you third period," he said, ignoring the question altogether. Then he turned and started toward the parking lot, tucking his one hardly cracked notebook under his arm. A group of girls from my English class giggled as they passed me, watching him. We'd been big news the last two weeks; a month ago I'd been Scarlett's friend Halley, and now I was Halley, Macon Faulkner's girlfriend.

At the end of second period, someone knocked on the door of my Commercial Design class and handed Mrs. Pate a slip of paper; she read it, looked at me, and told me to get my stuff. I'd been summoned to the office.

I was nervous, walking down the corridor, trying to think of anything I'd done that could get me in trouble. But when I got there the receptionist handed me the phone and said, "It's your mother."

I had a sudden flash: my father, dead. My grandmother, dead. Anyone, dead. I picked up the phone. "Hello? Mom?"

"Hold on," I heard someone say, and there were some muffled noises. Then, "Hello? Halley?"

"Scar—?"

"Shhhh! I'm your mother, remember?"

"Right," I said, but the receptionist was busy arguing with some kid over a tardy slip and not even paying attention. "What's going on?"

"I need you to come get me," she said. "At the clinic."

I looked at the clock. It was only ten-fifteen. "Is it over? Already?"

"No." A pause. Then, "I changed my mind."

"You what?"

"I changed my mind. I'm keeping the baby."

She sounded so calm, so sure. There was nothing I could think of to say.

"Where's Marion?" I said.

"I told her to leave me here," she said. "I said she was making me nervous. I was supposed to call her to come get me after."

"Oh," I said.

"Can you come? Please?"

"Sure," I said, and now the receptionist was watching me. "But, Mom, I think you have to tell them to give me a pass or something."

"Right," Scarlett said, all business. "I'm going to put my friend Mary back on the phone. I'm at the clinic on First Street, okay? Hurry."

"Right," I said, wondering how I was getting anywhere, since I had no car.

There were some more muffled noises, Scarlett giving instructions, then the same voice I'd heard earlier came back on. "This is Mrs. Cooke."

"Hold on," I said. I held out the phone to the receptionist. "My mom needs to talk to you."

She tucked her pen behind her ear and took the receiver. "Hello?"

I concentrated on the late sign-in sheet on the counter in front of me, trying not to look twitchy.

"She does? Okay, that's fine. No, it's no problem. I'll just give her a pass. Thank you, Mrs. Cooke." She hung up and scribbled out a pass. "Just show this to the guard as you leave the parking lot. And keep it to show your teachers so your absence is excused."

"Right," I said as the bell rang and the hallway outside started to fill up. "Thanks."

"And I hope the surgery goes well," she said, eyeing me carefully.

"Right," I said, backing into the door to push it open. "Thanks."

I stood outside of P.E., waiting for Macon. As he passed, on his way to dress out, I grabbed his shirt and pulled him back.

"Hey," he said, grinning. I still felt that rush whenever he looked so happy to see me. "What's up?"

"I need a favor."

"Sure. What is it?"

"I need you to skip P.E. with me."

He thought for about a second, then said, "Done. Let's go."

"Wait." I pulled him back. "And I need a ride somewhere."

"A ride?"

"Yeah."

He shrugged. "No problem. Come on."

We walked up to the parking lot and got into his car; he pushed a pile of stereo parts out of my seat. The car smelled slightly smoky and sweet, the same smell that followed him, faintly, wherever he went. He was always in a different car, which was also something he never felt it necessary to explain. So far I'd seen him in a Toyota, a pickup, and some foreign model that smelled like perfume. All of them had candy wrappers littering the floors and stuffed in the ashtrays.

Today he was in the Toyota.

"Wait a sec," I said as he started the engine. "This isn't going to work. You don't have a pass to get out."

"Don't worry about it," he said casually, grabbing something from his visor, scribbling on it, and starting up the hill toward the guardhouse. The security guy, an African-American guy we called Mr. Joe, came out with his clipboard, looking bored.

"Macon," I hissed as we slid to a stop. I doubted even the Jedi Mind Trick would fool Mr. Joe. "This will not work; you should just go back—"

"Hush," he said, rolling down the window as Joe came closer, the sun glinting off his store-bought security guard badge. "What's up, Joe?"

"Not much," Joe said, looking in at me. "You got a pass, Faulkner?"

"Right here," Macon said, handing him the scrap of paper he'd pulled down from the visor. Joe glanced at it, handing it back, then looked in at me.

"What about you?"

"Right here," Macon said cheerfully, taking my pass and handing it over. Joe examined it carefully, taking much longer than he had with Macon's.

"Y'all drive safe," Joe said, handing my pass back. "I mean it, Faulkner."

"Right," Macon said. "Thanks."

Joe grumbled, ambling back to his stool and mini-TV in the

guardhouse, and Macon and I pulled out onto the road, free.

"I cannot believe you," I said as we cruised toward town, playing hooky on a Friday. It was my first time, and everything looked different, brighter and nicer, the world of eight-thirty to three-thirty on a school day, a world I never got to see.

"I told you not to worry," he said smugly.

"Do you have a whole stack of those passes, or what?" I pulled at the visor and he laughed even as he grabbed my hand, stopping it.

"Just a few," he said. "Definitely not a stack."

"You are so bad," I said, but I was impressed. "He didn't even hardly look at your pass."

"He likes me," he said simply. "Where are we going, anyway?"

"First Street."

He switched lanes, hitting his turn signal. "What's on First Street?"

I looked over at him, so cute, and knew I'd have to trust him. We both would. "Scarlett."

"Okay," he said easily. And as I looked over, the scenery was whizzing past houses and cars and bright blue sky, on and on. "Lead the way."

Scarlett was sitting on a bench in front of the clinic with a heavyset woman in a wool sweater and straw hat.

"Hey," I said as we pulled up beside them. Now, closer, I

could see the woman had a little dog in her lap with one of those cone collars on its head to keep it from biting itself. "Are you okay?"

"I'm fine," she said quickly, grabbing her purse off the bench. To the woman she said, "Thanks, Mary. Really."

The woman petted her dog. "You're a good girl, honey."

"Thanks," Scarlett said as I unlocked the door and she slid into the backseat. "I paid her five bucks," she explained to me. The dog in the woman's lap looked at us and yawned. To Macon, in a lower voice, Scarlet said, "Go. Now. Please."

Macon hit the gas and we left Mary behind, pulling out of the shopping center and into traffic. Scarlett settled into the backseat, pulling her hands through her hair, and I waited for her to say something.

After a few stoplights she said quietly, "Thanks for coming. Really."

"No problem," Macon said.

"No problem," I repeated, turning back to look at her, but she was facing the window, staring out at the traffic.

When Macon stopped at the Zip Mart and got out to pump gas, I turned around again. "Hey."

She looked up. "Hey."

"So," I said. I wasn't sure quite where to start. "What happened?"

"I couldn't do it," she blurted out, as if she'd only been waiting, holding her breath, for me to ask. "I tried, Halley, really. I knew all the arguments—*I'm young, I have my whole life ahead of me, what about college*—all that. But when I lay down there on that cot and stared at the ceiling, just waiting for them to come do it, I just realized I couldn't. I mean, sure, nothing is going to be normal for me anymore. But how normal has my life *ever* been? Growing up with Marion sure wasn't, losing Michael wasn't. Nothing ever has been."

I watched Macon as he stood in line inside, tossing a pack of Red Hots from hand to hand. Two months ago, when Michael died, I hadn't even known him. "It isn't going to be easy, at all," I said. I tried to imagine us with a baby, but I couldn't picture it, seeing instead just a blur, a vague shape in Scarlett's arms. Impossible.

"I know." She sighed, sounding like my mother. "I know everyone will think I'm crazy or even stupid. But I don't care. This is what I want to do. And I know it's right. I don't expect anyone to really understand."

I looked at my best friend, at Scarlett, the girl who had always led me, sometimes kicking, into the best parts of my life. "Except for me," I said. "I understand."

"Except for you," she repeated, softly, looking up to smile at me. And from that moment, I never questioned her choice again.

We spent the whole day just driving around, eating pizza at one of Macon's hideouts, looking for some guy he knew for a reason that was never quite clear, and just listening to the radio, killing time. Scarlett called Marion and said she'd taken a cab home. Everything, for now, was taken care of.

Macon dropped us off a few streets over from our houses, so I could pretend I'd taken the bus, then drove off, beeping the horn as he turned out of sight. Scarlett steadied herself and went to wait for Marion, and I walked in the door and found a strange, uneasy silence, as well as my father, who darted out of sight the second he saw me. But not fast enough: Milkshakes. Big Time.

"I'm home," I called out. The house smelled like lasagna, and I suddenly realized I was starving, which distracted me until my mother stepped out of the kitchen, holding a dishtowel. Her face had taken on that pointy, angular look, a dead give-away that I was in trouble.

"Hi there," she said smoothly, folding the towel. "How was school today?"

"Well," I said, as my father passed by quickly again, into the kitchen, "It was . . ."

"I would think very hard before answering if I were you," she interrupted me, her voice still even and calm. "Because if you lie to me, your punishment will only be worse."

Busted. There was nothing I could do.

"I saw you, Halley, today at about ten forty-five, which I believe is when you're supposed to be in gym class. You were in a car, pulling out of the First Street Mall."

"Mom," I said. "I can—"

"No." She held up her hand, stopping me. "You're going to let me finish. I called your school and was told, to my surprise, that I had just spoken with someone to have you sent home due to a family emergency."

I swallowed, hard.

"I cannot *believe* that you would lie like this to me." I looked at the floor; it was my only option. "Not to mention," she went on, "cutting class and running around town with some boy I don't know, and Scarlett, who of all people should know better. I called Marion at work and she was equally furious."

"You told Marion that Scarlett was with us?" I said. So she knew; she knew before Scarlett would even have a chance to explain.

"Yes, I did," she snapped. "We agreed if this was a new trend for you two, it needed to be nipped in the bud, right now. I will not have this, Halley. You've been pushing it with Ginny and camp all summer, but today was the last straw. I'm not going to let you openly defy me when it suits you. Now go upstairs and stay there until I tell you to come down."

"But . . ."

"Go. Now." She was shaking, she was so mad. There'd been that strange uneasiness all summer, the rippling of irritation— but this was the real deal. And she didn't even know half of it yet.

I went up to my room and straight to the window, grabbing

my phone. I dialed Scarlett's number and just as it started ringing I saw Marion's car coming down the street. Scarlett answered right as she turned into the driveway.

"Watch out," I said quickly, whispering, "we're busted. And Marion knows you didn't do it."

"What?" she said. "No, she doesn't. She thinks I took a cab home."

"No," I said, and I could hear my mother coming up the stairs, down the hall, "my mother called her. She knows."

"She what?" Scarlett said, and I could see her garage door opening.

"Halley, *get off that phone!*" my mother said from outside my door, rattling the handle because thank God it was locked. "I mean *now!*"

"Gotta go," I said, hanging up quickly, and from my window I could see Scarlett in her kitchen, holding her phone and staring up at me as Marion burst in, her finger already pointing. My mother was outside my own door, her voice meaning business, but I saw only Scarlett, trying to explain herself in the bright light of her kitchen before Marion reached and yanked at the shade, making it fall crooked, sideways, and shutting me out.

Chapter Six

I had to sit and wait for my punishment. I could hear my parents downstairs conferring, my father's voice low and calm, my mother's occasionally bouncing off the walls, peaking and plummeting. After an hour she came upstairs, stood in front of me with her hands on her hips, and laid down the law.

"Your father and I have discussed it," she began, "and we've decided you should be grounded for a month for what happened today. You are also on phone restriction indefinitely. This does not count your birthday tomorrow; the party will go on as planned. But as far as anything else goes, you may go to school and to work but not anywhere else."

I was watching her face, how it transformed when she was angry. The short haircut that always framed her face looked more severe, all the angles of her cheekbones hollowing out. She looked like a different person.

"Halley."

"What?"

"Who was the boy who was with you today? The one who was driving?"

Macon flashed into my head, smiling. "Why?"

"Who is he? Was he the boy who cut the lawn that day?"

"No," I said. My father had either forgotten Macon's name or was choosing, wisely, to stay out of this. "I mean, it's not him, it was my—"

"He took you off campus and I need to know who he was. Anything could have happened to you, and I'm sure his parents would like to know about this as well."

The thought alone was mortifying. "Oh, Mom, no. I mean, he's nobody. I hardly know him."

"You obviously know him well enough to leave school with him. Now what's his name?"

"Mom," I said. "Please don't make me do this."

"Is he from Lakeview? I must know him, Halley."

"No," I said, and thought *You don't know everyone I know. Not everyone is from Lakeview.* "You don't."

She took a step closer, her eyes still on me. "I'm losing patience here, Halley. What's the boy's name?"

And I hated her at that moment, hated her for assuming she knew everyone I did, that I was incapable of life beyond or without her. So I stared back, just as hard. Neither of us said anything.

Then the phone rang, suddenly, jarring me where I sat. I started to reach for it, remembered about phone restriction, and sat back. I knew it was Macon. It rang on and on as she stood there watching me, until my father answered it.

"Julie!" he yelled from downstairs. "It's Marion."

"Marion?" my mother said. She picked up the phone next to

my bed. "Hello? Hi, Marion. . . . Yes, Halley and I were just discussing what happened. . . . What? Now? Okay, okay . . . calm down. I'll be right over. Sure. Fine. See you in a minute."

She hung up the phone. "I have to go across the street for a few minutes. But this conversation is not over, understand?"

"Fine," I said, but I knew already things would have changed by the time she got back.

Marion met her at the end of the walk, by the prickle bush, where they stood talking for a good five minutes. Actually Marion talked, standing there nervously in a mini-dress and wedge heels, chain-smoking, while my mother just listened, nodding her head. From across the street I could see Scarlett in her own window, watching them as well; I pressed my palm against my window, our special signal, but she didn't see me.

Then my mother walked inside with Marion, shut the door, and stayed for an hour and a half. I expected to see a ripple, a shock wave shaking the house when my mother was told the news; instead, it was quiet, like the rest of the neighborhood on a Friday night. At seven the Vaughns arrived, and by eight I could smell popcorn from downstairs. The phone rang only once more, right at eight o'clock; I tried to grab it but my father answered first and Macon hung up, abruptly. A few minutes later I heard the blender whirring as my father did his part to mend fences.

At eight-fifteen Marion walked my mother to the door, standing on the stoop with her, arms crossed against her chest. My mother hugged her, then crossed back to our house, where

119

my father and the Vaughns were already watching a movie with a lot of gunfire in it. A few minutes later she came up the stairs and knocked at my door.

When I opened it she was standing there with a bowl of popcorn and, of course, a milkshake. It was so thick with chocolate it was almost black, foaming over the edge of the glass. Her face was softer now, back to its normal state. "Peace offerings," she said, handing them to me, and I stepped back and let her in.

"Thanks." I took one suck off the straw in the shake but nothing budged.

"So," she said, sitting on the edge of my bed, "why didn't you tell me about Scarlett?"

"I couldn't," I said. "She didn't want anyone to know."

"You thought I'd be mad," she said slowly.

"No," I said. "I just thought you'd freak out."

She smiled, reaching over for a handful of popcorn. "Well, to be truthful, I did."

"She's going to keep it, right?" I asked.

She sighed, reaching back to rub her neck. "That's what she's saying. Marion is still hoping she'll change her mind and put it up for adoption. Having a baby is hard work, Halley. It will change her life forever."

"I know."

"I mean, of course it's nice to have someone that's all yours, that unconditional love, but with being a mother there are responsibilities: financial, emotional, physical. It will affect her education, her future, everything. It's not a smart decision to

Chapter Seven

the middle of a typical terrible Saturday rush,
up to my station and grinned at me.

d. "Happy birthday."

aid, taking as long as I could to scan his Pepsi
bars. Scarlett reached over to poke him and he

l, "How'd it go this morning? Did you pass, or

im. "Of course I did."

throwing his head back. "Halley with a license,
aying off the roads for a while."

y," I said, and he grinned.

answer the phone last night," he said, leaning
er and lowering his voice. "I called, you know."

id, hitting the total button, "is because I got

ou think?"

back. "Oh. Skipping school? Or helping Scarlett

take all that on now. And I'm sure that some of this is an attempt to hold on to a part of Michael, an extension of the mourning process, but a baby goes way beyond that." She was on a roll now, her voice getting louder and smoother.

"Mom," I pointed out, "I'm not Scarlett."

She was taking a breath, readying herself for another point, but now she stopped, sighing. "I know you're not, honey. It's just frustrating to me because I can see what a mistake she's making."

"She doesn't think it's a mistake."

"Not now, no. But she will, later. When she's tied down to a baby and you and all her other friends are going off to college, traveling abroad, living other lives."

"I don't want to go abroad," I said quietly, taking a handful of popcorn.

"My point is," she said, putting her arm around my shoulder, "that you have an entire life ahead of you, and so does Scarlett. You're too young to take on anyone else's."

From downstairs there was a hail of movie gunfire, then my father's chuckling. Another Friday night, at home with the Vaughns. My life before Macon.

"So, about what happened today," she said, but she'd lost the fire, the anger that had brought her up here earlier, ready to draw and quarter me. "We can't just let this go, honey. Your punishment will have to stand, even if you thought you were helping Scarlett."

"I know," I said. But it was clear; by the pure fact of not being pregnant, I'd escaped the worst of her wrath. Scarlett had saved me, again.

She stood up, brushing off her slacks. I could see her at Scarlett's kitchen table, a place that I considered mine, negotiating Marion and Scarlett to some kind of truce. My mother was good at all kinds of peace except my own.

"Why don't you come down and watch the movie?" she said. "The Vaughns haven't seen you for so long. Clara thinks you're just fabulous."

"Clara's five, Mom," I said. I tried another sip of the shake, then gave up and stuck it on my bedside table.

"I know." She stood at my open door, leaning against the frame. "Well, you know. If you change your mind."

"Okay."

She started to leave, then stopped in the doorway and said in a low voice, "Marion says that boy you were with is named Macon. She says he's your boyfriend."

Marion and her big mouth. I lay down on my bed, turning my back to her and pulling my knees up to my chest. "He's just this guy, Mom."

"You never mentioned it to me," she said, as if I had to, as if that was required.

"It's no big deal." I couldn't look at her, couldn't risk it. Her voice sounded sad enough. I had my eyes on the window, where the lights of a plane were coming closer, red and green blinking, the noise not quite loud yet.

Another sigh. Sometimes
left to speak. "Okay, then. Co

But she lingered there, may
that plane came closer and clo
growing louder and louder a
house, the panes in the wind
belly, coasting overhead, whit
its passing, the shaking and th
slipped out of the doorway and
back over, in sudden silence, s

At work
Macon step
"Hey," he
"Thanks,
and four ca
waved to h
"So," he
what?"
I looked
He laug
look out.
"You're
"You d
over my
"That,
busted."
"For v
"Wha
He th
go AWC

"Both." I held out my hand. "That'll be two fifty-nine."

He handed me a five, pulling it out of his back pocket all wrinkled. "How bad did you get it?"

"I'm grounded."

"For how long?"

"A month."

He sighed, shaking his head. "That's too bad."

"For who?"

The woman behind him was murmuring under her breath, irritated.

As I handed him his change he grabbed my fingers, holding them, then leaned over the register and kissed me fast, before I even had a chance to react. "For me," he said, and with his other hand slipped a candy bar into the front pocket of my Milton's apron.

"Really?" I said, but he just grabbed his bag and walked off, turning back to smile at me. Everyone in my line was watching, grumpy and impatient, but I didn't care.

"Really," he said, taking a few steps still facing me, smiling. Then he turned and walked out of Milton's, just like that, leaving me speechless at my register.

"Man," Scarlett said as my next customer stepped up, slapping a carton of Capris on the belt. "There's something wrong with that boy."

"I know," I said, still feeling his kiss on my lips, saving me from all the Saturdays ahead. "He likes me."

*   *   *

125

That evening we had my party at Alfredo's: my parents and me, Scarlett, and of course the Vaughns. Scarlett sat next to me; the way she told it, my mother had saved her baby. She said when Marion had come storming in she'd already made another appointment for the next day and planned to sit outside the operating room, chair blocking the door, if that was what it took to see it was done. They had a huge blowout, and she said she'd been packing a bag, ready to leave to go somewhere, anywhere, when my mother appeared at the front door in her red cardigan sweater like Mr. Rogers, ready to handle everything. She held Scarlett's hand and passed her tissues, calmed Marion down, and then mediated through the twists and turns of what Scarlett had done. In the end, it was decided: Scarlett would go through with the pregnancy, but would honor Marion's wishes of seriously considering adoption. This was the truce.

"I'm telling you," she said to me again as I ate my pasta, "your mother is a miracle worker."

"She grounded me an entire month," I said, keeping my voice low. "I can't even go out later."

"This is a very nice party," she said. "Noah looks especially happy for you."

"Shut up." I was already sick of my birthday.

"I'd like to propose a toast." My mother stood up at her seat, holding her glass of wine, with my father smiling from where he sat beside her. "To my daughter Halley, on her sixteenth birthday."

"To Halley," everyone else echoed. Noah still wouldn't look me in the eye.

"May this year be the best yet," my mother went on, even though everyone had already drank. She was still standing. "And we love you."

So everyone clinked their glasses again, and drank again, and my mother just stood there with her cheeks flushed, smiling at me, as if yesterday had never happened.

When we got home we opened presents. I got some clothes and money from my parents, a book from the Vaughns, and a silver bracelet from Noah, who just stuffed the box in my hand when no one was looking and ignored me for the rest of the evening. Scarlett gave me a pair of earrings and a keychain for my new car keys, and when she left to go home she hugged me tight, suddenly emotional, and told me how much she loved me. As I hugged her back I tried again to picture her with a baby, or even just pregnant. It was still hard.

I was getting ready for bed around eleven when I heard it. The slow, even rumble of a car passing slowly on the street, then pausing, the engine humming. I went to the window and watched, my eyes on the stop sign that faced my house. A few seconds later the car slid back into sight, facing my window, and blinked its lights. Twice.

I put on my shoes and crept down the stairs in my pajamas and jacket, past my mother's half-open bedroom door, past where my father was dozing on the couch in front of the TV. I opened the back door, mindful to go slow because of the creak it made halfway. I slipped outside, across the deck, and down around the house to the side yard, past the juniper bushes, to the sidewalk and across the street.

"Hey," Macon said as I leaned into his window. "Get in."

I went around and climbed into the passenger seat, pulling the door shut behind me. It was warm inside, the dash lights giving off a bright green glow.

"Ready for your present?" he asked.

"Sure." I sat back in my seat. "What is it?"

"First," he said, putting the car in gear, "we have to go someplace."

"Go someplace?" I took a panicked look at my house. It was bad enough to sneak out, but the further away I got the better chance I had of getting caught. I could see my father sticking his head in my room to say good night, seeing me gone. "I probably shouldn't."

He looked at me. "Why not?"

"I mean, I'm already in trouble," I said, and I sounded like a wimp even to myself, "and if I got caught—"

"Oh, come on," he said, already starting to head out of Lakeview. "Live a little. It's your birthday, right?"

I looked up at my dark house. I had just an hour left of my birthday, and I had the right to celebrate at least that much of it the way I wanted.

"Let's go," I said to him and he smiled, hitting the gas as we took the corner, tires squealing a little bit, carrying me away.

He took me all the way out to Topper Lake, a good twenty minutes from my house. We stopped about halfway and I drove, watching him as he squirmed, just like my dad, as the speedometer edged higher and higher.

"You nervous?" I asked him as we went across the bridge, the water black and huge all around us.

"No way," he said. But he was, and I laughed at him. I was barely doing the speed limit.

We passed all the boat ramps and docks, all the tourist traps, and finally went down a long dirt road that wound through woods and potholes and NO TRESPASSING signs into complete darkness. In the distance I could see the radio towers of my father's station, blinking red and green against the sky.

We got out of the car and I followed him through the dark, his hand holding mine. I could hear water but I couldn't make out where exactly it was.

"Watch your step up here," he said as we climbed a steep hill, up and up and up with me barely able to keep from falling. I was cold in my pajamas and jacket, disoriented, and out of breath by the time the ground beneath my feet got more smooth and stable. I still had no idea where I was.

"Macon, where are we going?" I said.

"Almost there," he called out over his shoulder. "Walk right behind me now, okay?"

"Okay." I kept my eyes ahead, on the blond of his hair, the only thing I could make out in the dark.

And then, suddenly, he stopped dead in his tracks and said, "Here we are."

I wasn't sure where *here* was, since I still couldn't see anything. He sat down, dangling his legs over the edge in front of us, and I did the same. I could still hear water, louder now.

"So what is this?" I said, shivering in my jacket.

"Just this place I know," he said. "Me and Sherwood found it, a couple of years back. We used to come out here all the time."

It was one of the only times he'd mentioned Michael, ever, in the whole time I'd known him. Michael had been on my mind a lot lately, with the baby. Scarlett said she had to get up her nerve to write his mom; whether she had moved to Florida or not, she had a right to know about a grandchild. "I bet you miss him," I said.

"Yeah." He leaned back against the thick concrete behind us. "He was a good guy."

"If I lost Scarlett," I said, not knowing if I was going too far or saying the wrong thing, "I don't know what I'd do. I don't think I could live without her."

"Yeah," he said, there in the dark. He turned his head, not looking at me. "You think that, at first."

So we sat there, in the pitch black, the sound of water rushing past, and I thought of Michael Sherwood. I wondered how this year would have been different if he hadn't taken that road that night, if he was still here with us. If Scarlett would be keeping that baby, if I'd ever have met Macon or come this far.

"Okay," he said suddenly, looking down at his glowing watch. "Get ready."

"Ready for what?"

"You'll see." He slid his arm around my waist, pulling me

closer, and I felt his warm lips on my neck. Right as I turned my head to kiss him, there was a loud whooshing noise and the world suddenly lit up bright all around us. It was blinding at first, and frightening, like a camera flash going off right in my face and turning the world starry. I pulled back from Macon and saw that I was sitting on a thin strip of white concrete, surrounded by DANGER DO NOT ENTER signs, my feet dangling over the edge into the air. Macon grabbed my waist as I leaned forward, still dazed and blinking, to peer over the edge and finally see the water I'd been hearing gushing past a full mile below. It was like opening your eyes and finding yourself suddenly in midair, falling. The dam was groaning, opening, as I twisted in Macon's arms, suddenly terrified, all the noise and light and the world so far below us.

"Macon," I said, trying to pull away, back toward the path. "I should—"

But then he pulled me back in, kissing me hard, his hands smoothing my hair, and I closed my eyes to the light, the noise, the water so far below, and I felt it for the first time. That exhilaration, the whooshing feeling of being on the edge and holding, the world spinning madly around me. And I kissed him back hard, letting loose that girl from the early summer and the Grand Canyon. At that moment, suspended and free-falling, I could feel her leaving me.

Chapter Eight

"Okay, let's see. . . . Food cravings."

"Check."

"Food aversions."

"Ugh. Check."

"Headaches."

"Check."

"Moodiness," I said. "Oh, *I'll* answer that one. Check."

"Shut up," Scarlett said, grabbing the book out of my hands and flopping back in her seat. We were in her car, before first bell; since I'd gotten my license, she let me drive every day. She was eating saltines and juice, the only things she could keep down, while I tried to eat my potato chips quietly and unobtrusively.

"Just wait," I said, popping another one in my mouth. "The book says morning sickness should end by the beginning of Month Four."

"Oh, well, isn't *that* special," she snapped. She had been moodier than hell lately. "I swear those chips smell so bad, they're going to make me *puke.*"

"Sorry," I said, rolling down my window and making a big

show of holding them outside, my head stuck sideways to eat free and clear of the confines of the car. "You know the doctor said it's normal to feel sick a lot of the time."

"I know what she said." She stuck another saltine in her mouth, swigging some juice to wash it down. "This is just crazy. I've never even *had* heartburn before and now I do, like, all the time, my clothes look terrible on me, I'm sweating constantly for some weird reason and even when I'm starving, everything I look at makes me feel sick. It's ridiculous."

"You'll feel better at Month Five," I said, picking up the book, which was called *So You're Pregnant—What Now?* It was our Bible, consulted constantly, and my job was usually to quote from it to rally and strengthen both of us.

"I wish," she said in a low voice, turning to glower at me with a face I hadn't even seen before Month Two, ever, "that you would *shut up* about Month Four."

I shut up.

Macon was waiting for me outside my homeroom, leaning against the fire extinguisher. Since my birthday, things had changed between us, almost imperceptibly; everything was a little bit more serious. Now just the sight of him gave me a sense of looking down and finding myself in midair, dangling lost above the world.

"Hey," he said as I came closer, "where have you been?"

"Arguing with Scarlett," I said. "She's so cranky lately."

"Oh, come on. Cut her some slack. She's pregnant." I'd told

him the night of my birthday. He was the only one besides my parents, Marion, and us who knew.

"I know. It's just hard, that's all." I stepped a little closer to him, lowering my voice. "And keep quiet about that, okay? She doesn't want anyone to know yet."

"I didn't tell anyone," he said. Behind me people were crowding into my homeroom, bumping backpacks and elbows against me. "Sheesh, what kind of a jerk do you think I am, anyway?"

"A big one," I said. He wasn't laughing. "She just wants to wait until she has to tell people. That's all."

"No problem," he said.

"Faulkner!" someone yelled from behind us. "Get over here, I gotta talk to you."

"In a second," Macon yelled back.

"You said you were going to homeroom today," I reminded him. "Remember?"

"Right. I gotta go." He kissed me on the forehead, quickly, and started to walk off before I could stop him. "I'll see you third period."

"Wait," I said, but he had vanished in the shifting bodies and voices of the hallway. I only saw the top of his head, the red flash of his shirt, before he was gone. Later, when I was hunting for a pencil in my backpack pocket and found a handful of Hershey's Kisses, I wondered again how he did so much without my noticing.

Later that morning I was in Commercial Design, the only

class I had with Scarlett, looking for some purple paper in the supply room. I heard someone behind me and turned around to see Elizabeth Gunderson shuffling through a stack of orange paper. She'd been slumming since Michael's death, quitting the cheerleading team, chain-smoking, and taking up with the lead singer for some college band who had a pierced tongue and a goatee. All of her copycat friends were following suit, casting off their J. Crew tweeds for ripped jeans and black clothes, trying to look morose and morbid in their BMWs and Mercedes.

"So, Halley," she said, moving closer to me, a sheaf of orange tucked under one arm. "I heard you're going out with Macon Faulkner."

I glanced out to the classroom, to Scarlett, who was bent over the table, cutting and pasting letters for our alphabet project. "Yeah," I said, concentrating on the purple paper in my hand, "I guess I am."

"He's a nice guy." She reached across me for some bright red paper. "But just between us, as your friend, I think I should warn you to watch out."

I looked up at her. Even with her ripped jeans and styled-to-look-stringy hair, Elizabeth Gunderson was still the former head cheerleader, the homecoming queen, the girl with the effortless looks and perfect skin, straight out of *Seventeen* magazine. She was not like me, not at all. She didn't even know me.

"I mean," she went on, stepping back and tucking her paper under her arm, "he can be real sweet, but he's treated a lot of

135

girls pretty badly. Like my friend Rachel, he really used her and then never talks to her anymore. Stuff like that."

"Yeah, well," I said, trying to get around her but she wasn't moving, just standing there with her eyes right on me.

"I got to know him really well when I was with Michael." She said his name slowly, so I'd be sure to get it. "I just didn't know if you knew what he was like. With girls and all."

I didn't know what to say, how to defend myself, so I just stepped around her, knocking my shoulder against a shelf just to slip by.

"I just thought you should know, before you get too in-volved," she called after me. "I mean—*I* would want to know."

I burst out into the classroom. When I looked back she was still watching me, standing by the paper cutter talking with Ginny Tabor, who practically had radar for these kinds of con-frontations. I threw my paper down next to Scarlett and pulled out my chair.

"You would not believe what just happened to me," I said. "I was in the supply room, and—"

I didn't get any further than that, because she suddenly pushed her chair back, clapped a hand over her mouth, and ran toward the bathroom.

"Scarlett?" Mrs. Pate, our teacher, was a little high-strung; outbursts made her nervous. She was supervising the paper cutter, making sure no one lost any fingers. "Halley, is she okay?"

"She's got the flu," I said. "I'll go check on her."

"Good," Mrs. Pate said, redirecting her attention to Michelle Long, who was about to sever at least half her hand with slap-dash cutting behavior. "Michelle, wait. Look at what you're about to do. Can you see that? *Can* you?"

I found Scarlett in the last stall against the wall, kneeling on the floor. I wet some paper towels at the sink and handed them to her, then said, "It's gonna get better."

She sniffled, wiping her eyes with the back of her sleeve. I felt so sorry for her. "Are we alone?" she asked.

I walked down the row of stalls, checking underneath for feet, and saw none. It was just us, the deep blue cinderblock of the girls' bathroom, and a dripping faucet.

She leaned back on her heels, dabbing her face with the wet paper towel. "This," she said in a choked voice, sniffling, "is the worst."

"I know," I said, telling myself not to talk about Month Four or the joy of birth or the little life inside of her, all things that had failed me in the past. "I know."

She wiped her mouth with the back of her hand, closing her eyes. "It's like, whenever I used to see pregnant women, they always looked happy. Glowing, right? Or on TV, in those big dresses, knitting baby afghans. No one ever tells you it makes you fat and sick and crazy. And I'm only three months along, Halley. It's just going to get *worse*."

"The doctor said—" I started, but she cut me off, waving her hand.

"It's not about that," she said softly, and she was crying

137

again. "It would be different if Michael was here or I was married with a husband. Marion doesn't even want me to have this baby, Halley. It's not like she's being that supportive. This is all me, you know? I'm on my own. And it's scary."

"You are not on your own," I said forcefully. "I'm here, aren't I? I've been holding your head while you get sick and bringing you saltines and letting you crab like crazy at me. I'm doing everything a husband or anyone would do for you."

"It's not the same." In the fluorescent light her face seemed paler than ever. "I miss him so much. This fall has been so hard."

"I know it," I said. "You've been really strong, Scarlett."

"If he was here, I don't even know what might have happened between us. We were only together for a summer, you know? Maybe he would have turned out to be a major jerk. I'll never know. But when it gets like this, and I'm miserable, all I can think is that he might have made everything okay. That he was the only one who understood. Ever."

I knelt down next to her. "We can do this," I said firmly. "I know we can."

She sniffled. "What about childbirth classes? What about when I have to give birth and it hurts, and all that? What about money? How am I going to support a whole other person scanning groceries at Milton's?"

"We've already talked about that," I said. "You have that trust your grandparents put aside, you'll use that."

"That's for college," she moaned. "Specifically."

"Oh, fine," I said, "you're right. College is much more important right now. This is your *baby*, Scarlett. You have to hold it together because it needs you."

"My baby," she repeated, her voice hollow in the cool deep blue of the stall. "My baby."

Then I heard it: the creak of a door opening, not the outside door either but closer, just behind me. I turned, already dreading what I'd see. A set of feet I'd somehow missed, belonging to somebody who now had heard everything. But it was worse than that. Much worse.

"Oh, my God," Ginny Tabor said as I turned to face her, standing there in a white sweater, her mouth a perfect O. "Oh, my God."

Scarlett closed her eyes, lifting her hands to her face. I could hear the lights buzzing. No one said anything.

"I won't tell anyone," Ginny said quickly, already backing up to the door, her eyes twitchy and weird. "I swear. I won't."

"Ginny—" I started. "It's not—"

"I won't tell," she said in a louder voice, backing up too far and banging against the door, her hand feeling wildly for the knob. "I swear," she said again, slipping out as it fell closed between us, a flash of white all I saw before she was gone.

By lunch we were getting strange looks as we walked to Macon's car. Everyone seemed to be eyeing Scarlett's stomach, as if since second period she'd suddenly be showing, the baby ready to pop out at any minute. We ate lunch in the Toyota, parked in the Zip Mart lot around back by the Dumpsters.

"It's weird," Scarlett said, finishing off her second hot dog, "but since I know everybody knows now, I'm starving."

"Slow down on those hot dogs," I said nervously. "Don't get overconfident."

"I feel fine," she said, and Macon reached over and squeezed my leg. All through P.E. I'd agonized about how it was all my fault, Ginny Tabor faking me out, then spreading Scarlett's secret like wildfire across the campus. "And I'm not mad at you, so stop looking at me like you're expecting me to fly into a rage at any second."

"I'm so sorry," I said for at least the twentieth time. "I really am."

"About what?" she said. "This isn't about you, it's about Ginny and her huge mouth. Period. Forget about it. At least it's over now."

"God," I said, and Macon rolled his eyes. I'd already planned several ways I could kill Ginny with my bare hands. "I really am *sorry.*"

"Shut up and pass those chips back here," Scarlett said, tapping my shoulder.

"Better pass them," Macon told me, grabbing them out of my lap. "Before she starts eating the upholstery."

"I'm hungry," Scarlett said, her mouth full. "I'm eating for two now."

"You shouldn't be eating hot dogs, then," Macon said, turning to face her. "At least not all the time. You need to eat fruit and vegetables, lots of protein, and yogurt. Oh, and vitamin C is important, too. Cantaloupe, oranges, that kind of thing. Green peppers. Loaded with C."

We just looked at him.

"What?" he said.

"Since when are you Mr. Pregnancy?" I asked him.

"I don't know," he said, embarrassed now. "I mean, I'm not. It's just common knowledge."

"Cantaloupe, huh?" Scarlett said, finishing off the bag of chips.

"Vitamin C," Macon said, starting up the car again. "It's important."

By the time we got back from lunch, everyone was definitely staring, entire conversations dissolving as we passed. Macon just kept walking, hardly noticing, but Scarlett's face was pinched. I wondered if we'd see those hot dogs coming up again.

"Oh, please," Macon said as we passed the Mouth herself, Ginny Tabor, standing with Elizabeth Gunderson, both of them staring, thinking, I knew, of Michael. "Like they've never seen a pregnant woman before."

"Macon," I said. "You're not helping."

Scarlett kept walking, facing straight ahead, as if by only concentrating she could make it all go away. I wondered what was more shocking, in the end; that Scarlett was pregnant, or that the baby was Michael's. Of course girls got pregnant at our school, but they usually dropped out for a few months and then returned with baby pictures in their wallets. Some carried their babies proudly to the school day care, where little kids climbed on the jungle gym on the right side of the courtyard, running to the fence to watch their mothers go by on their way to class. But for girls like us, like Scarlett, these things didn't happen. And if they did it was taken care of in secret, discreetly, and only rumored, never proven.

This was different. If we'd started to forget Michael Sherwood, any of us, it would be a very long time before we would again.

Chapter Nine

Then, in the middle of everything, we began losing my Grandma Halley.

It had actually started months earlier, in the late spring. She became forgetful; she would call me Julie, confusing me with my mother, forgetting even her own name. She kept locking herself out of her house, misplacing her key. My mother even convinced her to wear one on a string around her neck, but nothing worked. The keys just slipped away into cracks and crevices, sidewalks and street corners, thin air.

It got worse. She walked out of the Hallmark store with a greeting card she forgot to pay for, setting off all the alarms, which scared her. She started calling in the middle of the night, all anxious and upset, sure we'd said we were coming to visit the next day, or the previous one, when no plans had actually been made. For those calls her voice was unbalanced and high, scaring me as I handed the phone over to my mother, who would pace the kitchen floor, reassuring her own mother that everything was fine, we were all okay; there was nothing to be afraid of. By the end of October, we weren't so sure.

I'd always been close to my Grandma Halley. I was her namesake and that made her special, and I'd spent several summers with her when I was younger and my parents went on trips. She lived alone in a tiny Victorian house outside of Buffalo with a stained-glass window and a big, fat cat named Jasper. Halfway up her winding staircase was a window, and from the top sill she hung a bell from a wire. I always touched it with my fingers as I passed, the chiming bouncing off the glass and the walls around me. It was that bell that always came to mind before her face, or her voice, when I heard her name.

My mother had Grandma Halley's sparkling eyes, her tiny chin, and sometimes, if you knew when to listen for it, her singsong laugh. But my Grandma Halley was kind of wild, a little eccentric, more so in the ten years since my grandfather had died. She gardened in men's overalls and a floppy sun hat, and made up her scarecrows to resemble neighbors she didn't like, especially Mr. Farrow, who lived two doors down and had buck teeth and carrot-red hair, which fit a scarecrow nicely. She ate only organic food, adopted twenty kids through Save the Children, and taught me the box step when I was in fifth grade, the two of us dancing around the living room while her record player crackled and sang.

She was born in May of 1910, as Halley's Comet lit up the sky of her small town in Virginia. Her father, watching with a crowd from the hospital lawn, considered it a sign and named her Halley. It was the comet that always made her seem that much more mystical, different. Magic. And when I was named after her, it had made me a little magical too, or so I hoped.

The winter I was six, we made a special trip to visit her for the comet's passing. I remember sitting outside in her lap, wrapped in a blanket. There'd been so much hype, so much excitement, but I couldn't see much, just a bit of light as we strained to make it out in the sky. Grandma Halley was quiet, holding me tight against her, and she seemed to see it perfectly, grabbing my hand and whispering, *Look at that, Halley. There it is.* My mother kept saying no one could see it, it was too hazy, but Grandma Halley always told her she was wrong. That was Grandma Halley's magic. She could create anything, even a comet, and make it dance before your eyes.

Now my mother was suddenly distracted, making calls to Buffalo and having long talks with my father after I went to bed. I busied myself with school, work, and Macon; with my grounding over, I slipped off to see him for a few hours whenever I could. I went with Scarlett to the doctor, read to her from the pregnancy Bible, reminding her to get more vitamin C, to eat more oranges and green peppers. We were adjusting to the pregnancy; we had no choice. And after our being the scandal for a couple of weeks, Elizabeth Gunderson's tongue-pierced boyfriend fooled around with her best friend Maggie, and Scarlett and the baby were old news.

But each time Grandma Halley called again, scared, I'd watch my mother's face fold into the now-familiar frown of concern. And each time I'd think only of that comet overhead, as she held me in close to her, all those years ago. *Look at that. There it is*. And I'd close my eyes, trying to remember, but seeing nothing, nothing at all.

By the middle of November, Marion had been dating Steve the accountant for just about as long as I'd been seeing Macon. And slowly, he was beginning to show his alter ego.

It started around the third or fourth date. Scarlett noticed it first, nudging me as we sat on the stairs, talking to him and waiting for Marion to come down. He always showed up in ties and oxford shirts, nice sports jackets with dress pants or chinos, and loafers with tassels. But this night, suddenly, there was something different. Around his neck, just barely visible over his tie, was a length of brown leather cord. And dangling off the cord was a circular, silver *thing*.

"It is not a medallion," I hissed at Scarlett after he excused himself to go to the bathroom. "It's just jewelry."

"It's a medallion," she said again. "Did you see the symbols on it? It's some kind of weird warrior coin."

"Oh, stop."

"It is. I'm telling you, Halley, it's like his other side can't be held down any longer. It's starting to push out of him, bit by bit."

"Scarlett," I said again, "he's an accountant."

"He's a freak." She pulled her knees up to her chest. "Just you wait."

Marion was coming down the stairs now, her dress half-zipped, reaching to put in one earring. She stopped in front of us, back to Scarlett, who stood up without being asked and zipped her.

"Marion," she said in a low voice as we heard the toilet flush and the bathroom door open, "look at his neck."

"At his what?" Marion said loudly as he came around the corner, neat in his sports jacket with the leather cord still visible, just barely, over his collar.

"Nothing," Scarlett muttered. "Have a good night."

"Thank you." Marion leaned over and kissed Steve on the cheek. "Have you seen my purse?"

"Kitchen table," Scarlett said easily. "Your keys are on the counter."

"Perfect." Marion disappeared and came back with the purse tucked under her arm. "Well, you girls have a good night. Stay out of trouble and get to bed at a decent hour." Marion had been acting a little more motherly, more matronly, since she'd taken up with conservative warrior Steve. Maybe she was preparing to be a grandmother. We weren't sure.

"We will," I said.

"Gosh, give us some credit," Scarlett said casually. "It's not like we're gonna go and get pregnant or anything."

Marion shot her a look, eyes narrowed; Steve still didn't know about the baby. After only a month and a half, Marion figured it was still a bit early to spring it on him. She still wasn't dealing with it that well herself, anyway. She hardly ever talked about the baby, and when she did, "adoption" was al-

147

ways the first or last word of the sentence. Steve just stood there by the door, grinning blandly, distinctly unwarriorlike. It was my hope that he *would* metamorphose into Vlad, right before our eyes.

"Have a good night," I called out as they left, Marion still mad and not looking back, Steve waving jauntily out the door.

"Sheesh," Scarlett said. "What a weirdo."

"He's not that bad."

She leaned back against the step, smoothing her hands over her stomach. Though she wasn't showing yet, just in the last week she'd started to look different. It wasn't something I could describe easily. It was like those stop-action films of flowers blooming that we watched in Biology. Every frame something is happening, something little that would be missed in real time—the sprout pushing, bit by bit, from the ground, the petals slowly moving outward. To the naked eye, it's just suddenly blooming, color today where there was none before. But in real time, it's always building, working to show itself, to become.

Cameron Newton was probably the only person in school who was getting weirder looks than Scarlett that fall. He'd transferred in September, which was hard enough, but he was also one of those short, skinny kids with pasty white skin; he always wore black, which made him look half dead, or half alive, depending on how optimistic you were. Either way, he was having a tough time. So it didn't seem unusual that he was drawn across Mrs. Pate's Commercial Design class to Scarlett.

I'd missed one morning of school because of a doctor's appointment, and when we came in the next there was Cameron Newton, sitting at our table.

"Look," I said, whispering. "It's Cameron Newton."

"I know," she said cheerfully, lifting a hand to wave to him. He looked nervous and stared down at his paste jar. "He's a nice guy. I told him he should sit with us."

"What?" I said, but it was already too late, we were there and Cameron was looking up at us, in his black turtleneck and black jeans. Even his eyes looked black.

"Hey, Cameron," Scarlett said, pulling out the chair next to him and sitting down. "This is Halley."

"Hi," I said.

"Hello." His voice was surprisingly deep for such a small guy, and he had an accent that made you lean in and concentrate to understand him. He had very long fingers and was busy working with a lump of clay and a putty knife.

"Cameron's spent the last five years in France," Scarlett told me as we got settled, pulling out all of our alphabet letters and getting them organized. "His father is a famous chef."

"Really," I said. Cameron was still making me a little nervous. He had the jumpy, odd quality of someone who'd spent a lot of time alone. "That's neat."

Scarlett kicked me under the table and glared at me, as if I was making fun of him, which I definitely wasn't. Cameron got up suddenly, pushed out his chair, and stalked into the supply room. He walked like a little old man, slowly and deliberately. As he passed the paper cutter, a group of girls there dissolved into laughter, loud enough so I was sure he heard.

"You didn't tell me you made friends with Cameron Newton," I said in a low voice.

"I didn't think it was that big a deal," Scarlett said, cutting out an O. "Anyway, it was the coolest thing. I was here yesterday by myself, right? And Maryann Lister and her friends were talking about me. I could hear every word, you know, all about Michael and the baby and how I was a slut, blah blah blah."

"They said that?" I said, swiveling in my chair to find Maryann Lister, who just stared back at me, startled, until I turned away.

"I don't care now," she said. "But yesterday I'd been sick all morning and I was kind of blue and you weren't here and it just got to me, you know? So I start blubbering right here in Commercial Design, and I'm trying to hide it but I can't and right when I'm just feeling completely pathetic, Cameron scoots his chair over and puts this little piece of clay on the table in front of me. And it's Maryann Lister."

"It's what?"

"It's Maryann Lister. I mean, it's this perfect little head with her face on it, and the details were just amazing. He even had that little mole on her chin and the pattern of the sweater she was wearing."

"Why did he do that?" I said, glancing back to the supply room where Cameron was pacing the aisles, putty knife in hand, looking for something.

"I had no idea. But I just told him it was nice, and pretty, and he kind of ignored me and then handed me his history book. And he just puts it in my hand, but I still didn't know what he wanted me to do with it, so I handed it back to him. And right then she and her friends said something about him and me, like we would be perfect for each other or something."

"I hate her," I grumbled.

"No, but listen." She was laughing. "So Cameron, totally solemn, takes the book, centers the little clay Maryann on the table in front of us, and then lifts the book up, drops it, and flattens her. Just like that, *smoosh*. It was so funny, Halley. I mean, it just about killed me. And then I took the book and pounded her, and he did, and we just pummeled her into nothing. I'm telling you, he's a riot."

"A riot," I said as Cameron came out of the paper room with another wad of clay in his hands. He looked straight ahead as he walked, as if he was on a mission. "I don't know."

"He is," Scarlett said with certainty as he came closer. "Just wait."

I spent the rest of that week in Commercial Design getting to know Cameron Newton. And Scarlett was right: he *was* funny. In a weird, under-his-breath-as-if-totally-not-meaning-to way that made you think you shouldn't laugh, even when you wanted to. He was incredibly artistic, truly gifted even; he

Sarah Dessen

could make a clay face of anyone in minutes, completely accurate down to the last detail. He did Scarlett beautifully, the curve of her face and smile, her hair spilling across her shoulders. And he did me, half smiling, my face tiny and accurate. He had a way of being able to capture the world, perfectly, in miniature.

So Scarlett took Cameron in, the way she'd taken me in all those years ago. And Cameron grew on me as well; his low, quiet voice, his all-black ensembles, his strange, jittery laugh. I had nothing in common with Cameron Newton except for the one thing that counted: Scarlett. And that, alone, was enough to make us friends.

My mother still wasn't happy about Macon. There were things he did that she couldn't pin on him directly, but she was suspicious. Like the calls he made to me every night: when I didn't answer he either hung up or wouldn't leave a message. Sometimes he called late at night, the phone seeming to ring incredibly loud, just once, before I could grab it. Often she'd pick it up, and I could hear her, half-asleep, breathing on the other end.

"I got it," I'd say, and she'd slam it down. Macon would laugh, and I'd huddle deeper under the covers, and whisper so she couldn't hear.

"Your mom hates me," he'd say. He seemed to enjoy it.

"She doesn't even know you."

"Ah," he'd say, and I could feel him grinning on the other

152

end. "And to know me, as you have discovered, is to *love* me."

Because of this, and other frustrations, she started making new rules.

"No phone calls after ten-thirty," she said one morning, over her coffee cup. "Your friends should know better."

"I can't stop them from calling," I said.

"Tell them you'll get your phone taken away," she said curtly. "Okay?"

"Okay." But of course the calls didn't stop. I never was able to fully fall asleep, with one hand always on the phone. All this just to say good night to Macon, from wherever he was.

There were other things, too. Some nights, when Macon knew I couldn't see him, he'd drive by and just beep or sit idling at the stop sign across from my window. I knew he was waiting for me, but I could never go. I knew he knew that, too. But he still came. And waited.

So I'd just lie there, smiling to myself, goofily secure in the knowledge that he was thinking about me for those few rumbling minutes before he hit the gas and screeched away. This always brought on the light at the Harpers' next door, and Mr. Harper, neighborhood watch chairman, standing on his porch, glaring down the street. I don't know why Macon did it; he knew I was on thin ice anyway, that my parents were strict, a concept he clearly could not understand. Every time I heard a beep or a squealing of tires, I felt that same pull in my stomach, half exhilaration, half dread. And always my mother would look up from her book, her paper, her plate and look at me as if it was me behind that wheel, me hitting the gas, me terrorizing the neighbors.

Because of this, I had to devise new ways for him to pick me up. I'd leave the house most weekend nights, bound for Scarlett's, and cut through the woods behind her pool to meet him on Spruce Street. And from there, we went everywhere and anywhere. Slowly, I was beginning to see bits and pieces of the rest of his life.

One night, after a few hours of driving around, we pulled into a parking lot at the bottom of a huge hill. It faced a tall apartment building lit up with row after row of bright lights. The highest floor was all windows, and I could see people moving around, holding wine glasses and laughing, like a party on top of the world.

"What's this?" I said as we got out of the car and climbed the hill, then a winding flight of stairs with a thick iron rail.

"This," Macon said as we came to a row of glass doors, and a lobby with cream-colored walls and a huge chandelier, "is home."

"Home?" He held the door for me. When I stepped inside, the first thing I smelled was lilacs, just like the perfume my mother wore on special occasions. I looked at my watch: 11:06. I had fifty-four minutes to curfew.

Macon led the way to the elevator, hitting a triangle-shaped button with the back of his hand. The door slid open with a soft beep. The elevator was carpeted in deep green pile and even had a little bench against the far wall if you got tired of standing. He hit the button for P and we started moving.

"You live in the penthouse?" I turned in a circle, watching myself in the four mirrored walls.

"Yep," he said, his eyes on the numbers over my head. "My mother's into power trips." This was the first time he'd talked about her, ever. All I knew about was what I'd heard, years ago, when she'd lived in our neighborhood. She sold real estate and had been married at least three times, the last to a developer of steak houses.

"This is amazing," I said. "This elevator is nicer than my whole house." The beep sounded again as the doors slid open, onto another, smaller lobby. As we got out I saw, through a slightly open door, people moving, mingling, and voices mixed with the clinking of glasses and piano music.

"Down here," Macon said, leading me around a corner to what looked like a linen closet or maid's room. He pulled a keychain out of his pocket, unlocked it, and reached in to turn on a light. Then he stood there, holding it, waiting for me. "Well, come on," he said, reaching over to snap me on the side in the one spot where I was absolutely the most ticklish, "we haven't got all night."

The room itself was pretty small, painted a light sky blue; there was a single bed, neatly made, and a dresser and desk that looked brand-new. Beyond another door on the opposite wall, I could hear someone playing the piano. On a chair, at the end of the bed, there was a TV with something taped to the screen.

"This is your room?" I said, taking a few steps to the TV to get a better look at what was stuck to it. It looked like a photograph.

"Yep." He opened the door to the party, just a crack, then peeked out and shut it again. "Wait here," he said. "I'll be right back."

I sat down on the bed, facing the TV, and leaned forward to get a good look at the photograph. I thought how familiar it looked, and the setting, before it finally hit: it was me. Me, at the Grand Canyon with my mother, the same picture that sat framed on our mantel. But she wasn't in this picture, had somehow been cut out neatly, leaving only me with my arm reaching nowhere, cut off at the elbow.

I pulled the picture off the TV, turning it over. I was still holding it when Macon came back in, carrying two glasses and a plate of finger food.

"Hey," he said, "I hope you like caviar, because that's about the best thing they had out there."

"Where did you get this?" I asked him, holding up the picture.

He just looked at me, and I swear he blushed, even if only for a second. "Somewhere."

"Where?" It wouldn't have surprised me a bit to go home and find that frame on the mantel empty, everything else untouched and in its proper place. He was that slick.

"Somewhere," he said again, handing me a wine glass and the paper plate.

"Where, Macon?" I said. "Come on."

"Scarlett. I took it—borrowed it—from Scarlett. It was stuck to her mirror."

"Oh," I said. I flipped it over again. "You could have asked me for one."

"Yeah," he said, popping something small and doughy into his mouth and not looking at me.

"Well," I said, kissing his cheek where it was smooth and soft and smelled slightly cool, like aftershave. "I'm glad you like me enough to steal my picture."

Outside the music was still playing. In Macon's tiny room, we were like stowaways.

"You don't spend much time here, do you?" I asked him.

"Nope." He sat up and drained his glass. "Can you tell?"

"Yeah. It doesn't even look like anyone lives here. Where *do* you stay, Macon?"

"I don't know. I used to stay at Sherwood's a lot. They had an extra room, his dad was always out of town. His mom never cared. And I got other friends, other places. You know."

"Sure," I said, but I didn't. It was completely foreign to me, this nomadic existence, traveling from place to place, crashing wherever was convenient. I thought of my own room, filled to the brim with my trophies and pictures, my spelling-bee ribbons and schoolbooks, everything that made up who I was.

The only place in the world that had been all mine, always.

I looked over and he was watching me, then leaning over to kiss me as I closed my eyes and lay back, feeling his arms slide around me. With the party music in the background, and voices outside passing louder and softer, he kissed me and kissed me, the bed settling comfortably under us. The sheets smelled like him, sweet and smoky. Macon was a good kisser—not that I had much to compare him to—but I just knew. I tried not to think of all the practice he'd had.

Then, after what seemed like blissful hours, I saw his watch glowing and the time on it: 12:09.

"We have to go," I said suddenly, sitting up. My shirt was all twisted and out of place and my mouth felt numb. "I'm late."

"Late?" he said, all discombobulated and confused. "For what?"

"For my curfew." I grabbed my coat and jammed my feet into my shoes while he jumped up and turned on the light beside the bed, which had somehow been turned off though I couldn't remember when. "God," I said, shaking my head. "I'm dead."

We ran out of the elevator downhill to the parking lot, jumping into his car and squealing around corners and through stop signs, finally pulling up to the corner of my street at exactly 12:21. I could see the light from Scarlett's house, where I was supposed to be, through the trees.

"I gotta go," I said, opening the door. "Thanks."

"I'll call you tomorrow," he called out through the car window. I could see him smiling in the dark.

"Right," I said, smiling back as precious seconds went by. I waved, one last time, then cut through the trees and popped out by Scarlett's pool. I heard him beep as he drove off.

I walked up Scarlett's back steps, through the door and into the kitchen, where she was sitting at the table eating a hot-fudge sundae, with *So You're Pregnant—What Now?* propped up against the sugar bowl in front of her.

"You're late," she said distractedly as I passed through, heading straight for the front door. She had a smear of chocolate sauce on her chin.

"I know," I said, wiping it off with my finger as I passed her. "I'll see you tomorrow."

"Right." She went back to her book and I opened the front door and headed up the walk, across the street.

My mother was waiting for me inside, by the stairs. As I shut the door behind me I could hear Macon's engine rumbling, testing fate again. Bad timing.

"You're late," she said in an even voice. "It's past curfew."

"I know," I said, revving up for my excuse, "but Scarlett and I were watching this movie, and I lost track of time."

"You weren't with Scarlett." This was a statement. "I could see her sitting in her living room by herself, all night. Nice try, Halley."

Outside, Macon was still there, rumbling. He didn't know how much worse he was making it.

"Where were you?" she said to me. "Where did you go with him?"

"Mom, we were just out, it was nothing."

"Where did you go?" Now her voice was getting louder. My father appeared at the top of the stairs, watching.

"Nowhere," I said, as Macon's revving got louder and louder, and I clenched my fists. There was no way to stop it. "We were at his house, we were just hanging out."

"Where does he live?"

"Mom, it doesn't matter."

She had her stony face on, that look again, like a storm crossing over. "It does to me. I don't know what's gotten *into* you lately, Halley. Sneaking around, creeping in the door. Lying to me to my face. All because of this Macon, some boy you won't introduce to us, who we don't even know."

The rumbling got louder and louder. I closed my eyes.

Her voice rose too, over it. In the alcove, it seemed to bounce all around me. "How can you keep lying to us, Halley? How can you be so dishonest?" And she caught me off guard, sounding not mad, not furious, just—sad. I hated this.

"You don't understand," I said. "I don't want to—" and then the engine was tacking up higher and higher, louder and louder, God he wanted me to get caught, he didn't understand, as the tires squealed and screeched, burning, and he took off down the street, racing, stopping to beep as he rounded the corner. All this I knew, without even looking, as well as I knew Mr. Harper's light was already on, he was already out there in his slippers and bathrobe, cursing the smoke that still hung in the air.

"Did you hear that?" my mother said, twisting to look up at my father, who just nodded. "He could *kill* someone driving like that. Kill someone." Her voice was shaky, almost scared, just like Grandma Halley's.

"Mom," I said. "Just let me—"

"Go to bed, Halley," my father said in a low voice, coming down step by step. He took my mother by the arm and led her into the kitchen, flicking on the light as they went. "Now."

So I went, up to my room, my heart thumping. As I passed the mirror in the hallway I glanced at myself, at a girl with her hair tumbling over her shoulders, in a faded jeans jacket, lips red from kissing. I faced my reflection and committed this girl to memory: the girl who had risen out of that night at Topper Lake, the girl who belonged with Macon Faulkner, the girl who broke her mother's heart, never looking back. The girl I was.

Chapter Ten

"Look at this," Scarlett said, passing me the magazine she was holding. "By Month Four, the baby is learning to suck and swallow, and is forming teeth. And the fingers and toes are well defined."

"That's surprising," I said, "considering it's existing only on hot dogs and orange juice." It was the next day, and we were at the doctor's office for the fourth-month checkup. Scarlett had always been phobic of stethoscopes and lab coats and needed moral support, so I'd been pardoned from my most recent grounding, for (1) lying about being with Macon and (2) breaking curfew. I was becoming an expert at being grounded; I could have written books, taught seminars.

"I'm eating better, you know," she said indignantly, shifting her position on the table. She was in one of those open-back gowns, trying to cover her exposed parts. Behind her, on the wall, was a totally graphic poster with the heading *The Female Reproductive System*. I was trying not to look at it, instead focusing on the plastic turkey and Pilgrims tacked up around it; Thanksgiving was two weeks away.

"You're still not getting enough green leafy vegetables," I told her. "Lettuce on a Big Mac doesn't count."

"Shut up." She leaned back, smoothing her hand over her stomach. In just the last few weeks she was finally starting to show, her waist bulging just barely. Her breasts, on the other hand, were getting enormous. She said it was the only perk.

There was a knock on the door, and the doctor came in. Her name tag said Dr. Roberts and she was carrying a clipboard. She had on bright pink running shoes and blue jeans, her hair in a twist on the back of her head.

"Hello there," she said, then glanced down at her notes and added, "Scarlett. How are you today?"

"Fine," Scarlett said. She was already starting to wring her hands, a dead giveaway. I concentrated on the *Life* magazine in my lap; the cover story was on Elvis.

"So you're about sixteen weeks along," Dr. Roberts said, reading off the chart. "Are you having any problems? Concerns?"

"No," Scarlett said in a low voice, and I shot her a look. "Not really."

"Any headaches? Nosebleeds? Constipation?"

"No," Scarlett said.

"Liar," I said loudly.

"You hush," she snapped at me. To the doctor she said, "She doesn't know anything."

"And who are you?" Dr. Roberts turned to face me, tucking her clipboard under her arm. "Her sister?"

"I'm her friend," I said. "And she's scared to death of doctors, so she won't tell you anything."

"Okay," the doctor said, smiling. "Now, Scarlett, I know all of this is a little scary, especially for someone your age. But you need to be honest with me, for the good of yourself and your baby. It's important that I know what's happening."

"She's right," I chimed in, and got another death look from Scarlett. I went back to Elvis and kept quiet.

Scarlett twisted the hem of her gown in her hands. "Well," she said slowly, "I have heartburn a lot. And I've been dizzy lately."

"That's normal," the doctor said, easing Scarlett onto her back and sliding her hand under the gown. She ran her fingers over Scarlett's stomach, then put her stethoscope against the skin and listened. "Have you noticed an increase in your appetite?"

"Yes. I'm eating all the time."

"That's fine. Just be sure you keep up your proteins and vitamin C. I'll give you a handout when you leave today, and we can discuss it further." She took off her stethoscope and consulted the file again, tapping the clipboard with her finger. "Blood pressure is fine, we've gotten the urine sample already. Is there anything you'd like to talk about? Or ask me?"

Scarlett shot me a look, but I didn't say anything. I just turned the page, reading up on national politics, and pretended I wasn't listening.

"Well," Scarlett said quietly. "I have one. How bad does it hurt?"

"Does what hurt?"

"Delivery. When it comes. Is it really bad?"

Dr. Roberts smiled. "It depends on the situation, Scarlett, but I'd be lying if I said it was painless. It also depends on the course of childbirth you want to take. Some women prefer to go without drugs or medication; that's called 'natural childbirth.' There are birthing classes you can take, which I will be happy to refer you to, that teach ways of breathing that can help with the delivery process."

"But you're saying it hurts."

"I'm saying it depends," Dr. Roberts said gently, "but honestly, yes, it hurts. But look at how many people have gone through it and lived to tell. We're all here because of it. So it can't be that bad. Right?"

"Right," Scarlett said glumly, putting her hand on her stomach.

"You're gonna need major drugs," I said as we left, climbing into the car en route to our Saturday twelve-to-six shifts at Milton's. I was driving, and she settled into the passenger seat, sighing. I said, "They should just totally knock you out. Like with a baseball bat."

"I know," she said, "but that's bad for the baby."

"The bat?"

"No, the drugs. I think I should take a birthing class or something. Learn how to breathe."

"Like Lamaze?"

"Yeah, or something like that." She shuffled through the handouts the doctor had given us, packets and brochures, all with happy pregnant women on their covers. "Maybe Marion could go with me."

"I'm sure she would," I said. "Then she'd get to be there when it came. That would be cool."

"I don't know. She's still talking about adoption like it's for sure going to happen. She's already contacted an agency and everything."

"She'll come around."

"I think she's saying the same thing about me." We pulled into Milton's parking lot, already packed with Saturday shoppers. "Sooner or later, one of us will have to back down."

Later that afternoon, after what seemed like thousands of screaming children and gallons of milk, hundreds of bananas and Diet Coke two-liters, I looked down my line and saw my mother. She was reading *Good Housekeeping*, a bottle of wine tucked under one arm, and when she saw me she waved, smiling. My mother still got some small thrill at seeing me at work.

"Hi there," she said cheerfully when she got to the front of the line, plunking the bottle down in front of me.

"Hi," I said, scanning it and hitting the total button.

"What time do you get off tonight?"

"Six." Behind me I could hear Scarlett arguing with some man over the price of grapes. "It's seven eighty-nine."

"Let's go out for dinner," she said, handing me a ten. "My treat."

"I don't know," I said. "I'm real tired."

"I want to talk to you," she said. My line was still long, people shifting impatiently. Like me, they had no time for my mother's maneuvering. "I'll pick you up."

"But, Mom," I said as she grabbed her wine and change from my hands and started toward the door. "I don't—"

"I'll see you at six," she called out cheerfully, and left me stuck there face to face with a fat man buying two boxes of Super Snax and a bottle of Old English. Lately to get to me she'd had to hit hard and fast, rushing me, then tackling to the ground. For the rest of the afternoon, all I could think about was what she had planned, what trick was up her sleeve.

She picked me up at six, waiting in the loading zone with the engine running. When I got in the car, she looked over at me and smiled, genuinely happy, and I felt a pang of guilt for all the dreading I'd been doing all afternoon.

We went to a little Italian place by our house, with checkered tablecloths and a pizza buffet. After a half a slice of pepperoni and some small talk about Milton's and school, she leaned across the table and said, "I want to talk to you about Macon."

The way she said it you'd think she knew him, that they were friends. "Macon."

"Yes." She took a sip of her drink. "To be honest, Halley, I'm not happy with this relationship."

Well, I thought, *you're not in it*. But I didn't say anything. I could tell already this wasn't going to be a discussion, a dialog, or anything involving my opinion. I was an expert at my mother. I knew her faces, her tones of voice, could translate the hidden, complex meanings of each of her sighs.

"Now," she began, and I could tell she'd worked on this, planned every word, probably even outlined it on a legal pad for her book, "since you've been hanging around with Macon you've gotten caught skipping school, broken your curfew, and your attitude is always confrontational and difficult. Honestly, I don't even recognize you anymore."

I didn't say anything and just picked at my pizza. I was losing my appetite, fast. She kept on; she was on a roll.

"Your appearance has changed." Her voice was so loud, and I sunk lower in my seat; this wasn't the place for this, which was exactly why she'd picked it. "You smell like cigarettes when you come home, you're listless and distracted. You never talk about school with us anymore. You're distant."

Distant. If she couldn't keep me under her thumb, I was far away.

"These are all warning signs," she went on. "I tell parents to watch out for them every day."

"I'm not doing anything," I said. "I was only twenty minutes late, Mom."

"That's not the issue here, and you know it." She got quiet as the waiter came by with more bread, then lowered her voice and continued. "He's not good for you."

Like he was food. Not a green pepper or an orange, but a big sticky Snickers bar. "You don't even know him," I said.

"That's because you refuse to discuss him!" She wadded up her napkin and threw it down on her plate. "I have given you endless chances to prove me wrong here. I have tried to dialog—"

"I don't want to 'dialog,'" I snapped. "You've already made up your mind anyway, you hate him. And this isn't about him, anyway."

"This is what I know," she said, leaning closer to me. "He drives like a maniac. He's not from Lakeview. And you are willing to do anything for him, including but probably not limited to lying to me and your father. What I *don't* know is what you're doing with him, how far things have gone—if there are drugs involved or God knows what else."

"Drugs," I repeated, and I laughed. "God, you always think everything is about *drugs*."

She wasn't laughing. "Your father and I," she said, finally lowering her voice, "have discussed this thoroughly. And we've decided you cannot see him anymore."

"*What?*" I said. "You can't do that." My stomach was tight and hot. "You can't just decide that."

"Well, Halley, with your actions lately you've given us no other choice." She sat back in her chair, crossing her arms. This wasn't going the way she wanted, I could tell. This wasn't her office and I wasn't a patient and she couldn't just tell me what to do. But I didn't know what she'd expected. That she was do-

169

ing me a favor? "Halley, I don't think you understand how easy it is to make a mistake that will cost you forever. All it takes is one wrong choice, and . . ."

"You're talking about Scarlett again," I said, shaking my head. I was tired of this, tired of battling and putting up fronts, of having to think so hard about my next move.

"No," she said. "I am talking about you falling in with the wrong crowd, getting influenced to do something you aren't ready to do. That you don't *want* to do. You don't know what Macon's involved in."

I hated the way she kept saying his name.

"There's a lot of dangerous stuff out there," she said. "You're inexperienced. And you're like me, Halley. You have a tendency not to see people for what they really are."

I sat there and looked at my mother, at the ease in her face as she told me how I felt, what I thought, everything. Like I was a puzzle, one she'd created, and she knew the solution every time. If she couldn't keep me close to her, she'd force me to be where she could always find me.

"That's not true," I said to her slowly, and already I knew I'd say something ugly, something final, even as I stood up, pushing back my chair. "I'm not getting influenced, I'm not inexperienced, and *I am not like you.*"

It was the last thing that did it. Her face went blank, shocked, like I'd reached out and slapped her.

You wanted distance, I thought. *There you go.*

She sat back in her chair, keeping her voice low, and said, "Sit down, Halley. Now."

I just stood there, thinking of running out the door, losing myself in Macon's secret network of pizza parlors and arcades, side streets and alleys, riding up to that penthouse room and stowing away, forever.

"Sit *down*," she said again. She was looking over my head, out to the parking lot. She was blinking, a lot, and I could hear her taking deep, deep breaths.

I sat down, pulling in my chair, while she dabbed at her mouth with a napkin and waved over the waiter. We got the check, paid, and went out to the car without a word between us. All the way home I stared out the window, watching the houses slip past and thinking back to the Grand Canyon, vast and uncrossable, like so many things were now.

When we pulled into our driveway we passed Steve, who was getting out of his Hyundai in front of Scarlett's house. He was carrying flowers, his usual, and wearing yet another tweedish, threadbare jacket with patches on the elbows. But this time I didn't need Scarlett to point out the newest sign of Vlad's emergence: boots. Not just regular boots either, but big, leather, clunky boots with a thick heel and buckles that I imagined must be clanking loudly with each step, although my window was up and I couldn't hear them. Warrior boots, poking out from beneath his pants leg as if they'd just walked over the heads of dead opponents. He waved cheerfully as we passed, and my mother, still irritated, lifted her hand with her fake neighborhood wave.

We still hadn't said a word to each other as we came into the kitchen where my father was on the phone, his back to us. As he turned around, I could tell instantly something was wrong.

"Hold on," he said into the receiver, then covered it with his hand. "Julie. It's your mother."

She put down her purse. "What? What is it?"

"She fell, in her house—she's hurt bad, honey. The neighbors found her. She'd been there for a while."

"She fell?" My mother's voice was high, shaky.

"This is Dr. Robbins." He handed her the phone, adding, "I'll use the other phone and start calling about flights."

She took the phone from him, taking a deep breath as he squeezed her shoulder and headed down the hall, toward her office. I stood in the open doorway and held my breath.

"Hello, this is Julie Cooke. . . . Yes. Yes, my husband said . . . I see. Do you know when this happened? Right. Right, sure."

All this time, each word she said, she was looking right at me. Not like she was even aware of it or could see me at all. Just her eyes on me, steady, as if I was the only thing holding her up.

"My husband is calling about flights right now, so I'll be there as soon as I can. Is she in pain? . . . Well, of course. So the surgery will be tomorrow at six, and I'll just—I'll get there as soon as I can. Okay. Thanks so much. Good-bye." She hung up the phone, turning her back to me, and then just stood there, one hand still on the receiver. I could see her tense back, the shoulder blades poking out.

"Your grandmother's hurt," she said in a low voice, still not turning around. "She fell and broke several ribs, and she'll have to have surgery on her hip in the morning. She was alone for a long time before anyone found her." She choked on this last part, her voice wavering.

"Is she gonna be okay?" Down the hall I could hear my father's voice, asking questions about departures and arrivals, coach or first class, chances of standby. "Mom?"

I watched her shoulders fall and rise, one deep breath, before she turned around, her face composed and even. "I don't know, honey. We'll just have to see."

"Mom—" I started, wanting to somehow fix this, whatever I'd opened between us by not wanting to share Macon with her. By not wanting to share *me* with her.

"Julie," my father's voice came booming from down the hall, always too loud for small spaces, "there's a flight in an hour, but you have a long layover in Baltimore. It's the best we can do, I think."

"That's fine," she said evenly. "Go ahead and book it. I'll throw a bag together."

"Mom," I said, "I just—"

"Honey, there's no time," she said quickly as she passed me, reaching to pat my shoulder, distracted. "I've got to go pack."

So I sat on my bed, in my room, with my math homework in

my lap and the door open. I heard the closet door opening and shutting, my mother packing, my father's low, soothing voice. But it was the silences that were the worst, when I craned my neck, hoping for just one word or sound. Anything would have been better than imagining what was happening when everything was muffled, and I knew she had to be crying.

She came in and hugged me, ruffling my hair like she always had when I was little; she said not to worry, she'd call later, everything was okay. She'd forgotten about what I'd said, about what had happened at dinner. Just like that, with one phone call, she was a daughter again.

Chapter Eleven

With my mother gone, it was like I'd been handed a Get Out of Jail Free card. My father's morning show was still riding an Arbitron rating high, which meant he was busy almost every afternoon or evening with promotional events. In the past few months, he'd already lost an on-air bet with the traffic guy that resulted in him having to perform an embarrassing (and thank God, not complete) striptease at a local dance club, attended about a hundred contest-winner cocktail parties, and wrestled a man named the Dominator at the Hilton for charity. That one had left him bruised, battered, and with nose splints for a full week, which he'd loved. He'd discussed his drainage problems, complete with a million booger jokes, every morning while I cringed on the way to school.

The phone rang constantly, usually a nervous-sounding man named Lottie who organized my father's every waking moment, lining up another trip to the mall, meeting, or Wacky Stunt. My father, who my mother insisted was too old and too educated for any of this nonsense, hardly even saw me, much less kept careful track of what I was doing. At most, we passed each other late at night, as I walked past his bedroom to brush my teeth. We came to an unspoken understanding: I'd behave, show up when I was supposed to, and he wouldn't ask questions. It was only four days, after all.

Of course, I was always with Macon. Now he could pick me up for school and take me to work or home in the afternoons; Scarlett, who used to drive me, was as busy as my father. She was working extra shifts at Milton's so she could buy baby clothes and nursery items; plus, she was spending a lot of time with Cameron, who made her laugh and rubbed her feet. Finally, our guidance counselor, Mrs. Bagbie, had convinced her to join a fledgling Teen Mothers Support Group that met at school two afternoons a week. She hadn't wanted to go, but she said the other girls—some pregnant, some already with kids—made her feel a little less strange. And Scarlett, as I knew, could make friends anywhere.

Macon and I had fun. Monday we didn't go to school at all, spending the entire time just driving around, eating at McDonald's, and hanging out by the river. When the school called that night my father wasn't home, and I easily explained that I'd been sick and my mother was out of town. Macon had already mastered her signature, signing with a flourish every note I needed.

She called every night and asked me the basic questions about school and work, whether my father was remembering to feed me. She said she missed me, that Grandma Halley was going to be all right. She said she was sorry we'd argued, and she knew it was hard for me to break it off with Macon, but someday I would understand it was the right thing. At the other end of the line, phone in hand, I agreed and watched him back out of the driveway, lights moving across me, then heard him beep as he drove away. I told myself I shouldn't feel guilty, that she'd played dirty, changing the rules to suit her. Sometimes it worked; sometimes not.

The night before my father and I were leaving to go to Buffalo for Thanksgiving, Macon brought me home from work. The house was dark when we pulled up.

"Where's your dad?" he said as he cut off the engine.

"I don't know." I grabbed my backpack out of the back of the car and opened my door. "Doing radio stuff, probably."

As I leaned over to kiss him good-bye, he pulled back a bit, his eyes still on my dark house. Across the street Scarlett's front porch light was already on, and I could see Marion in front of the TV in the living room, her shoes off, feet up on the coffee table. In the kitchen Scarlett was standing at the stove, stirring something.

"Well," I said to Macon, sliding my hand around his neck. "I guess I'll see you when I get back."

"Aren't you going to ask me to come in?"

"In?" I drew back. He'd never asked before. "Do you want to?"

"Sure." He reached down and opened his door, and just like that we were walking up the driveway, past my mother's mums, to the front steps. The paper was on the porch and a few leaves were blowing around, making scraping noises. It was getting ready to rain.

I fished around in my backpack for my keys, then unlocked the door and pushed it open just as there was a loud rumbling overhead. Even without looking up I could feel the plane coming closer, the thin line of windowpanes on either side of the door already vibrating.

"Man," Macon said. "That's loud."

"It's bad around this time," I told him. "There are lots of early evening flights." The house was completely dark inside, and I felt across the wall for the light switch. Right as the light came on overhead there was a popping noise, a flash, and we were in the dark again.

"Hold on," I said, dropping my backpack as he stepped in behind me, a few leaves blowing in across his feet. "I'll find another light."

And then I felt his arms wrap around me from behind, his hand, cool, on my stomach, and in the dark of my parents' alcove he kissed me. He didn't seem to have any problem negotiating the dark of the empty house, walking me backwards to the living room and the couch, pushing me down across my mother's needlepoint pillows. I kissed him back, letting his hand slide up my shirt, feeling the warmth of his legs pressing against mine. Another plane was rumbling in the distance.

"Macon," I said, coming up for air after a few minutes, "my father could be home any second."

He kept kissing me, his hand still exploring. Obviously this wasn't as much of a threat to him as it was to me.

"Macon." I pushed him back a little. "I'm serious."

"Okay, okay." He sat up, bumping back against another stack of pillows. My mother was into pillows. "Where's your sense of adventure?"

"You don't know my father," I said, like he was some big ogre, chasing boys across the yard with a shotgun. I was running enough risk just having him there; my father finding us alone in the dark would be another story altogether.

I got up and went into the kitchen, flicking on lights as I went. All the familiar things looked different with him trailing along behind me. I wondered what he was thinking.

"Do you want something to drink?" I said, opening the fridge.

"Nah," he said, pulling out a chair from the kitchen table and sitting down.

I was bending into the fridge, searching out a Coke, when I suddenly heard my father's voice, as if he'd stepped up right behind me. I swear I almost stopped breathing.

"Well, we're over here at the new Simpson Dry Cleaners, at the Lakeview Mall, and I'm Brian and I gotta tell you, I've seen a lot of dry cleaners before but this place is different. Herb and Mary Simpson, well, they know a little bit about this business, and . . ."

I felt my face get hot, blood rushing up in sheer panic, even after I realized it was just the radio and turned around to see Macon smiling behind me, his hand still on the knob.

"Not funny," I said, pulling over a chair to sit down next to him. He turned the volume down and I could only hear my father murmuring, something about same-day service and starch.

He said he wanted to see my room, and I knew why, but I took him up there anyway, climbing up the steps in the dark with him holding my hand. He walked around my bed, leaning into my mirror to examine the blue ribbons I'd gotten in gymnastics years ago, the pictures of Scarlett and me from the photo booth at the mall, mugging and smiling for the camera. He lay across my bed like he owned it. And as he leaned to kiss me, I had my eyes open, looking straight over his head to the top of my bookcase, at the Madame Alexander doll Grandma Halley had given me for my tenth birthday. It was Scarlett O'Hara, in a green-and-white dress and hat, and just seeing it for that second before I closed my eyes gave me that same pang of guilt, my mother's face flashing across, telling me how wrong this was.

Outside, the planes kept going over, shaking my windows. Macon kept sliding his hand under my waistband, pushing farther than he had before, and I kept pushing him back. We'd turned on my clock radio, low, to keep track of my father's whereabouts, but after a while it cut off and it was just us and silence, Macon's lips against my ear coaxing. His voice was low and rumbly and right in my ear, his fingers stroking the back of my neck. It all felt so good, and I would feel myself forgetting, slipping and losing myself in it, until all of a sudden—

"No," I said, grabbing his hand as he tried to unsnap my jeans, "this is not a good idea."

"Why not?" His voice was muffled.

"You know why not," I said.

"No, I don't."

"Macon."

"What's the big deal?" he asked me, rolling over onto his back, his head on my pillow. His shirt was unbuttoned; one hand was still on my stomach, fingers stretched across my skin.

"The big deal is that this is my house and my bed, and my father is due home at any time. I could get so busted."

He rolled over and turned up the radio again, my father's voice filling the room. *"So come on down here to Simpson's Dry Cleaners, we've got some prizes and great deals, and cake —there's cake, too?—how can you say no to cake? I'm Brian, I'm here till nine."* He just lay there, watching me, proving me wrong.

"It's just not a good idea," I said, reaching over and turning on the light. All around me my room jumped into place, the familiar parameters of my life: my bed, my carpet, my stuffed animals lined up across the third shelf of my bookshelf. There was a little green pig in the middle that Noah Vaughn had bought me for Valentine's day two years before. Noah had never slid his hand further than my neck, had never found ingenious ways to get places I was trying zealously to guard. Noah Vaughn had been happy just to hold my hand.

181

"Halley," Macon said, his voice low. "I'm into being patient and waiting and all, but it's been almost three months now."

"That's not that long," I said, picking at the worn spot in my comforter.

"It is to me." He rolled a little closer, putting his head in my lap. I had a sudden flash, out of nowhere, that he had done this before. "Just think about it, okay? We'll be careful, I promise."

"I think about it," I said, running my fingers through his hair. He closed his eyes. And I *did* think about it, all the time. But each time I was tempted, each time I wanted to give up my defense and pull back my troops, I thought of Scarlett. Of course I thought of Scarlett. She'd thought she was being careful, too.

He left not long after that. He didn't want to stay and watch TV or just hang out and talk. Something was changing, something I could sense even though I'd never been here before, like the way baby turtles know to go to the water at birth, instinctively. They just *know*. And I already knew I'd lose Macon, probably soon, if I didn't sleep with him. He kissed me goodbye and left, and I stood in my open door and watched him go, beeping like he always did as he rounded the corner.

As I lost sight of him, I thought of that sketched black outline, the colors inside just beginning to get filled in. The girl I'd been, the girl I was. I told myself the changes had come fast and furious these last few months, and one more wasn't that big of a deal. But each time I did I thought of Scarlett, always Scarlett, and that new color, that particular shade, which I wasn't ready to take on just yet.

When I went over to Scarlett's to say good-bye, there was food out on the kitchen table and counters, and she was squatted on the floor with a bucket and sponge, scrubbing the inside of the fridge.

"Can you smell it?" she said before I'd even opened my mouth. She hadn't even turned around. Pregnancy was making every one of her senses stronger, more intense, and I swear sometimes she seemed almost clairvoyant.

"Smell what?"

"You can't smell it?" Now she turned around, pointing her sponge at me. She took a deep breath, closing her eyes. "That. That rotting, stink kind of smell."

I breathed in, but all I was getting was Clorox from the bucket. "No."

"God." She stood up, grabbing onto the fridge door for support. It was harder for her to get to her feet now, her stomach throwing her off balance. "Cameron couldn't smell it either—he said I was being crazy. But I swear, it's so strong it's making me gag. I've had to hold my breath the whole time I've been doing this."

I looked over at the pregnancy Bible, which was lying on the table, open to the chapter on Month Five, which was fast approaching. I flipped through the pages as she bent down over the vegetable crisper, nose wrinkled, scrubbing like mad.

"Page seventy-four, bottom paragraph," I said out loud, following the words with my finger. "And I quote: 'Your sense of smell may become stronger during your pregnancy, causing an aversion to some foods."

"I cannot believe you don't smell that," she muttered, ignoring me.

"What are you going to do, scrub the whole house?" I said as she yanked out the butter dish, examined it, and dunked it in the bucket.

"If I have to."

"You're crazy."

"No," she said, "I'm pregnant and I'm allowed my eccentricities; the doctor said so. So shut up."

I pulled out a chair and sat down, resting my arm on the table. Every time I was in Scarlett's kitchen I thought back to the years we'd spent there, at the table, with the radio on. On long summer days we'd make chocolate-chip cookies and dance around the linoleum floor with our shoes off, the music turned up loud.

I sat down at the table, flipping through Month Five. "Look at this," I said. "For December we have continued constipation, leg cramps, and ankle swelling to look forward to."

"Great." She sat back on her heels, dropping the sponge in the bucket. "What else?"

"Ummm . . . varicose veins, maybe, and an easier or more difficult orgasm."

She turned around, pushing her hair out of her face. "Halley. Please."

"I'm just reading the book."

"Well, you of all people should know orgasms are not my big concern right now. I'm more interested in finding whatever is rotting in this kitchen."

I still couldn't smell anything, but I knew better than to argue. Scarlett was handling things now, and I was proud of her; she was eating better, walking around the block for a half hour every day because she'd heard it was good for the baby, and reading everything she could get her hands on about child rearing. Everything, that is, except the adoption articles and pamphlets that Marion kept leaving on the lazy Susan or on her bed, always with a card from someone interested in Discussing the Options. Scarlett was playing along because she had to, but she was keeping the baby. Like everything else, she'd made her choice and she'd stick to it, everyone else be damned.

"Scarlett?" I said.

"Yeah?" her voice was muffled; she had her head stuck under the meat and cheese drawer, inspecting.

"What made you decide to sleep with him?"

She drew herself out, slowly, and turned to face me. "Why?"

"I don't know," I shrugged. "Just wondered."

"Did you sleep with Macon?"

"No," I said. "Of course not."

"But he wants you to."

"No, not exactly." I spun the lazy Susan. "He brought it up, that's all."

She walked over and sat down beside me, pulling her hair back with her hands. She smelled like Clorox. "What did you say?"

"I told him I'd think about it."

She sat back, absorbing this. "Do you want to?"

"I don't know. But he does, and it's not that big a deal to him, you know? He doesn't understand why it is to me."

"That's bullshit," she said simply. "He knows why."

"It's not like that," I said. "I mean, I really like him. And I think for guys like him—like that—it isn't that big of a deal. It's just what, you know, you *do*."

"Halley." She shook her head. "This isn't about *him*. It's about *you*. You shouldn't do anything you're not ready for."

"I'm ready," I said.

"Are you sure?"

"Were *you* ready?" I said.

That stopped her. She smoothed her hands over her stomach; it looked like she'd swallowed a small melon, or a pumpkin. "I don't know. Probably not. I loved him, and one night things just went farther than they had before. Afterwards I realized it was a mistake, in more ways than one."

"Because it came off," I said.

"Yeah. And for other reasons, too. But I can't preach to you, because I was sure I was doing the right thing. I didn't know he'd be gone the next day. Like, literally *gone*. But you have to consider that."

"That he might die?"

"Not die," she said softly, and there was that ripple again, the one that still came over her face whenever she spoke of him, and I suddenly realized how long it had really been. "I mean, I loved Michael so much, but—I didn't know him that well. Just for a summer, you know. A lot could have happened this fall. I'll never know."

"I can tell he wants to. Like soon. He's getting more pushy about it."

"If you sleep with him, it will change things," she said. "It has to. And if he goes, you'll have lost more than just him. So be sure, Halley. Be real sure."

Chapter Twelve

Grandma Halley was staying in a place called Evergreen Rest Care Facility. Some of the people were bedridden, but others could get around; women in motorized wheelchairs zoomed past us down the corridors, their purses clamped against their laps. Everything smelled fruity and sharp, like too much cheap air freshener. It seemed like every open piece of wall had a Thanksgiving decoration taped to it, turkeys and Pilgrims and corn husks, and you got the sense that holidays there were imperative, important, because there wasn't much else to look forward to.

I'd slept for most of the trip up, since my father wanted to leave at four A.M. to get the jump on all the other travelers. My father was always concerned with "getting the jump" when we traveled, obsessed with outsmarting other motorists; once in the car, he flipped the radio dial constantly, checking out his competition, something that drove me crazy since I never got to hear any music.

Before we left I lay awake most of the night, listening for cars outside. I was sure Macon would come by, even just to beep, to say good-bye again. He knew I was upset about my grandmother, but it made him uncomfortable; family stuff was not really his department. I didn't want to leave things the way we had, unresolved, and I pictured him in the few places I knew he went, with the few friends of his I'd met, and tried to tell myself he cared about me enough not to look elsewhere for what I wasn't giving him.

The first thing I thought when I walked into Grandma Halley's room was how small she looked. She was in bed, her eyes closed, and a square of sunlight was falling across her face from the window. She looked like a doll, her face porcelain and unreal, like the Madame Alexander Scarlett O'Hara she'd given me.

"Hi there." My mother stood up from a chair by the window. I hadn't even seen her. "How was the trip?"

"Fine," I said as she came over and kissed me.

"Fine," my father said, putting his arm around her waist. "We made great time. Really got the jump on everyone."

"Come outside," she said softly. "She's had a hard night and she really needs her rest."

Out in the corridor a pack of women in wheelchairs was passing, laughing and talking, and next to Grandma Halley's room, behind a half-closed door, I could see someone hooked up to a machine, a tube in his nose. The room was dark, the shades drawn.

"So how's everything?" my mother said to me, pulling me close. "I've missed you guys so much."

"How are you?" my father said, noticing as I did how tired

she looked, her face older and more drawn, as if just time in this place could age you.

"I'm okay," she said to him, her arm still around me. I was uncomfortable, my arm clamped in an odd position against my side, but this was important to her, so I didn't move. "She's doing much better today. Every day she just improves by leaps and bounds." Every few words she squeezed my shoulder again for emphasis.

When we went back inside I only spoke with Grandma Halley for a few minutes. At first, when she opened her eyes and saw me there was no flicker of recognition, no instant understanding that I was who I was, and that scared me. As if I had already changed into another girl, another Halley, features and voice and manners all shifting to make me unrecognizable.

"It's Halley, Mother," my own mother said softly from the other side of the bed, looking across at me encouragingly, since she couldn't squeeze my shoulder and pass this off as better than it was.

And then I saw it, flooding across my grandmother's antique, careful features: she found me in the strange face looking down at her. "Halley," she said, almost scolding, as if I was an old friend playing a trick on her. "How are you, sweetheart?"

"I'm good. I've missed you," I said, and I took her hand, so small in mine, and wrapped my fingers around it. I could feel the bones in it working, moving to grab hold, as I carefully squeezed it, emphasizing, reassuring, that everything would be all right.

*   *   *

Later, we watched Grandma Halley eat turkey and cranberry Jell-O off an orange plastic, cornucopia-decorated tray. The halls at Evergreen were packed with other relatives now, making pilgrimages; at one point when I passed the room next door, the man with the tubes and machines had a crowd around his bed, all talking softly and huddled together. Outside, in the hallway, a little girl in a pinafore and Mary Janes was playing hopscotch across the linoleum tiles. The halls had a different smell now, of air freshener mingled with hundreds of types of perfumes and hair spray, the outside world suddenly mixed in.

That evening we went to a hotel downtown and paid a flat twenty bucks each for a Thanksgiving buffet, rows and rows of steam tables full of mashed potatoes and gravy and cranberry sauce and pumpkin pie. Everyone was dressed up and eating at little tables, like a huge family broken up into pieces. My father ate three plates' worth and my mother, her face tired and lined from lack of sleep, talked the entire time, nonstop, as if enough words could make it less strange, less different from every other Thanksgiving we'd ever had. She asked me tons of questions, just to keep the conversation going, about Scarlett and school and Milton's. My father told a long story about some listener who'd stripped naked and run down Main Street for concert tickets, the station's latest coup. I picked at my mashed potatoes, smooth as silk, and wondered what Macon was doing, if he even had a turkey dinner or just a Big Mac in his empty

191

room and another party without me. I missed him, just like I missed the lumpy potatoes my mother made every Thanksgiving.

We settled into Grandma Halley's house, me in my old room from all those summers, my parents down the hall in the guest room with the blue flowered wallpaper. Nothing much had changed. The cat was still fat, the pipes still wheezed all night, and each time I passed the bell in the staircase window I touched it automatically, without thinking, announcing myself to the empty stairwell.

In the evenings I reread the few magazines I'd brought or called Scarlett. She'd cooked an entire traditional dinner for Cameron (whose family ate early) and Marion and Steve/Vlad, who showed up, she told me, in dress pants, with his clanking boots and medallion necklace and what she said could only be described politely as a tunic.

"A what?" I said.

"A tunic," she said simply. "Like a big shirt, with a drawstring collar, that hung down past his waist."

"He tucked it in, right?"

"No," she said. "He just wore it. And I swear Marion hardly even noticed."

This fascinated me. "What did you say?"

"What could I say? I told him to sit down and gave him a bowl of nuts. I don't know, Marion's crazy for him. She wouldn't care if he showed up butt naked."

I laughed. "Stop."

"I'm serious." She sighed. "Well, at least dinner went well. Cameron kept the conversation going, and I was highly complimented on my potatoes. Not that I could eat them. My back has been killing me and I've been feeling nauseous since last week. Something is rotting in the kitchen. Did I tell you that?"

"Yeah, you did," I said. "Did they have lumps?"

"What?"

"The potatoes. Did they have lumps?"

"Of course they did," she said. "They're only good if they have lumps."

"I know it," I said. "Save me a bowl, okay?"

"Okay," she said, her voice crackling across the line, reassuring as always. "I will."

I got to know my Grandma Halley a little better that weekend, and it wasn't through the few short visits I spent by her bedside, holding her hand. She was still in pain from her surgery and a little confused; she called me Julie more than once, and told me stories that trailed off midway, fading out in the quiet. And all the while my mother was there behind me, or beside me, finishing the sentences my grandmother couldn't, and trying to make everything right again.

In my bedroom at Grandma Halley's, there was an old cabinet made out of sweet-smelling wood with roses painted across the doors. One night when I was bored I opened it up, and inside were stacks of boxes, photographs, letters, and odds and ends, little things my grandmother, who was an intense pack rat, couldn't bear to throw away. There were pictures of her as a teenager in fancy dancing dresses posing with gaggles of other girls, all of them smiling. Her hair had been long and dark, and she wore it twisted up over her head, with flowers woven across the crown. There was one box full of dance cards with boys' names signed in them, each dance numbered off. I found a wedding picture of her and my grandfather bending over a cake, the knife in both their hands. It all fascinated me. I read the letters she wrote to her mother during her first trip abroad, where she spent four pages describing an Indian boy she met in the park, and every word he said, and how blue the sky was. And the later letters about my grandfather, how much she loved him, letters that were returned to her postmarked and neatly tied with string when her own mother died.

I went downstairs and found my mother at the kitchen table, drinking a cup of tea and sitting in Grandma Halley's big green chair by the window. She didn't hear me come in and jumped when I touched her shoulder.

"Hey," she said. "What are you still doing up?"

"I've been reading all this stuff of Grandma Halley's," I said, sliding in beside her. "Look at this." And I showed her the dance card I had tied to my wrist, and the wedding picture of them dancing past the band, and my birth announcement, carefully saved in its own envelope. Hours had passed as I'd sat going through my grandmother's life, stored in boxes and envelopes, neatly organized as if she'd meant for me to find it there all along.

"Can you believe she was ever so young," my mother said, holding the wedding picture to the light. "See the necklace she's wearing? She gave that to me on my wedding day. It was my 'something borrowed.'"

"She fell in love with an Indian boy the summer she was nineteen," I told her. "In a park in London. He wrote to her for two years afterwards."

"No kidding," she said softly, her fingers idly brushing across my hair. "She never told me."

"And you know that bell she keeps in the window halfway up the stairs? Grandpa bought her that at a flea market in Spain, when he was in the service."

"Really?"

"You should read the letters," I said, looking down at my own name on the birth announcement: *Welcome, Halley!*

She smiled at me, as if remembering suddenly when moments like this between us were not noticed for the very fact of how rare they were.

"Honey," she said, gathering up my hair in her hands, "I'm sorry about that night at the restaurant. I know it's hard to understand why we can't let you see Macon. But it's for the best. Someday you'll understand that."

"No," I said. "I won't." And then, just as easily as it had closed, the distance opened up between us. I could almost see it.

She sighed, letting my hair drop. She felt it, too. "Well, it's late. You should get to bed, okay?"

"Yeah, okay." I got up and walked toward the stairs, past the framed front page of the local paper, announcing the comet's arrival. HALLEY MAKES ANOTHER VISIT, it said.

"I remember when the comet came through," I said, and she walked up behind me, reading over my shoulder. "I sat in Grandma's lap and we watched it together."

"Oh, honey, you were so little," she said easily. "And it really wasn't clear at all. You didn't see anything. I remember."

And that was it; it was so easy for her. My own *memories* did not even belong to me.

But I knew she was wrong. I had seen that comet. I knew it as well as I knew my own face, my own hands. My own heart.

The next morning we locked up the house, fed the cat and left money for the petsitter, then piled into the car for one last visit with Grandma Halley. Evergreen was quiet then, with the visitors already having hit the road, getting the jump on each other. My father said his good-bye quickly and went out to the parking lot to stand by the car, eyes on the freeway ramp, his head ducked against the wind. Inside, behind the sealed-for-your-own-safety windows, we couldn't even hear it blowing.

I sat for a long time next to Grandma Halley's bed, her hand in mine, with my mother on the other side. She was coherent, but barely; she was tired, the drugs made her woozy, and she kept closing her eyes. Her cheek was dry when I kissed it, and as I pulled back she put her hand against my face, her fingers smooth and cool, smiling at me but saying nothing. I remem-

bered the girl in the pictures, with the roses and the long dancing dresses, and I smiled back.

I waited in the hallway while my mother said good-bye. I
stood against the wall, under the clock, and listened to it tick-
ing. Inside, my mother's voice was low and even, and I couldn't
make out any words. Next door, the man with the tubes was
alone again, the equipment by his bed beeping in the dark. The
TV over his bed was showing only static.

Finally, after about twenty minutes, I walked back to the
half-open door. My mother had her back to me, one hand on
Grandma Halley's, and as I looked closely I could see Grandma
Halley had fallen asleep, her eyes closed, breath even and soft.
And my mother, who had spent the entire holiday weekend almost manic with reassurance, squeezing my shoulder and smiling, forcing conversation, was crying. She had her head down,
resting against the rail of the bed, and her shoulders shook as
she wept, with Grandma Halley sleeping on, oblivious. It scared
me, the same way I'd been scared the night I came home from
Sisterhood Camp and found Scarlett in tears on her porch,
waiting for me. There are some things in this world you rely
on, like a sure bet. And when they let you down, shifting from
where you've carefully placed them, it shakes your faith, right
where you stand.

Chapter Thirteen

Now that it was Month Five, there was no hiding anymore that Scarlett was pregnant. With her stomach protruding and her face always flushed, even the drab green Milton's Market apron couldn't keep her secret. The first week of December, she got called in to talk to Mr. Averby. I went along for moral support.

"Now, Scarlett." Mr. Averby looked over his desk and smiled at us. He was about my dad's age, with a bald spot he tried to cover with creative combing. "I couldn't help but notice that you have some, uh, news."

"News?" Scarlett said. She had this little game she played with people; she liked to make them say it.

"Yes, well, what I mean is that it's come to my attention—I mean, I've noticed—that you seem to be expecting."

"Expecting," Scarlett said, nodding. "I'm pregnant."

"Right," he said quickly. He looked like he might start sweating. "So, I just wondered, if there was anything we should discuss concerning this."

"I don't think so," Scarlett said, shifting her weight in the chair. She could never get comfortable anymore. "Do you?"

"Well, no, but I do think that it should be acknowledged, because there might be problems, with the position, that someone in your condition might have." He was having a hard time getting it out, clearly, that he was worried about what the customers might think of a pregnant sixteen-year-old checkout girl at Milton's, Your Family Supermarket. That it was a bad example. Or bad business. Or something.

"I don't think so," Scarlett said cheerfully. "The doctor says it's fine for me to be on my feet, as long as it's not full time. And my work won't be affected, Mr. Averby."

"She's a very good worker," I said, jumping in. "Employee of the Month in August."

"That's right." Scarlett grinned at me. She'd already told me she wouldn't quit for anything, not even to save Milton's embarrassment. And they couldn't fire her. It was against the law; she knew that from her Teen Mothers Support Group.

"You *are* a very good worker," Mr. Averby said, and now he was shifting around in his seat like he couldn't get comfortable either. "I just didn't know how you felt about keeping up your hours now. If you wanted to cut back or discuss other options or—"

"Nope. Not at all. I'm perfectly happy," Scarlett said, cutting him off. "But I really appreciate your consideration."

Now Mr. Averby just looked tired, beaten. Resigned. "Okay," he said. "Then I guess that's that. Thanks for coming in, Scarlett, and please let me know if you have any problems."

"Thanks," she said, and we stood up together and walked out

of the office, shutting the door behind us. We made it through Bulk Foods and Cereal before she started giggling and had to stop and rest.

"Poor guy," I said as she bent over, still cackling. "He never knew what hit him."

"Nope. He thought I'd be glad to leave." She leaned against the rows of imported coffees, catching her breath. "I'm not ashamed, Halley. I know I'm doing the right thing and they can't make me think any different."

"I know you are," I said, and I wondered again why the right thing always seemed to be met with so much resistance, when you'd think it would be the easier path. You had to fight to be virtuous, or so I was noticing.

As December came, and everything was suddenly green and red and tinseled, and holiday music pounded in my ears at work, "Jingle Bells" again and again and *again*, I still hadn't made any real decision about Macon. The only reason I was getting out of it was the pure fact that we hadn't seen each other much, except in school, which was the one place I didn't have to worry about things going too far. I was working extra holiday shifts at Milton's and busy with Scarlett, too. She needed me more than ever. I drove her to doctor's appointments, pushed the cart at Baby Superstore while she priced cribs and strollers, and went out more than once late in the evening for chocolate-raspberry ice cream when it was crucially needed. I even sat with her as she wrote draft after draft of a letter to Mrs. Sherwood at her new address in Florida, each one beginning with *You don't know me, but*. That was the easy part. The rest was harder.

Macon was busy, too. He was always ducking out of school early or not showing up at all, calling me for two-minute conversations at all hours where he always had to hang up suddenly. He couldn't come to my house or even drop me off down the street because it was too risky. My mother didn't mention him much; she assumed her rules were being followed. She was busy with her work and arranging Grandma Halley's move into another facility, anyway.

"It's just that he's different," I complained to Scarlett as we sat on her bed reading magazines one afternoon. I was reading *Elle;* she, *Working Mother*. Cameron was downstairs making Kool-Aid, Scarlett's newest craving. He put so much sugar in it, it gave you a headache, but it was just the way she liked it. "It's not like it was."

"Halley," she said. "You read *Cosmo*. You know that no relationship stays in that giddy stage forever. This is normal."

"You think?"

"Yes," she said, flipping another page. "Completely."

There were still a few times that month, as Christmas bore down on us, when I had to stop him as his hand moved further toward what I hadn't decided to sign over just yet. Twice at his house, on Friday nights as we lay in his bed, so close it seemed inevitable. Once in the car, parked by the lake, when it was cold and he pulled away from me suddenly, shaking his head in the dark. It wasn't just him, either. It was getting harder for me, too.

"Do you love him?" Scarlett asked me one day after I told her of this last incident. We were at Milton's, sitting on the loading dock for our break, surrounded by packs upon packs of tomato juice.

"Yes," I said. I'd never said it, but I did.

"Does he love you?"

"Yes," I said, fudging a bit.

It didn't work. She took another bite of her bagel and said, "Has he told you that?"

"No. Not exactly."

She sat back, not saying any more. Her point, I assumed, was made.

"But that's such a cliché," I said. "I mean, *Do you love me*. Like that means anything. Like if he did say it, then I should sleep with him, and if he didn't, I shouldn't."

"I didn't say that," she said simply. "All I'm saying is I would hope he did before you went ahead with this."

"It's just three words," I said casually, finishing off my Coke. "I mean, lots of people sleep together without saying, 'I love you.'"

Scarlett sat back, pulling her legs as best she could against her stomach. "Not people like us, Halley. Not people like us."

*   *   *

My mother, who is serious and businesslike about most things, is an absolute fanatic about the holidays. Christmas begins at our house the second the last bite of Thanksgiving dinner is eaten, and our Christmas tree, decorated and sagging with way too many ornaments, does not come down until New Year's Day. It drives my father, who always loudly proclaims himself a Christmas atheist, completely bananas. If it was up to him, the tree would be dismantled and out at the curb ten seconds after the last gift was opened—a done deal. Actually, if given his choice, we wouldn't have a tree, period. We'd just hand each other our gifts in the bags they came in (his chosen wrapping paper), eat a big meal, and watch football on TV. But he knew when he married my mother, who insisted on a New Year's Eve wedding, that he wouldn't get that. Not even a chance.

I figured Grandma Halley's being sick would make the holidays a little less important this year, or at least distract my mother. I was wrong. If anything, it was more important that this be the Perfect Christmas, the Best We've Ever Had. She took a day, maybe, after we got home from Thanksgiving before the boxes of ornaments came out, the stockings went up, and the planning was in full swing. It was dizzying.

"We have to get a tree," she announced around the fourth night of December. We were at the dinner table. "Tonight, I was thinking. It would be something nice to do together."

My father did it for the first time that year, a combination of a sigh and something muttered under his breath. His sole holiday tradition: The Christmas Grumble.

"The lot's open until nine," she said cheerfully, reaching over me for my plate.

"I have a lot of homework," I said, my standard excuse, and my father kicked me under the table. If he was going, I was going.

The lot was packed, so it took my mother about a half hour, in the freezing cold, to find the Perfect Tree. I stood by the car, more frustrated by the minute, as I watched her walk the aisles of spruces with my father yanking out this one, then that one, for her inspection. Overhead, what sounded like the same Christmas tape we had at Milton's played loudly; I knew every word, every beat, every pause, mouthing along without even realizing it.

"Hi, Halley." I turned around and saw Elizabeth Gunderson, standing there holding hands with a little girl wearing a tutu and a heavy winter coat. They had identical faces and hair color. I hadn't seen her much lately; after the scandal with her boyfriend and best friend, she'd been away for a couple of weeks "getting her appendix out"; the rumor was she'd been in some kind of hospital, but that was never verified either.

"Hey, Elizabeth," I said, smiling politely. I was not going to make a mute fool of myself again.

"Lizabeth, I want to go look at the mistletoe," the little girl said, yanking her toward the display by the register. "Come *on.*"

"One second, Amy," Elizabeth said coolly, yanking back. The little girl pouted, stomping one ballet slipper. "So, Halley, what's up?"

"Not much. Doing the family thing."

"Yeah, me, too." She looked down at Amy, who had let go of her hand and was now twirling, lopsidedly, between us. "So, how are things with Macon?"

"Good," I said, just as coolly as I could, my eyes on Amy's pink tutu.

"I've been seeing him out a lot at Rhetta's," she said. "You know Rhetta, right?"

The correct answer to this, of course, was "Sure."

"I've never seen you over there with him, but I figured I was just missing you." She tossed her hair back, a classic Elizabeth Gunderson gesture; I could still see her in her cheerleading uniform, kicking high in the air, that hair swinging. "You know, since Mack and I broke up, I've been spending a lot of time over there."

"That's too bad," I said. "I mean, about you and Mack."

"Yeah." Her breath came out in a big white puff. "Macon's been so great, he really understands about that kind of stuff. You're so lucky to have him."

I watched her, forgetting for the moment about being cool and friendly, about maintaining my facade. I tried to read her eyes, to see beyond the words to what might really be happening at Rhetta's, a place I'd never been. Or been invited to. Elizabeth Gunderson obviously hadn't been grounded, her life controlled by her mother's hand. Elizabeth Gunderson could *go* places.

"Elizabeth!" We both looked over to see a man standing by a BMW, a tree lashed to the roof. The engine was running. "Let's go, honey. Amy, you, too."

"Well," Elizabeth said as Amy ran over to the car, "I guess I'll see you tomorrow in class, right?"

"Right."

She waved, like we were friends, and her dad shut the door behind her. As they pulled away, their headlights flooded my face, making me squint, and I couldn't tell whether she was watching me.

"We found one!" I heard my mother say behind me. "It's just about perfect and it's a good thing because your father was almost completely out of patience."

"Good," I said.

"Was that one of your friends from school?" she said as Elizabeth's car pulled out.

"No," I said under my breath. The Christmas Mumble.

"Do I know her?"

"No," I said more loudly. She thought she knew everyone. "I *hate* her, anyway."

My mother took a step back and looked at me. As a therapist, this was almost permission for her to pick my brain.

"You hate her," she repeated. "Why?"

"No reason." I was sorry I'd said anything.

"Well, here's the damn tree," my father said in his booming radio voice; a few people looked over. He walked up and thrust it between us so I got a face full of needles. "Best of the lot, or so your mother is convinced."

"Let's go home," my mother said, still watching me through the tree. You'd think she'd never heard me say I hated anyone before. "It's getting late."

"Fine," my father said. "I think we can stuff this in the back, if we're lucky."

They went around to the back of the car and I sat in the front seat, slamming the door harder than I should have. I did hate Elizabeth Gunderson, and I hated the fact God gave me virginity just so I'd have to lose it someday and I even hated Christmas, just because I could. In September I'd told Scarlett that Macon belonged with someone like Elizabeth, and maybe I'd been right. I wasn't ready to think about the other yet: that it wasn't that I wasn't right for Macon, but that maybe he wasn't right for me. There *was* a difference. Even for someone who things didn't come so easy for, someone like me.

The next afternoon, when I was supposedly at work and Macon and I were over at his house, his hand crept back again to our familiar battleground. I grabbed it, sat up, and said, "Who's Rhetta?"

He looked at me. "Who?"

"Rhetta."

"Why?"

"I just want to know."

He sighed loudly, dramatically, then flopped back across the bed. "She's just this friend of mine," he said. "She lives over on Coverdale."

"You go over there a lot?" I knew I sounded petty and jealous, but there was no other way to handle this. I was prepared, soon, to hand over something valuable to him. I needed to be sure.

"Sometimes." He traced my belly button with one finger, absently. To him, this was obviously no big deal. "How'd you know about her?"

"Elizabeth Gunderson," I said. I was watching his face closely for a sign, any suspicious ripple at the sound of her name.

"Yeah, she's over there sometimes," he said casually. "She and Rhetta are friends, or something."

"Really."

"Yeah." I was watching him, and he just stared back, suddenly catching on, and said, "What, Halley? What's your problem?"

"Nothing," I said. "I just thought it was weird you never mentioned it. Elizabeth said she'd seen you there a lot."

"Elizabeth doesn't know anything."

"She acts like she does," I said.

"So? Is that my fault?" He was getting angry. "God, Halley, it's *nothing*, okay? Why is this important now?"

"It isn't," I said. "Except half the time I don't know where you are or what you're doing and then I hear from Elizabeth you're off somewhere you never told me about hanging out with her."

"I'm not hanging out with her. I'm at the same place she is, sometimes. I'm not used to being accountable to anyone. I can't tell you what I'm doing every second, because half the time I don't even know *myself.*" He shook his head. "It's just the way I am."

Back in the beginning, when P.E. was my life and nothing had happened between us yet, it wasn't like this. Even two months ago, when I'd spent my afternoons just driving around with him, listening to the radio under a bright blue fall sky, there hadn't been these issues, these awkward silences. We didn't talk or laugh as much anymore, or even just play around. Everything had narrowed to just going to his house, parking out by the lake and battling for territory while arguing about trust and expectations. It was like dealing with my mother.

"Look," he said, and he slid his arm around my waist, pulling me close against him. "You've just got to trust me, okay?"

"I know," I said, and it was easy to believe him as we lay there in the early winter darkness, him kissing my forehead, my bare feet entwined with his. It all felt good, real good, and this is what people *did;* all people, except me. I felt closer than ever to telling him I loved him, but I bit it back. He had to say it first, and I willed him to just as I'd willed him to come over to me in P.E. when it all began.

Feuilleton, feuilleton, I thought hard in my head as he kissed

209

me. *Feuilleton, feuilleton.* Kissing him felt so good and I closed my eyes, feeling his skin warm against mine, breathing him in.

Feuilleton, feuilleton, as his hand crept down to my waistband. *I love you, I love you.*

But I didn't hear it, just like I always hadn't. I pushed his hand back, trying to keep kissing him, but he pulled away, shaking his head.

"What?" I said, but I knew.

"Is it me?" he asked. "I mean, is it just you don't want to do it with me?"

"No," I said. "Of course not. It's just—it's a big deal to me."

"You said you were thinking about it."

"I am." *Every damn second*, I thought. "I am, Macon."

He sat back, his hands still around my waist. "What happened with Scarlett," he said confidently, "that's, like, an impossibility. We'll be careful."

"It's not about that."

He was watching me. "Then what is it about?"

"It's about me," I told him, and by the way he shifted, looking out the window, I could tell that wasn't the right answer. "It's just the way I am."

We had come to the same place we always did, a place I knew well. Just standing across the battle line, eye to eye, no further than where we'd started. A draw.

Christmas was coming, and everyone seemed suddenly giddy. All the mothers came into Milton's in sweatshirts with wreaths and reindeer on them and even my boss, congested Mr. Averby, wore a Santa hat on the day before Christmas. My parents went to party after party, and I lay in bed and listened to them as they came home, half drunk and silly, their voices muffled and giggly downstairs. Grandma Halley's move to the rest home was all set, and my mother was going up there in early January to help. I thought of my grandmother in that tiny room, small in her bed, and pushed the thought away.

We had our tree, all the presents beneath it, and the Christmas cards lined up on the mantel. We had lights strung up across the porch and Christmas knickknacks on every free bit of table or wall space. My father kept breaking things. First, with a too-bold arm movement, he sent the chubby smiling porcelain Santa off the end table and into the wall, and later one of the three Wise Men from the crèche under the tree rolled across the floor and was flattened, easily, as he walked through the room. *Crunch.* This happened every year, which explained why all of our Christmas sets were short something—a baby Jesus, one reindeer, the tallest singing caroller. The Christmas Victims.

Scarlett and I did our shopping together at the mall, in the evenings; she bought an ABBA CD for Cameron, his favorite, and I got Macon a pair of Ray-Ban sunglasses, since he was always losing his. The mall was crowded and hot and even the little mechanical elves in the Santa Village seemed tired.

I felt like I saw Macon less and less. He was always running off with his friends, his phone calls shorter and shorter. When he did pick me up or we went out it wasn't just us anymore; we were usually giving someone a ride here or there, or one of his friends tagged along. He was constantly distracted, and I stopped finding candy in my pockets and backpack. One day in the bathroom I overheard some girl saying Macon had stolen her boyfriend's car stereo, but when I asked him he just laughed and shook his head, telling me not to believe everything I heard in the bathroom. When he called me now, from noisy places I wondered about, I got the feeling it was only because he felt he had to, not because he missed me. I was losing him, I could feel it. I had to act soon.

Meanwhile, my mother was so happy, sure that things were good between us again. I'd catch her smiling at me from across the room, pleased with herself, as if to say, *See, wasn't I right? Isn't this better?*

On Christmas Eve, after my parents had left for another party, Macon came over to give me my present. He'd called from the gas station down the street and said he only had a minute. I met him outside.

"Here," he said, handing me a box wrapped in red paper. "Open it now."

It was a ring, silver and thick, that looked like nothing I would have picked out for myself. But when I slid it on, it looked just right. "Wow," I said, holding up my right hand. "It's beautiful."

"Yeah. I knew it would be." He already had the sunglasses; I wasn't good at keeping secrets. He'd convinced me to give him his present the day I got it, begging and pleading like a little kid. They were only half his present, but he didn't know that yet.

"Merry Christmas," I said, leaning over and kissing him. "And thanks."

"No problem," he said. "It looks good on you." He lifted up my hand and inspected my finger.

"So," I asked, "what are you doing tonight?"

"Nothing much." He let my hand drop. "Just going out with the fellas."

"Don't you have to do stuff with your mom?"

He shrugged. "Not tonight."

"Are you going over to Rhetta's?"

A sigh. He rolled his eyes. "I don't know, Halley. Why?"

I kicked at a bottle on the ground by my feet. "Just wondered."

"Don't start this again, okay?" He glanced down the road. One mention of this and he was already twitchy, ready to go.

But I couldn't stop. "Why don't you ever take me there?" I said. "Or any of the places you go? I mean, what do you guys do?"

"It's nothing," he said easily. "You wouldn't like it. You'd be bored."

"I would not." I looked at him. "Are you ashamed of me or something?"

"No," he said. "Of course not. Look, Halley. Some of the places I hang out I wouldn't *want* you to go. It's not your kind of place, you know?"

I was pretty sure this was an insult. "What does that mean?"

"Nothing." He waved me off, frustrated. "Forget it."

"What, you think I'm too naive or something? To hang out with your friends?"

"That's not what I said." He sighed. "Let's not do this. Please?"

I had a choice here: to let it go, and wonder if that what was what he meant, or keep at him and be sure. But it was Christmas, and the lights on the tree in our front window were twinkling and bright. I had a ring on my finger, and that had to mean something.

"I'm sorry," I said. "I really like my ring."

"Good." He kissed me, smoothing back my hair. "I gotta go, okay? I'll call you."

"Okay."

He kissed me again, then went around to the driver's side of the car, his head ducked against the wind. "Macon."

"What?" He was half in the car, half out.

"What are you doing for New Year's?"

"I don't know yet. Why?"

"Because I want to spend it with you," I said. Even as I said it I hoped he understood what I was saying, how big this was. What I was giving him. "Okay?"

He stood there, watching my face, and then nodded. "Okay. It's a plan."

"Merry Christmas," I said again as he got in the car.

"Merry Christmas," he called out, then turned on the engine, gunning it, and backed out of the driveway. At the bottom he flashed his lights and beeped, then screeched away noisily, bringing on Mr. Harper's front light.

So that was that. I'd made my choice and now I had to stick to it. I told myself it was the right thing, what I wanted to do, yet something still felt uneven and off-balance. But it was too late to go back now.

Then I heard Scarlett's voice.

"Halley! Come here!"

I whirled around. She was standing in her open front door, hand on her stomach, waving frantically. Behind her I could see Cameron, a blotch of black against the yellow light of the living room.

"Now! Hurry!" She was yelling as I ran across the street, my mind racing: something was wrong with the baby. The baby. The baby.

I got to her front stoop, panting, already in crisis mode, and found her smiling at me, her face excited. "What?" I said. "What is it?"

"This." And she took my hand and put it on her stomach, toward the middle and down, and I felt her skin, warm under my hand. I looked up at her, wondering, and then I felt it. A ripple under my hand, resistance—a kick.

"Did you feel that?" she said, putting her hand over mine. She was grinning. "Did you?"

"Yeah," I said, holding my hand there as it—the baby— kicked again, and again. "That's amazing."

"I know, I know." She laughed. "The doctor said it should happen soon, but when it did, it just freaked me out. I was just sitting on the couch and *boom*. I can't even explain it."

"You should have seen her face," Cameron said in his low, quiet voice. "She almost started crying."

"I did not," Scarlett said, elbowing him. "It was just—I mean, you hear about what it's like to feel it for the first time, and you think people are just dramatic—but it was really *something*, you know. Really something."

"I know," I said, and we sat down together on the stoop. I looked at Scarlett, her face flushed, fingers spread across the skin of her belly, and I wanted to tell her what I'd decided. But it wasn't the time, so just I put my hand over hers, feeling the kicks, and held on.

Chapter Fourteen

My mother spent the whole day of New Year's Eve madly cleaning the house for her annual New Year's Anniversary Party. She was so distracted it wasn't until late afternoon, as I lifted my legs so she could get to a patch of floor by the TV, that she concerned herself with me.

"So what are your plans tonight?" she asked, spraying a fog of Pledge on the coffee table and then attacking it with a dust-cloth. "You and Scarlett going to watch the ball drop in Times Square?"

"I don't know," I said. "We haven't decided."

"Well, I've been thinking," she said, working her way over to the mantel, and then around the Christmas tree, which regardless of my father's loudest grumbling was still standing, dropping what seemed like mountains of needles anytime anyone passed it. "Why not just stay here and help me out? I sure could use it."

"Yeah, right," I said. I honestly thought she was joking. I mean, it was New Year's Eve, for God's sake. I watched her as she sanitized the bookcase.

"The Vaughns will be here, and you can keep an eye on Clara

for us, and you and Scarlett always like helping out at the party—"

"Wait a second," I said, but she kept moving, dusting knick-knacks like her life depended on it. "I have plans tonight."

"Well, you don't sound like you do," she said in a clipped voice, lifting up the Grand Canyon picture and dabbing at it with the cloth, then setting it back on the mantel. "It sounds like you and Scarlett don't even know what you're doing. So I just thought it would be better—"

"No," I said, and then suddenly realized I sounded more forceful than I should, more desperate, as I felt the net start to close around me. "I can't."

I half expected her to spin around, rag in hand, point at me and say, *You're going to sleep with him tonight!* proving she had somehow managed to read my mind, and once again making my choice for me before I had a chance to think for myself.

"I just think you and Scarlett can watch TV and hang out over here as easily as you can over there, Halley. And I would feel better knowing where you were."

"It's New Year's Eve," I said. "I'm sixteen. You can't make me stay home."

"Oh, Halley," she said, sighing. "Stop being so dramatic."

"Why are you doing this?" I said. "You can't just come in here at five o'clock and forbid me to go out. It's not fair."

She turned to look at me, the dust rag loose in her hand. "Okay," she said finally, really watching me for the smallest flicker of wavering strength on my part. "You can go to Scarlett's. But know that I am trusting you, Halley. Don't make me regret it."

And suddenly, it was so hard to keep looking at her. After all these months of negotiating and bartering, putting up strongholds and retreating, she'd used her last weapon: trust.

"Okay," I said, and I fought that sudden pull from all those days at the Grand Canyon and before. When she was my friend, my best friend. "You can trust me."

"Okay," she said quietly, still watching me, and I let her break her gaze first.

As I got dressed to go out that night I stood in front of the mirror, carefully studying my face. I blocked out the things around my reflection, the ribbons from gymnastics, honor-roll certificates, pictures of me and Scarlett, markers of the important moments in my life. I rubbed my thumb over the smooth silver of the ring Macon had given me. This time, I had only myself and what I would remember, so I concentrated, taking a picture I could keep always.

I stopped at Scarlett's house on the way to Spruce Street, where Macon was picking me up. This was one of the first New Year's Eve we hadn't spent together; I'd made my decision, but for some reason I still felt guilty about it.

"Take these," Scarlett said to me when I came in, stuffing something into my hand. Marion came around the corner, smoking, her hair in curlers, just as I dropped a condom right on the floor by her foot. She didn't see it and kept going, stepping over the half-assembled stroller—none of us could understand the directions—and I snatched it up, my heart racing.

"Um, I don't think I'll need this many," I said. She'd given me at least ten, in blue wrappers. They looked like the mints hotels give you on your pillow. I could see Cameron sitting at the kitchen table. He was cutting up a roll of refrigerated cookie dough into little triangles and squares. Scarlett had been scarfing cookies like crazy lately; usually she didn't even wait until the dough was cooked, just eating it by the handful out of the wrapper.

"Just take them," Scarlett said. "Better to be safe than sorry." One of my mother's favorite sayings.

She was looking at me as we stood there in the kitchen, as if there was something she wanted to say but couldn't. I pulled out a chair, sat down, and said, "Okay, spit it out. What's the problem?"

"No problem," she said, spinning the lazy Susan. Cameron was watching us nervously; he'd recently branched into wearing at least one thing that wasn't black—Scarlett's idea—and had on a blue shirt that made him look very sudden and bright. "I'm just—I'm just worried about you."

"Why?"

"I don't know. Because I know what you're doing, and I know you think it's right, but—"

"Please don't do this," I said to her quickly. "Not now."

"I'm not doing anything," she said. "I just want you to be careful." Cameron got up from the table and scuttled off toward the stove, his hands full of dough. He was blushing.

"You said you'd support me," I said. "You said I'd know when it was right." First my mother, now this, thrown across my path to keep me from moving ahead.

She looked at me. "Does he love you, Halley?"

"Scarlett, come on."

"Does he?" she said.

"Of course he does." I looked at my ring. The more times I said it, the more I was starting to believe it.

"He's said it. He's told you."

"He doesn't have to," I said. "I just know." There was a crash as Cameron dropped a cookie sheet, picked it up, and banged it against the stovetop, mumbling to himself.

"Halley," she said, shaking her head. "Don't be a fool. Don't give up something important to hold onto someone who can't even say they love you."

"This is what I want to do," I said loudly. "I can't believe you're doing this now, after we've been talking about this for weeks. I thought you were my friend."

She looked at me, hard, her hands clenched. "I am your *best* friend, Halley," she said in a steady voice. "And that is why I am doing this."

I couldn't believe her. All this talk about trusting myself, and

221

knowing when it was time, and now she fell out from beneath me. "I don't need this now," I said, getting up and shoving my chair in. "I have to go."

"It's just not right," she said, standing up with me. "And you know it."

"Not right?" I said, and I already knew something hateful was coming, before the words even left my lips. "But with you it was right, Scarlett, huh? Look at how *right* you were."

She took a step back, like I'd slapped her, and I knew I'd gone too far. From the stove I could see Cameron looking at me, with the same expression I saved for Maryann Lister and Ginny Tabor and anyone who hurt Scarlett.

We just stood there, silent, facing off across the kitchen, when the doorbell suddenly rang. Neither of us moved.

"Hello?" I heard a voice say, and over Scarlett's shoulder I saw Steve, or who I thought was Steve, coming into the room. The transformation, clearly, was complete. He was wearing his cord necklace, his boots, his tunic shirt, thick burlaplike pants, what appeared to be a kind of cape, and he was carrying a sword on his hip. He stood there, beside the spice rack, a living anachronism.

"Is she ready?" he said. He didn't seem to notice us outright staring at him.

"I don't know," Scarlett said softly, taking a few steps back toward the stairs. She wouldn't look at me. "I'll go see, okay?"

"Great."

So Vlad and I stood there together, both of us fully evolved, in Scarlett's kitchen at the brink of the New Year. I heard Scarlett's voice upstairs, then Marion's. On the table in front of me I could see the pregnancy Bible, lying open to Month Six. She'd highlighted a few passages in pink, the pen lying beside.

"I have to go," I said suddenly. Vlad, who was adjusting his sword, looked up at me. "Cameron, tell Scarlett I said goodbye, okay?"

"Yeah," Cameron said slowly. "Sure."

"Have a good night," Vlad called out to me as I got to the back door. "Happy New Year!"

I got halfway across the backyard before I turned around and looked back at the house, the windows all lit up above me. I wanted to see Scarlett in one of them, her hand pressed against the glass, our old secret code. She wasn't there, and I thought about going back. But it was cold and getting late, so I just kept walking to Spruce Street, Macon's car idling quietly by the mailbox, and what lay ahead.

The party was at some guy named Ronnie's, outside of town. We had to go down a bunch of winding dirt roads, past a few trailers and old crumbling barns, finally pulling up at a one-story, plain brick house with a blue light out front. There were a few dogs running around, barking, and people scattered across the stoop and the yard. I didn't recognize anyone.

The first thing I thought when I stepped inside, past a keg set up at the front door, was what my mother would think. I was sure the same things would jump out at her: the fake oak paneling, the coffee table crammed with full ashtrays and beer bottles, the yellow and brown shag carpet that felt wet as I walked over it. This house wasn't like Ginny Tabor's, where you knew in its real life it was a home, with parents and dinner and Christmas.

A bunch of people were lined up on the couch, drinking, and beside them the TV was on with just static, a soundless blur. I couldn't hear, the music was so loud, and I kept having to step over people sitting on the floor and backed against the walls, as I followed Macon to the kitchen.

He seemed to know everybody, people reaching out to slap his shoulder as he passed, his name floating over my head in different voices. At the keg he filled up a cup for me, then himself, while I tried to make myself as small as possible to fit in the tiny space behind him.

Macon handed me my beer and I sucked most of it down right away out of nervousness. He grinned and filled it again, then motioned me to follow him down a hallway, past a trash can overflowing with beer cans, to a bedroom.

"Knock-knock," he said as we walked in. A guy was sitting on the bed, and there was a girl with him, leaning over the side. The room was small and dark, with just a candle lit on the headboard, one with cabinets and shelves, like in my parents' room.

"Hey, hey," said the guy on the bed, who had short hair and a tattoo on his arm. "What's up, man?"

"Not much." Macon sat down at the foot of the bed. "This is Halley. Halley, this is Ronnie."

"Hi," I said.

"Hello." Ronnie had very sleepy eyes and his hair was short and spiky, black, his voice low and gravelly. He slid his hand across the bed to the leg of the girl beside him, who gave up on whatever she was looking for on the floor and started to lift her head out of the shadows.

"I lost my damn earring," she said, as her hair slid across her face, and I could make out her mouth. "It rolled under the bed and I can't reach it." As she sat upright, her features all falling into place, she looked at me, and I looked right back. It was Elizabeth Gunderson.

"Hey," she said to Macon, doing that hair swing, so out of place here. "Hi, Halley."

"Hi." I was still staring at her. She was wearing a T-shirt that was too big on her and shorts, obviously not what she'd come to the party in. Elizabeth Gunderson worked fast.

Ronnie reached down beside the bed, on the floor, and picked up a purple bong, which he handed to Macon. I sucked down the rest of my beer, just to have something to do, as he took the hit and handed it back.

"You want one?" Ronnie asked me, and I could feel Elizabeth watching me as she lit a cigarette. I wondered what her father, with his Ralph Lauren looks and BMW, would think if he could see her. I wondered what my father would think of me. As she watched me, in the dark, I could have sworn she was smiling.

225

"Sure," I said, pushing the thought of my father away as quickly as it came. I handed Macon my empty cup and took the bong, pressing it to my mouth the way I'd seen it done at other parties. He lit it and I breathed in, the smoke curling up toward my mouth, thicker and thicker, until there was a sudden rush of air and my lungs were full, hot. I held it until it hurt and then blew it out, the smoke thick against my teeth.

"Thanks," I said to Ronnie, handing it back as Macon slid his hand across my back. He'd been wrong. I could fit in here. I could fit in anywhere.

After a while Ronnie and Macon went outside to do something and left me and Elizabeth alone in the dark together. He handed me his beer as he left, which I downed half of because I was suddenly so thirsty, my tongue sticking to my lips. I'd never been stoned before, so I didn't know what to think about what I was feeling. I wasn't about to ask Elizabeth Gunderson, who had taken three bong hits before I lost count and was now stretched out across the bed, smoking, examining her toes. I was still perched at the foot, looking at the shag carpet which was suddenly fascinating, and wondering why I'd never tried this before.

"So," she said suddenly, rolling over onto her stomach. "When's Scarlett due, anyway?"

"May," I said, and my voice sounded strange to me. "The second week, or something."

"I can't believe she's having Michael's baby," she said. "I mean, I didn't even know they'd hooked up."

I licked my lips again, taking a tiny sip of beer, then looked around Ronnie's room, at the towels hung over the window for a curtain, at the *Penthouse* magazine by my foot, at the litter box that was by the door. I didn't see any cat.

Then I remembered I was talking to Elizabeth, so I thought back to what we'd been saying, which was hard, and then said, "They didn't hook up. They went out all summer."

"Did they?" Elizabeth said. Her voice didn't sound strange at all. "I had no idea."

"Oh, yeah," I said, taking another precious sip of my beer, which was warm and flat. "They were really in love."

"I didn't know," she said slowly. "They must have been awfully secretive about it. I saw Michael a lot last summer, and he never mentioned her."

I didn't know what to say to that. I had the feeling we were getting into sticky territory, so I changed the subject. Scarlett didn't belong in this room, in this place, any more than my mother did. "So is Ronnie your boyfriend?"

She laughed, like she knew something I didn't. "Boyfriend? No. He's just—Ronnie."

"Oh."

"It's funny that she's keeping the baby," Elizabeth said, pulling Scarlett right back between us. "I mean, it's going to ruin her life."

I was looking at that litter box, wondering about the cat again. "No, it won't. It's what she wants to do."

"Well," she said, and there was that hair flip as she sat up, pulling another cigarette out of the pack on the headboard. "If it was me, I'd just kill myself before I'd have a baby. I mean, I'd know enough to realize there was no way I could handle it."

I decided, at that moment, that I truly hated Elizabeth Gunderson. It was all clear to me now; she was evil. She lived her life to swoop down and catch me off guard, dropping bombs and walking off, leaving them to explode in my face.

"You're not Scarlett," I said.

"I know it." She got off the bed, tucking her cigarettes in her pocket. "Thank God for that, right?" She walked to the door, brushing past me, and pushed it open. "You coming?"

"No," I said, looking back at her, "I think I'll just—" But she was already gone, the door left half-open with light spilling in, and I was alone.

I sat there on the bed by myself for a long time, the music drifting in from the hallway along with voices and noise, girls giggling, the bathroom door slamming. I lost all track of time and I was sure hours had passed, that I'd missed the New Year altogether, when Macon finally slipped back through the door, locking it behind him.

"Hey," he said. I could only see his teeth in the dark, just a mouth coming toward me. "You okay?"

I leaned forward, determined to make out his face. As he got closer I was relieved to see he looked the same. My Macon. My boyfriend. Mine. "What time is it?"

"I don't know." He looked at his watch, glowing green in the dark. "Eleven-thirty. Why?"

"I just wondered," I said. "Where have you been?"

"Mingling." He handed me the beer in his hand, which tasted good and cold going down. I'd lost track of how many I'd had. I felt liquid and warm, and I curled up against him on the bed, kissing his neck as he wrapped his arms around me. As I closed my eyes the world began to spin in the dark, but he held me tight, his hand already moving up my leg, to my waistband. This was it.

I kept kissing him, trying to lose myself in it, but the room was hot and small and the bed smelled bad, like sweat. As we went further and further, I kept thinking that this wasn't how I'd imagined it would be. Not here, in a smelly bed, when my head was spinning and I could hear each flush of the toilet in the room next door. Not here, in a room with a dirty litter box and *Penthouse* magazine on the floor, where Elizabeth Gunderson had preceded me. Not here.

I started to get nervous, jumpy, and as Macon kept on, unsnapping my jeans, the noise from the bathroom only got louder, and outside some girl was coughing, and I felt something pressing against my bare back, something hard. When I reached around I felt it cool against my palm, and held it up over Macon's head to the dim light. It was an earring, a gold teardrop; the one Elizabeth had lost. Scarlett had the same pair.

"Wait," I said suddenly to Macon, pushing him up and away from me. We were very close, almost there, and I could hear him groan even as I squirmed out from beneath him.

"What?" he said. "What's wrong?"

"I feel sick," I told him, and it wasn't really true until I said it, and then I thought of all those beers and that bong hit and being here in this sweaty stinky bed and the reeking litter box. "I think I need some air."

"Come on," he said, sliding his hand up my back but it felt cold and creepy, suddenly, "lay back down. Come here."

"No," I said, jerking away from him and standing up, but I was off-balance and everything slanted off to one side. I leaned against the door, fumbling with the lock. "I think—I think I need to go home."

"Home?" He said it like it was a dirty word. "Halley, it's early. You can't go home."

I couldn't get the door open, the lock slipping past my fingers as I tried to find it, and suddenly I could feel everything on its way up, slowly. "I have to go," I said. "I think I'm going to be sick."

"Wait," he said. "Just calm down, okay? Come here."

"No," I said, and I was crying suddenly, scared in this strange place and I hated him for doing this to me, hated myself, hated my mother and Scarlett for being right, all along. And then I heard it: voices, counting down. *Ten, nine, eight,* and I was sick and lost and the lock wouldn't budge even as I felt everything coming up, the first taste in my mouth, and then finally the door was somehow open and I was running, *seven, six, five,* down the hallway, busting past the people crammed and chanting the numbers in the kitchen and living room and out into the cold, down the steps and the driveway *four, three, two* and into the woods and then, as the *one* came and everyone cheered, I was finally, violently, sick, alone on my knees in the woods, as the New Year began.

Chapter Fifteen

He didn't speak to me for the first part of the ride home. He was mad, as if I'd elaborately planned getting sick. When he found me in the woods I was half asleep, wishing I was dead, with leaves stuck to my face. He put me in the car and peeled out down the driveway, going way too fast and fishtailing as we headed out onto the main road.

I was huddled against my window, my eyes closed, hoping I wouldn't get sick again. I felt terrible.

"I'm sorry," I said after about five miles, as the lights of town started to come into view. Every time I thought of that litter box, and those sheets, my stomach rolled. "I really am."

"Forget it," he said, and the engine growled as he changed gears, careening around a corner.

"I wanted to," I told him. "I swear, I was going to. I just drank too much."

He didn't say anything, just turned with a screech onto the highway that led to my house, gunning the engine.

"Macon, please don't be like this," I said. "Please."

"You said you wanted to. You made this big deal about spending New Year's with me and what that meant, and then you just change your mind." We were coming up on the main intersection to my neighborhood now, the stoplight shining green ahead.

"It's not like that," I said.

"Yes, it is. You never really wanted to, Halley. You can't just play around like that."

"I wasn't playing around," I said. "I wanted to. It just wasn't right."

"It felt fine to me." The light was turning yellow but he kept pushing it, and we were going faster and faster, the mall shooting by in a blaze of lights.

"Macon, slow down," I said, as we came up to the intersection, faster and faster. The light turned red but I knew already we weren't stopping.

"You just don't get it," he said, punching the gas as we got closer, under the light now, and I turned to look at him, wondering what was coming next. "You're just so—"

I was wondering what he was going to say, what word could sum me up right then, when I saw the lights come across his face, blaringly yellow, and suddenly he was brighter, and brighter, and I asked him what was happening, what was wrong. I remember only that light, so strong as it spilled across my shoulders and lit up his face, and how scared he looked as something big and loud hit my door, sending glass shattering all across me, little sparks catching the light like diamonds as they fell, with me, into the dark.

Chapter Sixteen

This is what I remember: the cold. The wind was blowing in my face and it was shivery cold, like ice. I remember red lights, and someone's voice moaning. Crying. And lastly, I remember Macon holding my hand, tightly between his, and saying it finally, in the wrong place at the wrong time, but saying it. *I love you. Oh, God, Halley, I'm sorry. I love you, I'm right here, just hold on. I'm right here.*

When the ambulance came, I kept telling them to just take me home, that I'd be okay, just take me home. I knew how close I was, all the landmarks. I'd traveled that intersection a thousand times in my life; it was the first big road I'd crossed alone.

I tried to keep track of Macon, his hand or his face, but in the ambulance, on the way to the hospital, I lost him.

"He had to stay at the accident scene," a woman with red hair kept telling me in a steady voice, each time I asked. "Lie back and relax, honey. What's your name?"

"Halley," I said. I had no idea what had happened to me; my leg hurt, and one of my eyes was swollen shut. I couldn't move my fingers on my left hand, but it didn't hurt. That was strange.

"That's a pretty name," she said as someone shot something into my arm, a slight prick that made me flinch. "Real pretty."

At the hospital they put me in a bed with a sheet pulled around it and suddenly people were hovering all over me, hands reaching and grabbing. Someone came and leaned into my ear, asking me my phone number and I gave her Scarlett's. Even then, I knew how much trouble I would be in with my parents.

After a while a doctor came and told me I had a sprained wrist, lacerations on my back, stitches to bind the cut by my right eye, and two bruised ribs. The pain in my leg was just bruising, she said, and because I'd also banged my head they wanted to keep me overnight. She said again and again how I was very, very lucky. I kept asking about Macon, where he was, but she wouldn't answer, telling me to get some sleep, to rest. She'd come back later to check on me. Oh, and by the way—my sister was waiting outside.

"My sister?" I said, as they parted the curtains and Scarlett came in, looking like she'd just rolled out of bed. She had her hair pulled back in a ponytail and was wearing the long flannel shirt I knew she slept in. Her stomach was bigger than it had been just hours ago, if that was possible.

"Jesus, Halley," she said, stopping short a few feet from the bed and looking at me. She was scared but trying not to show it. "What *happened* to you?"

"It was an accident," I said.

"Where's Macon?" Scarlett said.

"I don't know." I felt like I was going to cry, suddenly, and now everything was beginning to hurt all at once. "Isn't he outside?"

"No," she said, and now her mouth was moving into a thin, hard line, her words clipped. "I didn't see him."

"He had to stay at the accident," I told her. "He said he'd be right here. He was really worried."

"Well, good," she snapped. "He almost killed you."

I closed my eyes, hearing only the beeping of some machine in the next room. It sounded just like the bell halfway up Grandma Halley's stairs, chiming.

"I didn't do it," I said to her after a long silence. "In case you were wondering."

"I wasn't," she said. "But I'm glad."

"When my parents find out about this, I'm dead meat," I said, and I was so sleepy it was hard to even get the words out. "They'll never let me see him again."

"He's not even here, Halley," she said softly.

"He's at the accident," I said again.

"That was over an hour and a half ago. The cop was in the waiting room, too. I talked to him. Macon left."

"No," I said, fighting off the sleep even as it crept over me. "He's on the way."

"Oh, Halley," she said, and she sounded so sad. "I'm so, so, sorry." But she was getting fuzzier and fuzzier and the beeping quieter, as I drifted away.

*   *   *

When I woke up next, the first thing I saw was a quarterback going out for a pass on the TV over my head. The ball was flying, curving through the air, as he just reached up, grabbed it, and began to dodge through the bodies and helmets, running, while the crowd screamed behind him. When he hit the end zone he spiked the ball, high-fived one of his teammates, and the camera zoomed into his smiling face, his fist pumping overhead. Touchdown.

"Hi there," I heard my mother say, and I turned to see her sitting beside me, her chair pulled close. "How are you feeling?"

"Okay," I said. My father was on the other bed in my room, still in the tacky Mexican shirt he always wore for the New Year's party. "When did you get here?"

"Just a little while ago." I looked at the clock on the wall as she reached over and brushed my hair out of my face, smoothing her fingers over the bandage on my eye. It was three-thirty. A.M.? P.M.? I wasn't sure. "Halley, honey, you really, really scared us."

"I'm sorry," I said, and it was work just to talk, I was so tired. "I ruined your party."

"I don't care about the party," she said. She looked tired too, sad, the same face she'd had that whole week we were with Grandma Halley. "Where were you? What happened?"

"Julie," my father said from the next bed, his voice thick. "Let her sleep. It's not important now."

"The policeman said you were with Macon Faulkner," she went on, and she sounded uneven, as if she was running over broken ground. "Is that true? Did he do this to you?"

"No," I said, and it was coming back to me now, the cold and the bright light and all the stars, falling. I was so drained, I closed my eyes. "It was just—"

"I knew it, I knew it," she said, and she was still holding my good hand, squeezing it now, hard. "God, you just can't listen to me, you just can't understand that I might be right, I might know what's best, you always have to prove it to yourself, and look what happens, look at this. . . ." Her voice was getting softer and softer, or maybe I was just slipping off. It was hard to say.

"Julie," my father said again, and I could hear him coming around the bed, his steps moving closer. "Julie, she's sleeping. She can't even hear you, honey."

"You promised me you wouldn't see him," she whispered, close to my ear now, her voice rough. "You *promised* me."

"Let it go," my father said. Then, again, so soft I could hardly hear it, "Let it go."

I was half asleep, wild thoughts tangled in with the sounds around me, pulling me away. But right before I fell off entirely, or maybe I was already dreaming, I heard a voice close to my ear, maybe hers, maybe Macon's, maybe just one I made up in my head. *I'll be right here*, it said as I drifted off into sleep. *Right here.*

Chapter Seventeen

January was flat, gray, and endless. I spent New Year's Day in the hospital and then went home with everything aching and took to my bed for the next week, staring out the window at Scarlett's house and the planes overhead. My mother took complete control of my life, and I let her.

We didn't talk about Macon. It was understood that something had happened to me that night before the accident, something big, but she didn't ask and I didn't offer. Instead she rebandaged my eye and wrist, and gave me my pills, bringing me my meals on a tray. In the quiet of my house with her always so close by, Macon seemed like a dream, something barely visible, hardly real. It hurt too much to even picture him.

But he was trying to get in touch with me. My first night home I heard him idling at the stop sign, our old signal, and I lay staring at my ceiling and listened. He left after about ten minutes, turning the corner so that his headlights traced a path across my walls, lighting up a slash of my mirror, a patch of wallpaper, the smiling face of my Madame Alexander doll.

Then he beeped the horn, one last chance, and I turned again to the night sky and closed my eyes.

I didn't know what to think. That night was a mad blur, beginning with my fight with Scarlett and ending being cold cold cold on the side of the road. I was hurt and angry and I felt like a fool, for my wild notions, for turning even on Scarlett, the only one who really mattered, when she tried to tell me the truth.

Sometimes when I lay in bed that week I still felt for the ring he'd given me, forgetting they'd cut it off at the emergency room. It was on my desk, in a plastic baggie, next to the saucerful of candy I'd never touched. He wasn't what I'd thought he was; maybe he never had been. I wasn't what I'd thought *I* was, either.

Of course, some of us had already formed our opinions.

"He's such a *jerk*," Scarlett said after the first week, as we sat at my kitchen table playing Go Fish and eating grapes. We never discussed our argument on New Year's Eve; it made both of us uncomfortable. "And today he kept asking about you at school. He would *not* leave me alone. Like he couldn't come over and visit you himself."

"He came by again last night," I said. "He sits out there like he's waiting for me to sneak out."

"If he gave a crap, he'd be at your door on his knees, begging for forgiveness." She made a face, shifting in her seat. Now she really was huge; she couldn't even sit against the table, her walk reduced to what could only be politely called a waddle.

"I'm so hormonal right now I could kill him with my bare hands."

I didn't say anything. You can't just turn your heart off like a faucet; you have to go to the source and dry it out, drop by drop.

It was around midnight a few nights later when I heard something *ping* off my bedroom window. I lay in bed, listening to pebble after pebble bounce off until I finally went and opened it up, sticking my head out. I could barely see Macon in the shadows of the side yard, but I knew he was there.

"Halley," I heard him whisper. "Come out. I have to talk to you."

I didn't say anything, watching my parents' window for the sudden light that meant they'd heard too, and I almost hoped they had.

"Please," he said. "Just for a second. Okay?"

I shut the window without answering, then walked down the back stairs and even let the screen door slam a little bit behind me. I didn't care about being careful anymore.

He was in the side yard, by the juniper bushes, and as I came around the corner he walked toward me, stepping out of the shadows. "Hey."

"Hi," I said.

A pause. He said, "How are you feeling? How's your wrist?"

"Better."

He waited, like he expected me to say more. I didn't.

"Look," he began, "I know you're mad that I didn't show up

241

at the hospital, but I had a good reason. Your parents would've been upset enough without having to see me. Plus I had to walk to a phone and get a ride because my car was totaled, and . . ."

As he talked I just watched his face, wondering what it was that I'd ever thought was so magical about him. I had been fascinated by the things he'd shown me, but they were all just sleight of hand, quarters pulled from children's ears. Anyone can do that trick, if they know how. It's nothing special.

He was still talking. ". . . and I've been coming by all week 'cause I wanted to explain, but you wouldn't come out and I couldn't call you, and . . ."

"Macon," I said, holding up my hand. "Just stop, okay?"

He looked surprised. "I didn't mean to hurt you," he said, and I wondered which hurt he meant, exactly. "I just freaked out. But I'm sorry, Halley, and I'll make it up to you. I need you. I've been miserable ever since this happened."

"Yeah?" I said, not believing a word.

"Yeah," he said softly, and reached out to put his arms around my waist, brushing my bruised ribs and hurting me again. "I've been going crazy."

I stepped back, out of his reach, and crossed my arms against my chest. "I can't see you anymore," I said to him.

He blinked, absorbing this. "Your parents will get over that," he said easily, and I knew he'd said this many times before. Everything, each line I'd held close to my heart, had been said

SOMEONE LIKE YOU

a million times to a million other girls under their windows and in their side yards, on back streets and in backseats, in dark rooms at parties, with the door locked tight.

"This isn't about my parents," I said. "This is about me."

"Halley, don't do this." He ducked his head, that old hangdog P.E. look. "We can work this out."

"I don't think so," I said. The truth was I knew, after all those flat January days, that I deserved better. I deserved *I love you*s and kiwi fruits and flowers and warriors coming to my door, besotted with love. I deserved pictures of my face in a million expressions, and the warmth of a baby's kick under my hand. I deserved to grow, and to change, to become all the girls I could ever be over the course of my life, each one better than the last.

"Halley, wait," he called out after me as I backed away. "Don't go."

But I was already gone, working a little magic of my own, vanishing.

I didn't see her right away as I came inside the back door, easing it shut behind me. Not until I turned around, in the dark, and the room was suddenly bright all around me. My mother, in her bathrobe, was standing with her hand on the light switch.

"So," she said, as I stood there blinking. "Things are right back to the way they were, I see."

"What?"

243

"Wasn't that our friend Macon?" She said it angrily. "Does he ever come around in broad daylight? Or does he only work under cover of darkness?"

"Mom, you don't understand." I was going to tell her then that he was gone, maybe even that she was right.

"I understand that even that boy almost *killing* you is not enough for you to learn a lesson. I cannot believe you would just go right back out there to him, like nothing had changed, after what happened to you. After what he *did*."

"I had to talk to him," I said. "I had to—"

"We have not discussed this because you were hurt, but this is *not* going to happen. Do you understand? If you don't have the sense to stay away from that boy, I will keep you away from him."

"Mom." I couldn't believe she was doing it again. She was taking this moment, this time when I was strongest, away from me.

"I don't care what I have to do," she said, her voice low and even. "I don't care if I have to send you away or switch schools. I don't care if I have to follow you myself twenty-four hours a day, you will *not* see him, Halley. You will not destroy yourself this way."

"Why are you just assuming I'm going back to him?" I asked her, just as she was drawing in breath to make another point. "Why don't you ask me what I said to him out there?"

She shut her mouth, caught off guard. "What?"

"Why don't you ever wait a second and see what I'm planning, or thinking, before you burst in with your opinions and ideas? You never even give me a *chance.*"

"Yes, I do," she said indignantly.

"No," I said. "You don't. And then you wonder why I never tell you anything or share anything with you. I can never trust you with anything, give you any piece of me without you grabbing it to keep for yourself."

"That's not true," she said slowly, but it was just now hitting her, I could see it. "Halley, you don't always know what's at stake, and I do."

"*I will never learn,*" I said to her slowly, "*until you let me.*"

And so we stood there in the kitchen, my mother and I, facing off over everything that had built up since June, when I was willing to hand myself over free and clear. Now, I needed her to return it all to me, with the faith that I could make my own way.

"Okay," she said finally. She ran a hand through her hair. "All right."

"Thank you," I said as she cut the light off, and we started upstairs together, her footsteps echoing mine. It was still all settling in, this deal we'd made. It was like learning another way of something instinctive, like walking or talking. Changing something you already thought you'd mastered and figured out on your own.

As we got to the top of the stairs, to split off into our different directions, she stopped.

"So," she said softly. "What did you tell him?"

Outside, across the street, I could see Scarlett's kitchen light, yellow in the dark. "I told him he wasn't what I'd thought he was," I said. "That he let me down, and I couldn't see him anymore. And I said good-bye."

I knew there was probably a lot she wanted to ask or say, but she only nodded. We would have to learn this slowly, making the rules up as we went. It was undiscovered country, as wide as the Grand Canyon, as distant as Halley's Comet.

"Good for you," she said simply, and then she went inside her room, shutting the door quietly between us.

You can't just plan a moment when things get back on track, just as you can't plan the moment you lose your way in the first place. But standing there alone on the landing, I thought of Grandma Halley and how she'd held me close against her lap as we watched the sky together. I'd always thought I couldn't remember, but suddenly in that moment, I closed my eyes and saw the comet, finally, brilliant and impossible, stretching above me across the sky.

Part III

GRACE

Chapter Eighteen

"Oh, honey, you look so wonderful! Brian, come in here with the camera, you've got to see this. Stand here, Halley. No—here, so we get the window behind you. Or maybe—"

"Mom," I said, reaching behind me again for the itchy tag that had been scratching my neck since I'd put the damn dress on, "please. Not now, okay?"

"Oh, but we've *got* to take pictures," she said, waving me over by the potted plant in the corner of the kitchen, "some of you alone, and some when Noah comes."

Noah. Every time I heard his name, I couldn't believe I'd gotten myself into this. Not just the prom, not just a too-poofy dress with a tag that would drive me insane, but the prom with the dress with the tag with Noah Vaughn. I was in hell.

"Oh my goodness," my mother said, looking over my shoulder, one hand moving up to cover her mouth. She looked like she might cry. "Look at *you!*"

I turned around to see Scarlett, much as I'd left her upstairs minutes ago, except maybe larger, if that was possible. She was at nine months almost exactly, her belly protruding up and outward so it was always the very first thing you noticed when she came into a room. Her dress had been made especially by Cameron's mother, a seamstress, who was so happy Cameron was actually going to the prom that she spent hours, *days*, making the perfect maternity prom dress. It was black and white, with a semi-drop neck that showed off Scarlett's impressive bosom, an empire waist, and it fell gently over her knees. She really did look good, if huge. But it was the smile on her face, wide and proud, that made it perfect.

"Ta-da!" she said, sweeping her arms over herself and back down again, as if she was a prize on a game show. "Crazy, huh?"

She just stood there, grinning at me, and I had to smile back. Since we'd decided we would go to the prom and fulfill our *Seventeen* daydreams, nothing had been normal. But then, nothing had been normal, or even close to normal, for a while.

Since January, something had changed. It was all subtle, hard to see with the naked eye, but it was there. The way my mother held her tongue when I knew she was dying to offer an opinion, to dominate a conversation—to be my mother. She'd take a breath, already gathering words, and then stop, let it out, and look hard at me as something passed between us, imperceptible to the rest of the world. She'd backed off just enough, focusing on other things: selling Grandma Halley's house and visiting her often, as well as the new book she'd started writing about her experiences being a daughter again. Maybe I'd be in this one. Maybe not.

As for Macon, I hadn't talked to him much since that night in my side yard. He seemed to be coming to school even less, and when he did I was skilled at avoiding him. But I still felt a pang whenever I saw him, the way I still felt a soreness in my wrist every morning, or a pain in my ribs when I lay a certain way at night. In March, when I heard his mother had kicked him out, I worried. And in mid-April, when I heard he was dating Elizabeth Gunderson, I cried for two days straight.

I made myself concentrate on something more important: the baby. I saw it, small and hardly recognizable, when we had the ultrasound during Month Six. It had hands and feet and eyes and a nose. The doctor knew the sex, but Scarlett didn't want to know; she wanted it to be a surprise.

We had a baby shower at my house, inviting Cameron and his mother, the girls from the Teen Mothers Support Group, and even Ginny Tabor, who bought the baby a huge stuffed yellow duck that quacked when you squeezed it. But something was wrong with it, and it quacked whenever you picked it up, and then wouldn't shut up until you took its head off, an option we never had with Ginny herself. Cameron's mother sewed a beautiful layette set, and my parents gave Scarlett ten babysitting coupons, for whenever she needed a break. For my gift, I had blown up a recent picture of me and Scarlett, sitting on her front steps together. Scarlett's belly was huge, and she had her hands folded over it, her head on my shoulder. I had it framed and Scarlett immediately hung it over the baby's crib, where she or he would see it every day.

"The three of us," she said, and I nodded.

And then we just waited, circling in a holding pattern, while the due date got closer and closer.

We planned. We bought a baby name book and made lists of good ones: something simple, not bringing to mind someone else, like Scarlett's, or needing a paragraph of explanation, like mine. We both knew how far a name could take you.

We went to Lamaze classes, me sitting in a long row of fathers, her head in my lap. We were the youngest ones there. We breathed and we pushed, and I tried to tell myself that I could handle this when it happened, that I could do it. Scarlett was scared and tired, with all that huffing and puffing, and I always nodded at her, confident.

And Marion had come around. She acted like she was firm on adoption until about Month Seven, early March, when I walked in on her in the nursery. The sun was slanting through the window, warm and bright, bouncing off the yellow walls, and the constellations Cameron had painted on the ceiling. Everything was ready: the clothes all folded in the drawers, the crib and changing table in place, the stroller finally assembled (with the help of a neighbor, who was an engineer and the only one who could figure out the instructions). She was just standing there, arms crossed, surveying it all with a smile on her face. And I knew it then. There'd never been a question of where this baby was going or who it belonged with. Of course, when she saw me she turned around and scowled, muttering something about paint fumes, and hurried out. But that was Marion. I knew what I had seen.

And lastly, I walked with Scarlett to the mailbox as she carried the letter we'd worked and re-worked, all these months. *Dear Mrs. Sherwood*, it began, *You don't know me, but I have something to say.* She dropped it in, the mailbox door clanked, and there was no going back. If we heard from her, we heard from her. If not, this baby had enough love to carry on.

And now, on May twelfth, we were going to the prom. I was doing this for Scarlett; it was important to her. When Cameron asked her, I had to go, too. Which is how I ended up with Noah Vaughn.

Actually, it was my mother's fault. She brought up the prom one Friday night when the Vaughns were over, Mrs. Vaughn lit up like the sun, and it went from there. *Of course I keep telling Halley she should go*, my mother said, *I mean, it's the prom. Well, Noah, I can't believe you haven't mentioned this*, said Mrs. Vaughn. *Well, Halley's best friend is going, you know Scarlett, but Halley hasn't been asked*, said my mother, and now I was realizing what was happening, how awful this could be, as Noah watched me from across the table and my father giggled at his plate. *But Noah doesn't have a date either*, said Mrs. Vaughn, *so I don't see why you two couldn't . . .* And then my mother, who had learned something, looked across the table, realizing too late, and said quickly, *Actually I think Halley might have plans that weekend*, but of course now it *was* too late, way too late, and Mrs. Vaughn was already clapping her hands together excitedly, and smiling big, and my mother kept trying to get me to look at her but I wouldn't. All I could see was Noah

253

across the table, eating a slice of pizza, with cheese all over his chin.

Of course Scarlett was ecstatic. She dragged me out to buy a dress and shoes, and insisted we get ready together. And I went along, trying not to complain, because I knew somehow that this was the end of something for her, before the baby came and everything changed.

"Smile!" my mother said, stepping back across the kitchen with her camera's red light blinking. My father was leaning against the kitchen door, making faces at me. "Oh, you two look just great. So glamorous!"

Scarlett put her arm over my shoulder, pulling me closer, tighter in for the shot. I saw the red in her hair, her easy smile, the small sprinkling of freckles across her nose.

"Okay!" my mother said, now against the far wall, crouching down. "Now say prom night!"

"Prom night!" Scarlett said, still smiling.

"Prom night," I said, more softly, my eyes on her, and not the camera, as the flash popped bright all around me.

I could tell that Noah was drunk the minute he crossed the living room holding the corsage.

"Hi," he said as he got close, reaching out with the pin toward my bodice, his breath hot and sweet. "Hold still."

"I'll get it," I said, taking it from him before he stabbed me while Mrs. Vaughn, who obviously hadn't gotten close to him lately, and my mother, who looked like she might bust with happiness, watched from across the room. Beside us Cameron was carefully attaching Scarlett's corsage, a group of pink roses and baby's breath, to her ample bustline. Cameron looked very small and very dapper in his tuxedo and cranberry-colored cummerbund and socks. Very European, my mother had said when he arrived, with Noah in his rented tux and too-short pants with gym socks peeking out beneath. I stuck my corsage on, barely missing poking myself in my haste, and settled in for another round of pictures.

"Wonderful!" Mrs. Vaughn said, circling us with the video camera while Noah snaked his arm around my waist. The liquor had obviously emboldened him. "Halley, smile!"

"One more," my mother said, going through at least another roll of film, flash after flash. "What a great night you'll have! Terrific!"

Marion was there, with one of those disposable cameras, taking picture after picture of Scarlett in her dress. She was going to a medieval tournament with Vlad that night, and was already dressed for the part in a long velvet dress with puffy sleeves that made her look like Guinevere, or maybe Sleeping Beauty. She'd gotten into Vlad's weekend hobby, bit by bit, and she seemed to like it, tagging along to tournaments and drinking mead while he jousted. Scarlett was embarrassed, but Marion just said being someone else was kind of nice, every once in a while.

"Scarlett," she called out, waving one hand over her head. "Over here, honey. Perfect. Perfect!"

After we'd been satisfactorily documented, we finally got out the door and to the limousine, on loan from the hotel where Cameron's father worked. Cameron, for all his quirkiness, really knew how to make an evening. I couldn't exactly say the same for *my* date.

"Where's the bar?" Noah slurred as soon as we shut the door and drove off. "There's supposed to be a bar in these things, right?"

Scarlett was just eyeing him, settling her dress around her, and I said, "He's wasted. Ignore him."

"I am not," Noah said indignantly. Already he'd talked more to me, total, than he had in the entire year and a half we'd been broken up. "But there *is* supposed to be a bar."

"I'm sure they just took it out," Cameron said quietly. "Sorry."

"Don't be sorry," Scarlett said to him, squeezing his arm. "We don't care."

"I don't need it anyway," Noah said loudly, pulling a plastic juice container from his inside pocket. "Got it all taken care of, right here."

I just looked at him. "Noah," I said. "Please."

"Wow," Scarlett said as he opened the container and guzzled down a bit, dribbling on his shirtfront. "That sure is classy."

"Works for me," Noah said snippily. He stuck it back in his pocket, wiping his mouth, and put his arm over my shoulder, which I shrugged off as best I could.

By the time we got to the prom, Noah was completely

loaded. The limo dropped us off in the bus parking lot, by the cafeteria, and I just started to walk inside, leaving him to stumble along behind me. He'd downed the last swallow of his stash, dropped the container on the sidewalk, and reached out to grab me; instead, he got my dress, tearing it at the waist. I felt cool air on my back and legs and stopped walking.

"Ooops," he said as I turned around. He had something white and shiny, formerly part of my dress, in his hands and he was giggling. "Sorry."

"You jerk," I snapped, grabbing behind me to bunch the fabric together, covering myself. Now I was at the prom with Noah Vaughn *and* half-naked. There was no end to my shame.

"Halley, what's going on?" Scarlett called from the front entrance to the cafeteria. I could see Melissa Ringley, prom chairwoman, sitting at a table watching me. "Hurry up."

"Go in without me," I said. "I'll be right there."

"Are you sure?"

"Yes."

She shrugged, handing Melissa their tickets, and she and Cameron disappeared inside. I could hear music playing, loud, and people kept walking past, on their way in. I backed into the shadow of the science lab to do something about my dress.

"Here," Noah said, stumbling in behind me, "let me help."

"You cannot help me," I told him. "Okay?"

"You don't have to be a bitch," he snapped, still reaching around to the back of my dress, his hand brushing my skin. "You know, you've changed so much since we went out."

"Whatever, Noah," I said. I needed a safety pin, badly. I could not go inside and moon my entire class, not even for Scarlett.

"You used to be nice, and all that," he went on, "but then you started thinking you were all cool, hanging out with Macon Faulkner and all. Like you were too good for everybody all of a sudden."

"Noah," I said. "Shut up."

"You shut up," he said back, loudly. Two girls in white dresses and heels looked over at us, trying to make us out in the dark.

I ignored him, reaching around the back of my dress again, when suddenly he was right up against me, his breath in my face when I turned around. I didn't remember him ever being so tall. He slid his arm around my waist, reaching back to the gaping fabric, and stuck his hand down my dress, brushing over my underwear. I just stared at him, dumbstruck, and watched his face get closer and closer, eyes closed, tongue starting to stick out—

"Get *off* me," I said loudly, pushing him away. He stumbled, tripped over a tree stump and landed on the sidewalk just as another group of people started to pass by. I leaned against the wall, not caring anymore about my dress, or this night, and tried to hide myself.

"Whoa," a guy in the group said as he stepped over Noah, who was still prone, blinking. "You okay, buddy?"

"She's just—she's such a . . ." Noah sputtered as he got to his feet, unsteadily, and started to weave back around the side of the building, muttering to himself. The guy and his date just watched him go, then laughed a little nervously and headed across the courtyard to Melissa Ringley and the cafeteria. And I was alone.

I thought about going home. I had money and could easily call a cab, or my father, and just give up entirely. But Scarlett would worry, I knew, so I bunched together the back of my dress, holding it that way, and went to tell her myself.

I found her on the dance floor, with Cameron. They couldn't dance that close but they did what they could, her stomach between them. All around her were these perfect girls, hair swept up and wearing lipstick and high heels, with their dates in dark tuxedos and dress shoes. I saw Ginny Tabor and Brett Hershey, wearing Prom King and Queen crowns, making out by the punch table. And Regina Little, one of the fattest girls in school, in a huge white dress with a hoop, dancing with a guy in a military uniform who looked at least thirty. And lastly, in the corner, I saw Elizabeth Gunderson and Macon, not dancing or smiling or even talking, just standing there staring at the crowd, same as me.

Macon saw me, and right then I felt it for the first time in so long, that rush and craziness, that feeling I'd had at Topper Dam. He looked good and he grinned at me, and I thought that in this desperate moment, alone at the prom, he could take me away.

It was too much, all of a sudden, everything rushing at me. The prom and Michael and my mother and the baby. Macon and Ronnie's house and that night in the car, with the glass shattering around my head. Elizabeth Gunderson and her sly smile, the cold of the woods as I'd gotten sick on New Year's Eve, Grandma Halley's hand, thin and warm, in mine. And finally, Noah coming closer and closer to me, his tongue sticking out, and now Scarlett on the dance floor, right before my eyes, swaying to the music and smiling, smiling, smiling.

I pushed through the crowd, still holding my dress, thinking only of getting out, getting away, something. I pushed past girls in their princess outfits, past clouds of cologne and perfume, past Mrs. Oakley, the vice principal, who was eyeballing everyone on the lookout for drugs and drunks. I didn't stop until I reached the bathroom door and ran inside, letting it slam behind me.

The first person I saw was Melissa Ringley, standing in front of the mirrors with a lipstick in her hand. She looked at the mirror in front of her, and me beyond it, and turned around, her mouth still in a perfect O.

"Halley, my goodness, what is wrong?" She put the lipstick down and walked toward me, lifting her dress off the ground so it wouldn't brush the floor. It was black, with a full skirt and a modest neckline. She had a small gold cross hanging from a chain around her neck. "Are you okay?"

I did look crazed, wild even. My hair, so carefully crafted into a perfect French twist by Scarlett, had somehow come untucked and was sticking up like a lopsided Mohawk. My face was red and my mascara smeared and that didn't even include my dress, which was bagging open in the back now that I had let go of it. Two other girls, checking their makeup, brushed past me, glanced at my exposed underwear and clucked their tongues as they pushed the door open, leaving me and Melissa alone.

"I'm fine," I said quickly, moving to the sink and wetting a paper towel, trying to do something about my face. I pulled my hair down, bobby pins spilling everywhere. "Just a rotten night, that's all."

"Well, I heard Noah was drunk," she said, whispering the last word and taking a furtive look around. "You poor thing. And what happened to your dress? Oh my God, Halley, turn around. Look at that!"

"I *know*," I said, my teeth clenched. I couldn't believe I was mooning Melissa Ringley. "I just want to get out of here."

"Well, you can't go out there like that," she said, moving around behind me. "Here, hand me some of those bobby pins, I'll see what I can do."

So I stood there, with Melissa behind me muttering to herself and stabbing bobby pins into my dress, all the while wondering how the night could get any worse. And then, it did.

Elizabeth Gunderson was wearing a tight black dress and spike heels that I could hear clacking outside before she even opened the door and came into the bathroom itself. When she saw me she narrowed her eyes and looked me up and down before moving to another sink and leaning into the mirror.

"Well, this should at least get you through the rest of the night," Melissa said cheerfully, coming out from behind me and

261

tossing the extra bobby pins into the trash. "Just don't try any radical movements or anything."

"Okay," I said, staring at my reflection. I could feel Elizabeth watching me. I told myself it was only fitting she was with Macon; they deserved each other. This didn't really make me feel better. "Thanks, Melissa. Really."

"Oh, no problem," she said in her chirpy little can-do voice, fluffing her blond bob with her fingers. "It's all part of being prom chairwoman, right?" She waggled her fingers at me as she left, the sound of music—something slow and easy—coming in as the door opened and then drifted shut behind her.

Beside me, Elizabeth was putting on eyeliner, leaning in closer to the mirror. She looked tired, worn out, now that I was looking at her more closely. Her eyes were red and her lipstick was too dark, making her mouth look like a gash against her skin.

I took one last look at myself, decided there wasn't much I could do under the circumstances, and started to leave. I had nothing left to say to Elizabeth Gunderson. But then, just as I was reaching for the door, I heard her voice.

"Halley."

I turned around. "What?"

She pulled away from the mirror, brushing her hair over her shoulders. "So." She wasn't looking at me, instead down at the purse in her hands. "Are you having a good night?"

I smiled, in spite of myself. "No," I said. "Are you?"

She took a deep breath, then ran a finger over her lips, smoothing out her lipstick. "No. I'm not."

I nodded, not sure what else to say, and reached for the door again. "Well," I said, "I guess I'll see you later."

I was halfway out, the music loud enough that I almost didn't hear her when she said, "You know, he still loves you. He says he doesn't, but he does. He does."

I stopped and turned around. "Macon?" I said.

"He won't admit it," she said quietly, but her voice was shaky, and I thought of how I'd envied her that night at Ronnie's, stretched out across the bed examining her toes. I didn't now. "He says he doesn't even think about you, but I can tell. Especially tonight. When he saw you out there. I can tell."

"It's nothing," I said to her, realizing how true it was. It was just a feeling, a whooshing in my ears. Not love.

"Do you still love him?" In the bathroom her voice echoed strangely, louder and then softer all around us.

"No," I said quietly. And I caught a glimpse of myself in the mirror, my wild hair, my ripped dress. You could even see the scar over my eye where the makeup had brushed off. But I was okay. I was. "I don't," I said.

And Elizabeth Gunderson turned from the sink, her hair swinging over her shoulder just it had before she tumbled off a million pyramids at a million high-school football games. She opened her mouth to say something more but I didn't hear it, never got a chance, because just then the door slammed open and Ginny Tabor burst in with a blast of pink satin, her voice preceding her.

"Halley!" She stopped, fluttering one hand over her chest while she caught her breath. "You've—you've got to get out here."

"Why?" I said.

"Scarlett," she gasped, still breathing hard. She held up a finger, holding me there, while she gulped for air. "Scarlett's having the baby."

"*What?*" I spun around to look at her. "Are you serious?"

"I swear, she and Cameron were getting their picture taken and Brett and I were next in line and right when the flash went off, she just got this look on her face and then boom it was happening—"

"*Move,*" I said, pushing past her out into the cafeteria, around the dance floor and the people drinking punch, past the band and to the edge of a crowd gathered around the tiny wooden drawbridge where everyone had been posing for pictures. There was a buzz in the air and a photographer with a huge camera wringing his hands and finally, with her face bright red and way too many people pressed around her, Scarlett. When she saw me, she burst into tears.

"You're fine, you're fine," I said, sliding around to her other side, by Cameron who was looking kind of ashen. Someone was shouting about an ambulance and the music had stopped and I couldn't even remember the breathing patterns we'd learned in Lamaze class.

Scarlett grabbed me by the neckline and jerked me toward her; she was surprisingly strong. "I don't want an ambulance," she said. "Just get me the hell out of here. I am not having this baby at the prom."

"Okay, okay," I said, looking to Cameron for support but he was leaning against the edge of the drawbridge, fanning himself with one hand. He looked worse than Scarlett. "Let's go, then. Come on."

I helped her to her feet, her arm around my shoulder, and started to push through the crowd. Mrs. Oakley was on one side of me, saying she'd already called someone, to stay put, and somewhere in an explosion of pink was Ginny Tabor, yelling about boiling water, but all I could think of was Scarlett's hand squeezing my shoulder so damn hard I could hardly even see straight. But somehow, we were making headway.

"Where's Cameron?" Scarlett said between gasps as we burst out the door into the courtyard. "What happened to him?"

"He's back there somewhere," I told her, dragging her along beside me, her grip still tight on my skin. "He looked a little nauseous or something."

"This is no time for that!" she screamed, right in my ear.

"We're fine, we're fine," I said, and now that we were getting closer to the parking lot it suddenly occurred to me that we had no mode of transportation, since the limo wasn't due back until midnight. By now we'd lost most of the crowd, all of them hanging back by the cafeteria door with Mrs. Oakley shouting about how we should wait for the ambulance, it would be here any second.

"I don't want an ambulance," Scarlett said again. "I swear, if they put me in one I will fight them tooth and nail."

"We don't *have* a car," I told her. "We took the limo, remember?"

"I don't care," she said, clutching at my shoulder even harder. *"Do something!"*

"I will get us a ride," I said, looking around the parking lot for any poor sucker who just happened to be driving off at that moment. "Don't worry," I told her. "I have it under control."

But this was nothing *Seventeen* magazine had ever covered. We were on our own.

Just then I heard a car screech around the corner, and I leaned out and waved my arm frantically, as much as I could while still supporting Scarlett. "Hello!" I called. "Please, God, please stop."

"Oh, no," Scarlett said quietly. "My water just broke. Oh, man, what a mess. This dress is a goner."

"Please stop!!" I screamed at the car as it came closer, already slowing down, and of course as it slid to a stop beside us, engine rumbling, I knew who it was.

"Hey there," Macon said, smiling from the driver's seat as he hit the button to unlock the door. He was in a different car this time, a Lexus, Elizabeth next to him. "Need a ride?"

"Of course we need a ride!" Scarlett screamed at him. "Are you stupid?"

"That would be nice, thank you," I said smoothly as Elizabeth reached behind her to open the back door and we piled in, Scarlett all sticky and me scattering bobby pins everywhere because these were definitely radical movements. We were pulling away when Cameron ran up and we had to stop to let him in, too; he was huffing and puffing and still looked kind of pale.

"What happened to you?" I asked as Scarlett bore down on my bad hand, squeezing so hard my fingers were folding in on each other.

"I passed out," he said quietly.

"What did he say?" Scarlett bellowed from my other side.

"He didn't say anything," I said. "He's fine. Now, let's work on our breathing. Deep breaths, in and out—"

"I don't want to breathe," she said in a low voice. "I want drugs and I want them *now*."

From the rearview, I could see Macon grinning back at us, and I had a sudden flash of the last time we'd been together in a car, speeding toward town. But I couldn't think about that now.

"Breathe," I said to Scarlett. "Come on now."

"I'm scared," she said. "Oh, God, Halley, it *hurts*."

I gripped her hand harder, tighter, ignoring my own pain. "Think about what we learned in class, okay? Peaceful thoughts. Uh, oceans and fields of flowers, and country lakes."

"Shut *up!*" she said. "God, listen to yourself."

"Okay, fine," I said, "don't think about that. Think about

good things, like that trip we took to the beach in sixth grade, remember? When you got stung by the jellyfish?"

"That was good?" Her brow was wet, sweaty, and her hand in mine was hot. I tried not to look scared, but it was hard.

"Sure it was," I said, and Macon was still watching me as we sped down Main Street but I ignored him, going on, "and remember baking cookies in your kitchen all those summers, and dancing to the radio, and last summer with Michael, and going to the lake, and . . ."

"Kiwi fruit," she said, gasping. Beside me Cameron looked like he was ready to pass out again.

"Right," I said, ready to run with anything, "kiwi fruit. And remember the day you got your license? And the first thing you did was back into my house, right there by the garage door? Remember?"

"Your dad said most people stick to just hitting other cars," she said, her voice raspy, hand still gripping mine. "He said I was special."

The lights of the hospital were coming up now, closer. I could hear an ambulance, somewhere. "I know he did," I said, brushing the damp hair off her forehead. "Just hold on, Scarlett, okay? We're almost there. Just hold on."

She squeezed my hand, hard, and closed her eyes. "Don't leave me, okay? Promise you won't."

"I won't," I said as we pulled into the parking lot, past the front entrance to Emergency. "I'll be right here. I promise."

They put Scarlett in a wheelchair, shoved a bunch of forms in my hand, and pushed her through a set of double doors with a bang, leaving me and Cameron at Admitting with a bunch of Boy Scouts who'd had a camping accident, an old man with a bleeding forehead, and a woman screaming in Spanish with a baby planted against her hip. Cameron went over and sat down, putting his head between his knees, and after I scribbled what I could on the forms, I went to the pay phone to call Marion.

Of course she wasn't home. She was off jousting, or doing medieval dances, or whatever she and Vlad did on their theme weekends. The phone rang and rang before the machine came on, and I hung up and did what came instinctively. I called my mother.

"Halley?" she said, before I even finished my hello. "Where *are* you? Mrs. Vaughn just called and said Noah had been found drunk in the school parking lot and Norman had to go down there to pick him up from the principal, she's completely hysterical and no one knew what happened to you. . . ."

"Mom."

"I trusted you not to drink, and I don't know what got into Noah, he's never been in trouble before and John was just livid, apparently . . ."

"Mom," I said again, louder this time. "The baby's coming."

"The baby?" There was a sudden silence. "What, now? Right now?"

"Yes." Beside me the Boy Scouts were banging on a candy machine, grumbling about being gypped, and Cameron was a few seats down with his eyes closed, slumped in a plastic chair. "I'm at the hospital, they just took Scarlett away and I don't have time to explain about Noah right now, okay? I can't get in touch with Marion, so when you see her come home, tell her where we are. Tell her to hurry."

"Is Scarlett okay?"

"She's scared," I said, thinking of her alone wherever they'd taken her, and how I'd promised to stay right with her, no matter what. "I have to go, okay? I'll call you later."

"Okay, honey. Let us know."

"I will." I hung up the phone and rushed back to Admitting, my dress dragging across the floor, one lone bobby pin still holding it together in the back. As I passed the front entrance I saw Macon and Elizabeth still in the car. They were talking, Macon's mouth moving, one finger pointing, angrily. Elizabeth was just staring out the window, her arm hanging down the side of the car, a cigarette held loosely in her fingers. She didn't even see me.

I went to the Admitting desk, told them I was Scarlett's sister and Lamaze partner, and got led back through the double doors, past the emergency-room cots and curtains, to where they had Scarlett on a bed, the fetal monitor already hooked up and beeping.

"Where have you *been?*" she shrieked as soon as I came

around the corner. She had a plastic cup full of ice in her hand and a green gown on, her prom dress tossed over a chair in the corner. "I am *freaking* out here, Halley, and you just vanish into thin air."

"I did not vanish," I said gently. "I was calling Marion and handling things at the front desk. I'm here now."

"Well, good," she said. "Because I really need—"And then she stopped talking and sat up straight, holding her stomach. She made a low, guttural moaning sound, rising and rising louder and louder, and I just stared at her, not even recognizing her face, and knew all at once I was in way over my head.

The door opened behind me and the doctor came in, all cheerful and easygoing, taking her time walking up to the bed while Scarlett huffed and puffed and grabbed for my hand, which she immediately squeezed so hard I felt bone meeting bone, crunching.

"So," the doctor said easily, grabbing a chart off the end of the bed, "looks like we're having a baby."

"Looks that way," Scarlett said between gasps. "Can I have some drugs, please?"

"In a minute," the doctor said, moving to the end of the bed and lifting the sheet, moving Scarlett's legs into the stirrups attached to the side of the bed. "Let's see how far along you are."

She poked and prodded, and Scarlett ground the bones in my hand to powder.

"Okay," the doctor said, patting the sheet back down, "we're getting close. It shouldn't be too long now, so I just need you to relax, and work your breathing with your partner here. Leave the rest to us."

"What about the drugs?" Scarlett said urgently. "Can I get the drugs?"

"I'll send someone in shortly," the doctor said, smiling like we were cute. "Don't worry, honey. It'll be over before you know it." She slipped the chart back into its place on the end of the bed, tucking her pen behind her ear, and walked out the door, waving as she went.

"I *hate* her," Scarlett said decisively through a mouthful of ice. "I mean it."

"Let's do our breathing," I suggested, pulling a chair up beside the bed. "Deep breath in, now, okay?"

"I don't want to breathe," she snapped at me. "I want them to knock me out, completely, even if they just hit me on the head with something. I can't do this, Halley. I can't."

"Yes, you can," I said sternly. "We're ready for this."

"Easy for you to say." She sucked down more ice. "All you have to do is tell me to breathe and stand there. You've got the easy part."

"Scarlett. Hold it together."

She rose up in the bed, spitting frozen shards everywhere. "Don't tell me to hold it together, not until you have felt this pain, because it is unlike anything—" And then she stopped talking, her face going pale again as another contraction hit.

"Breathe," I said, doing it myself, *puff puff puff,* inhale deep, *puff puff puff.* "Come on."

But she wasn't breathing, only moaning again, that low scary noise that made me back away from the bed, literally scared for my life. I was wrong. *We weren't ready for this.* This was big, and scary, and I understood suddenly how Cameron must have felt, woozy and terrified all at once. I wished I was out in the waiting room, with the Boy Scouts and the candy machine, pacing and waiting to light up a cigar.

"Stay here," I said to her, backing away from the bed, step by step, as she stopped moaning suddenly and watched me, eyes wide. "I'll be—"

"Don't leave!" she cried, trying to sit up straight, reaching for the sides of the bed. "Halley, don't—"

But I let the door swing shut behind me and I was suddenly alone, in the corridor, the cool wall pressing against my back where my dress was gaping open. I tried to shake the fear off. I could hear Scarlett on the other side of the door, moaning. Just when she needed me, I was falling apart.

Then, I heard it. The sound of footsteps coming closer, louder and louder, *clack clack clack,* all businesslike as they rounded the corner. I looked to my left and coming toward me, purse tucked under her arm and eyes straight ahead, was my mother.

"Where is she?" she said as she got closer, switching her purse to the other arm.

"In there," I said. "She's freaking out."

"Well, let's go." She reached for the doorknob but I hung back, pressing myself harder against the wall. "Halley? What's wrong?"

"I can't do this," I said, and my voice sounded strange, high. "It's too crazy, and she's in pain, and I just think—"

"Honey." She looked at me. "You need to be in there."

"I can't," I said again, and my throat hurt when I spoke. "It's too much to deal with."

"Well, that's too bad," she said simply, grabbing my shoulder and pushing me toward the door, her hand guiding me from behind. "Scarlett is counting on you. You can't let her down."

"I'm no help, she wouldn't want me there, I'm a mess," I said, but she was already opening the door, pushing it with her free hand.

"You are the *only* one she wants," my mother said, and then we were crossing the room, her arm clamped around my shoulders, back to the bed where Scarlett was sitting up, clenching the sheet in her hands, tears streaming down her face.

"Hi, honey," my mother said, crossing to the bedside and smoothing down Scarlett's hair. "You're doing great. Just great."

"Is Marion here?" Scarlett said.

"Not yet, but Brian is over at your house, waiting for her. She'll get here any time now. Don't worry. Now, what can we do for you? Anything?"

"Just don't leave me," Scarlett said quietly as my mother

settled in next to her, laying her purse on the chair with the prom dress. "I don't want to be alone."

"You won't be." My mother was eyeing the chair on Scarlett's other side, so I took my place carefully, ashamed. "We're here."

I looked across the bed, past Scarlett's tired, shiny face as my mother leaned close to her ear, whispering words I couldn't hear. But I knew what they were, what they had to be: the same ones I'd heard after all those bad dreams, all those skateboard and roller-skating accidents, all the times the little fiendettes chased me home on pink bicycles. I watched my mother do what she did best, and realized there would never be a way to cut myself from her entirely. No matter how strong or weak I was, she was a part of me, as crucial as my own heart. I would never be strong enough, in all my life, to do without her.

Chapter Nineteen

The doctor looked up at us, nodding.

"Here it comes, Scarlett, I can see the head. Just a couple more big pushes and it's out, so get ready, okay?"

"Not long now," I whispered to her, squeezing her hand harder. "Almost there."

"You're doing so great," my mother said. "Very brave. Much braver than I ever was."

"It's the drugs," I said. "Since then it's been a piece of cake."

"Shut up," Scarlett snapped. "I swear, when this is over, I am going to *kill* you."

"Give me another good push!" the doctor said from the foot of the bed. "Get ready!"

"Breathe," I said to her, taking a deep one myself. "Breathe."

"Breathe," my mother repeated, her voice echoing mine. "Come on, honey. You can do it."

Scarlett braced against me, her hand twisting mine, and I watched her face swallow up her eyes, her mouth fall open, as she pushed harder than she had all night, with every bit of strength she had left.

"Here it comes, it's coming, look at that." The doctor was smiling from the end of the bed, excited. "Oh, push once more, just a little one, Scarlett, just a tiny one . . ."

Scarlett pushed again, gasping, and I watched as the doctor reached down with her hands, groping around, and then, suddenly, she was holding something, something small and red and slimy with kicking feet and a tiny mouth that opened up to wail, a tiny, tiny voice.

"It's a girl," the doctor said, and the nurses were wiping her off, cleaning out her mouth, and then they put her in Scarlett's arms, against her chest. Scarlett was crying, looking down at her against her skin, closing her eyes. She'd been with us since that summer, growing and growing, and now she was here, real as we were.

"A girl," Scarlett said softly. "I knew it."

"She's beautiful," I told her. "She has my eyes."

"And my hair," she said, still crying, her hand brushing the top of the baby's head and the red fuzz there. "Look."

"You should be very proud," my mother said, reaching to touch one tiny little hand. "Very proud." And she looked over and smiled at me.

"I'm going to name her Grace," Scarlett said. "Grace Halley."

"Halley?" I said, amazed. "No kidding."

"No kidding." She kissed the baby's forehead. "Grace Halley Thomas."

When I looked down at Grace, I was overwhelmed. She was our year, from the summer with Michael to the winter with Macon. We would never forget.

Scarlett was just beaming, rocking Grace in her arms and kissing the tiny fingers and toes, asking everyone if they had honestly ever seen a more beautiful baby. (It was agreed that no one had.) After we all cooed over her, and Scarlett nodded off to sleep, I went out to the waiting room to deliver the news. What I saw, as I rounded the vending machines and water fountains, was enough to stop me dead in my tracks.

The room was bright and packed. On one side, grouped around the Emergency Room door, was at least half of our class, all in dresses and tuxedos, leaning against the walls and sitting on the cheap plastic sofas. There were Ginny Tabor and Brett Hershey, girls from our Commercial Design class and their dates, Melissa Ringley and even Maryann Lister, plus tons of people I didn't even know. All in their finest, eating candy bars and talking, waiting for news. I didn't see Elizabeth Gunderson, but I did see Macon, leaning against the candy machine and talking to Cameron, who had finally gotten some color back in his face.

And on the other side of the waiting room, segregated by some chairs and modern time, were Vlad, a breathless Marion, and at least twenty other warriors and maidens, all decked out in full medieval regalia. Some were carrying swords and shields. One was even wearing chain mail that clanked as he paced back in forth in front of Admitting.

Then, all at once, they saw me.

Marion ran across the room, dress swishing madly across her feet, with Vlad and a handful of warriors right behind. The nurse at Admitting just rolled her eyes as I passed, with Marion approaching from one side and Cameron and Ginny Tabor fast closing in on the other, Ginny in her shrieking pink followed by a slew of girls in pastels and boys in tuxes, all crowding in. Everyone else had stopped talking, rising from their seats and gathering closer, watching my face.

"So?" Ginny said, skidding to a stop in front of me.

"How is she?" Marion asked. "I just got here, I was late getting home—"

"Is she okay?" Cameron said. "Is she?"

"She's fine," I said, and I smiled at him. I turned to the assembled crowd, the prom-goers and Cinderellas, the maidens and ladies and warriors and knights, not to mention the odd Boy Scout and security guard, all carefully keeping their distance. "It's a girl."

Someone started clapping and cheering and then everyone was talking at once, slapping each other on the back, and the tuxedos and warriors were intermingled, shaking hands and hugging, as Marion went back to see her granddaughter and

Cameron followed her and Ginny Tabor kissed Brett Hershey just for show. The Admitting nurse told everyone to quiet down but no one listened and I just stood and watched it all, smiling, committing everything to memory so that later I could tell Scarlett, and Grace, every single detail.

Much later, I sent my mother home and sat with Scarlett, watching her sleep. This had been our Special Night, just not the one we'd expected. I was so excited about the baby and what was coming next, I wanted to wake her up and talk about everything, right then, but she looked so peaceful that I held back. And as I left, I walked past the nursery and looked in on Grace, curled up so tiny in her bassinette. I spread my fingers on the glass, our signal, just to let her know I was there.

Then I walked downstairs and out into the night to go home. I didn't want anyone to start this journey with me.

I bent down and took off my shoes, hooking the straps over my wrist, and started down the sidewalk. I wasn't thinking about Macon, or my mother waiting at home for me, or even Scarlett dozing behind one of those bright hospital windows. I was only thinking of Grace Halley with each step I took, in my prom dress (safety-pinned tight, now), barefoot, heading home.

I wondered what kind of girl she'd be, and if she'd ever see the comet that was her name, and Grandma Halley's, and mine. I knew I'd try, one day, to take her and show her the sky, hold her against my lap as I told her how the comet went overhead, how it was clear and beautiful, and special, just like her. I hoped that Grace would be a little bit of the best of all of us: Scarlett's spirit, and my mother's strength, Marion's determination, and Michael's sly humor. I wasn't sure what I could give, not just yet. But I knew when I told her about the comet, years from now, I would know. And I would lean close to her ear, saying the words no one else could hear, explaining it all. The language of solace, and comets, and the girls we all become, in the end.

Turn the page to read a chapter from
Sarah Dessen's

what happened to goodbye

One

The table was sticky, there was a cloudy smudge on my water glass, and we'd been seated for ten minutes with no sign of a waitress. Still, I knew what my dad would say. By this point, it was part of the routine.

"Well, I gotta tell you. I see potential here."

He was looking around as he said this, taking in the décor. Luna Blu was described on the menu as "Contemporary Italian and old-fashioned good!" but from what I could tell from the few minutes we'd been there, the latter claim was questionable. First, it was 12:30 on a weekday, and we were one of only two tables in the place. Second, I'd just noticed a good quarter inch of dust on the plastic plant that was beside our table. But my dad had to be an optimist. It was his job.

Now, I looked across at him as he studied the menu, his brow furrowed. He needed glasses but had stopped wearing them after losing three pairs in a row, so now he just squinted a lot. On anyone else, this might have looked strange, but on my dad, it just added to his charm.

"They have calamari *and* guac," he said, reaching up to

push his hair back from his eyes. "This is a first. Guess we have to order both."

"Yum," I said, as a waitress sporting lambskin boots and a miniskirt walked past, not even giving us a glance.

My dad followed her with his eyes, then shifted his gaze to me. I could tell he was wondering, as he always did when we made our various escapes, if I was upset with him. I wasn't. Sure, it was always jarring, up and leaving everything again. But it all came down to how you looked at it. Think earth-shattering, life-ruining change, and you're done. But cast it as a do-over, a chance to reinvent and begin again, and it's all good. We were in Lakeview. It was early January. I could be anyone from here.

There was a bang, and we both looked over to the bar, where a girl with long black hair, her arms covered with tattoos, had apparently just dropped a big cardboard box on the floor. She exhaled, clearly annoyed, and then fell to her knees, picking up paper cups as they rolled around her. Halfway through collecting them, she glanced up and saw us.

"Oh, no," she said. "You guys been waiting long?"

My dad put down his menu. "Not that long."

She gave him a look that made it clear she doubted this, then got to her feet, peering down the restaurant. "Tracey!" she called. Then she pointed at us. "You have a table. Could you please, maybe, go greet them and offer them drinks?"

I heard clomping noises, and a moment later, the wait in the boots turned the corner and came into view. She looked like she was about to deliver bad news as she pulled out her order pad. "Welcome to Luna Blu," she recited, her voice flat. "Can I get you a beverage."

"How's the calamari?" my dad asked her.

She just looked at him as if this might be a trick question. Then, finally, she said, "It's all right."

My dad smiled. "Wonderful. We'll take an order of that, and the guacamole. Oh, and a small house salad, as well."

"We only have vinaigrette today," Tracey told him.

"Perfect," my dad said. "That's exactly what we want."

She looked over her pad at him, her expression skeptical. Then she sighed and stuck her pen behind her ear and left. I was about to call after her, hoping for a Coke, when my dad's phone suddenly buzzed and jumped on the table, clanging against his fork and knife. He picked it up, squinted at the screen, put it down again, ignoring the message as he had all the others that had come since we'd left Westcott that morning. When he looked at me again, I made it a point to smile.

"I've got a good feeling about this place," I told him. "Serious potential."

He looked at me for a moment, then reached over, squeezing my shoulder. "You know what?" he said. "You are one awesome girl."

His phone buzzed again, but this time neither of us looked at it. And back in Westcott, another awesome girl sat texting or calling, wondering why on earth her boyfriend, the one who was so charming but just couldn't commit, wasn't returning her calls or messages. Maybe he was in the shower. Or forgot his phone again. Or maybe he was sitting in a restaurant in a town hundreds of miles away with his daughter, about to start their lives all over again.

A few minutes later, Tracey returned with the guacamole and salad, plunking them down between us on the table. "Calamari will be another minute," she informed us. "You guys need anything else right now?"

My dad looked across at me, and despite myself, I felt a twinge of fatigue, thinking of doing this all again. But I'd made my decision two years ago. To stay or go, to be one thing or many others. Say what you would about my dad, but life with him was never dull.

"No," he said now to Tracey, although he kept his eyes on me. Not squinting a bit, full and blue, just like my own. "We're doing just fine."

× × ×

Whenever my dad and I moved to a new town, the first thing we always did was go directly to the restaurant he'd been brought in to take over, and order a meal. We got the same appetizers each time: guacamole if it was a Mexican place, calamari for the Italian joints, and a simple green salad, regardless. My dad believed these to be the most basic of dishes, what any place worth its salt should do and do well, and as such they provided the baseline, the jumping-off point for whatever came next. Over time, they'd also become a gauge of how long I should expect us to be in the place we'd landed. Decent guac and somewhat crisp lettuce, I knew not to get too attached. Super rubbery squid, though, or greens edged with slimy black, and it was worth going out for a sport in school, or maybe even joining a club or two, as we'd be staying awhile.

After we ate, we'd pay our bill—tipping well, but not extravagantly—before we went to find our rental place. Once we'd unhitched the U-Haul, my dad would go back to the restaurant to officially introduce himself, and I'd get to work making us at home.

EAT INC, the restaurant conglomerate company my dad worked for as a consultant, always found our houses for us. In Westcott, the strip of a beach town in Florida we'd just left, they'd rented us a sweet bungalow a block from the water, all decorated in pinks and greens. There were plastic flamingos everywhere: on the lawn, in the bathroom, strung up in tiny lights across the mantel. Cheesy, but in an endearing way. Before that, in Petree, a suburb just outside Atlanta, we'd had a converted loft in a high-rise inhabited mostly by bachelors and businessmen. Everything was teak and dark, the furniture modern with sharp edges, and it was always quiet and very cold. Maybe this had been so noticeable to me because of our first place, in Montford Falls, a split-level on a cul-de-sac populated entirely by families. There were bikes on every lawn and little decorative flags flying from most porches: fat Santas for Christmas, ruby hearts for Valentine's, raindrops and rainbows in spring. The cabal of moms—all in yoga pants, pushing strollers as they power walked to meet the school bus in the mornings and afternoons—studied us unabashedly from the moment we arrived. They watched my dad come and go at his weird hours and cast me sympathetic looks as I brought in our groceries and mail. I'd known already, very well, that I was no longer part of what was considered a traditional family unit. But their stares confirmed it, just in case I'd missed the memo.

Everything was so different, that first move, that I didn't feel I had to be different as well. So the only thing I'd changed was my name, gently but firmly correcting my homeroom teacher on my first day of school. "Eliza," I told him. He glanced down at his roll sheet, then crossed out what was there and wrote this in. It was so easy. Just like that, in the hurried moments between announcements, I wrapped up and put away sixteen years of my life and was born again, all before first period even began.

I wasn't sure exactly what my dad thought of this. The first time someone called for Eliza, a few days later, he looked confused, even as I reached for the phone and he handed it over. But he never said anything. I knew he understood, in his own way. We'd both left the same town and same circumstances. He had to stay who he was, but I didn't doubt for a second that he would have changed if it had been an option.

As Eliza, I wasn't that different from who I'd been before. I'd inherited what my mother called her "corn-fed" looks—tall, strawberry blonde, and blue-eyed—so I looked like the other popular girls at school. Add in the fact that I had nothing to lose, which gave me confidence, and I fell in easily with the jocks and rah-rahs, collecting friends quickly. It helped that everyone in Montford Falls had known each other forever: being new blood, even if you looked familiar, made you exotic, different. I liked this feeling so much that, when we moved to

Petree, our next place, I took it further, calling myself Lizbet and taking up with the drama mamas and dancers. I wore cut-off tights, black turtlenecks, and bright red lipstick, my hair pulled back into the tightest bun possible as I counted calories, took up cigarettes, and made everything Into A Production. It was different, for sure, but also exhausting. Which was probably why in Westcott, our most recent stop, I'd been more than happy to be Beth, student-council secretary and all-around joiner. I wrote for the school paper, served on yearbook, and tutored underachieving middle school kids. In my spare time, I organized car washes and bake sales to raise funds for the literary magazine, the debate team, the children in Honduras the Spanish club was hoping to build a rec center for. I was that girl, the one Everyone Knew, my face all over the yearbook. Which would make it that much more noticeable when I vanished from the next one.

The strangest thing about all of this was that, before, in my old life, I hadn't been any of these things: not a student leader or an actress or an athlete. There, I was just average, normal, unremarkable. Just Mclean.

That was my real name, my given name. Also the name of the all-time winningest basketball coach of Defriese University, my parents' alma mater and my dad's favorite team of all time. To say he was a fan of Defriese basketball was an understatement, akin to saying the sun was simply a star. He lived and breathed DB—as he and his fellow obsessives called it—and had since his own days of growing up just five miles outside campus. He went to Defriese basketball camp in the summer, knew stats for every team and player by heart, and wore a Defriese jersey in just about every school picture from kindergarten to senior year. The actual playing time on the team he eventually got over the course of two years of riding the bench as an alternate were the best fourteen minutes of his life, hands down.

Except, of course, he always added hurriedly, my birth. That was great, too. So great that there was really no question that I'd be named after Mclean Rich, his onetime coach and the man he most admired and respected. My mother, knowing resistance to this choice was futile, agreed only on the condition that I get a normal middle name—Elizabeth—which provided alternate options, should I decide I wanted them. I hadn't really ever expected that to be the case. But you can never predict everything.

Three years ago my parents, college sweethearts, were happily married and raising me, their only child. We lived in Tyler, the college town of which Defriese U was the epi-center, where we had a restaurant, Mariposa Grill. My dad was the head chef, my mom handled the business end and front of house, and I grew up sitting in the cramped office, coloring on invoices, or perched on a prep table in the kitchen, watching the line guys throw things into the fryer. We held DB season tickets in the nosebleed section, where my dad and I sat screaming our lungs out as the players scrambled around, antlike, way down below. I knew Defriese team stats the way other girls stored knowledge of Disney princesses: past and present players, shooting average of starters and second stringers, how many Ws Mclean Rich needed to make all time winningest. The day he did, my dad and I hugged each other, toasting with beer (him) and ginger ale (me) like proud family.

When Mclean Rich retired, we mourned, then worried over the candidates for his replacement, studying their careers and offensive strategies. We agreed that Peter Hamilton, who was young and enthusiastic with a great record, was the best choice, and attended his welcome pep rally with the highest of hopes. Hopes that seemed entirely warranted, in fact, when Peter Hamilton himself dropped into Mariposa one night and liked the food so much he wanted to use our private party room for a team banquet. My dad was in total DB heaven, with two of his greatest passions—basketball and the restaurant—finally aligned. It was great. Then my mom fell in love with Peter Hamilton, which was not.

It would have been bad enough if she'd left my dad for anyone. But to me and my dad, DB fanatics that we were, Peter Hamilton was a god. But idols fall, and sometimes they land right on you and leave you flattened. They destroy your family, shame you in the eyes of the town you love, and ruin the sport of basketball for you forever.

Even all this time later, it still seemed impossible that she'd done it, the very act and fact still capable of unexpectedly knocking the wind out of me at random moments. In the first few shaky, strange weeks after my parents sat me down and told me they were separating, I kept combing back through the last year, trying to figure out how this could have happened. I mean, yes, the restaurant was struggling, and I knew there had been tension between them about that. And

I could vouch for the fact that my mom was always saying my dad didn't spend enough time with us, which he pointed out would be much easier once we were living in a cardboard box on the side of the road. But all families had those kinds of arguments, didn't they? It didn't mean it was okay to run off with another man. Especially the coach of your husband and daughter's favorite team.

The one person who had the answers to these questions, though, wasn't talking. At least, not as much as I wanted her to. Maybe I should have expected this, as my mom had never been the touchy-feely, super-confessional type. But the few times when I tried to broach the million-dollar question—why?—in the shaky early days of the separation and the still-not-quite-stable ones that followed, she just wouldn't tell me what I wanted to hear. Instead, her party line was one sentence: "What happens in a marriage is between the two people within it. Your father and I both love you very much. That will never change." The first few times, this was said to me with sadness. Then, it took on a hint of annoyance. When her tone became sharp, I stopped asking questions.

HAMILTON HOMEWRECKER! screamed the sports blogs. I'LL TAKE YOUR WIFE, PLEASE. Funny how the headlines could be so cute, when the truth was downright ugly. And how weird, for me, that this thing that had always been part of my life—where my very name had come from—was now, literally, part of my *life*. It was like loving a movie, knowing every frame, and then suddenly finding yourself right inside of it. But it's not a romance or a comedy anymore, just your worst freaking nightmare.

Of course everyone was talking. The neighbors, the sports-writers, the kids at my school. They were probably still talk-ing, three years and twin little Hamiltons later, but thankfully, I was not around to hear it. I'd left them there, with Mclean, when my dad and I hitched a U-Haul to our old Land Rover and headed to Montford Falls. And Petree. And Westcott. And now, here.

×   ×   ×

It was the first thing I saw when we pulled in the driveway of our new rental house. Not the crisp white paint, the cheerful green trim, or the wide welcoming porch. I didn't even notice, initially, the houses on either side, similar in size and style, one with a carefully manicured lawn, the walk lined with neat shrubs, the other with cars parked in the yard, empty red plas-tic cups scattered around them. Instead, there was just this, sitting at the very end of the drive, waiting to welcome us per-sonally.

We pulled right up to it, neither of us saying anything. Then my dad cut the engine, and we both leaned forward, looking up through the windshield as it loomed above us.

A basketball goal. Of course. Sometimes life is just hi-larious.

For a moment, we both just stared. Then my dad dropped his hand from the ignition. "Let's get unpacked," he said, and pushed his door open. I did the same, following him back to the U-Haul. But I swear it was like I could feel it watching me as I pulled out my suitcase and carried it up the steps.

The house was cute, small but really cozy, and had clearly been renovated recently. The kitchen appliances looked new, and there were no tack or nail marks on the walls. My dad headed back outside, still unloading, while I gave myself a quick tour, getting my bearings. Cable already installed, and wireless: that was good. I had my own bathroom: even better. And from the looks of it, we were an easy walking distance from downtown, which meant less transportation hassle than the last place. I was actually feeling good about things, basketball reminders aside, at least until I stepped out onto the back porch and found someone stretched out there on a stack of patio furniture cushions.

I literally shrieked, the sound high-pitched and so girly I probably would have been embarrassed if I wasn't so startled. The person on the cushions was equally surprised, though, at least judging by the way he jumped, turning around to look at me as I scrambled back through the open door behind me, grabbing for the knob so I could shut it between us. As I flipped the dead bolt, my heart still pounding, I was able to put together that it was a guy in jeans and long hair, wearing a faded flannel shirt, beat-up Adidas on his feet. He'd been reading a book, something thick, when I interrupted him.

Now, as I watched, he sat up, putting it down beside him. He brushed back his hair, messy and black and kind of curly, then picked up a jacket he'd had balled up under his head, shaking it out. It was faded corduroy, with some kind of insignia on the front, and I stood there watching as he slipped it on, calm as you please, before getting to his feet and picking up whatever he'd been reading, which I now saw was a textbook of some kind. Then he pushed his hair back with one hand

and turned, looking right at me through the glass of the door between us. *Sorry,* he mouthed. Sorry.

"Mclean," my dad yelled from the foyer, his voice echoing down the empty hall. "I've got your laptop. You want me to put it in your room?"

I just stood there, frozen, staring at the guy. His eyes were bright blue, his face winter pale but red-cheeked. I was still trying to decide if I should scream for help when he smiled at me and gave me a weird little salute, touching his fingers to his temple. Then he turned and pushed out the screen door into the yard. He ambled across the deck, under the basketball goal, and over to the fence of the house next door, which he jumped with what, to me, was a surprising amount of grace. As he walked up the side steps, the kitchen door opened. The last thing I saw was him squaring his shoulders, like he was bracing for something, before disappearing inside.

"Mclean?" my dad called again. He was coming closer now, his footsteps echoing. When he saw me, he held up my laptop case. "Know where you want this?"

I looked back at the house next door that the guy had just gone into, wondering what his story was. You didn't hang out in what you thought was an empty house when you lived right next door unless you didn't feel like being at home. And it was his home, that much was clear. You could just tell when a person belonged somewhere. That is something you can't fake, no matter how hard you try.

"Thanks," I said to my dad, turning to face him. "Just put it anywhere."

YA DESS
Dessen, Sarah.
Someone like you /

BRIDE OF ISRAEL,
MY LOVE

Books by Richard Llewellyn

BRIDE OF ISRAEL, MY LOVE
THE NIGHT IS A CHILD
WHITE HORSE TO BANBURY CROSS
BUT WE DIDN'T GET THE FOX
THE END OF THE RUG
DOWN WHERE THE MOON IS SMALL
SWEET MORN OF JUDAS' DAY
A MAN IN A MIRROR
UP, INTO THE SINGING MOUNTAIN
CHEZ PAVAN
MR. HAMISH GLEAVE
A FLAME FOR DOUBTING THOMAS
A FEW FLOWERS FOR SHINER
NONE BUT THE LONELY HEART
HOW GREEN WAS MY VALLEY

Juveniles

WARDEN OF THE SMOKE AND BELLS
THE FLAME OF HERCULES
THE WITCH OF MERTHYN

BRIDE OF ISRAEL, MY LOVE

Richard Llewellyn

Doubleday & Company, Inc., Garden City, New York
1973

This book could not have been written without the help of my editor, LeBaron Barker, whose introduction to Herman Wouk led to Zvi Bresh, Press Attaché of the Israeli Embassy in Washington, D.C., and on to Ben Horion in the Israeli Embassy in Rome and finally to Mme. Ben Yosef of the Ministry of Information in Jerusalem. I express deepest gratitude to them all as well as to Mr. and Mrs. Nathan Shacham of Beitaleph, my first Israeli hosts.

ISBN: 0-385-05551-X
Library of Congress Catalog Card Number 74–186038
Copyright © 1973 by Richard Llewellyn
All Rights Reserved
Printed in the United States of America

Mothers of Israel!
> *Your sons have fought as lions . . .*
> *General Moshe Dayan*
> *Post-Battle Valedictory*
> *June 1967.*

This book is dedicated to
> The Mothers of the Lions, yesterday, today, and
tomorrow—to
> THE WOMEN OF ISRAEL
> With respect and admiration and with love

Eilat
Israel
March First
1972.

BRIDE OF ISRAEL,
MY LOVE

ONE

The land's fertile peace lulled, the warm Negev breeze held a lull, and the sky, a blue of the first firmament, of bluest delphiniums, glowed a wondrous lull, and working a seventy-two-hour week and sometimes more, Israeli-style, made its own lull, and day by day I felt myself returning to a commons of good life, saner, kindlier than I had known, remote from the lunatic strut I left with such relief. Yet, if anyone had told me those few months ago that near midnight on the eve of my next birthday I would be reaching out on a rickety ladder, picking olives in a grove above the road from Beersheba to Gaza, I might have stared the gloomy eyes of a stray dog. In that day, gloom sat beside me, and stray was what I felt. Life seemed to have no purpose, or any hope of promise for better use of time on earth.

It was long after that night, when I realized I had begun thinking about myself, what I was doing, what I intended to do, on that ladder. Reaching out may have helped, a sprout began climbing in mind, blooming in

1

spirit, a small warm wonder of hope, a desire to do more, a sudden and intense feeling I had other things to do, though I had no idea what.

I was well aware of all I might and could do, and what I had done. I had vivid memory of the day I left my office, leaving three months' separation pay for the staff, handing the keys to the building superintendent, calling the storage people to collect the furniture, carpets, filing cabinets, the junk, and going to the airport without so much as hand luggage, and taking a flight to Paris. It sounded good. It was. Wherever I wanted to go, I went, and then I was in Lod Airport almost as if nabbed by pincers, and I wandered out and got the bus to Jerusalem, and by some glory of fortune sat next to Arye, the secretary of our Collective, out on his monthly round of paying accounts.

A light for a cigaret led to talk about the news, and the funny weather, and I told him I was in Israel only half an hour and looking for somewhere to settle, work, do anything.

Listen, he said. You want a word in the right ear? What you do, you take the bus on. Don't stay nowhere. Sleep the night. Plenty small hotels. Keep going. See the country. Look for where you want. We all know. Once we know, we don't want any place else. You don't find it? Come on down to Beersheba. Call me. That's the phone. Listen, you talk Hebrew?

No, I said. I had training when I was a boy. I have the alphabet, but what I heard here, and the signs, I don't know a thing.

Damn right, he said. We came from Vilna. Old man went to New York. I was there three-four years of age. Came here when he died. I was ten-eleven maybe. Lived in tents. We never spoke Hebrew. Never saw nobody them days. No buses. Nothing. Spoke either Yiddish, or Polish, or English. Or a mix-up. So here I am, I speak Russian, Polish, Yiddish, all pretty good. English, well, sort of so-so. Hebrew? I try. Like the rest of us down there. Can't "get" the Hebrew. Sure, we all got a few words. We have something nice, it's called the Ulpan. Sort of class where they try putting it into you. Ever had a tooth out? Tried putting one back in? That's us. Only when I went in the Army, I got some of it. But not comfortable. Down there where I am, we speak English. Like in other places they speak French. Or Russian. It's easier for the life, see? Try to get a language, boy, it kind of breaks you up inside. Can't say what you mean? Other guy can't tell you? So you all get together. Like us, down there. It's pretty good. Come see us. What's your job?

Well, I said. I'm not sure what you could put me down as. A nut, number one, I suppose. A mathematician, perhaps. Long word, doesn't mean all that much. Bit of a hand at tronics.

Hell's that, he said. Tronics? That's new.

New in space exploration, I said. It's miniature circuits for electrical power. I had enough, that's why I'm here.

Look, he said. You're an electrician, you got all the work you can handle and real good money. We can use you right now.

He was shorter than me, but stocky, thirties, black hair and sideburns, bright grey eyes that *flicked!* here and there, and a real boney hawk face, thin nose, carved cheekbones, and good hands, short fingers, squared-off nails, white-clean.

Not what I want, I said. It's not why I'm here. I'd like farm work. Anything quiet. Where I can get my mind back.

3

Anything you say, he said. I think I know what you mean. Just come down to us. I'll put you in a work squad. You start from the bottom. Only thing is, we don't have hours. We start a job, we finish it. More you do, more you get paid.

That was how I got on that ladder, without any regret in the world, perfectly happy among those trees, some a thousand years old, and all of them heavy with the black marvel, most large as a damson. We either thrashed long sticks to knock them down, or went up ladders to shake branches, careful of scorpions, spiders, dwellers in our land, and strict as us in defence of their right to live at peace.

The grove belonged to the Commune above us. We had the glean after they gathered the main crop, and we had to leave a further glean for the Arabs down in the village, and if our harvest was less than careful, even so, our baskets were many, and heavy, and we worked on, in the late night. Our team had only that one day, and those olives were part of breakfast, and a few hours more meant that in months ahead, cream cheese with that black succulence would make richer tables, happier mornings.

Yeke, our squad boss, went from tree to tree, testing the weight of the baskets, telling us when we had enough. As an old hand at the glean, he was fair judge at telling how far we could go without stripping, though in that or in anything else, he never had much to say. His gesture was all. Only once we talked, after I complained about water without ice and he turned pale grey eyes, a quick pierce, and said, Look, when I came to Israel, we had the stars to live in, see? Don't tell me you got a difficult life. Today, the water, turn a tap. The gas, to cook, turn a tap. The light, press the switch. The ice? The icebox.

4

Who is born? *Warm* water? Seven miles, the tank, the oxen, them days. Who talks? Got time to talk? Who gave it? We. We lived under stars. Stars we got in the heart. Give thanks.

I certainly gave thanks for a girl I could think poetry about, and I knew, and I was warm in knowing, she waited at home for me. She worked between the vegetable pickers' squads, and the greenhouses or in the turkey or chicken sheds, wherever the work list sent her, and often there was a happiest day when we worked together. Work was all. We lived for work, and work was tiredness, pain in the body, sweat, and a surety of satisfaction to see so much done, so much less to do. An orchard picked and crated, a stretch ploughed, a field sown, the herd milched, eggs gathered, a path cleared of stones, the young green planted, sand conquered, beauty growing where desert was before, this was our joy, enchantment, succour.

Yeke's squad of seven was known to be the best in the area, and I was lucky, after those first back-breaking months, to have a place, junior even to the Arab water-carrier, but still prizing the honour. We always had the pick of the work and the best pay, and we worked all the days of the week except sometimes when Yeke took a couple of days off to repair the machines. The collective had no real religion. Some were strictly observant of the basic law, but most had no belief one way or another, and many, Yeke among them, were implacable atheists, though arguments were few enough, and the atmosphere was simply live and let live and keep your mouth shut. Yeke said that time, Look, we suffered enough. Now we have peace, so quit and leave us alone. How is there a god, he kills millions of us, no help? Forget it. Just enjoy what you got. You worked for it.

Zvi, his second man, a Belgian, had served with the British Army, and changed his name from Abramson to Bar Avram. Yeke had taught him over the years, and his skin-and-bone struggle to do better I found at first almost pathetic. But he never stopped trying, and working beside him sweated all the snoot out of me, and in its place there grew respect. Sometimes I paired with the third man, Dov, a roly-poly from London's Bow Road. He spoke with a Russian accent and worked like a small bull. His surname, Zinsky, he changed to Rimmon, which means pomegranate, and he looked like one, and he had a smile that seemed to glow brighter the more the sweat ran, and often, in packing a truck with bags or crates, I stood aside, dead, and watched those tireless muscles and that smile for me, that said, Don't worry, son. I can do your work as well. It was always a take-down, but I knew where I stood. Lower than the Arab water-carrier.

But nobody swore at me, and Yeke kept me on.

Moshe Ben Yoseph had been Joe Joseph of Bloemfontein, South Africa. There might have been a Negro somewhere in his line, because in all except colour, he could pass for Mr. Africa himself, though we took little enough notice. We all had our own troubles, and anyway, work was enough. He stood over six foot, but his muscles were so big that he looked small unless you stood near him. He said he got the padding down at the building yard, lifting sacks of cement. He never went to school, and his one delight was to write his name in Hebrew characters, just two, that he practised anywhere, in any pause, with a twig in the earth, a stone on stone, a piece of brick on a wall, a burnt stick on whitewash. That secret smile of his, as though knots were being undone, stayed with me.

Yitzah, short, a frizz of gingery hair to his shoulders,

6

beard and moustache, and the most surprising eyes, of cognac held to sunlight, came from Argentina with Gad, tall, fair, pointed beard, clipped moustache, and they worked together as one, and Yeke said they did the work of one, but one is better than none. They both had a lot of *mañana*, and they lost many a job because the bed, or a girl, was more important. Yeke liked them because they were always apologetic in the old caballero style, all bows and gestures, making him laugh, and he said such people were the salt and sugar, leave them.

Lod had been a priest, though of which sect only Arye knew, and since no detail escaped the files in his office we had to enjoy curiosity. He was an older man, white about the tonsure, calm brown eyes, a wonderful smile, and an appetite for sheer labour that made him Zvi's only rival. He worked with Gil, a firefly, Yeke called him, because one eye was bluish and the other brownish and in the sun they could seem a strange green. He came from Morocco, spoke French and Arabic, and Lod taught him English when he would listen, but he preferred not to speak, and Lod protected him.

Shmuel, the saddest human I ever met, seemed to rouse Yeke to make a special job of helping him, though I never understood why. He seemed a stringbean, all bumps, and bent in an arc, as if he carried unseen weight. Watery eyes, a straggly beard and moustache, and that sad look made him appear a biblical patriarch in late youth, the more so because he wore the long grey gown of the Bedouin. Dan, his partner, a tall ex-Marine, veteran of Vietnam, close-cropped, carrying the Corps' unmistakable stamp in all he did, acted as an older brother, even at times as a father when Shmuel had one of his "down" days and the world turned black. At those times Yeke took special pains to find them a job apart from us.

7

Beneath the ladder in black shadow the moon made filigree, and the basketmen moved as ghosts, silent in white sprinkle, and the dry frisk of shaken branches were small waves lapping the stars.

Ahmed, of the Druse patrol, pattered down the rock steps, holding a lamp shining white gems in his eyes. He spoke to Yeke, and turned off for the tractor park, and on Yeke's nod, the first team lifted their baskets and went up the steps, and we began clearing the area, stacking the long sticks and binding the ladders.

Move careful, Yeke whispered. No noise. We got a woman to look for, and Moshe said, What woman? and Yeke said, Patrol got a message. Some people, a chain they should have, the neck. How many times, you tell them, look, don't walk around, the night, it's dangerous?

Hold on, Dov said. A car down there?

We listened. Night breeze tickled the leaves, and I heard only that, but Zvi pointed below, towards Beersheba, and whispered, It's stopped. Go down there? and Yeke lifted a hand, and put an index to his ear, looking up at the branches, and we heard the voice, a whisper, but as she climbed the song was clearer, in pace with the walk, as if she sang to keep herself company, and we saw her shadow a little way off, coming closer.

Yeke called in Hebrew, and her voice hooked up in fear, broke in a shaky whisper.

I only speak English, she said, and Yeke said, So you got plenty here you can talk. No worries. All right, everybody. Enough. Bring your baskets here. And you, what's the trouble?

She stood beside him, tall, a dark plait below the jacket, long legs outlined in tight canvas trousers, a wide-brimmed hat on the back of her head, and even that time of night, dark spectacles.

8

I don't have any trouble, but where *is* this? she asked, while we lined up the baskets and ladders, and Yeke said, About halfway between Beersheba and Hatserim. How do you just go off? The alarm's out. You know the Police looking for you?

Not a thing about it, she said, opening mouth and eyes. Nobody said anything? I was trying to find Kfar-Sidon. I met a lot of Bedouin, and they gave me some tea, and pointed to this road. So I walked on, and heard you talking, and came on up. What should I have done?

Yeke nodded at the steps as if they asked the favour of reply, and an owl spoke, oo-oo, round as its eyes, down in the grove.

You speak Arabic? Zvi asked, and she said, No, and he said, So how do you know who is a Bedouin? He was in a tent?

She shook her head, and her eyes startled in sudden light.

Enough, Yeke said. Questions we don't ask. If questions, we don't answer. Tonight, you sleep with our girls. Tomorrow the truck takes you to Kfar-Sidon. It's a long way. The man told you this is terrorist country at night? and she said, No, and Moshe said, You didn't see the night patrol? and she shook her head.

They certainly saw *you*, Dov said. Also it will be known who your Bedouin "friend" was, and she turned to Yeke, and said, Wait a minute. They were kind. It was a family. They had camels and goats, and Moshe said, You come in a car? and Yeke said, Listen. Why she have to answer questions? Courtroom we got here? and she said, But isn't it true you don't like any kind of Arabs? Palestinian, or anyone else? and Yeke said, You been in the country long enough, you know it's a rotten kind of lie. Original.

9

And she said, I've been told so often you hate them, and Yeke said, Now, *I* ask the question. By *who?*

She looked away, and we stood silent.

Why should people want to *hate?* Yeke said, and shook the baskets for us to lift. Why should *I* hate? *Every*body must be born to hate? To be living right we must actually *hate* somebody? Greeks hate Turks. Turks turn around and hate Armenians. Who does the Armenian get out of bed in the morning to hate while he is lacing the boots? So he can feel satisfied with his life, he *has* to hate? So why I should hate an Arab?

It is in the Scripture, Lod said. Beloved is Man, for he was created in the image of God. Is an Arab also of the Image? We hate him? So we hate God? It's possible we should be such fools?

If the Arabs are shown, and they are helped, they work well, Yeke said. If I teach, and I pay, why *should* he hate me?

Well, you have their land, she said. That's what all the trouble's about. Everybody says so.

Don't tell me *e*verybody, Yeke said. Tell me the names. I want a talk with them. Man to man, using the head. Look, the top of these steps, we found a tomb. A father I had, a good man. I had a mother, my love follows her. *We* all had a father and a mother. *They* all had a father and a mother, going back to the people of that tomb. How do we know? The language, the Hebrew, *Ivrit,* it's there. Four thousand years, *our* people. Not the others. With the vines and olives, and the milk and honey, every man his fig tree, you should want more. We find their pots up there. They handled those pots. They had the food and drink. The baskets to carry, we found them. The beads for the neck, the wrists, a woman, real, live, she *warmed* them. A man loved her.

But how can you *know* that? she said.

So how does she have the beads? Yeke asked her, laughing. Beads, a present, it's not love? A man thinking? More beauty she should have, here, take it, wear it. Think of me. Listen, the school, they gave you history?

She walked, looking up at the sky, and we were six in line carrying five baskets, and she shook her head and held out a hand to the moon.

Not enough, she said, and Yeke said *Down*, and we eased shoulders, and Abu brought the tray of jars, and dipped mugs of sweet lemon. She drank in gulps, and ran a forefinger over her forehead, easing the bright drops falling with ours.

You work hard, she said. This time of night? It's slavery. Surely.

Not, Yeke said, and we shook our heads. Do we look like slaves? For extra money, we work. Extra stores. It's not our grove. The commune gave us the glean. Glean, you call it? What is left when everything is gathered. Now we leave the rest for the Arabs. The commune leaves to us. We also have a duty. Arabs have a share. The commune is rich. We shall be. The others, Arabs, not, and she said, Why? and Moshe spat, and said, They don't work. Don't have the idea. Only the women do anything. Follow the goats, milk, make cheese. It's enough? and she looked at Yeke, and said, But you just told me Arabs work well, and Yeke said, When they want. Too little, the men. They ride the camel. Sell the goats, spend the money. Plant tobacco. No work, no water needed, and the crop they sell. Why work? and she laughed, and said, Why do *you* work? and Yeke looked around for a moment, and said, Well, I like to *be*. What I plant, I like to see *grow*. The trees, my friends, they wait for me to turn the water. If pest, I take away. Wheat, crops, I plough. I seed. Everything my father and his fathers could *never* do. That is what I *do*. I think of *them*. But this collective, it needs money. The commune can borrow. We can, also. But not so much. A collective is not a commune.

If I could see the difference, she said, in a woman's way, in the air.

Be patient, Yeke said, flat hand out. In the commune, everybody has the same share, everything. Food, lodge, dress. No money. Everything in a common fund. In the collective, we work together, we share together the money. We work, we get. We don't work, we don't get. We use money. In the pocket. Of the conscience, we are not a prisoner. Over the tyrant we have a victory.

Tyrant? she said. Work?

You will learn, Yeke said, and nodded. Work, it's a brother. Six days we work together. On the seventh, we rest. Work and you. Conscience is the tyrant. I must act so. I must do so, this, that. Or what will the others think? What will *I* think of *me*? Here, you find us friendly with ourselves, first. It follows we are friendly to the next.

You speak English *and* Hebrew? she said, and the big hat was between me and her eyes.

I am born Hungarian, Yeke said, soft, not to offend the night. I worked in England, and America. I speak also French, Italian, Spanish, not much. Arabic, Hebrew. I spoil them all. Ah, but Russian, good. Call me *Ye*-kee. Israeli now, and happy at last. *Up*.

We lifted to walk on, to the stone steps, and out of the grove to a moon that could make us silver inside, and the hills pale-green, grey with rock all about us, and our foreheads crowns of diamonds, and the lights of our houses egg yolks, a white bullseye above the gate, and a ruby high on the radio mast.

12

So calm, this place, she said. Here, I could grow, and Yeke said, As we are. We have room, and time. And your friends in Kfar-Sidon?

They don't know I'm in Israel, she said, almost laughing. I like it here.

Join us, Yeke said, in her tone. We could use the hands.

If only I knew where I am, she said, and danced, arms out in little turns.

You are in the collective of Uriel, Yeke said, to a daughter. We are about eighty men. More women. Children, I shall say fifty or less. I am here before you are born. Everything what you see was stones. Everything by the horse. Beersheba, you walk. Six, seven hours. The horse, it's only for work. Today, we take a bus, one hour. But we are still what we were.

What? she asked, like breaking a stick.

Down, Yeke said, and we stretched the ache. Nowhere else can we find a place, all of us, here. We speak only English. Hebrew, not much. We have no religion. We are not for the Communist. Not for the Orthodox. We are not for anybody except ourselves. And work. Work, we like. In the land we like. The work of our people, in the land of our people. Reasonable?

Sounds so to me, she said, and looked along our line, and Yeke said, Good. Another heard from. The water-carrier is Abu. Arab. The only one. We are Europe or America. Abu has no talk. He lost his tongue in a punishment. It was nailed to wood, and cut. In his own land. Where they are so kind, the heart. And if they come here, they will be kind also to us? The women? The children?

I don't even want to think about it, she said, turning her face away.

So many like you, Yeke said, in the throat. *Up.* You

look the moon? It's good? Men walking on it. Driving a car up there. It's possible? Such brave men.

Weren't *you* brave to come here? she said, all woman in the voice, the turn to him.

We dreamed, and so we came, Yeke said, at the light. Same reason. Next to you, with the ladders, that's Traul. He was born not speaking or hearing. He teaches Abu the talk of the fingers. Such a way to be born, it's not a blessing. So we let Abu stay here. To talk. It's company.

Isn't that dangerous? she said, hands together. An Arab?

We all laughed, and set down the baskets, and Traul magicked his fingers, stabbing a forefinger fast as rain-pelts, and Abu opened his mouth, spittle frothing down both sides of his chin, rattling the swollen bit of his tongue, and danced, in a thump-a-thump of feet, knees out, toes a-kick, in flappy white linen trousers tucked in socks, a drunken cockerel.

Last year he was not friends with his books, Yeke said, eyebrows up, nodding. He came with a party of Arab students. They come more and more every year. We teach, they learn. We pay, they like. Abu found Traul. They have no tongues, but Abu has ears. We should separate them, they put their arms round each other? Now they learn agronomy, plant the Negev. The talking fingers, the desert should speak. What they do, it's well done. More, you can't ask.

Way you talk, you seem to favor Arabs, she said, almost in contempt.

Well, I like many, yes, Yeke said. Plenty, *no*. I don't trust. *Next* question. Somebody behind take my place. She goes with me to the girls. Come. What is your name? and she said, Aliya, and Yeke said, Ah, Aliya. Aliy*at*.

The in-coming. Coming home. Like us. So. With me, please.

Moshe took Yeke's place, and we lifted and turned for the storehouse.

Great girl, Zvi said. Twenty-two-three? Can't tell these days. Educated. Fine talkers.

Sweet talkers, Moshe said. Who is listening? A wanderer. Belongs on the beach at Eilat. Seen too many.

Too many told you piss off, maybe? Zvi said, dark-faced, white moonsmile in his eyes. You couldn't be wrong? Coming up that road takes a lot of guts. Wanderers don't have it. And the voice. So soft, you should look for your mother. And the legs.

Fell in love with her, dope, Yitzah said. That shape, betch, Zvi told the moon. Ai. The way I dream.

She shouldn't be on the road this time of night, Dan said. None of us would. It's dangerous, and Shmuel said, Ah, come off it. What the hell, she stealing chickens? Patrol take care of her.

Not what we're talking about, Dan said. Girl like that, high-assing down that stretch? For the time of night, I wouldn't. You can be shot by your own patrol.

She had legs like you got, I go along, Zvi said. And believe me, I'm your friend.

I never heard Yeke *talk* before, Shmuel said, Couple years I'm here, a dozen words. It's too many. Sure, Zvi said. She turned him on. Turned? Dov said, Boy, she sure spun me. Maybe it's the time of night. Or she got her own music. She walks, it sparks off.

You hear it, Zvi said. She hears it. Like it says, gals six, or sixty, they run to the sound of the timbrel.

O-ohh. Here come the Philistines, Shmuel said.

Ah, can that stuff, Gad said. Don't let's get Mosaic. Hell's that? Yitzah asked. Mosaic? You mean that floor

15

up there? Bits of coloured glass, is it? Stone? Okay. So what? and Shmuel said, Look, don't let's get into it.

But what's this mosaic got to do with it? Yitzah said. All I want to know.

Avraham and Moshe—not me—and them, they passed right by here when this road wasn't even a track, Moshe said, thin, over the rumble. Them old guys, they had all the secrets, arts and stuff. One of the reasons Pharaoh didn't want them to go. Losing know-how. They had the ideas. Knew what was going on. Had the time those days.

And the bread, Zvi told the pouring olives. Look at what the Romans socked them for. And they certainly knew how to build.

I take what's new anytime, Shmuel said. Give me high-rise. Cement. That old stuff, they should keep it how it was? What's so wonderful, a heap of rocks?

Like Yeke said, Moshe shouted over the olive thunder. If your father four thousand years ago was here, well, so you got the *right* to be here. Listen, big guy he likes to belt little guys? Little guy got muscle, won't stand for it, he's going to piledrive that big sonnabitch.

This is supposed to be us and the Gippos? Shmuel said, lifting the basket. Don't follow. I believe like my dad, see? Everything got crisscrossed. Everybody, the old ones, they made a goddam mess before I was born. Listen, I'm Sabra. I don't owe nobody a cent, except my dad. And he won't take even the cent. He sent me through college. I flunked? I'm so proud of it? Hell I am. You don't think I wanted to come back here with the picture to hang on the wall? I give anything pass them exams. I just got nervous, see? Didn't get the questions. Couldn't spell a word, couldn't ask nobody. I try to see it in English, in Hebrew. Not a hope. So I'm sitting there, wasting money? Them questions tough to read, see?

That's when I quit. I come back. I know what I can *do*, here. It's the place. Here, it's all friends. I dig the scene. It's Israel. I'm Israeli. I got a place. I done my Army service. I'm strictly Sabra. So don't go giving me a bunch of goop about tombs. That's for the museums. Y'know, the tourists. Not me.

We all heard it before, and all of us turned aside from the trembly voice, and we let the olives talk in the throat of the chute.

Wasn't for the tombs, you couldn't be here, Zvi said, loud. The tombs, Torah, Talmud, three T's, that's it. Take them out, who in hell are you? What kind of a Jew?

Listen, Shmuel said, and took his hands from the basket on the hopper's brim. *I am no Jew.* I'm Israeli. I don't even want to know about that, y'know, when Israel was in Pharaoh's land. I heard the lot. I had a couple of years listening to it. The *goyim*. On the guitars. Plonk, plank. I hear *one*, I'm round the goddam bend. It's music? Five hundred miles? Nine hundred miles? Brother, a moonshot from me's too close.

So how can you be Israeli and not a Jew? Zvi said. It's what your papers say. If you're no Jew, you can't be Israeli. One, it's one, and one is all, and evermore shall be so. Remember the song?

Song *and* papers, I wipe myself, my inconsequential *ass*, Shmuel said, opening a hand to guide the olive pour. I'm no Jew. I'm from birth Israeli. I don't want no trouble, see? I just want to live. In peace?

Tell the others, Zvi said, and lifted the basket. You are born American, how are you here?

Me, I'm not born American, Shmuel said. If my mother lives there, it don't make *her* American. She comes here with my father. I'm born *here*. Israeli. So how am I American?

17

Talk to the guys with the rubber stamps, Moshe said. You got to be a Jew, first. Your mommy, she's the guarantee. Aliens, they get born, they get the passport of their old man. Not here. You got what y'mommy gave you. Because she's Jewish. Jew first, Israeli second, and Shmuel said, Israeli, I tell you. I don't want none of that other crap. Dan, he's the same. Right, Dan?

Right on, Dan said, quiet, lifting a basket, no effort. Plenty more of us, and Moshe said, Look, we don't wear no fur hats, see? No Sephardics, no Ashkenazim. We're no zealots, right? But there's a whole lot back there, it's sacred. My grandaddy, my old man, they both be*lieved*, see? So do I. It's why we're here. We'll take care of it. O.K. by you?

Listen, Shmuel said, and put the basket down. We can always get another job. Someplace else, what's the difference? You don't want us, all you got to do's say so. The religious stuff, we had. Whole scene's a blackout, goddammit.

What's all the shouting down here? Yeke called, two-stepping the flight. Even a whisper, it's on the hilltops. You, they hear in Beersheba. So?

Ah, Shmuel said. Him and this religious bunk.

Enough, Yeke said. Here, it's work. No time. Keep it for the cultural center. Where you like, not here.

Wasn't an argument, Moshe said. He says he's not a Jew.

Damn' right, I'm not, Shmuel said. I couldn't even *say* it. I'm straight Israeli, no trim. And I don't budge. I *won't.*

So what's so special? Yeke asked us. He don't want the use of his mother's body, I should pick a quarrel? Up to him.

Body, hell, Shmuel said. I don't want her dragged in

18

this. I'm just saying. I came back from the States. I failed, that's all. Tears I couldn't cry, all inside. So I changed. Somebody I could like better, and Yeke said, So? Rat dives one hole, one colour, out the other, another colour? Same rat? and Shmuel said, No. I *changed*, I tell you. Another type human I can like. What I never was. Here, I *am*. No job here I can't do. Cattle, poultry, plough, name it.

Blowing the *shofar*, Yeke said. I didn't see no walls come down. You got a whole lot to learn. Right, everybody. Five-thirty, the tractor park.

Moshe tipped the last basket in the chute, and the others went out with the moon in their hair.

How's that girl? he shouted over the noise, and Yeke said, Fine. Just what I hoped. She's in Shoshana's. Making her blintzes when I came out. Around that one, you don't starve, and Moshe said, Say any more about the Bedouin, and Yeke said, No. Tight lip. You don't believe her? and Moshe said, Why should I? I been here long enough. She has a play.

Her business, Yeke said, piling baskets one in the other. She's entitled. That Shoshi, took her two minutes for the whole story. Not even a month, you listening? This one, Aliya, she's married. Canopy, big scrolls, the whole deal. Get it? Not even one month it lasts? Such a girl? and Moshe said, He die? and Yeke said, No. Run off with somebody, and Moshe looked at me, and laughed, and said, Holy cow. She must have been *something*.

Yeke let the pour go down, and turned off the current.

No *she*, he said, in the quiet. The male cult of prostitutes. Hear about *them*?

Ah, come on, Moshe said. Hit me. Really *hit* me. A *fruit*? She crying? and Yeke sat against the hopper, chewing a little finger, and said, I don't get it. She was laughing, like, you know, it had to happen to her. Game got switched. Why she changed her name. Quit what she was doing. Come here. Threw it all out. Cat vomit. No more. Wanted to be somebody new, she said. Why she's Aliya. O.K.? Five-thirty, tractor park? and I said, I'll be on my own. Girl's in the greenhouse. 'K? and Yeke said, 'K. *Laila Tov.* Nicest way to say good night. *Shalom.*

Nicest? Moshe said. Been picking melon seeds? and Yeke laughed, and said, Aliya told Shoshi, it's the nicest way she ever heard to say good night. So I'll keep it. *Laila Tov,* and Moshe said, *Shalom, shalom.*

Peace in peace, Yeke said, on his way out. It's good. You two got four hours' sleep, and Moshe said, You, too. Sleep blind.

While we put our coats on, he nodded at the footsteps going up the stairway.

Not good, he said, and I said, What's not good? and he said, That one, Aliya, she calls herself? She reeled him in, and I said, So what's wrong with it? And he said, Look, I'm Police Reserve. Why I'm here. You got them years training, you can smell it, and I said, So? Others can't smell? and he laughed, and said, Damn' right. That's why the patrol got the word. Police, in Beersheba. Nervous kind of place. But she has Yeke in the basket. Never seen him fired up. And these guys talking. Talk, talk, talk. Always the same. Nothing else to talk about? That Shmuel. Times I heard it, I can stand in, every word whole cloth. I tell you, one day I sink a boot. Way him and that Dan top off, and that skirt and all, I probably lose it.

I'll worry about myself and three hours-something sleep, I said. I'll catch hell from the girl. *Laila Tov,* and he said, Listen, don't say nothing, but I bet they opened a file on her. They don't phone a patrol for nothing. And Ahmed and them didn't show? Boy, that's bad. They're just waiting. *Shalom.*

I was too tired to worry about it, and anyway, if there happens to be anything better than tiptoeing into a house, and washing quietly, and getting into a bed warmed by a naked marvel of a girl, let me know.

That, too, I had to be thankful for.

TWO

We were *one,* no you, no me, no mine, no yours, dreaming, thinking, talking together, *one,* living, treasuring, working together, *one.* We often tried to think of ourselves before, if only to measure the blissful difference, but "before" was some other sort of life we thankfully put aside, and even our memories failed in picking the moment when the I-and-You decided to become *Us.* There must have been an instant, though neither of us knew exactly when.

We were in the orchard that day. I was on the fruit-picker platform machine taking us to the top of the tree, and down, branch by laden branch, for our hands to garner. Towards evening I lowered to a rumple of plump, green-striped scarlet apples, and I was looking at the legs of somebody standing on a strong fork, but the legs, the hips, were so wondrous in beauty that I could only stare, and put out a finger to touch a rill of sweat in the muscle's valley, taste, *salt!* and look, a couple of feet up, at the eyes of a maleficent cat ready with claws, and the flooding-out of rage was flooding-in of another glory, and I put my hands beside her knees, and caressed to the bones below her waist, and she bent to put her arms about me, and We became Us.

We think that was when, but we were never sure. We remembered seeing each other in the dining hall, and the library. I remember her red-gold head caught in sunstream making a halo, and trying to imagine if the medieval painters had borrowed the idea to illumine their saints, and so leave a lit wound in the memories of all of us looking at them down the generations. The wonder of her legs were always walking away from me. I wanted hungrily to kiss the pink bulb of the heel, up, past the pinched Achilles, to the bones of the mountains of the moon, and back, and hungrily, I hungered. Not only for her, but to possess her beauty which was part of the sun's light, and air. I saw her deft hands plaiting a child's mop, thinking of the carven tresses of Roman women in the museum at Naples, seeing, too, that thick plait of vital bronze hanging its swing below her waist. And hungrily, I hungered for her, until my hands enfolded, and I lifted her down, and we kissed in the scent of apples, and our sweat ran together, *salt!* and Eden's warmth in the mouth, a luscious sweet of lazy tongues, an electrical ripple in space unknown, an urge far beyond the joyous, and the wondrous sculpt of a woman's body, a merge and melt in other galaxies, echoes of dreams. For me a new existence was born in tenderness I never knew existed.

Perhaps it was then that We became Us. We incline to think it was before, because she decided that I was hers, though I could never find out when she thought so. This was the small difference between us, that she had little secrets, and I, none. We got used to calling our-

23

selves We in all we did. We lost the I, the You, the Me. We became A plus 1 and A minus 1, so that in terms we were $A+1=2A+A-1$, which, to us, shone out as a caballistic theorem of portentous significance, though of what, we were unsure except that *We* were *Us*. Neither of us had been married, but We were Us from the moment We kissed, and Shoshana gave Us a room, and so We loved her, and among our friends there was no question.

Perhaps that was partly why We felt a special, secret sorrow for Aliya, though she never knew, possibly because we had so much, and she so little. She was alone with brutal memory. We helped, all of us, and Shoshana found her the small-store, where we bought writing paper and stamps, and soft drinks, and sweets that made a bump in the face We loved, and all the other little things that tempt the hand in a pocket.

Small-stores had been the charge of an old German woman branded with the sallow furrows and sad eyes of Auschwitz, barely glimming Us through thick lenses that almost covered blackish sacs she might have kept pennies in. Her quietness left us for a hospital in Tel Aviv, and so Aliya had her place. Years-lain dust went out with the hose, and for three days she worked, and we in our spare time helped, and at about nine o'clock on the third day, we looked at a fresh-painted, scrubbed-clean, shelves-filled place we had never known, and there was pleasure going in, and a fatness coming out, for she got on the telephone, and many new items made us feel more a part of the world beyond, not that we needed or wanted, but we simply took comfort in minor blessings enjoyed elsewhere by others of our time.

But the day beamed when a truck backed in, and the *espresso* machine burst out of sawdust, and Sam and his garage squad hammered and spannered to put plumbing and electricity in, and just after eight o'clock that night, we had the best cup of coffee in the land. But the crush left no room to sit, even if there had been a chair.

Aliya went into Tel Aviv for a couple of days, and Shoshana made the coffee, with us at the washup, but we felt the lack.

Shoshana said it all, for all of us, when she piled her hair, and let it fall, and said Hell, how long she going to be? I got used to her. I don't feel good, she's not here.

She came in the evening with a truckload of small white-topped tables and black chairs with red backs and seats, and a lot of crates, and another truck piled with flagstones and cement. We asked no questions, but she knew we were happy to see her, and Shoshana opened big arms and hugged her close, and we all did a ring-a-roses dance, and Abu did his feet-up fandango, and Aliya said, How is he as a gardener? and Yeke said Fine, what I saw. He can learn.

Tell him I'd like him to look after the garden, she told Traul. Can't hear, Yeke said. And besides he doesn't have that much English. I'll tell him.

Traul watched the mouth, and the frown flew in a foxgrin, and he nodded from the neck, and Abu made a grab for Aliya's hand and kissed the palm and the bones up to the wrist before she could stop him, and she let him, because he wept, and took him by the hand to the *expresso*, and made him a special coffee, with a splash of cognac. Traul looked a whimper, head on one side, and she let him in for another, and then flung up her hands, and we all went in. Such good coffee gave us a feeling that everything had become better.

Why, we supposed we would never know, but there was always that secret sorrow for Aliya. Tall, she stood, and with the middle fingers she combed back the hair

25

to fall behind her ears, and looked the grey-blue eyes in a tilt of the chin, all men her servants, any woman her friend, because she had no man, made no play, cast no eyes, worked as though anything she did would be her last on earth, and was herself, remote.

She sensed we put our arms round her. Her servant, but absolute, Traul, followed her. She told him what she wanted, he watched her mouth, and in the sudden fox-grin, leapt to serve. Abu was his shadow, and she always had a special kindness for him, almost maternal, though at distance, but it was she who discovered his talent.

He refused to help build a wall at the back of the stores and outbuildings, lean-tos, stacks of planks and props, dust-ridden, sun-shrunk, hopelessly tangled in weeds and overgrown shrubs.

He drew in the earth at her feet a plan of the area, a large terrace in front and extending to both sides of the café, steps down to a rock walk, gardens both sides and canted walls making a rock garden. He pointed to the carobs, and in signs made us see stretches of lawn, shrubs replanted, pomegranates left there, flower beds everywhere, and five small fountains in stone basins to cool the air.

She nodded her pleasure, keeping her hands behind, and said, That's it, and Abu took charge, and Traul became *his* shadow, spokesman, and sweating labourer.

We helped in spare time, trying not to see how the place was changing, only to keep for ourselves the pleasure of seeing it finished. Yeke ran plaster in Abu's earth-sketch, and later took the design in one piece, stuck it to a six-foot square of apple, olive, and rosewood in odd sections, framed it with an aluminum band, and one night brought it in, and Aliya took back her hair to look, pointed to the one white wall, turned, stood a moment, and walked away.

Yeke showed fine teeth and blinked at Us, a happy one.

For the next couple of weeks, we gathered grapes from early morning to dusk, and after a bath and a meal, there was no time for Aliya, except to go there for coffee. Abu knew what he was doing. He finished here and there, but left planks, pickets, wire and debris all about so that none might see what had been done, and people began saying If you want to waste money, trust an Arab. Yeke heard Dov say it, and shouted, Keep shut the mouth. Truth, it's not there. I want advice about trust, I don't ask *you*. I hear it again, you finished with me. *Mouvan?* which in Hebrew is Understand? and Dov said *Ken,* which is Yes, as a beaten dog.

Across the room, Moshe looked at me brows-up, no smile, and something was in the eyes that disturbed me. He was of the Police, whether Reserve or not, and they had only half the power of the Army, and that meant twice the power of all else, and I was worried, because they *knew.*

I said nothing to Plus A.

THREE

When the vineyard was stripped, and the last baskets of grapes were in, we took a day off before the Sabbath, and went to Aliya's for the luxury of morning coffee and a croissant. Then we saw how cunning a man Abu was, for instead of all that dust and gravel the place was finished, in order, shining.

Red and black flagstones made a wide frame all round the café, and big windows slid to enter from the terraces, pink-cream stone walls made rock gardens along the stairways, flower beds were in bud, five small fountains blossomed light, trees had been pruned, a few replanted, shrubs trimmed, grass clipped, weeds gone, and We stood there, glad for Aliya, for Us, and everybody. But the day before the Sabbath was Friday, Abu's day of rest as a Moselm, and Traul served at the tables of four black-and-red chairs, little islands of comfort, even so early, almost filled. Aliya called Traul a black thumb. He slopped, he dropped, he sweated, tripped on chair legs, and all in a haste to please and an air that said, I am a beast, but can I do more than try? In those early days any coffee-stained shirt was called a Traul, and seeing one, he put hands together, shut one eye, one shoulder up, staring over the wearer's head.

And so it was a moment for Zuz to appear with the rug-bag, one evening, along the road from Beersheba, a patriarch in cast-offs, sandals slapping little puffs, skull-cap covering the bald patch, and an affably lofty air of no concern, a disregard in majestic terms for all that went on. It was exactly the air of one risen above the squalor of the ghetto.

He saw us up there, and looked about, at the terraces, the stairways, the tables, chairs, us, the shining *espresso* machine, and the bar, and opened his eyes in such amazement that he might have seen the Throne, and all Glory. The bag fell, the hands went into his lap, and he bent his head, and we knew he prayed, and we stood. Even the unbeliever, Shmuel.

He came up in quick steps, staring the black eyes of purpose, and walked to the bar, and Aliya looked down at him with the little smile that said Pity, Love, Tell Me.

He spoke in Hebrew, and Aliya said, Sorry. Only English, and he said, *Va bene,* I am here. Who is the owner? in English with the scent of Italian. What can I do for you? Aliya said.

I am Zuzoni, and I wish for a place here, he said. To do my work. Or I *die.*

Aliya took time in the smile.

What can you do? she asked.

I am of the school of Giandomenici, and Cassati, and Verga, he said. I know the cities of the world. Restaurants, cafés, where you like. Waldorf-Astoria, New York, Ritz, London, Plaza Athénée, Paris, Grand Hotel, Venice, Florian's.

It's enough, Aliya said. Do you have a white coat?

Everything, and my work, I got, he said, holding up the bag. Show to me, please, the place to dress. I like to shave. Half hour, I'm here.

Back way, second door on the left, Aliya said, Now I'll stop losing my cups and glasses.

Everything I saw, he said, on the way out, in a frowning glare at Traul. A *ho-r-r*-se. A shoe*make*r. You send, please? *Vai. Mascalzoni.*

And so, Traul went back to the garden, and happily.

We had not known what a café was until Zuz took charge. No more the clatter of crockery or rattling spoons, odd crashes of china, scraping chairs, tables squeaking, the thud of boots, dripping forehead, sweatniff, blundering hands.

Dapper, white shirt, black bow, white jacket, black trousers, polished shoes, we saw Zuz go to work, and knew a master. No more coffee in a slopped saucer, sugar stains in the pot, sugar stuck hard, no spoon, croissants handled in the fingers, puddled tables. We had a feeling we were at one of the world's best, and Zuz one night said he would make it so. He had the ideas of experience. He told Aliya. She listened.

Green and white striped canvas came in rolls, and a couple of sailmakers from Haifa made awnings all round, and sewed an outer cover for a woven silk Bedouin tent, in blue, white, gold and red, the gift of Abu. When it was up, mothers and children ate ice cream and had tea in free time, always apart from us, and Zuz trained three girls to serve. His own help took longer to find. He was exacting, impatient, and Aliya said he was Impossible—with the smile—and he said, You are Israeli too soon. You like to be served by a hor-rr-se, a shoe*make*r, a foot*ball*er, it's the same for you? This is the Café Aliya. Here I work.

Here, it will be done so, as I have lived to know. I know, or I don't know?

You know, all right, Aliya said. *Alora,* Zuz said. What I do, it will be as I say, as I learn with Giandomenici, and Montefiore, and Renzi, and more, the school of *maestri.* If a shoemaker, shoes make, if a *maître, be* a maître. *D'accord?* Do it your way, she said. I just hope the help stays, that's all.

If the help is not my way, it is not help, he said, white, shaking, and his passion reached Us. A man should know his business. He should be correct. What he learns he must put in his life. Or what life? I will walk in the roads, but I will find what my life tells me. He pointed to the floor. It was here. I said This, or I *die.* You like I should die?

No, Aliya said, Too few of you. Handle it the way you want. I love a pro. A pro, what is? Zuz asked. A professional, Aliya said. Somebody won't take the easy way.

Zuz flipped the napkin over his cuff, bowed short, and pointed to the jugs of coffee and milk. Cold, he said. You please change. They're cold because you talked, Aliya said. You pay for them. I pay, Zuz said, and brought out a purse. What I say, it was worth more. So I pay half, Aliya said, and bent for her handbag, nodding at the cash register. That's the boss. He does the talking.

Zuz lined out the coins, and leaned over the bar. To say you are a *won-der-*ful, it is nothing. To say you are a *mar-a-vig-lia,* only a little, he said. You are Aliya. It's enough? Look, she said, These coffees get cold again, you pay for the lot.

The tray went, level with the right ear, and Zuz reigned at the small service table in chew of his moustache, a noble sweep of grey parted over the top lip and combed out to peaks almost under the eyes. The croissants were served with tongs out of a napkined basket, the butter from a lidded dish, jams and jellies in their several pots, cheeses in ordered slices, and the sugar bowl gave free, white.

With her chin on two fingers, and two up her cheek, Shoshana looked at it all, and found it good. She made the blintzes of cream cheese, any kind of jelly, or shredded chicken, turkey, lamb in season, and cheesecakes with, and without, blackcurrant, or greengage, or black cherry filling.

In the orchards, the groves, the fields, we thought of them, and put our arms round each other when we broke to drink, and whispered we would go there after the bath, because we knew that blintzes or cheesecake meant love afterwards, and Shoshana's black eyes held knowledge when she slid the copper pan, and pointed the palette at us for Zuz to serve.

It is nice? he often said, and We said, Yes, it's very nice. I am nice, also? he said, that afternoon, in the short bow. Nobody nicer, one of Us said. We think you are, *really*, a *maître*. He looked up, through the awning, raising a hand that tremored. I have my beautiful answer, he said, and the kitchen bell took him away.

Shoshana worked there in free time. It was not work, she said. To cook and see smiles, I am born, she told us. But she also earned extra money, and other women began to work, and soon, we could buy chicken pies, turkey pies, patties, *vol-au-vent*, sausage of any kind, and then the pastries, but all of them had to pass the test of Zuz. It was no easy one. He wanted three separate bakings on three successive days to ascertain correct standard, and quality.

We were there when the éclairs came in from Orfa,

32

and he spat out the first mouthful. For *canaglia*, he shouted, spitting again. Éclair, it is *the* most *delicate*. The case, a virgin's breath, the cream it must be of the thick, with a lover's touch of *vanille*, and the chocolate, completely without a bitter, or a rough. Please, you give to the chickens. They laugh.

That's it, Aliya said, tranquil, at the bar. The master hath spoke. Go ahead, Orfa. Show him.

But it took seven bakings before Orfa got them as Zuz wanted, and she was in such a temper, she would have died before giving in, and when Zuz chewed, eyes shut, on the afternoon of the seventh baking, and kissed his fingers, and said *Eccelente*, she kissed *him*, and we had the world's finest éclair, and the best of everything else.

Orit sometimes played for us on the Bechstein, and often Zvi, violinist, Lubet on viola, Sam, cello, Rachel, flautist, and Avram, double-bass, gave us a night of music and we sat under the stars to listen. At those times, Zuz sat with us, because Aliya refused to serve. But she also refused to sing. The smiling shake of the head was strong as a shouted No.

We said she would lose her voice.

Let me lose it, she said. I lost more. I found more. What I have is more than enough. Right?

It must be right for you, We said. But for us, we lose a dream.

Worthless, she said. I know.

And still she had no man. If she went to Beersheba or Tel Aviv by bus, she was alone, coming back with the truck driver. She wore the short dress, long hair down her back, and Yeke called her Shunnamit, but all he got was a turn-away smile. She could look at any man and talk to him from a yard away, but the distance was a

33

mile, and every man was aware, knowing too well that mis-behaviour would cost him his place in the collective, and certainly time in a hospital bed.

Some thought the mystery solved when a dozen girls, all beauties, came one night by car, and stood in the doorway, and Aliya threw up the fingers, and said Ah, and ran to them, and kissed them all both cheeks, and they stood with their arms about each other, and We tried not to listen.

But My loves and Darlings filled the air, and in a strange smile, Shmuel looked down at Us and held out the flat of his hands. Orit began to play "Summertime," and we lost the talk.

They went in a group to the back, where Aliya lived, and Zuz had to move his sleeping place next to the potting shed so that four could sleep in there, and eight on the floor of Aliya's two other rooms. Shoshana saw it all, elbow on the bar, two fingers flat up the cheek, two and the thumb under the chin, eyebrows up, eyes shut, opening in the little shrug, and a move to the grill.

What goes on shouldn't interest nobody, Yeke said.

I should be an elephant, I got the curler so far in there, Shoshana said. I heard of it. I never saw it before. Ah, now, Shoshi, Zvi said. It's nobody's business.

Wrong again, Shoshi said. I like to know. Something new. I could be one.

We yelled, and Orit stopped playing, shut the piano, and Yeke went after her to say we were sorry, and come on back, please. But she gave him the shoulder, goodbye, and it was days before we heard her again, and we had time to find out what we lost.

Nobody, not even Shoshi knew if we were right or wrong about the girls. We made up Our mind not even to think about it, but we did, and Shoshi said the cleaning

34

woman, an Arab from the village had found nothing except the floor-beds neatly folded in the mornings, and no sign that Aliya had not slept in her own bed, less that anybody had slept with her.

Yeke said, But for the love of God, we trying to think like the no-goods outside? What has she done for us? It's so terrible we speak with a whisper? What are we thinking? Why you don't ask honestly, as a friend? Please, you are of Lesbos? You are a Sappho? And if she tells, instead, to go to hell, yes, I am of Lesbos, what? The coffee, it's not the same? Everything is different? Something is dirty? Why? The love of women, it's not clean? If we say *we* are dirty in the head and the heart, yes, we are right. Who speaks so of Aliya?

Better watch it, Shoshana said. I'm listening. Four blintzes, Zuz, top table.

Got, Zuz said, and turned, black eyes wide in quiet fury, pointing to himself. Listen, I hear this, I *kill*. It's everybody the life *their* business. Who else must live in the body?

Blintzes getting cold, Shoshana said. Vols ready.

Two more here, We said. Blackcurrant, please.

Subito, Zuz said. What I say, I mean. I hear? I kill. *Ecc'*. We should help to sing. If she is born to sing, it is from God. Talk, blab-blab-blab, what is? *Sporcaccioni*.

Walking home, breathing roses, Plus A said, I have an awful feeling he's right. We ought to *do* something. Not our pigeon, I said. But don't lose the idea. Getting her back where she belongs can't be wrong. Have to make it good. Here's where law school pays off.

Pays off, how? she asked. What's that got to do with it? You're not suing her? and I said, Don't tell me lady lawyers never wrote a brief? That's what this has to be. Clause by clause. Each clause a stepping stone to build

35

the argument. You don't know a thing about it, she said, and put her arm round my waist. But it's an idea. Just let me think.

I'm doing the thinking, I said. It's pretty good. Solid. How long's it going to take you to get in bed?

I just want to make some notes first, Plus A said. Like to see how it looks on paper. Wonder if she's still married? Not a thing in this world to do with it, I said. You have to get her singing. Marriage made her quit. Or what came of it. How's a brighty like that get caught? Couldn't she *see* it?

Oh I don't know, Plus A said, bumping hips. I've known a few. You couldn't tell. It was always a shock. I mean, to find out. Perhaps she thought she could cure him, or something. She's the maternal look-after-everybody type, that's for sure, Or maybe she just didn't *know*. Or like now, nobody wanted to say anything. Didn't take her long to find out, though.

How long'll it take you to find out about me, Minus A said, opening the door. I could find out right now, Plus A said. But I want to write those notes. And I agree. Solid's the word. Many a gal's said yes for less.

Ouch, Minus A said, in no pain. Do I rate in the marriage mart? I'd say so, Plus A said, leaning. But I have a bias, and Minus A said, Best I ever saw. Prettiest. I'd like to take a lease on it. Legally. Signed. Sealed. The bit, entire, freehold. This is making me want to *nestle*, she said, and nestled. I suppose we *did* ought to do something about the paper. He'll want a name, won't he? I don't want a *mamzer*.

He won't be, Minus A said. A *mamzer*'s a product of an adulterous union. Or no marriage, if the woman's not a Hebress. A *mamzer* can't marry according to the Law. It says in the Book "unto the tenth generation."

Sounds too long to me, she said. I wouldn't want to make him a present of any of that. So what do we do?

I've been thinking, A-Minus said. How long's Boiler Room Billy going to give us?

Well, he hasn't done much grumbling yet, she said, opening a notepad. I'd say six, seven months, and I said, We can't get married here. How would you like the night boat from Haifa to Cyprus, get the paper, and fly to Sharm el-Sheikh for a few days' fishing?

Nodding down at the pad, turning into a hold-on cuddle, Sounds right, she whispered. I believe those notes'll do later, don't you? Isn't all that hurry. Darling. I'll never let go. Never. Hear me?

FOUR

Early every morning Aliya's guests went off to visit ancient sites, and got back late at night. They never took table-space but had their meals in Aliya's room. She sometimes went with them, and in the strangest way, the café lost light, and the ends of Zuz's moustache seemed to droop and Shoshi piled her hair this way and that, and every-body knew better than to break her silence, never mind how hungry.

But when Aliya came in, Zuz leapt as a hare, hands at his waist, fingers twiddling, short bow, *'piacore,* Donna Aliya, you like something? and she, in that smile said, So good to see you, Zuz. Yes, please. Shoshi, you look great, baby. How's about the chicken blintzes, and a coffee and a cheesecake? Let them choose, and coffee and a cognac for everybody. My room would be lovely, Zuz. Hi, everybody.

We saw the girls only at those times, for in the morn-ing we were at work. They were like Aliya, in height, the

38

same slimness, almost the same legs, and the same way of standing, one foot behind, toes out.

Shoshana, again, brought our minds to health and our hearts to a normal pulse. The girls were of a ballet from Germany, all American, British, French, and she knew, because she got it from an official guide, and he got it from a Passport officer at the airport, and they were all going back four days from the moment. The cleaning woman had nothing to say. The beds were always folded. Aliya's bed was slept in by herself alone, and Shoshana, chief at the laundry, controlled the linen.

Yeke drank the coffee, turned his back and walked out.

Zuz served whatever came with the same bland line of mouth. We pretended we took no notice, but we did. That special sorrow for Aliya seemed to be stronger but without our knowing why. The feeling puzzled us. We felt it curious that she could keep ten lively ones to herself. But then we found we had small minds, village minds, or no minds at all.

The fountain's knee-high water blossoms blew cool in the late afternoon, and Aliya told Shoshana to pass the word that her guests, with help of Orit and her musicians, would dance for us after supper. Zuz asked us not to use the larger terrace and we helped him stack tables and put chairs in rows, and Traul brought in plants to line the wall with flowers. When night came, with starlight on pinky-cream stone, lighting the fountains on each side, scarlet and white lilies, marguerites and roses in mass, the girls came out in white *tutus*, satin slippers, garlands in their hair, eye shadow, and we were shocked by a strange beauty, as if the Lord God had sent His angels, and many, not used to ballet, cried out for wonder.

They danced to Bach, Smetana, Rimsky-Korsakoff, and We sat close enough to see the sweat burst jewels down

39

spines and faces, knowing the full beauty of Eve's thighs in a frill, shouting encores led by Zuz, and Yeke's bull-roared *Bis*. Afterwards they sat with us, and we got them towels for their shoulders and Zuz served them as princesses, and Aliya came to our table, a rare privilege, and we talked of Europe, and the change in past years, of fat bellies and full pockets, new cities, TV and sex films.

They'll get tired of it, Aliya said. You've seen one, you saw the lot. Body's a simple thing. Not too many things you can do. But you have to do them right, with some-*body* right. Then you have a beautiful time on earth, and when you're old, you remember. Not too old. I wouldn't want to live past the time I couldn't stroll around.

You like strolling, Yeke said. You strolled in here.

Of course, she said. And I knew I was home. It's why I stayed. And I'm so glad, I can't tell you. All that matters, Yeke said. You made a difference here. What we do without you, who knows?

Look, Aliya, Avi, one of the dancers sitting between Us, said. A lot more of us want to come here. I have to say this. We think we imposed a whole lot on you, and you know, made a lot of trouble.

Not, Aliya said. Been wonderful having you here. Sort of caught up with myself. I couldn't face the idea of going back. You taught me that. I know the life. I know just what you're going to see. Where you'll be. I just don't *want* it. For me, it's over. Going back, it just makes me ill.

And the life you had, Cygal said, the tall girl sitting between Neb and Lod. We don't know how you could give it up, you want to know the truth.

Truth? Aliya said. It's here. Look, don't let's talk about it. It's over, gone.

She was upset, frowning, and Yeke said, I see you stole my partner. *Now* who do I work with? He finished with me. I should blame him, he picked such a boss?

He's wonderful in that garden, Aliya said. I'm selfish. I didn't think of you. He's in the best place, Yeke said. I didn't know he knew all that about a garden. Been wasting his time. Let him stay.

Yeke, you've been a good friend, Aliya said. Been? he said. What's wrong? I got thrown out?

Who will you find to work with? she asked. It's going to bother me.

Listen, Yeke said. Traul as a partner, all right, good worker, no let-up. But can I talk to him? It's good to talk. Sometimes, you got to. Say small things. Questions, they ache in the head. Know what I mean? So now I got to find somebody can talk. Who, it's a question.

Where's Abu, these days? Zvi asked. I didn't see him in a month or more.

Got more than he can handle, Yeke said. He finished this place, the commune wanted him to fix a place up there. He gets that, he's got half dozen other places waiting. Can't keep a good man down. On his way up.

So how was he carrying jars here, and just flicking fingers with Traul? Neb asked. We're stupid, that's why, Yeke said. We wanted water jars, he's nearest. Don't ask what he did before.

What? Aliya said, I thought, a little frightened.

Ah, just a graduate, Beirut, couple of years Paris, London, Yeke said. Political crime, they cut his tongue, can't talk, can't give orders. So? Carrier of water jars. He kissed your hand. Came to life, Natural? This place woke him up.

It's beautiful, Avi said. Never saw anything to compare. Reminds me of the Kranzler in Berlin. How about Sacher,

41

in Vienna? Lod asked. Well, yes, for the pastries, Avi said. I go there, I gobble. Minimum two kilos every time. The cherry *tart*lets. Umm.

Come here in four months, Aliya said. I'll give you cherries *this* size. And nobody beats us for pastry. Right, Zuz?

He raised his eyes to the roof, and pointed a forefinger. *Nessuno,* he whispered. The most beautiful women, the best everything, it's *here.* Café *Aliya. Ecc'.*

Aliya, Avi said. Couldn't you just sing *once* for us?

No, she said. I pulled out the stopper. Not again. The lungs, they stay closed. I wanted out, I'm out. I don't go back.

Yeke, even he, was silenced by the tone, so harsh, so unlike the kindly one we knew. She was strict with herself. It held in silence. Avi looked at Cygal, and they got up.

Couldn't we have a nice, private cup of coffee, and let us say how sorry we are for even trying? Avi said. The girls asked me to.

Cygal put an arm about Aliya's shoulder. It's mass guilt, she said. We just wanted to hear once, that's all. Gone, Aliya said. No more. Let's have the coffee.

We all got up, and Aliya waved to Zuz, and he made the short bow.

Why won't she sing, such a voice? Moshe said. I like to hear.

Ah, let her be happy the way she wants, Yeke said. Who are we, we got so much to say?

Tell you who she reminds me of, Lod said. Just thought. Look, no make up, no silk, none of that stage business, who's the number one somebody should frame her?

He raised open hands. The *real* Shunnamit.

That was a real piece, Yitzah said.

42

So who the hell's that? Zvi said.

Another didn't read the Book, Moshe said. Zuz, a coffee here.

Subito, Zuz said. This one, Shunnamit, what is?

King David's nurse, Lod said. She laid with him to keep him warm when he was old. But he knew her not.

Mm, Moshe said. That's how you get when the age hits so. So what happened?

Well, King David died, and Solomon was the king, and this Shunnamit, her name was Abishag, she was still around, Lod said. So his older brother, Adonijah, he went to Batsheva, his mother and Solomon's, and asked her to ask the king for permission for him to marry the Shunnamit.

They were brothers, he had to do business through his ma? Moshe said.

Well, you know how it is, Lod said. He must have known there was a little action around there.

Sol was getting his, so he wanted to hog the lot? Shmuel said.

No, wait a minute, here, Lod said. Well, his mommy, she went to Solomon, and she must have known what was going to happen. Part of the story I don't get. How does a mother just take and throw her first-born son in the pit? Anyway, Solomon called for a chair, and put it at his right hand, and he said, What can I do for you? and she said, Don't refuse me, and he said, Say on. So she said, Adonijah wants to marry Abishag, the Shunnamit. Well, Solomon, he blew his windberries. Listen, he says, why doesn't he ask for the kingdom? So he sent Benaiah, his Chief of Staff, to prune at the neck.

Boy, Moshe said. Was he stupe. If he kept the trap shut, and made her behind a door, he be living yet. Anything happen to her?

43

Don't hear much about her after that, Lod said. But she was what a brother killed a brother *for*. Why does it remind me of Aliya?

What's wrong with the Book, Zvi said, elbows on knees. Says just so much, then somebody got to explain it. Like these Torah *meshugeners*.

Not *meshugeners*, Lod said. Long line, the scholars. Goes back five thousand years. More. The proof we have. It's their business.

They make a business *of* it, Zvi said.

Torah *crap*, Sam said, looking down at craggy hands in charge of the tractor garage. Them and their six hundred and thirteen laws, and the buses can't run on the Shabbath, and their students can't serve in the Army, that bunch of high-class dung. Listen, that old goat in New York, the *schtunk*. He won't have his holy boys and girls in the Army? So me and my boy, we got to sit down there on the Suez? My daughter, she has to serve that much longer than what they said? What *is* this? They don't want to serve? So they can throw stones at buses on the Shabbath? That's picking on people don't have a car, taking them to see their families, the day of rest? Listen, I was a bus driver, I take the Uzzi, give 'em the long burst. And that old goat in New York, and them goats we got, I skin 'em for waterbags.

Only doing what they think's right, Lod said.

Right, my ass, Sam said. I got to *work* here. My son, he has. My daughter, *she* has. But not this *yeshiva* klatch? Just got to learn books, and throw stones? The wasps, they should nest in the whiskers, the old *goat*.

It's how you look at it, Lod said. Because of the Rabbis, that's why we're here.

Hell it is, Zvi said. Think that's why *we* came here? We never even saw one. Except the once. When I was a

44

kid. He give everybody the business for working Saturdays, and eating wrong, and all that stuff. Boy, was my old man ever mad. Don't know the facts of life, he's telling *them?* Who's going to pay 'em for a five-day week? I mean, in them days? You had to go the other end of town for kosher. Who had the time? Ma, eight kids and her sister, arthritis? So O.K., you think we lived like the *goyim?* Hell we did. My ma was strict, I tell you.

So was mine, Moshe said. Kept me at school. The books, get to the books. That's her. Loafers, they can go. I can still hear it.

They all the same, Shmuel said. Mine, too. Listen, now we here, you think they be satisfied?

Mine wouldn't be, Zvi said. She was ambitious. I wasn't.

Hell with ambition, Shmuel said. What I'm doing, I like.

Going to do it the rest of your life? Moshe asked. Me, no.

You said that, same words, last year, Zvi said. You still here.

I had the same idea, Shmuel said. I'm still here. You get to where you like what goes on. You can do what you have to good as anybody. Sometimes a whole lot better. My book, you can't beat it.

Going to do it the rest of your life? Yitzah asked. Me, no.

You said that last year, too, Zvi said. You're still here? What happened? Sipporah? and Yitzah said, Look. She wants to do her Army service first. That's maybe three years.

The holy girls don't help, Shmuel said. Going to wait? and Yitzah held out his hands, and said, Why not? For such a girl it's painful? But you just said you wanted a piece like this Shunnamit, Zvi said. She dogging you? Dogging nothing, Yitzah said. Listen, there's a world and another world. One world you're in, the other you can't get in, right? So? I got the other world, I should scream?

Maybe Sipporah should, Moshe said. But about Aliya, it's another world, that's for sure. Feel it, hear it, see it. Don't matter she's freaking.

Wait a minute, Zvi said. Call this freaking?

Ah, come *on*, Moshe said. Coffee and ice cream, take a look at her. Look what come to see her. Listen, I never saw that kind of a dance before. I love it. I don't know how she could leave it, it should stay in your heart.

How do you know she left it? Yeke said. They wanted her to *sing*. She probably *was* a singer. What she was, leave it. Her own business. What she thinks, it hurts? Put your arm around. Help. Be kind. Listen. You want to earn extra? Six tomorrow night, the packing sheds. Peaches. Who wants?

All the hands went up.

No, Yeke said. Six is enough. Toss the coin. Zuz got them, Moshe said. We're broke. This many *Ivrim* anywhere in the world, not a coin? It's possible?

Listen, Sam said. A matchbox, the label, it's heads.

Roll 'em, Zvi said. Wonder what they talking about in there?

Own business, Yeke said. Look, I'm up four-thirty. Settle it yourselves. Six of you, packing sheds, six tomorrow night. And listen, Aliya and her friends, be nice. Got it? They know they come home. They have to go away. Not like us. We stay. We're home. Why?

Take five thousand years to answer the question, Lod said. Me, I'm in the vineyard at five. *Shalom.*

We were all going out, and Avi came in, both hands full of cassettes held against her breasts, a vision in mauve silk, a leotard wrist to ankle, white feet tiptoe, honey-hair piled in a double bun, flowers on top, and Zuz, bunching fingers, looked to heaven, and breathed *Dio mio, ma che bellezza* and he was right, and we were grateful. He let the air out of our tires.

Look, she said, to Us. We brought these, but somehow we never got around to playing them. Wouldn't you please take them as a little sort of, y'know, memory of us? And play them sometimes? Some of the things we've loved. Danced to. We'd love you to have them.

Ours, we said. We'll play them and think of you. We'll give them to Orit tomorrow. She's in charge of the stereo.

Just so we know you're all going to hear them, Avi said. Wish we weren't going. Love you all. Good night.

Laila Tov, we said. Come back. We love all of *you.*

I saw the way you looked at her, the one-of-Us-with-the-little-secrets, said. You tired of me?

Why be ridiculous? A-minus said. Certainly I looked at her. Nothing underneath? Great.

I'm so ugly? A-plus said. You didn't see me underneath?

I certainly did. Listen, what *is* this? I look at a gal, I'm wrong? She wants to show, I'm going to look. I *will* say this. In the dairy department, you come first.

I'm too small, A-plus says, pulling her arm away.

Look, A-minus says, the Greek, Praxiteles, he made them just your size, that's classic.

But you like the bra-busters, A-plus said. Oversize. The droolies.

Doll, A-minus says. Oversize, *no.*

Flops, A-plus says.

47

Twee, A-minus says. There are times when flop is distinctly acceptable. Especially that type of flop. Which, incidentally, is *not*. That nipple, starboard or larboard, stuck out like my little finger.

Tell you what to do with it, A-plus said. I think I made a mistake.

So I look at somebody wants me to see her, and I'm Bluebeard? A-minus says. Sister Annie, Sister Annie, who do you see?"

It's ungrammatical, A-plus says. "Whom" is what you are looking for.

I'm looking for nothing, 'oddammit, A-minus said. Listen, gal like that, dressed so, I don't look at her, I'm unhealthy.

My secret thought, A-plus says. You had half a chance, you'd be down the kindergarten.

What about you? A-minus almost whined. Looking at that Zvi, the big legs, the mop, the muscle? How about that?

Well, A-plus says, looking up at Mars. You sort of dream about the tangle, know what I mean?

So what the hell, A-minus says. I don't think about tangling? Baby, I could really ball up the skein.

You never balled up my skein? A-plus says. I certainly did, A-minus says. You have the balling-uppingest. If there's one thing I love, it's balling you up.

But it's only because of *that*, A-plus says. You'll meet somebody like that bitch, and you'll leave me.

Hell I will.

Why?

Got the best there is.

Wish I thought you meant it.

Ever know a moment I didn't?

When you look at. Well.

48

Well, what? When I look at you coming out of the bath. *Look* at you. Who's as beautiful?

They're so. Sort of. Dressed up. They don't have to work in the. Darling.

That's enough. We're Us. I catch you looking at.

Darling, no. Please. Let's go home, baby.

Baby. *Baby?*

Well, it's next. Let's go home. *Home.* Beautiful word. With you. *Shalom.*

Shalom, my sweet. You beauti-bitch. Bitch. *Bitch.* Come *here.*

FIVE

Before dawn was our favorite time, a breathing of loam and greensweet, blue silence, a small breeze singing itself awake, birds still too sleepy to chirrup, flying to drink at puddles and preen, the sun not yet alight in green and mauve desert shadow, and We, in Eros-languor, not tired, but lax, in luxury of $A+1=2A+A-1$.

We made coffee in the flask and took it with us to drink when we reached the starting tree, and sat there, sharing a cigaret that always tasted better from her mouth, waiting for sunlight, and the others. No talk at those times, but a prayer of thanks for the marvel of being alive, and to know that evening and night were one, as we were, and they would be with us, once again, after work, after the bath, when the bed glowed white in shadow and Solomon thought that Thy belly is like unto a heap of wheat.

Avocado pears, of the pelt smoothly silk as hers, that day, and we plucked, and drank, and packed, and drank, and before midday, we shared the sandwiches, the salad, the beer icy from the well, Shoshi's cheesecake with the lime and honey dress, and Turkish coffee made in the old black saucepan, a veteran of pioneer days, swanking its bruises as warriors show scars, but ready with a brew, nothing like Aliya's *espresso,* yet with a comfort all its own.

It belonged to the soil, to the men and women of the Beginning, those sleeping under the stars, no roof, no tent, no thing for tomorrow except hope, and prayer, in how many languages, for food, even unto the day. Those were the old ones, and we followed on, we hoped, with their strength, their faith, at least with that tenacity which shaped the land, and now we used their saucepan, battered as they, as forthright, down the days of sweat and hope, the useful made beautiful by work.

Dov came to our fire, and said, Heard this stuff about Aliya? and we said No. What? Making too much profit and not paying her share, he said. Borrowed the money from the fund, and didn't pay it back. Arye won't be out of the Army for another month. What's your idea, they try putting her out?

How, out? We said.

It's our land, Dov said. Building's ours. We could run it, or Shoshi and Zuz could, just as well. And we take the profits. Nice piece of coin, that's what they say.

Who's they? We asked.

Ah, some of the, y'know, some of the others. What you say?

When we hear more about it, we'll let you know, We said. But we'll fight it. So let "they" know. If it's a gang-up, they're out of luck. It won't do.

He went off, kicking stones, and we looked surprise at the saucepan. We never thought that Aliya's success could have made hidden enemies. We never heard that sort of talk. She, in those few months, made us one with her, and in fact we disliked any thought that except for chance, she might never have been with us. We thought of our lives without her, and shook our heads. But is a good cup of coffee, a table and chair, an ice cream, cheesecake, pies, tartlets, Zuz and his napkin, and the music of ideas, in starlight always, or under a moon sometimes, a necessity, or why should it be, or is it so much? For what we did, and where, looking at a world map, yes, it was. We were with—we were among—and even in front—of most of our kind elsewhere. There were few Cafés Aliya anywhere on earth. Those of us travelling abroad came back to tell it, and knowing made us feel more a part of our world.

A look at the map showed us where we were. That little dot made us feel lonely, apart, cut off, even though we knew we could be in Beersheba in an hour, in Jerusalem in another couple, Tel Aviv a little more. It made no difference. The map showed the distance. Sometimes, on some maps, there was no dot, and we felt we had vanished. But with the Café we were brought into Western air, to the streets, the smells of cities, and the happy aroma of our kind, in Aliya's goodness and the hearts of Shoshi, and Zuz, and Orfa and the others, and in Traul's foxgrin, planting here or there overnight, taking out a near-wilt after we went home, that in the morning became a mass of something new, in bud.

Our people taking a vacation abroad never told us— grateful—even shudderingly joyous—almost on their knees —why they were happy to be back with us again, and when we asked, they said this was home, and outside was a wilderness, a hugeous grunt, Lod said, of Gadarene swine in slither towards the brink, but nobody told us why.

See for yourselves, they said, and turned their backs.

52

In past months, Abba and Shoshi, Avram and Tikva, Sam and Miriam were among them, but not one had anything to say, except that the trip was all right for stretching the muscles, and teaching them the rich extent of what they had left behind with us.

The journeys were always fruitful, because most of them had relatives they called on, and few came back without a recruit or two, either with them or following, and oftener, parties of students for a month's work, good for them, and us. We had need of those hands, the hours, and the clearing rakes and spades to bring Israel's hidden garden from a thousand years of desert.

We knew why they were glad to come back to us, with or without recruits. We knew too well those streets at night, crinkled paving, lamp posts, traffic lights, greenish, bluish, front doors, windows, side doors, gates, fences, buses, shops, miles and curving miles, eating places, billboards, light poles, gasholders, coal heaps, bridges, tunnels, canal locks, pools, mud, drizzle, love in corners, the lonely entranced, a crowd *aut*, traffic screech, petrol-stink and a black bane of fuel oil, a steady drip of mawkish futility, a final deathly spew, a fists-to-heaven rage, cut, and go.

We knew that was why, but we never pressed. For others there had been the hounding, for some, a denial of common right. But the majority fled the towns, cities, the *goyim* ghettos. We had no need to ask why they came back. The fear of what they had escaped was in their faces for days, and then the hills held them again, the orchards nursed them, the gardens rested, birds got them out of bed, Negev sunlight brightened their eyes, lifted their souls, and we put our arms about them, and they knew themselves home.

Never again, not even to see the child, not me, Shoshi

said. They can come here. Plenty to do, more to see. Me, go back there? The last days I'm sick to my stomach, I should come home, a stretcher? Outside of this land I don't go. Take it or leave it? *Bfui*.

We were enjoying a blackcurrant pancake and she came round the bar and sat down at the table, unusual for her. Listen, she said, flat face, the stone stare. You hear any of this talk about Aliya? *You* know. Borrowing from the fund and not paying it back? Putting the profit in the pocket, nobody getting a share? You did? When?

Couple of weeks ago, A-plus said. And you didn't say nothing to her? Shoshi said, smooth, no tone. Not a word?

Not our business, A-minus said. We *did* say, if we were asked, we'd be with her.

Not good enough, and not friendly, she said, and stood. You should have told her first, and straight. Give her the chance put a hayfork in that snake, like now, it's all over, and people believe it, nobody arguing her favour? I *know* it's not true.

So why didn't *you* say something, A-plus told her. Are we the only ones?

Listen, I just heard, she said. Zuz goes down the village for Turkish coffee, and they told him—imagine? —he's losing his boss and his job. The collective's throwing her out and somebody else going to run it. Well, he come back here, thought he was going to faint, the temper. So now he's sharpening a razor.

What do we *do*? A-plus asked.

Saturday night's coming, Shoshi said. The meeting, she's got a paper. The facts, the accounts, the money, where it comes. They want a *schtunk im der shtetl*, they got it. Take it from me, this is strictly *Yiddisher Wirtschaft*. We make an example, you see.

The example came after the meeting, that Saturday,

without an absent member. We were crowded in the library, and the usual business brought the arguments and show of hands. When it was over, nobody made a move. By the guilty sweat of their faces, we knew who waited for a victim to howl at, or to stone.

Order of business, Yeke said, from the platform. I stand in for Arye. Doing his Reserve. He said nothing of this. Nothing in his desk. Nothing on file. Nothing in the bank accounts. So how does Aliya borrow money from the fund without anybody telling us? Would Arye do a thing like that? So Aliya, you tell it.

First of all, I want to say I really feel ashamed of this, she said, down front, standing, looking round, and the hair hung. Anything I spent here is my own money. Waste of time reading all this. It's going on the main board. Read it for yourselves. These are the accounts, what I spent, and how. This is my bank statement, to date. Not a cent of the collective's money has been used. I paid for the alterations, the garden, the furniture and the café fixtures. I pay the wages of Shoshi and the women working with her, as well as for Zuz, Traul, and the off-duty workmen, the driver and the electrician. You never spent a cent. When the profits of the café have returned my capital, I want a normal agreement for a share to go to the common fund. Until my capital's back in the bank, you can't expect that. If you want me to leave, say so. That's all.

Yeke stood, hand upheld.

The vote? he called.

Avram raised a finger at the back. Question, he said.

Speak, Yeke said.

So she spent her own money, no permission, no guarantee? Avram shouted. We have to have a new school. Why can't the money be spent there? It's for the children.

55

This coffee stuff, it's so important? We come here to drink coffee? Sit around? Listen, I was here first, you couldn't get a drink of water. So what's about coffee? Get it at home. Cost nothing. Here, we spending money we don't have.

I have, Aliya said. It's mine. I spend as I want. When I came here, nobody got a cup of coffee. Except the instant, at home. It's coffee? If I give you a rubber woman, same shape, same size, you'd be satisfied? The school, that's your problem and the bank's. I don't have any problems. You don't want me here, I can go. But I take what's mine. That's the café as it stands, the flagstones, the watering system, the garden, everything around. That what you want?

We stood up, and said No. She raised both hands.

I have to be careful, she said. This can come again. The type is common. Let me make it clear. I came here to live again. To work with my hands, scrub my own floors, take care of something that's mine. To give coffee, ice cream, it's so small? To work with Shoshi, and Orfa, and Sipporah, and Zuz, and Traul, it's nothing? Look, I use my own money. I ask nobody. Nobody said no when I started here. Who says no, *now?*

Silence.

What makes the feeling, the hair stands up?

Let's have the word, Yeke said. Raise.

All the hands were up.

Pass, Yeke said. Aliya, put up the papers. Let them read. Now, what we have to find, who started the talk? Who is the mouth?

Her own money, so she's insulted? Shoshi said, beside Us, and everybody *mmm-d.* Listen, see that?

Years over the washtub had grown the muscle of Gath,

and she made a fist, bent the elbow, and a mound of power sheened in a bicep not many of us could match.

One welt, a leak in the head, thumb-sucking mother, she said. That missile-*drekker*, I should put the finger, he goes straight up.

Only somebody could get in a word with crowbars, the rush to tell Aliya what an angel she turned out to be, and when we followed her out to the café, we saw what had been the small-store, a planked, dusty corner in overgrown shrubs, a screen of honeysuckle and jasmine, dust, rocks, weeds, and now an oasis, flowered, ordered, lit, a hunger bin for the spirit.

We gave thanks for an Aliya.

SIX

Orit came to us one night with that gone stare.

What? we said. Sit down. Those cassettes, she said. I had music exams. Never had time to spin them. You hear them? Any of them?

No, We said. Why?

Look, come on over my place. Hear them. Tell me what you think. I don't believe they ought to be played here.

Why? A-plus said. Something wrong?

They're marvellous, she said. Finish your coffee. Come on over. Listen to one or two. And tell me.

We went with her across the flagstones, down the path to the stonelaid avenue through the lawn, to the rose garden, and the cactus twist, and the steps up to her apartment. She opened the door without using the key. A para-blouse hung over a chair, and a young man, barefoot, in khaki longs, to the buff, looked at us, nodded, and went on reading, one hand behind his neck, plainly in from days in the desert, and his high para-boots leaned tired against each other in the corner.

I'll play this, and you tell me, she said, and fed the cassette, thumbed the tab. Nothing on the label. No name. The orchestra's top ten, no need to tell you. Listen.

La Bohème but not the tenor. A soprano, a voice to drink. Orit thumbed the tab, took out the cassette, put in another. *La Traviata,* the soprano again, and the para-boy put the paper down, and said, Why take the other off? It was good. Listen to this, she said. We listened to a few bars, and she touched the tab. Ah, let it play, the para-boy said. I just wanted them to hear, Orit said. What do you think? Beautiful, we said. Couldn't be anything better we'd want. Why?

Whose voice is it? she said. Would we know her? Let's think we're lucky. Who?

That's Aliya, she said. You can hear it.

So?

Might hurt her. She wants to get away from it.

All you have to do is play one, A-plus said. She doesn't want it, she says so. That's that. Be honest with her, she can be honest with you.

Play it tonight?

Play it now. Let's go.

We took the short cut across the lawn. Looking back, we saw the footsteps dark in the dew, and Avi seemed close to us, and we wondered if she had an idea.

We held up six fingers to Shoshi in the cool air of the café, and six-and-three to Zuz, which meant two blackcurrant blintzes each, and a cup of coffee. Orit went out to the stereo box.

A first deep chord pulsed, held, and violins niddered, flutes piped, and in a crescendo, a voice floated.

Aliya, between the *espresso* machine and the cash register, lifted middle fingers to part the hair, and turned her back, walked, leaning on the table, running a hand up the jamb, out.

Yeke stood, hands out to Orit, and she touched the tab, and in the silence he said, It's necessary you have a cannon, shoot the head? What is in the mind, such people? The girl tells you. She *tells* you. She finished. You, a musician, *gifted,* how can you do this? What is behind the idea? If it was a man, there would be here a murder.

Orit pushed up the switch with the butt of her hand, took out the cassette, and ran.

Don't put the blame on her, We said. We heard it. It's beautiful. We thought Aliya might like it.

Yeke raised the palms and looked up.

Why she should like it? he whispered. She left it. You know why she left it? You know? So why she should want to hear? Twenty-four hours, she has it in the throat. We don't hear it. Why not? She threw in the garbage. *She* suffers, she hopes she forgets, you kick her the teeth? In the teeth, it's good?

Don't let's get mixed up, Lod said. We know how she feels. We have respect. But there's a talent. It belongs to all of us. Given to one, for everybody. Who denies it?

Talent, fine, Yeke said. But the person? Not important? *Most* important? The soul?

Talent, that's soul, Lod said. You have useful talent? You have soul. Ability is something else. Talent, it's like the heavens. Over all of us. A gift. Nobody has the right to withhold. Colours life.

Wait, Yeke said. She has the right, yes or no?

Punishing herself, she punishes us, Lod said. Unjust. Doing herself harm. How, doing herself harm? Yeke said. It's hers. Do what she likes with it.

60

No, Lod said. It was given to her. For all of us. Without the talented people, what *is* life? How would living be without the talent? No poets, no singers, no musicians? Orit, how much pleasure does she give us? Take it away, where are we? Talent, you have to practise. Work. Sweat. To rob yourself, rob everybody. Because something happened, a bad temper, denial, it's enough? Here, she has a café. All right, all right, it's fine. I'm not saying it's no good. But it's an excuse. It's a toy. Something to play with. The talent, it has to be used. It's what I say. She does *us* harm. She does herself a whole lot more. She invites punishment.

Yeke weighed both hands at the roof.

Please, punishment, he whispered. *What* punishment? From the sky? The Lord God, he takes her by the ear?

Lod looked at him with the mica-shining grey eyes, and nodded.

It's the people with the talent, they won't use it, they perish, he said. They, they only, are the chosen. As the people of Israel once were. Chosen. Chosen to take the Law among mankind. Make it known to all men. What did they do? Sat fat, dressed up, slaughtered animals for sacrifice, took the coin. Had themselves a great time making laws. Six hundred and thirteen they still have. So after they get through, they don't have time for anything else. They were so holy, so chosen, they put on the airs. They probably forgot they had a whole slew of pagans all around. So they were always getting beat up. Taken prisoner. Babylon. Rome. All over. Temple destroyed. I mean, knuckleheads. They couldn't see what they were doing to them*selves*. Withholding a talent from everybody else.

But what the hell, talent? Yeke said. What talent they *have*?

61

The talent of the Law, Lod said. They kept it to themselves. Took a guy called Jesus to spread it. Yeshua. He was a Rabbi. Taught in the synagogues. In the Temple. But he taught ordinary people. Anybody wanted to know, he told them. But the guys up top, they wanted to keep it all to themselves. Wouldn't share the talent.

Listen, so what the hell does this have to do with *her?* Yeke said. She has the right.

She has *no* right, Lod said. She brings the Armageddon upon herself.

It's big words, Yeke said, tired. Who is interested? How does she bring down this stuff?

If you want to know, any talent is the Lord God's especial gift to only a few, Lod said. You work at it, you work with it, you sweat, you suffer, finally you produce. Everybody knows. Everybody's rejoicing. Everybody has what they want. Life is that much better, they hear, or they see, and they dream that much more. And the younger, also with the talent, they have an example to follow.

So all right, Yeke said. She could change her mind.

Better be soon, Lod said. *You* can stand still, except I never saw you. I can, but I have enough to do. Look, the sun doesn't stand still. The moon doesn't. This earth doesn't. Even *we* don't. You think the Lord God does?

I am no believer, Yeke said. I think we getting into something else here. Putting it plain, I don't tie-in.

Too bad, Lod said. You deal with the evidence every day.

What evidence? Yeke shouted. What's the proof?

Diaspora, Lod said. Three thousand years and more. Thrown out. In the desert five thousand years ago. Wander forty years. Long enough for the old generation to die off, the dirty habits, the worship of false gods. So then the Law, the Tablets, the talent. Listening? The talent. Should have been spread. But they kept it to themselves. So? Suffer. Like *she* must. *Got* to happen.

I had enough, Yeke said. Me, I don't believe it. While I got a breath to pull, to her nothing happens. *Laila Tov.*

He went out, Zuz brought the coffee, and we were looking anywhere.

So, Lod said. Everyone must take sides. For, against. Let her go on depriving herself, and us. Or get her to sing. Not because she's afraid, or to keep herself company, But for herself, for us, to the Glory.

Listen, Moshe said. You Orthodox?

Nothing like it, Lod said.

So what's this about the Glory? Moshe said, one eye shut, irritated. Listen, you know we don't swallow the mix?

Glory is what you're living, Lod said. Die, you went some place else. But open your eyes, that's glory. All around.

Ah, come *on*, Moshe said. Lot of stuff you say, I'm with you. But this glory. *What* glory? Listen, what *glory?*

Use your eyes, Lod said. Use the ears. Look at people. Look at girls. Look where you like. It's *given* to you. You don't have to call for it. Don't have to pray for it. No getting down on your hands and knees. It's *there*. All around. Wherever you want to look. Who put it there? Did *you?* You just happen to be living. Open your eyes every morning as if you had the right. Well, you do. Till your time comes. That's marked. You'll go. No argument. You'll just go. So? Who is in charge? You, or somebody else?

Listen, I don't know where we getting, here, Moshe said. I don't like the, y'know, what's going on. This started out with Aliya.

63

Just plain miserable, Lod said. She's doing what she wasn't born to do. What she was born *to* do, it's like flowers don't get water. Dries up. It's good? Like the idea?

No business of yours or anybody's, Moshe said. What's everybody else think?

I think he's right, Shoshana said, two fingers up the cheek, two under the chin. You don't do what you *know* you ought to, you living ridiculous. Never thought of it before.

So tell her, Moshe said. She listens to you.

None of my business, Shoshi said, and pointed to her nose. It stays in the plate.

SEVEN

We decided that Plus A would know what to say to Aliya, and keep to herself any reply, not a word of it known to any other, even to me, or that an effort was made. We thought that proper. Meddling, for any reason, in another's affairs was distasteful to begin with, and gossip little less than pismire.

An opportunity came, we thought, when Plus A had to go into Beersheba with Shoshana to buy material for chair covers, and Aliya asked if she could go with them. We said nothing to each other, but Plus A's eyes changed—more light, or a darker tint?—and when I saw them off on the 7 A.M. bus, there was a kiss on the cheek, and a shake for the arm, because Shoshi told us she was going to her sister's for a couple of hours, and meet at the 2 o'clock bus, he goes without me, that no-good *bum*, fuy*a*, I give the shoe.

All day we raked leafall in the citrus groves, and heaped a compost pit in layers with stable manure, turkey droppings, leaves, and cut grass. Everything rots fast in that sun, and after a month, with a few turnovers, Yeke said, we had good planting material for the new shoots. But it was a sad day for the shoulders, and worse for the hands. They still blistered and broke, never mind what I put on them.

Hands of a woman don't take work, Yeke said, dabbing iodine. Miss your partner? Certainly did, I said. But today would have been too tough for her. She has to have light work from now on.

I say nothing, Yeke said. It should say everything. Shall I say I'm happy? A good, sweet girl, a fine mother is making. And Minus A said, When could we have ten days off? and Yeke said, We got the apricots, We got the pears. There's the lettuce. The potatoes. Plough number three. I don't see how to let you go before the end of the year? and I said, Make up your mind. You lose us Friday-night-week for ten days. We'll be back in order. Nobody knows. Not even you. We in tune?

Everything it's wonderful, Yeke said. Tune, it's lovely. So I lose eight of my team the next ten days, a month? Who does the work? Why eight? I said. We're only two, and Yeke said, You do the work of four. Plus there's also Moshe, another two, and Zvi. Going to Tel Aviv, the university, they have to find out something. Why they don't telephone? Take too long, cost fortunes. Why they don't write a letter? They writing so many, the Post Office quits. Such a subject they have to pick? Now they talk to the brains. Who knows what for? Why they don't just work? Healthy. Books, you go nuts.

You have enough, I said. Walls of them. That's agronomy, Yeke said. The land. Growing the good food. Trees. Soil. That's the substance of the Spirit. Work is the Spirit. Substance, it's music. What you standing on. Neh?

66

Maybe right, I said. Sounds good. Since when were Zvi and Moshe such partners? No questions, no answers, Yeke said. It's good for one, for everybody it's good. *"Lul, Shaphan, Anigron, and Anirdaphon, I sit amidst the stars, I walk among lean and fat men."* In another's window I don't put the head. Get it?

Bit of the Talmud there? I said, uncomfortable in ignorance.

Talmud, it's wisdom, like the earth, Yeke said. Looks the same? Make the analysis, it's different. The Talmud, it's words, also. Analysis, the Book. It's words? Look for the meaning. The difference. The chemist, he tells the kind of earth. What you have to put in, take out. Rabbis tell the same from the Book.

Out of my reach, I said.

You don't believe? She, too?

We don't. God, creative spirit, all right. Judges, prophets, ancient disciplines, yes. But the rest, no. Says nothing for thousands of years of conscious growth. Using your term, we don't tie-in. Since when are you so religious?

Religious, not. Orthodox, not. I believe, yes. The. Well. The. Look. What makes the seed grow a green wing? Makes it keep on coming up? What *is* the power? Ah, *nature?* Tell me, what is the meaning? Or explain to me the energy of the leaf. Or a field of potatoes. Nature? Look, there, the wheat. In the hand, look the seed. Dry. Nothing. Throw it in the ground. Use water. First the beautiful green flag. Then the stalk. The ears. Where from? Look, already nearly a mile, the wheat. How? Nature? We shouldn't worship?

Well, I said, drawn against will. Nothing against it.

So kind. Big the heart. And this power? It has nothing

for you? It does nothing? Nothing is growing because of you? Why do you marry? Sorry. I know nothing. What grows? How? Not from love? And love, what is?

You're rocking a boat. Taking these hands to the nurse before there's an infection. See you at Aliya's. Meeting the bus. What's on tomorrow?

Six o'clock, the apricots. Wonderful, the goodness, the fat flesh. The smell, it's from the day of the Psalmist. "That I may rejoice in the gladness of thy nation." All right with you?

Six is good, I said. *Shalom.*

Nurse Delia's tsk-tsk seemed to take the pain from my hands, and the lotion dried the blisters.

You have to get other work, she said. I'll talk to Yeke. Thinks you made by Singer, he should treadle. Kind of dub built the pyramids. Won't build none here. When you had your bath, pour this on, and use these. All set? Hurt? Not for long.

Curious, the lonely feeling going in the house, nothing moving, nothing in place, nobody singing in the bathroom, no scrub for my back, nobody's back to scrub, nobody to kiss, fondle, paining inside, aching, reaching out for her in that bus, trying to sniff any small scent of her, finding a long hair in the comb, shining, a bright ray in late sun, holding the shape of her, using her towel that had known her silk and her thighs' honeysuckle, and I became myself, no longer A or minus, but one, hungry, thirsty, even desperate for sight and sound and touch of her, my *Lulu,* that in Hebrew means lust, she, one, mine, and I lusted from love, and prayed for her soon.

Soon.

Beautiful word.

The bath was nothing to crow about and my hands

were raw, sore. Why did I work like that, I wondered. I could say no, give me something else. But how could I say it, and Yeke working like a dozen, singing under his breath. He never talked like that before, or, at any rate, to me. He was close-mouth. Do it, don't say it, he often told us, and days went by without a word except to greet in the morning and *Shalom* when we finished. The rest was nods or signs. We supposed he got into the habit by working with Traul. But now Traul worked in the café's garden, each week spreading further beds and plots, and each week the paths were longer, a pleasure to walk.

Nobody seemed to know where Abu was. We had a boy carrying the water jars, but his mix of lemon, sugar and water was sad, and odd jobs were never done. He was a good boy, idle as dreamers are, and with us only until the Army took him in.

While that bus came towards me, and I Band-Aided my palms, I wondered what I was doing with *my* talent, and on the same tack, what my Lulu was doing with hers. She passed her law examinations about the same time I graduated top with a Master of Science, plus a few patents I had done nothing with, useful sometime, perhaps. But what were we doing, working as labourers? *Was* knowledge of law, and applied mechanics, a product of talent? Or was it memorised fact pushed into us? Get the right answer, pass. Can't remember, fail. I thought of those days. Nothing meant anything. The parchment seemed a caricature. What did I *know?* Beside unschooled Yeke, I was a child.

I remembered Shmuel, a good lad, splendid workman, no harm in him, and his agony, the drunkenness, the constant hurt of failure because of examination papers he failed to read. But if his professors had never realized it, what sort of teachers were they? I found it hard to believe. Yet here he was, back in Israel, a labourer.

Like us.

But we were more than graduates. What *did* the parchments mean?

Out in the groves and fields, in the turkey and chicken sheds, in the cattle pens and milch stalls, the tractor park and machine shop, the orchards and fishponds? Nothing.

Up in the hills, down in the wadis, among the stones of the tobacco patches, less. In that fine air, under the sun of the Judean wilderness, in blow of Negev breeze ruffling the green growth of new-planted Israel, what *did* a parchment mean?

We had to forget more than we learned.

I spoke to Arye about starting a workshop before he went for his term with the Reserve. I showed him the drawings, blueprints, patent files, and he said it was worth looking into. Young people were growing up, and once they finished Army service they wanted good jobs, but not always on the land. Some loved it. They came back. Others wanted the towns, the crowds, lights.

They burn incense on the high places, he said. Any wonder they get in trouble? But you're not Orthodox? I asked him, and he said, Hell I am. But I believe in the Book. What it has to say, certainly. It's why I'm here. But which part of it *don't* you believe? I asked, and he said, There's no part of *it*. It's all the other stuff they tacked on. Pretending to be different. I don't go for it. See, there's a lot of people dress funny. You take them Kings and Queens over there, them feathers and all like that? O.K. They like it? Nothing to do with me. I got no say. So when these goats wear a fur cap, and all the trimmings just to talk to God, I still got nothing to say.

It's the way *they* want to be. What they want to *do*.
It's what they *come* here to be. And *do*. They got as
much right as we have to make a goddam nuisance of
themselves, see? I uphold it. But, boy. There's a limit.

What limit would you set? I asked him. Because it
was the first time I realized there was a serious difference.

Don't know, he said, taking time. But it's getting pretty
damn' serious. They even have a ghetto in their own
country. Mea Shearim. The Hundred Gates. Sound terrible? Imagine? Right in Jerusalem. As if we didn't have
ghetto burned in the belly, they have to *build* one. To
separate themselves from their own people? Something
wrong, I don't like it. Lots of others don't. What to do
about it, don't ask *me*. Listen, this idea of yours I like.
Wait till I get back. See, there's a lot of people think
we're doing too much manual labour. They rather have
something brainier. Sit-down jobs. Less sweat. And more
money. So hang on. I believe you have something.

I had known so little of the quarrel between the Orthodox and the secular before that time. Strangely, very few
at Uriel could say what the difference was, and the
rest preferred to know nothing, say less. Lod said the
Orthodox were Ashkenazim of the European order.

They came from Germany and Poland, he said. They
probably saved the whole people. They hung together.
Suffered. Pogroms. Torture.

Avram denied him that noon, at sandwich time.

They think they better than anybody, he said. They
put the big hat, the shawl, boy, they in business. Rest of
us, we came here nineteen thirty-two, didn't have a thing
here, no money, not a tool, we don't count? We started
it. When we got it going, had enough to eat, what happens? This bunch comes in, starts telling us what to do.
They don't even believe in the State of Israel. Independ-

ence Day comes, they hold out the black flag. We going to stand for it? Like hell. Listen, my son got his own bus in the co-operative, they won't let him drive Shabbat? All these families, day of rest, they want to go to the beach, they can't? Who says so? The ghetto bugs. Orthodox. Day of rest? O.K. Why not? But if my son-in-law wants to drive families to the sea, their day off, why can't he? Oh, no. They break his windows, stones and bottles. What the hell *is* this? A way to live, you should have a war every weekend, you want to take the babies to the beach? Or the girl, maybe? What kind of a country? They police, or something?

Believe they have that idea, Zvi said. Social force. Moral.

Throw it out, Avram said. Modern country don't get to live that way. Fur hats, fine. Go and dodder at the Wall, O.K. But stop other people doing what *they* want? Nuts.

They think they hold the secret, Dov said.

What secret? Avram shouted, Goddammit, we had it plain for the past five thousand years. Look the calendar. Five thousand, seven hundred and thirty-odd. What's so secret if you had it that long? Everybody *knows* the dates, everybody has flowers and prayers *on* the dates. *What* secret?

Well. They think things aren't strict enough, Dov said. According to the Law.

Listen, Avram said. We come in here without the law, see? We come back to *our* land. We come *home*. Can't you feel you're *home*?

That's exactly what I feel, Lod said. Take more than them to put me out.

So, Avram whispered, glass up. What's the law? *What* law? Except what we made? If we didn't come here, would they have the chance to pick up a rock and throw at my son-in-law? You know what *he* says? Him and the other drivers? This *megillah,* forget it. Deal with them when we have to. They won't stand a chance.

We spoke about it at home, when we were by ourselves, and she became Plus A, and I, Minus A. It was different from being simply us, in our own names. We were free of all memories, something more than mundane plods, and intent in the joy of another existence we dreamed about and wanted far more than any we had known. Elegiac algebraics, she called us.

But what's the difference between working in an office or a vineyard, or an orchard, or grubbing for oranges? she said. Sometimes I think of a quiet desk, and a nice, big air conditioner, and a hamburger and a cup of coffee. And going home on the subway and grilling a steak. Why am I here?

You *want* to be. You *know* why you're here. Could you live anywhere else?

Boy, she said, wistful as pale pink flowers, I could certainly use a steak. Strictly non-*kosher*. That the thing to say? Look, a grilled pork chop and apple sauce, and some crepe suzette, let's say.

We can go to Aliya's.

No pork chop. No non-*kosher* steak.

Ever ask her?

Afraid to. She sounds *kosher* to me.

Nobody's found out.

Maybe they didn't ask. After all, you can't go up to somebody and ask if they keep all the dietary laws. Here, they should. But I know they don't. At least, they're sly about it.

Darling, you're raising questions a lot of people wouldn't want to answer, Minus A said. Let's just say we

73

don't eat meat with milk or cheese. Or oysters. Or shrimp. Don't seethe the flesh of the kid in its mother's milk. That's core of the reasoning.

Well I agree it's a horrible idea, Plus A said. But just show me a steak, and a *real* Alaska. I'll show you how *kosher* I am. I believe that's what most people here want. Just to be left alone. At last. Do what they want. Don't you?

Anything you say. But it's against the Book.

The people say that, they're old. You have to under-*stand* the Book, that's all. Wasn't written for old people. They just followed on. So they died. Now *we*'re here. Lots of kids growing up. Will *they* want it? Bet most of them won't.

But the fur caps kept the idea going. Generations.

For *them.* I don't believe they kept anything going for my family or for me. We just *knew,* and that was enough. How about you?

Just about that. *If* that. Perhaps the religion kick's dying out. People have no use for it. More use for the brain. More educated.

I wonder. Mommy had no education to speak of. Not as I had. But she's a lot better woman. More principle.

Are there better than you? I never met any.

Only saying that.

Mean it. Turn around. That zip annoys me.

Thinking about all that down at the bus stop, and looking at the long black road looping, suddenly I tried to see how Aliya could have come all the way from Beersheba that night. Nobody, so far as I knew, had tried to verify the story. Moshe seemed to have forgotten his doubt. No word had ever been said in front of me.

Yet, standing there, looking at the road's black stripe

74

against the pale gold desert, I tried to imagine Aliya walking those miles. She might have had a lift to the turn.

But then where would the Bedouin come from? They never travelled the roads, day or night, because of the traffic. I never heard of them taking goats, sheep, camels and asses across country by night. One of the Druse patrol? They were a different type of Arab. But would he offer tea? If he took her back to the Patrol tent, he could have used the telephone and asked for a jeep. But she told us she saw nobody except the Bedouin. I wondered what Yeke thought about it, but then the bus came around the last bend and started the long climb. Which reminded me that beyond sweating that night, she showed no mark of a journey. I noticed the pearl coat on her toenails, and the hair shone even by moonlight.

A dozen of our people got off, then Shoshi, Plus A looking eatable, and Aliya, helping each other with bags. I got a little kiss, stacked all their parcels and them in the jeep, and drove up to the café, and the handclapping of the usual crowd, and Zuz almost dancing. I dropped Aliya's smile, gave her parcels to Traul and Zuz, and went on to Shoshi's.

Listen, she said to Plus A, when we turned down for her place. You say anything kind of gummy to her, or something? Never saw anybody change so. One minute laughing like you cut a watermelon, next thing you know, the icebox got a partner. Well, yes, I did, Plus A said, looking in front. I asked if she'd sing at concerts for a fund to build the school, and we'd sell tapes. You had it right. Ice. That's all. And listen. I never want to hear about it again. If you hadn't asked, I'd have said nothing.

Won't get a toot out of me, Shoshi said. *I* wouldn't have had the nerve. Great idea, though. Real brainy way to raise cash. And she won't? Even for the kids? Guy really did hurt her, didn't he?

Right the way through. I never want to talk about it. That's all.

Abba waited to help Shoshi, and we went on to our place.

Looks good, Plus A said. Hadn't noticed how that blue convolvulus peeps in that climber. Wonderful to come home. To you. But I don't want to say another word. Ever. 'K? and I said 'K. I'll take the jeep back to the park and have a look at tomorrow's work list. Be in bed when I get here, and she said, That's the only medicine'll do me any good. Oh, darling. What a *horror* she can be. Not a word more. All I'll ever say.

I found myself partnered with Dan, the ex-Marine, and I was certainly not displeased. He worked, rarely spoke, never evaded the extra job. Yeke had Zvi as partner, probably the best of us all. We were straw-binding on Number Five, a job that could take a good week or longer, not too hard since we worked the machines, but rough on the physique because of the sun, overhead most of the day, heat rising from the earth, and the hot desert wind raising gritty dust, blowing cool only in shadow.

Plus A was down for the greenhouses, a job she loved, anyway.

I should have been a botanist, she said, and I said, So why don't you study? and she said, I'm learning. And when Boiler Room Bill's a naked fact, and properly weaned, maybe I'll go to Tel Aviv and study. You'd like that, wouldn't you?

I could go for the agronomy degree and be with you, I said. We could come home weekends.

So the chee-ild stays with the nurse all week? she said.

In the crèche, where it belongs, I said. Like the rest. They don't suffer. Looked after a whole lot better than they'd be at home.

I'd have to think that one over, Plus A said. Plenty of time yet. But I don't like the idea of having just another part-statistic in Israel's labour force. If I'm going to have a baby, he's going to be mine. Part of me. Us. Brought up that way.

But listen, Minus A said. By the time, say two years, we graduate, he'll be just ripe to know it's us. What's a baby know before?

Look, if it takes any baby of mine a couple of years to know it's me, I'm giving him back, right off, Plus A said.

Supposing he's a she? Minus A said.

None of that, Plus A said, and stood. If I thought a child of mine would be an Aliya, I'd go on the pill, and Minus A said, I mean a *real* she. Like you.

Back to me, she shook her head.

I have an idea, she said, and held out her hand. Come massage a little.

EIGHT

Yeke was called that because he never talked beyond a word or two. *Yeke-Yeke-Yeke* meant one talking too much, and so calling him Yeke we joked, and he seemed to enjoy it. Possibly only Arye, our Secretary and Treasurer, knew the proper name, but never used it, and when he came back that Saturday in the middle of the weekly meeting, they threw their arms about each other and we shouted welcome.

Arye was thinner, black from the sun, and the khaki shirt and trousers were sweat-curled, and salt stains crawled white. But he wore the silver wings of the parachutist, and the women crowded to kiss him, even Plus A, and I was jealous. As an alien I had no hope of joining the Armed Services or of volunteering. We don't need foreigners, I was told when I tried. And if you become a citizen you'll still have trouble. You don't have the Hebrew. Go to school instead. Any disturbance, God forbid, you'll find plenty to do, don't worry.

Arye came over warm from being kissed and pulled up a chair.

Listen, I talked about your idea, he said, and sounded excited, though that might have been the kisses. Come with me Tuesday. We have a date in Tel Aviv. He's big. You have the papers, details ready? and I said, Everything, and the blueprints.

I told him we could employ minimum twenty to start, he said.

Correct? and I nodded.

Right, well you'll be in charge, Arye said. He'll put in somebody take care the books. I told him we didn't want to handle that side. We'll have the car. Want to bring the girl, she can do some shopping with Dalia.

Too much frenzy for us in Tel Aviv, reminder of what, and why, we packed up, both, to find ourselves where we were. It was a nudge in the ribs from a sharp elbow that all we asked of life was peace, and time to enjoy Us in a green place we helped to grow.

The girls went off, and we took an elevator to the fifteenth floor.

Everybody got the high-up complex, Arye said. They got to have a desk in the sky and a front door to a penthouse, see? Got to. They like to live near the Lord God. Breathe His breath? More bang? Have angels in for coffee, give ideas maybe? Show any these guys a shovel, he's flat on his can just looking.

We waited in carpet, oils on the walls, a fine girl took our names and asked us to take a seat, Mr. Baum had a client.

Arye looked at the oils, one after another, and at me, and hunched a second's-long shrug.

I should complain? he said. How much do I know, I

have to sit here to talk to a guy he loans me money? *I* should have the money, *he* should wait. Frame of mind, see? You want money, you wait, I give the terms, you say yes, else you go out and look at the pictures some more. Frame of mind. So make the pictures terrible, I give up, pay seventy-eight per cent compound, sell the furniture, Dalia should pawn her diamonds, I don't have to look at them goddam pictures any more. I come out in debt till I'm dead. But I get the money, see? That's business. Up here, in some of the world's healthiest smog. Rich, real Tel Aviv juice. Bottle it, they make a fortune from bad breath. Eau de Ecology. Somebody's missing out.

The fine girl moved the legs and held open the door.

Mr. Baum will see you, she said.

Arye, passing her, looked again, and said, Chooki. Isn't it you? Remember me? Tanks? Ovot? and her lashes almost unstuck, and she opened the mouth and said, Why, yes, Who did you say? and Arye said, Beard and moustache, come *on*, Chooki. *Now* you remember, and they wrapped each other and she was dancing. *Ar*ye, she said. Oh, how *won*derful. How have you *been*? and Mr. Baum, an egg in collar and tie behind the desk, said, What's going on out there? I don't have all morning, and the girl said, We served together, sorry Mr. Baum, and he said, All right, come on in.

Arye did the talking, and I gave him folders of type, unrolled drawings, put a flower pot, two ashtrays and a book on four corners of the blueprints, and picked up what they were talking about.

Take a year, easy, Baum said. Permits alone. Just the buildings, and Arye said, I have the best builders in the country. We could go to work tomorrow morning, and the egg wagged side to side. Forget it, he said. Idea's good. I'd want a working model. I don't say it can't be

80

done. Just that it's going to take time. See, every guy behind a desk, he's civil service, he acts like he's a burgomeister. Stuff piles up till he lets it go. No way of straightening him out. He's Moses and Solomon and Abe Spicehandler, or Menahem Ben-Zion, and he's by God the boss, see? Civil Service, even the lavatory cleaners, all you big guys, you know so much, bow down. Abe's the Gauleiter. Think I'm kidding? Go ahead. Apply for the permits. See how far you get. Listen. Leave the papers here. I'll get a tech expert on it. Be in touch, two, three weeks maybe?

Maybe not, Arye said. Sorry we both wasted our time.

Listen, Baum said, All I want to do's help. Capital's available, like I told you. It's the detail, the permits. *Can't* do a job like this straight off. There's steps you got to take, see? Damn right, Arye said. I'll take my own steps like I always did. *Shalom.*

While he talked, I packed, and we were out of there, and the fine girl came down the corridor. Listen, she said to Arye. Tell you what to do. Call me in ten minutes. I heard what went on. I know the money. Forget the other stuff. Right? and Arye said, Chooki, I'm married seven times seven, but we have to have a grapefruit, just us, and she said, Call me. *Shalom.*

That's the Army, Arye said, when the doors clicked. Can't top it. She was in communications down there, on the Strip. Gaza, just outside, this shitty dump, hot, you should fry eggs on your head, and she says, do something for me? and I said, Name it, and she said, You're going up the coast? You pass a pharmacy, could you get me a cologne and this cream, and she give me the flat-out tube, see? So we got in Gaza, and I'm chasing around, and this cop says, Listen, place you want's down here to the right. It's closed. Go around the back. He'll look at

81

you out the peephole. He's had a few attempts. Tell him what you want. So I did, and I got a whole flagon of the cologne, and a box of them tubes, and when I took them back, she looked at them, and she put her arms on my shoulders, and leaned the head. Know something? I'm seven times seven married. But I'll always feel the heavy head. She rested. *She* was *me*. What I call beautiful. The wife know, she'd murder. But I need the grapefruit. Hang on.

He called from a booth on Ben Yehuda Street, and I saw him writing, and his chin moving, and almost felt the way he was smiling. He came out as if he just finished a race.

Listen, he said. I have to go for this grapefruit. Meet you this address, thirty minutes? Right? Going to tell on me? and I said, Certainly.

He got in a cab, and I watched him go, wondering if any girl could give me a grapefruit instead of Plus A, and I laughed, no. Out. I strolled, looked in a bookshop, at windows, at the nonsense people seem to buy, had a coffee at a sidewalk table, bought a paper, scanned the heads, and went to the address five minutes before time.

Arye came late, looking as if he blundered, and led into an office block, an elevator, a dozen people, no word until we were in a waiting room, three other men. The secretary, forties, nodded, pushed up the glasses, Mr. Merom see you in a minute, she said. Sit down.

We stood up, and Arye said, Listen, this is her Daddy. Batte's. He likes the idea. What she wants, he goes for. Know who he is? Brains behind the fund raising. Y'know? The money. Appeal. U.S. South Africa. Just say what you said, show him the designs. This time it's *right*.

How was the grapefruit? I asked, and he said, Out of a bottle. In a street kiosk. Most time on the phone.

Shows you. You get to think one thing, it's nothing like how it turns out.

Mr. Merom will see you now, the secretary said in Russian-English, and opened a glass-panelled door to a short corridor, and a double door at the end. She knocked, and a small door let-in the right hand leaf opened, no sound. We went in, and the door shut in a *fwap!* and I saw the foot come off a pedal under the desk.

Eyes looked at Arye, and swung to me, no move of the head. The feeling was like being torn apart, each part checked, put back wrong. Pale blue, very pale, those eyes, the steady glare of power. Small head, white bristles, pink skin tight over the cheekbones, clean shaved, no jacket or tie, hands like a woman's, delicate in the handle of paper.

The air conditioner played quiet drums.

All right, he said, and leaned back. What can I do for you? Sit down.

Arye nodded to me, and I emptied out the tubes with the graphs, drawings and blueprints, and they talked. Mr. Merom held each drawing as if it would fall apart. I never saw paper treated with such respect.

I like the whole project, he said. What we need. How much are you looking for?

Arye pointed the pencil at the figures in his file.

I see, Mr. Merom said. This is the follow-up? Sounds about right. This building. Tubular construction, asbestos roof, block walls, yes. If you get the go-ahead now, when do you want to start? and Arye said, Tomorrow morning. We don't need permits. Land's the collective's. We pay a nominal sum. Here. This column. Workmen, we have, and we take on extra Arabs. Start clearing to-morrow. I'll have the digger and bulldozer ready for foundations next Monday. They tell me I can have the

tooling machines the end of the mouth. Cash. For training the operators. They'll be our people. All we want's
the go-ahead.

You got it, Mr. Merom said, and sat back, arms behind
his neck. Didn't you serve with my daughter? Down
there, someplace, a hellhole? and Arye said, Yes. Great
girl.

You did her a favour, Mr. Merom said. Went clear
out of your way. Well, anybody does *her* a favour does
me a thousand. She isn't my daughter for nothing. Leave
these papers with me. Don't worry about construction.
Three of these companies you got estimates from, I own.
Couple more here, I control.

But, Arye said, I thought. Well, Mr. Baum told us it
could take a couple of years, and Mr. Merom took his
glasses off, and said, Mr. Baum is a financial middleman.
He looks around for capital and takes a rake-off. Useful
to me because I know who's asking for money and what
for. Me, I don't have to ask for a thing. You go on back,
start clearing. Check'll be in the Beersheba branch of
Leumi in the name of Uriel Collective, three days' time.
Call me here when the money's in. I'll be down there one
day next week to see what's doing. Now, if you'll excuse
me. Thanks again for what you did. She's never forgotten you. *I* won't.

We went out without saying a word, or looking at each
other, and in the street it seemed we were in a strange
place, richer, brighter, wonderful with people singing.
Arye looked at me as if he expected me to vanish.

I don't believe it, he said. He could be just another of
them. Talk. Keep you hanging on. Ego milk. I'm going
to call *her*.

He went in the corner booth, and I lounged along to a
sports shop, trying to see myself behind a trout rod, but

84

still up in the air, the one time I ever *felt* the meaning of euphoria.

Arye came out with the laugh in his breath. It's all right, he said. I don't believe it. But she says it's all right. We only have three days to wait. How will I tie myself down? Let's go and give the gals some lunch. I *still* don't believe it.

So don't think about it, I said. Just let it think for itself. Let it do what *it* wants. What can *you* do?

That's the trouble, Arye said. What?

The girls were in this new place, small tables and chairs, lights making a white circle over, hamburgers and franks, salads, cheese, beer, and we got a tray and filled up, slid the tray along and paid at the end.

Listen, let's go home, Dalia said, dark, small, beautiful. This you can have, and Plus A nodded. I'll take Jerusalem any time.

Give me Beersheba, Arye said. My town. But home, that's better than any place. We got three hours on the road. So fill up.

What happened? Dalia said. Get what you wanted? and Arye said, Do I know? People talk. You believe them?

That kind of a deal, Dalia said. Maybe I spent too much. But I enjoyed it. Got plenty to remember. Listen, who was this piece we saw you with? and Arye said, Piece? and Dalia said, Along Rothschild, and Arye said, Daughter of who's lending us the cash. She was on the phone. To him. No piece.

She married? Dalia asked, lemon-juice, holding a long way back.

Do I know? Arye said. We're in the Army together, and Dalia said, You never told me about her? and Arye says, Why do I have to? The best, why talk?

She looked a smart one, Plus A said.

85

But why wouldn't she call from her own office? Dalia asked, and Arye said, If she's Daddy's ear, why would she? Listen, they all got their own way of doing things. Main thing is, we got the cash.

You *think*, Dalia said, looking through the window. Not the same as cash in the bank, and Arye said, It'll be there, I tell you. Want to give me a bad time?

Bad *time?* Dalia said. What kind of time you think I had seeing you with that monkey?

No monkey, Arye said. Ask *him*, and I said, I was waiting on the corner, there. She put us on to this.

What? Dalia nearly screamed. A put-on?

Keep talking like this, you be sorry, Arye said. Look, I just left a couple of hundred like her where I was. In the desert. Never gets any better. Don't call 'em monkeys. They're the best. Finish?

Voice, eyes warned. Arye was quiet, but he could be a bad one. Dalia had that smile in her eyes, not the laugh.

We heard all about *them*, she said. No wonder you never came home the weekends.

First place, I never got one, Arye said. Second, how could I get there and back? What do you want me to do? Get thirty days in the wire? and Dalia said, I rather have you in there than running wild with them she-asses.

Listen, Arye said. Quit. I don't like the name-calling, and Dalia said, *You* don't? Supposing you saw me with another man? and Arye said, I didn't. Now shut the gas. Making these two uncomfortable.

Do I care? Dalia said. I'm not talking to them.

Ah, listen, Arye said and stood, bringing out some notes. Take yourself back. I'm tired of this.

You're tired? Dalia said. How do you figure I feel?

Any way you want, Arye said, and waved to us, going for the door.

Dalia grabbed the money, winked at Plus A, and ran after him, and Plus A said, He had a guilty look about him, and I said, Come on. Let's catch a nice quiet bus to Jerusalem, and another quiet one to Beersheba. We'll be in the café drinking a cold beer around six o'clock. I'm glad you don't nag, and Plus A said, Don't let me catch *you* with someone else. That's all, and she walked off as if *I* had the grapefruit.

I said, Godammit, she was wrong, anyway. She's asking for him to leave her, and it'll be her fault, and Plus A said, Not while she feels the way *she* does. She's all right. I don't know how I stopped her getting out of that cab. Only because of the traffic and the cab driver was so rude. By *that* time, we were too far, and I said, By what time? and Plus A said, By the time she'd told him his entire family's fortune, in spades, to way back. And *he* was rude? I said, and Plus A said, In four languages. I won't need a hair-job for weeks.

We got a long-distance taxi, by luck, direct to Beersheba, and I slept on her shoulder some of the way, she slept on mine, we had a drink at the halfway, and sure enough, we sat down at the café table just on five-thirty.

The girl brought the drinks, and someone else stood in her place, and I looked up at Sergeant Bar-Ezra, of the Police.

You heard? he said, and I said, Heard what?

Arye and his wife, he said. What about them? I said. We just left them in Tel Aviv, and he said, They got a grenade along the coast road. Car burned out.

I didn't look at Plus A.

Thanks, Sergeant, I said. Can we do anything? and he shook his head.

Nothing left, he said.

Plus A put her head slowly on the table and coughed her tears, a lost one.

I hope, oh, I hope they kissed before, she said, in those torn breaths. Please, God. They *had* to kiss before.

I put a hand on the warm hair, the praying bone, and we wept together, and people saw us, and they knew, and looked away.

Look down, Lord God, upon thy little ones.

NINE

Well, the check was in the bank, and I was off the work list, and without anything to do except put the models together, I felt like a loose button, not on, not off. To make things wonderful, Plus A felt sick. She went to the doctor that morning, and came back looking worse.

He's given me a note to the hospital, she said. Have to go in this afternoon, and I said, I'll drive you. No need, she said. The nurse has to go in, anyway.

No gain in to-and-fro talk, and I saw them off, and went down to the site, and found it almost clear for the digger. That was when I began working. I called the company, and the manager told me everything was set, and the trucks were bringing the machines out late that night for an early start. I said I had lodging for the drivers. The estimating had been done.

All I did was follow the detail in Arye's book. The more I saw of his work, the more I knew the kind of man we lost. The collective wanted me to become secretary, but I told them the new plant would take all my time, and Arye had made it clear that I would be in sole charge, no other duties. All he would have done was supervise finance, which I wanted nothing to do with, and after we had a talk over the phone, Mr. Merom took charge.

Nurse tapped on the door while I was pouring a glass of beer, and she joined me, thirsty from the ride. Plus A had to stay in the hospital annex for two or three days for a check, nothing wrong, but to make sure. I tried not to listen, but I had to. I was frightened. I wanted to go to her.

That would be silly, she said, and she never knew how I hated the comfortable way she settled to drink. After all, she's not born here. No medical record. *These* kids got records back to the minute Mommy went to the doctor. She has nothing. So they want a thorough check. She sent her love. Mustn't forget to tell you. Good gal. What's she, New York? Forgot to ask. Listen, uh. Better now than later. Start again. These things, who can tell? First one's nearly always a problem. But it's always all right next time around. Question of acclimatisation, that's all. Well, I have patients. Thanks for the drink. Set me up. *Shalom.*

Sick of the voice, the unbearable presence, poor old soul, and I should have been grateful, but I could think only of my wondergal, lonely in the hospital. I knew how she must feel. I went down to the secretary's office, but Sam had the key. The only other telephone was in the small-store, and I trotted across the lawn to the café.

Don't get worry, Shoshi said, when she saw me. I had the same thing, come through it like a bird. She be out of there brand new before you know it. Thanks, I said. Aliya, could I use the phone? Come on in, she said, and took

90

out the keys. Make yourself comfortable. She unlocked
the door and I went in.

The small-store had changed. It was up-to-the-moment
in glass, display and variety, but my mind was on that
bed, and I dialled the hospital, talked to the operator,
and she put me on to the night interne.

Just saw her, he said, no panic. She's in good shape.
Asleep at the moment. Just a routine check, normal schedule, that's all. You could see her any time after eight any
morning. Take it easy. *Shalom.*

All right for *him.*

I sat there, in the silence of all those things on the
shelves, each with a name, all of them with a clatter of
thought and planning behind them, perhaps with an
Arye and Dalia among them, all the little houses and
children kept together by them, and I thought about Us,
and if we had made a mistake to come and live in Israel.
Especially here, on the edge of the desert.

But then I realized I was thinking nonsense. It was
here I so-thankfully met her, and she was at Uriel some
weeks before I got there. It seemed to me I was prone
to become a self-blamer and I wondered if, in some sub-
conscious way, I accused myself of being responsible
for Arye's death, and poor Dalia, or if Plus A was sick
in knowing, as I did, that we might have stopped the
argument one way or another and brought them on with
us.

But again I heard the tone of their voices. Banter would
have been out of place, and commonsense went against
interference. A domestic quarrel in public was poor fod-
der for humour, and anyway nobody foresaw the grenade.

Aliya came in and pulled me out of a decline.

Cheer up, she said. She'll be all right. Shoshi was on
to the hospital earlier. All her friends, there. Zuz is bring-

ing you a coffee and cognac. Sit there and have a smoke.
Come out and join us when you feel like it. No hurry.

I nodded thanks. There was a note in that voice I
needed, warm, sustaining, an empathy I had no idea how
to respond to, and I watched her go out, in a sudden
shocking moment aware of her exceeding beauty. Zuz
came in while I watched my mind in somersault.

Thank you, I said, and I heard his *Niente*. I hope she
is better. She is not here, it is empty, the room.

He went out, and the door whispered shut, but I still
thought of Aliya, her beauty, trying to pin down why,
after all this time I should suddenly, at such a moment,
notice, became aware.

What, after all, *was* beauty? I thought Plus A beautiful, had from the moment of seeing her. But why? The
hair, the skin, the eyes, nose, mouth, the figure, her manner of walking, the voice, the smile. So many facets, all
at one moment, herself, wonderful at any time. There
was taint of disloyalty in thinking of Aliya in the same
way. I thought of Dalia, wondering what Plus A and she
would say if my mind were opened in front of them, and
what sort of defence I might offer.

I thought of Plus A, honest enough to tell me about
dreaming of the tangle. But dreaming of a "tangle" with
Aliya seemed the remotest form of idiocy. I became aware
that Plus A and Minus A no longer had a 2A. A worm
had entered, and at a time when she was helpless. I tried
to fight, argue, but instinct knew better. I had to go on
with the outer form. No other conduct was possible. A
hypocrite, born?

In disgust I tried to clear my mind. This Aliya business
might have been a sudden nightmare, a transformation,
seeing in some twisted way Plus A's beauty and sub-
stituting Aliya's. But had I seen it clearly as that, I could

never have felt those moments as I had. I must have known I was thinking, imagining, a baseless phantasy. I was warned by instinct. Intuition seemed too shapeless a word. I got up, stamped impatience, shrugged off all thought, drank the cognac in a gulp, coughed, waited to let the frog out of my throat, and went, carrying the tray, to the back of the bar. Aliya was not there. I felt an immediate, angry sense of loss.

How about a game of canasta? Shoshi said. Won't be many more in till the cine show's over. There's Sam and Gerda. You and me. Right? Take your mind off.

There seemed something sane about it, a game, a form of concentration, thankfully, relieving the brain of what I still felt was nonsense.

Fine, I said. Fill up till bedtime. Another coffee, please.

Won't sleep, Shoshi said.

It's a sleeping pill and a hammer for me, I said. Coffee, any time.

Sam dealt, and I saw the hand in white light, able to think of nothing else. Gerda, my partner, watched me pile the suits, helped sometimes, but luck was mine. The game seemed to pass in moments, and I was walking over the lawn, going home. The note stuck in our—*our?*—door flushed me as a douse of ice-cold water.

Mr. Merom called, in Sam's scrawl. Call him any time.

The note was on a Police pad.

I ran around to the post in the tractor park and found Khalid on duty. I called the number and the receiver *clicked!*

Merom, the voice said, as if there were nobody else in the world.

I had to swallow.

You asked me to call you, I said, and he said, Ah, yes. Glad you did. I understand you have the machines com-

93

ing in tonight? I just wanted to tell you congratulations. Start of a new job. I believe you have a real future. We'll talk more about it when I get down there. My best wishes. I heard the girl you're going to marry's in the hospital? In Beersheba? I hope you don't mind, I sent flowers. Girl in hospital gets kind of awful lonely. Flowers can do a lot. See you soon. *Shalom.*

He left me staring at the receiver. I almost saw his face. I had forgotten the incoming machines. I thanked Khalid, looked at the time, and walked down to the tractor park gate on the main road.

I saw the headlights down on the last loop before the climb.

I had forgotten. He, not.

But who told him I was to marry, or that Plus A was in hospital? Which hospital? Who told him the machines were due in that night? He seemed to have a grape vine. It gave me a feeling in the belly.

I was suddenly, by a force within myself, taken almost by the neck. I ran up to the café and sighed to find it open.

Shoshi, I said. Help out. I forgot. I'm sorry. I've got eight hungry drivers coming in to start work tomorrow. Would you feed them tonight, about twenty minutes' time, and give them each a flask of hot coffee for the morning?

Oh, sure, she said, two fingers up the cheek, two under the chin. What's the trouble?

Nothing, I said. Nothing at all. Except I could have forgotten, and she said, Why not? You got a lot on your mind. Just bring them right in.

I went back to the tractor park, and Khalid and Ahmed had seen the long procession of headlights, and waited, watching. I told them where I wanted them

94

parked, and Ahmed signalled them in, and Khalid backed them into their lanes. But I had fourteen to feed and lodge, not eight. Arye had overlooked relief drivers, assistants on the digger, and the two dynamite men. But they all followed me, and while Shoshi fed them, I ran from door to lodging door, making sure there were beds, and there were. By luck.

I thanked Merom.

I went back to the café. Zuz piled chairs on the tables, ready for the cleaner.

How about a glass of cold beer? I said. *Subito,* he said, and went behind the bar. You work late, I said. Always late, my life, he said. The café, it's the night. Here, people they work early, it's not so late. But early, late, I like.

Zuz, I said, caught in a rare thought. Why *do* you work here? You could open your own place. Tel Aviv. Jerusalem. Make a fortune.

You please to look the window, he said, at the hills in starlight, a velvet of grey and green. Where else I find? I *had* a fortune. What is?

He tugged at a pocket, making a jingle. It's enough, no? Where I spend? For what? No family, nobody, *nessuno,* why a fortune? Here I like. *Basta.*

I saw him back to his room beside the café's new store shed and garage. Aliya's windows were dark, and again I wondered what sort of insanity had come upon me in those moments, standing, now, at distance, in cool air from the garden, but still in fear of an unwanted, till then unknown, excess of desire more savage than I had ever felt for Plus A. But as I thought of her, lonely in that hospital, I could have wept, though my eyes were dry, and when Zuz invited me in for a good-night cognac my voice was steady, and I felt that never again could I be assaulted, or if I were, I would dominate.

His room was large, high ceilinged, panelled in white wood, a carpenter's bench and tools in the far corner, a bed, table, chairs, and on the floor tiles, a Bedouin rug of many stripes and colours.

It is the idea of Aliya, he said. I make the walls. She buy the wood. Years ago I have a few years in the carpenter shop. I like. But the café, for me it's better. The people, talk, it's for me a good life. And if I am near Donna Aliya, what I should want more? But soon, my friend, I think she will go.

Go where? I asked, and he looked at me.

How can such a place hold so much? he said, bunching his fingers in a question. Some *body*, some *thing, psst!*—she goes. Finish. Me, every minute I enjoy. I am afraid when she go in the car. At night. Now. She is out. Where you go? I say to her. Out, she says. Breath of air.

I remembered Arye. Dalia. Supposing.

Look, Zuz, I said. Does the patrol know this?

Patrol, what is? he said. She takes notice, patrol? *Magari.*

It explained the dark windows. But I thought it reckless to point of idiocy. Terrorists sometimes managed to squirm across the border from the East, or they came across, West, from Gaza, and a shot from ambush, a mine, or a grenade was simple enough, especially at night, and a passing car made an easy target.

Where can she go at night, so late? I said.

He waved a bony-knuckled hand, and said, Go, it is fresh air, forget the day. No? Sometimes I go. Shoshi, Orfa. Keep the company. Tonight, it's late, she goes she says, half hour. I say good, go.

But how about terrorists? I said, and his broadened upper lip made the moustache tips almost reach his ears.

Bedouin, they don't like, he said. They find, they kill. Here, both sides, plenty Bedouin. So? *Laila Tov.*

He held the door open and the stones were lit almost to our door, and I went in, to a stinging quiet, and again I thought of Aliya, but those minutes might have happened to someone else. I was cold to her, and scarred in pride to think I could be such a poor fool. I showered, and slept as I always did, with barely a move, and woke before five, knowing I dreamed, but unable to remember.

I went to Sam's house and he gave me the key in a good smell of coffee, and pointed to a cup, but I was impatient to reach the telephone, and coffee could wait. The hospital operator said number one-one-three would be ready to leave at eight o'clock but the cleaners were in, and ward telephones were not in use till seven-thirty. It's a private room, I said, and the voice said, Seven-thirty. *Shalom.*

I booted weeds down to the site, happy to see what had been done only in that hour. Dynamiters were drilling holes in the rocks, and the bulldozers piled earth for the lift to fill the trucks. I went up to the café, and the Druse cleaner gave me a cup of coffee and a warmed croissant, and I sat at leisure to listen to the news, a whisper, on her radio.

Sun was not yet alight on the hills, but the tips were gold, and the trees up there blazed little flames of green, and blue shadow poured down to the violet of the valley, and a stream, silver, frothed over the waterfall to the fish ponds still pink in dawn.

But the hills never sang with half the music, and trumpet and timbrel were never so sweet as sound of her voice from Beersheba.

Come get me, she said, About eight-thirty? Then I'll do some shopping, and home we go. Did you miss me?

I'll show you how much, I said, with memory of the night before starting a worm. Did you get some flowers from Mr. Merom? *Did* I? she said. They didn't have enough vases. Had to use buckets. I'm bringing some with me. What a wonderfully *kind* man. He wrote, "These cheered me up. They ought to do a lot more for you and I'll pray for it." I'm looking forward to meeting him. Not me? I said, still feeling the worm. Show you how much, she said. Come get me.

I went over to the tractor park and found the team boss filling the time sheets. Going in to Beersheba? he asked. Give me a lift? Have to get a couple of spares and a few things, and I waved him in. We turned out, and I free-wheeled the long hill and picked up speed over the bridge.

Going up to the rise and the start of the hills, the team boss shouted, Listen, just up here we blew a tire last night. We all stopped and you know the drill, lead truck kept headlights on, we had working lights, and the taillights, see? Well, it didn't take all of us, and some of us were having a smoke, and this car comes over the top of the hill with the radio on. So we thought. Went by at eighty, easy. Well, we watched it down to the floor, there, and it stopped. It's a big bowl, down there. We're coming to it. Well, somebody, must have been a woman, she got out and walked about, we couldn't see her, and she was singing her kettle off. There's a marvellous echo down there. She could hear herself seconds after, perfect. Scales, you know, ah-ah-ah—I can't do it. Don't do justice. Anyway, somebody met her down there. But she never passed us coming back.

Any idea who it was? I asked, and he said, Too far down there, European car, that's certain. Not a Mercedes. Could have been B.S.U. or one of the French. Or a Saab.

Nobody got a good look. It was dark, anyway. Who could it be? And I said, No idea.

Look, he said, and pointed. Here's where we were. Down there, all the way, that culvert, that's where *she* was. I mean, you think of the risk, it's kind of straight mad, and I said, It certainly is. But I haven't any idea. Erring wife meeting a lover?

You might be so right, he said, and settled back. While the old man's working? You can't get nuttier than that. Anyway I hate, it's a cheat.

I could almost see that worm, and I surely knew its crawl.

TEN

Plus A had to take things more than easy, so I put her in the office for a couple of hours in the morning till noon, and from four to six in the evening, answering the telephone, keeping the work diary, wage sheets, and store lists. The office had an air conditioner, and we brought in a comfortable chair with a cushion, and Zuz ran across with coffee, she said she felt she owned the place.

Certainly she was herself again, eager and wonderful. But the doctor told me to take it easy. Too much of this or that could tip the scale. Be *cir*cumspect, he said, and so every time, she raised a finger, speaking in his manner, and said, *Re*ally circum*spect*, and I had to conform, but it was like taking one bite out of Atlantida's apple. It lessened the appetite. Or time made it ravenous, and that was worse. Circum*spect* became a word to slink from. We both knew it, and in a way it may have been the only answer, because each time, we had to conserve ourselves, ration emotion, stop when it was wonderful, separate, and look at each other, or at night touch, and go to sleep.

Curious way to live, she said, that afternoon. I think I'm going back to the hospital. See if they changed their opinion. Or I *could* go to Jerusalem and see somebody there. This is like having one teat.

I'll take you in tomorrow, I said. How about that Haifa boat to Cyprus?

Like *this*? she said. What's the use? and I said, The name, and she said, Let's wait a little. Might not be necessary.

I had to put my arms around her, and she hung on, tight, but no tears, no words.

I believe she cried herself dry in the hospital.

We were finishing work for the Sabbath, and the *Mukhtar* came to me in the grey-and-white robe, shaven sharp-edged around the beard, white headdress, tall, dignified, distant.

Sir, he said, in his good English. We are not at work today, and I said, Yes, but why?

Sir, he said, our Sabbath is today, Friday. The men wish to work tomorrow, the Hebrew day of rest. They will also work on Sunday, when the Christians rest. There is plenty for us to do, even when the machines rest.

I must first of all see if we hurt any feelings, I said. Come back, please, in an hour.

I went first to Sam in the secretary's office, and asked him, and he said, They want to work, go ahead. Great, and I said, Supposing the others object? and he said, Who? Listen, talk to Avram, and Mordechai in the cannery, and Yeke, and Ya'acov over in the eggs tester. They say it's all right, you come out in the clear. We got no Orthodox here, but there's feelings. You're right to find out. We never had this kind of work before.

I called them by telephone. Avram said, Listen, long as I don't see nobody, it's all right. I won't go no ways near. Yeke said, Why not? We have to finish. It's not their day, anyway. Who's worried? Ya'acov said, Look, just don't bother me who works. I have to work tomorrow else we lose eggs. They don't stop laying because it's Sabbath, and Mordechai said, You asking me? When did I ever have the day of rest, ours, Christian's or anybody else? Forget that bunk. Rest when you can, that's all. Listen, this country takes a half day Tuesday off, the half day Friday, then Saturday all day? That's a five-day week. We can afford it? So let the *Goyim* get the work. So long it's done on time, who's wearing sackcloth?

When the *Mukhtar* came back I said, All right, work tomorrow and Sunday, and he said, But for double pay, and I said, Why? and he said, We work on days of rest, and I said, But you *had* your day of rest. The other days are normal.

But, he said, if the Christian works on his day he gets double pay, and I said, That is the Christian. You are not. Moreover, it is not your day of rest. Do you want to work on the Hebrew *and* the Christian days or not? Remember, on *your* day, Hebrews and Christians earn normal pay. If you work on *your* Sabbath, *then* you earn double the normal rate. Now, you work tomorrow, normal rates, and Sunday? Or not?

We work, he said. But we will not work on our day of rest.

Nobody asks you, I said. *Shalom.*

Not long after, a Cadillac turned into the space beyond the glow of bougainvillea that Plus A had insisted must be saved, and Mr. Merom was helped out of a special seat by his driver.

So how's everything? he said. That gal still in the hospital?

She's in the office, I said. Come and have a cup of coffee. I want to thank you for sending the flowers.

Nothing of it, he said. You seem to made lots of progress here.

Good workmen, I said. We'll be ready for the construction material by the end of the week, and he said, It's not here Friday midday, call me.

The tall man coming around the car had Government written all over him, white shirt, no tie, small panama hat, and a brief case too full to close.

Mr. Efram Olim, Mr. Merom said. He's the tech finance chief. Come to look at the set-up. You said you'd have the models ready?

Over here, I said, and led into the office.

Plus A looked her usual jewel self, I put the chairs out, and went over to order coffee and reserve a table for an early lunch.

When I got back, Plus A and Mr. Merom were talking as friends of years, and Olim had the models spread on the table, comparing them with the blueprints.

Keep *him* company, Mr. Merom said. He's the one you have to convince, and I said, You mean, you got into this without finding out? I *thought* there was something wrong, and he laughed, and said, Look, I checked those papers, didn't I? They're in that brief case. On surface, fine. But I'm always looking for sites. I have three or four projects fit this place. So convince Mr. Olim, and you take the lead.

I felt like an office boy sent to wash teacups.

Just explain this to me, will you? Olim said, pointing to an armature. I can see most of it. Wonderful idea. But this, and this, I don't get, and I said, All right, let's look at what the computer found out, first, and Plus A said, Look, you two keep working and I'll show Mr. Merom the place.

Meet you in the café for lunch, midday, I said. Table's reserved.

No, Mr. Merom said, without turning round. We due for lunch at the Ben-Gurion library, Sde Boker. One o'clock. Pick you up at twelve-thirty, Efram? and Olim said, I'll be around.

Not for the first time I noticed that never mind who, nobody said sir, or gave any account of position. While I showed Olim folios of paper Mr. Merom never saw, I wondered how a man could decide to finance a venture without knowing the detail. I asked Olim, and he laughed.

Trust him, he said. He knows what he's looking for. He's been over your background. You already got a whole slew of important patents, right? So this is protected? O.K. What's he risk? Listen, if I turn this down, he's got a couple of things he can put in here right away. Places like this, no drawbacks? Hard to find. You got the work force here, don't have to build housing, no transport problem, it's all gravy. Listen, I think this'll go. Bound to. Just explain this, here, and tell me what sort of jigs you're going to want.

They're being made, I said. First thing I did. We have the machines coming in at the end of next month. Start training right after.

He nodded, and turned a couple of pages.

What's the nod worth? he said. I have the figures here.

In those seconds of fury I thought of Arye, Dalia, the grenade, a generation of martyrs.

Worth nothing, I said. You realize this has to go before the collective for the general vote? and he said, This is Merom's job. Doesn't need any vote. Wrong, I said.

Here, things are done by consent of the majority. But even though we don't make a nod, and haven't thought of a model, I'll ask them what they think it's worth, and take a vote. Now get the hell out of here. I think I know what kind of a technician *you* are.

He laughed, pushing papers in the brief case.

You should have run a tape, he said. We don't all make a fortune. But listen, if things get rough, remember the time *and* the date. Don't worry about coming out, and I said, You take your own advice.

He went out to the car and got in. Plus A and Mr. Merom were coming over the lawn from the café. I looked at my watch. Almost perfect co-ordination. I began to wonder about Mr. Merom. I turned back to the car, and waited for them to reach me.

Well, young fella, everything good? he called.

So far as I know, I said. Mr. Olim wanted to know what the nod was worth. I said I'd have to put it to the vote, here, and he told me if things got rough to remember the time *and* the date. I told him to get the hell out.

He gave me the steady, pale, pale-blue-power-glare the whole time, and then he laughed, shaking his head.

You're all right, son, he said. If you offered him anything, I know you're a seed. If *he* can plaster you, I know what *I* can do. He can't? It's warning? Now we know who we're dealing with.

Funny way to do business, I said. I don't like it, and he said, Listen, it's the simple catalyst does the trick soonest. Let it sink in. It's a small country. Lot of smart people. Some, a lot *too* smart. There's only one way to find out. Simple as using litmus. I'll tell you this. If you *had* paid him off, you finished with me.

But just a minute, I said. He told me to remember the time *and* the date, and Mr. Merom spread his mouth and said, Why not? You didn't go the first shove, you might *just* go the second. You didn't? I'm happy about it. Anything here doesn't go right, call me.

While he talked to Plus A, I went to the car window.

Olim laughed at me, folded hands between his knees, and reached to open the window.

Thought I had you, he said. Glad I didn't. Know something? Too many do. They're no good, and I said, Listen. I'm remembering the day *and* the date. Anything goes wrong, I'll come looking for *you*, and he said, O.K. Only, remember, my brother's an Inspector in the Police, and I said, What's this? Another threat? and he sprawled, hat over his eyes, laughing, and said, You'd have to pay *him* off, too.

Mr. Merom got in the big chair beside the driver, waving to Plus A, turning to me, nodding, pointing to Plus A, and the driver slowly passed us, and turned for the road down the slope. She took my arm, and we walked toward the café.

What a curious man, she said. He only talked about Arye, and his daughter. Wanted to know if she ever came here. Or if they were friends. I said, I didn't know his daughter, and Arye was married. He wanted to know where Dalia lived, and I said, in northern Galilee. I didn't know where it was, and I asked around, but nobody knew exactly. They thought it was near Rosh Pina. He said, Don't bother. I'll find out. Then he said, Listen, what's wrong with you, you're in the hospital? And I said, Oh, just gal trouble, and he said, Look, you have problems, come to Tel Aviv, I have the hospital in my pocket, say the word. Call me, any time, day or night. I don't sleep good. Then he got on to Aliya. He saw her, She was in for a couple of minutes. He wanted me to call her over. I said she's busy, and he said, Nobody's too busy to come talk to me. So I said, You have the wrong idea, and I called Shoshi, and I said, This gentleman wants to talk to Aliya, and she knew from the way I looked at her, and she said, Aliya, she's in the stores, no talk, not even her own mother, the leg in plaster. So Mr. Merom looked at his watch and said, I have to go, but I'll be back. Sometimes I like him, other times I don't, and I said, Why not? and she said, Well, sometimes you think somebody's you know, nice, and you can talk, and then they say something and they're not so nice as you thought? What did he say? I asked. Well, she said. You have somebody sings here? he asked me, that was with the second cup of coffee, and I said, I never heard anybody sing except after the Saturday night get-together, then we all sing, sometimes. He said, The gal owns this café, and I said, The collective owns, she rents, and he said, All right, owns, rents, who is she? I said, Ask her. I don't know. It's her business. Why are *you* so curious? and he said, I like to know what goes on. Wasn't she a TV star? And I said, I never heard of her. I don't follow TV. Then he started talking about all the things he'd done, and what he was doing in Africa, and a whole lot of other places. It all *sounded* right. I believe he's a lonely man. Just wants somebody to talk to. He wants me to go to Tel Aviv. See a top physician. Friend of his.

You want to go, go, I said, and she said, Believe I will. I'd like another opinion. We can't go on like this. Either you'll go mad or I will.

When do you want to go? I said.

She looked off, at the hills.

I can catch that two o'clock bus, she said. I'll be there before five.

You had this planned, I said, and she nodded.

107

What's going on isn't us, she said. I have to find out why. Mr. Merom's getting me the room. Not costing us a cent, and I said, That doesn't interest me. What *does*, is what happens to you, and she said, Just let me get to that hospital and find out. This way, we get nowhere.

What do you mean, nowhere? I said. Doesn't it matter a damn I love you? and she said, Ah, baby, don't you think I'd rather *know*, and not be frightened? I'm frightened, the way I feel. I go on fooling in that office. Pretending. I won't. I'm going. And look. You stay here. You have a job. Forget me till I'm back, and some use to you.

I tried to hold her, but she half-turned away.

Let's say *I* was sick, I said. Would you let me go off this way? and she said, That's different. You're a man. You have work you're responsible for. I'm no help. So let me go.

I can't keep you, I said. We have no paper, and she flung herself against me, and we kissed as if we never had, and she broke, hands to face, hurrying, almost running, and called, Let me go by my*self*. *Please.*

I looked up, and the Negev's silent blue suddenly filled with a rhab of demons shrieking in darkness, and the hills wisped incense at the peaks, and the Eye of Satanas was red upon me, and I felt apart, accursèd, and ashes filled my mouth.

Dynamite blast shook the ground, and clapped my ears, and the dust ruffled golden-red, and strong breeze pushed it off. In the singing of my ears the sense came back, and I was cold in thought. I went to the office, and deliberately, to take time, I looked through all the files, the books, the diary and journal, and the accounts, all in Hebrew, unintelligible. By the time I shut the ledger, the bus had long gone, and I knew that even if I wanted to, there was no hope of catching it, and—why would that be?—I was comforted.

I drove the jeep slowly into Beersheba, kissing the ground she had covered, almost hearing Aliya singing when I crossed the culvert, thinking no more of her but only of Plus A, those tears, the voice.

At the bank I did the company's business, drew the wages, signed papers, shook hands with the manager, smiled, talked as though nothing in this world was wrong. But I almost ran to the hospital.

Her physician took me to his office, and I asked him what was wrong with her.

If she didn't tell you, it's not the sort of question I can answer, he said, in a brisk, English way. She was asked to come here twice a week for an injection. She hasn't been. If patients won't do as they're told, of course, it's up to them, and I said, She's gone to a hospital in Tel Aviv, and he said, Then she's no longer my patient. I have even less to say.

He stood, waiting for me to go. Can't you tell me if it's serious? I said.

Any illness can become serious if it's not treated, he said, walking to the door.

Can't you give me *any* sort of answer? and he said, No. Ask at the hospital she's in, and I said, I don't know which it is, and he said, It can only be one of two. Each has far more facilities than we have, here. Probably better off, and I said, Why *is* it you people are so *bloody* harsh? If that's the word. Not just you. You seem so kind on the outside. All smiles. *Shalom.* You know what I mean? But just not even a tone of voice, you change. Becomes damn' near brutes. Why?

Look here, he said, closing the door, and coming back to the desk. I've got work to do. But I'll take a couple of carefully selected moments. My ex-patient has left you. You try to imagine how she could possibly do such a thing? Perfect male reaction. But there's another side of this, d'you see? You're dealing with an ancient people. They aren't ordinary people in that sense. They're perfectly ordinary to each other. But their reflexes are quite different from anyone else's. I've said an *ancient* people. They have the ages in their genes. They've never been deflected from being them*selves*. They insist, under any circumstances, on *be*ing themselves. As such, many of them are often psychic quicksilver, but self-willed, untamed, and obdurate to point of self-murder. What has this to do with your question? Everything. She made up her mind. She'll do exactly what she knows she *must*. For *every*body's good. You follow?

I think I do, I said, and moved. Hadn't occurred to me. Thank you.

Absolutely nothing, he said. You're not Orthodox, I take it? and I said, My mother was Gentile, and he said, Yes. Difficult situation. Well. Good luck. *Shalom.*

I would have given everything to say that word, or any word, anything to get the ache out of my throat. Behind his voice, I seemed to hear him trying to encourage me, and I resented it for some reason I made no attempt to analyse, though I knew it to be childish.

Lord God, help her, help me, I prayed, but the trucks, the cars, the women with their children and shopping bags, and the Army girls, and blind beggars, all laughed at me.

And I laughed with them, because, in Beersheba, City of Seven Wells, if you look at a map, why not?

ELEVEN

Batsheba at the Baum office I found without trouble, and I told her about Plus A, and said I was not at all sure about Olim.

Look, she said, Just stop worrying, will you? I'll find out where she is and I'll let you know. As to Olim, you have to let my father know his own business. He does things *his* way. They never go wrong. So take it easy. Any trouble call me. He's in Europe at the moment. Is everything else on the line?

Everything's great, I said. Just that I'm worried.

Don't be, she said. I'll call you.

I waited. Other than that, I had more than enough to do. The buildings went up as if by a trick. Day after day, I could hardly believe it. What was waste ground, before, now held five long one-storey buildings. I asked Aliya if Traul could plant the gardens for me, and she sent him, and he stood there, looking, and I tried to talk to him, but he turned away and walked towards the café.

I had classes for the operators, mornings, late afternoons, and at night, and at the end of every day my
head seemed to gape, and I went home and slept. Shoshi
sent in a woman to clean, and look after laundry, and
Zuz came over with meals at midday, and at night,
and one night, he was clearing the tray, and there was
a rap on the door, and he opened it wide.

Abu smiled, Traul behind, and Moshe making three.
Abu wore Arab dress, a long brown garment, a wrap
of hand-made Bedouin linen, and the maroon-and-white
checkered headdress and black cords.

Look, Moshe said. Aliya asked me to come across and
translate. You want the garden planted here? and I said,
Yes. Ask his own price, and he said, He's going to tell
Traul, and sometime this week, he's sending the plants.
His office'll call me, and I'll call you. Payment on delivery.
O.K.? and I said, With me, it's settled.

Abu knelt down in the white moon, and pointed, and
scratched in the ground, and Traul's foxgrin nodded, and
the fingers flew, and hands brushed each other in whispers of primal chatter. At the end we walked Abu back to
his truck in the park. He refused a drink in the café, and
we watched him turn down for Beersheba.

They tell me he's got a real business going, Moshe said.
Gardens, and that. Good luck to him. He works hard.
Come out here, a favour. Won't take money. We'll see
about that, I said. I'll leave it to Traul.

All you can do, Moshe said. Aliya wants for you to
come over. You been missing too long, and I said, I'll
release the class first.

I went in the makeshift classroom, and looked at the
clock, only three minutes off the end of the session.
Twenty-eight girls were learning how to coil wire, and
eleven men cut aluminium and copper sheets in micro-

sizes. I used a tester on the girls' work, and got a flash in all of them, to their delight, and tried calipers on the men's work and found them correct, a useful week's training, and I told them so, and wished them Good night, and got a chorus of *Laila Tov*. I too often forgot to speak Hebrew.

For the first time in almost a month, I went in the café, to Shoshi's arms-wide welcome, and Zuz's figure-of-eight flick of the napkin at the vacant table. People crowded to ask how things were going, most of them mothers and fathers wanting to know how their daughters were getting along, and I had to tell all of them, in the long sh-h-h-h for silence, that they were all more than up-to-scratch, and they all had a job when we were ready.

When is this likely to be? Sam said, with both his daughters in class, and I said, Towards the end of the month, when the machines are bedded. We don't know yet, and he said, Anything likely to hold it up? and I said, I don't see anything. The machinery's all here. Just wants fitting.

Everybody started talking, and that was when I felt lonely, and I knew it was why I had avoided the café.

I was by myself.

I wanted to quit. Not just the café, but the place. Many times in past weeks I had been at point of walking out of the office, driving the jeep to Beersheba, leaving it in the Square, and taking the first bus north, anywhere. But I was held by a sense of duty to those rows of lustrous heads engrossed in strange work between brain and fingers, and the heart was not in me to leave them.

Batsheba had never called. I could never reach her, however many times I tried at all hours of the day. She was out, or gone on vacation, or visiting her family, until

I knew the tone in the voices of the various secretaries. I had no time to go to Tel Aviv later in those early weeks. Twice, I went, each time to call at hospitals. I found no trace of Plus A. Nobody knew a thing about her.

After that I was held at the site. Too many were dependent on me. I accepted. But going back to that house at night was like entering a silent, screaming inferno. I saw her, felt her, dreamed, hungered, and I was tired, and I needed her.

But then, not.

That morning, I knew, because the air was sharp in the nostrils, and I wakened as to the trump of doom, no longer the yearning half-dead or mutely howling bereft of love, but silently, savagely, myself.

Along the wall of the main building, an Arab mason plastered the last partition. Thin mewls brought him about, and he dropped the trowel to pick up a bundle, rummage inside, and bring out a baby's bottle, tip it, and move, one foot to another, in soothe. He looked around at me, half-smiled, half-nodded an excuse, and I put a hand on his shoulder, seeing black curls, small fists, milk bubbles, and an idea sprang.

Shoshi stood at the parcel tables when I went in the laundry, and I told her, and she called a girl, and we walked back to the main building. The baby lay in a swaddle of blue goat's-wool, and the father worked, pausing when he saw us, almost with fright in his eyes. The girl calmed him in Arabic.

Tell him I'll have the baby down at the crèche, Shoshi said, taking the child. He'll get soaped and nappied, and a clean bottle on time. How can he work and look after him?

The girl spoke, the man talked for moments, and the girl said, His wife went back to her family on the west bank. He say he goes there to find her. He will cut her throat.

Oi, a gentleman, Shoshi said.

He comes on the bicycle every morning, the girl said. The family won't look after the baby. The woman and him never married.

Ask him what he wants to do, I said. Leaving the child at the crèche costs him nothing. He'll be looked after by professional nurses.

The girl spoke, the man questioned, and she said, He is afraid they will kill it, and Shoshi said, Tell him he's one of his own asses. Certainly I'm going to kill him. Make a pie. You tell him I'll take care of him. Anything happens, he can kill me, he should duck. Tell him, find me in the laundry, three o'clock.

The girl spoke, the man looked at his son, with a little finger touched a fist, looked at Shoshi, the size of her, and nodded. Shoshi took the bundle, crooned, and walked towards the crèche.

In the quiet morning, we heard her all the way down in the rose garden, and the mason trembled, flat-faced, crying, and the girl tried to wipe the tears, but they ran, dripped in light.

I patted his shoulder, and went on, to the office, and sat there, and it came as a dream that I never wanted to see Plus A again. A desert was in me to think that a son could have been mine. I tried to imagine what had happened to that passion between us, the strength, the words.

Lies?

I decided then, never to think, or waste a thought.

Salah, one of the Druse girls in the office, came to say that the Absorption Center for placing incoming specialists had sent us seventeen, all in on the bus, and would I see all of them? and I said, One at a time.

English, French, Italian, German, Polish, Russian, Romanian, Czech, they came, each with credentials more imposing than mine, one, a Georgian, recently a physicist in Bialystok. I put them all on the payroll, knowing they were cleared by our Intelligence, and became a guide, showing them what I intended to do, and how I foresaw the unit's growth. Only two understood a little Hebrew, but they all spoke good English, and several other languages, and Mayerkopf said, That is why I applied. Everybody else wanted Hebrew. But after all, English can be learned. Hebrew comes only with the skin. It's in the womb, or not, and Arendts said, But the Israeli, it's a language? and Nahum said, Not even in the time of a generation, they created a land for themselves, *and* a language? Out of the desert? Don't look a healthy Phoenix in the mouth, my friend. It's only a miracle, and the Russian, Mayerkopf, said, It's good I hear this.

They all went to work, taking the machines out of the crates, and I went, of course, to Shoshi to find them lodgings, and where to eat, and she and Abba took the jeep to Beersheba to buy overalls and working shoes for them and the girls.

There came a morning, and Mayerkopf waited for me. Thirties, spectacles, short, bald, he seemed apart, subject and emperor of his own world. You mind I speak? he said, and I said, Say on, and he said, This layout, here. You don't do better this way? and I saw from the diagram he was right.

You were a planning engineer? I asked, and he said, It was my thesis. You take charge of emplacement, I said. Choose your own staff.

And so, in the quiet of the Negev Hills, among the rocks, and in brightest blue of sun-dry skies, we built day after day, speaking little, living full.

One morning, we were ready, and the clock we made began the strike of six.

In silence we stood, all the girls at their tool desks, men at the machines, Arendts at the board, looking at me, one hand on the power switch, and on the fifth chime I nodded, and he pushed contact on the sixth.

All the coloured lights glowed, all the machines hummed, all the tool desks lit, and all of us, without any sign, joined hands, and we sang, though I shall never know the song, and we danced, and I had never danced before, and we kissed, and at last I knew that these were the pure in heart, the children, and I remembered the Word, They Shall Inherit The Earth.

But those were dreams, no stranger than reality.

We were making timing units in the Land of Simeon, and giving eyes and feelers to deep-sea ships and coastal fishing boats, oil rigs and water drills, cutters for cloth, and metals, and all from the clever hands of girls, and the blessed heads of men, all of them brought back to a land by a Voice in the blood.

At noon, Mayerkopf came to me with the sixth-hour report.

We are twelve percent over estimated production, he said, and put a paper on the desk. We could triple our staff, and I said, We shall wait for the daily average of the first month. In the meantime, I shall ask the *Mukhtar* to bring in Arab girls. Let us see if they have the intelligence.

I found him in the village café, at a table apart, smoking the hookah, and I told him, through Bir Ramlah, the interpreter, that I could employ thirty of his women, and supply transport to and from, and food, and I showed what their wages would be.

But he shook his head.

They would earn more than the men, he said. There would be trouble. With so much, would they wish to marry? And I said, I will find work for the men. I will pay them more. But for every woman, only one man. You will be responsible to me. If the women are not suitable the first week, they will not be employed. For every woman sent back, one man will go with her, and he said, No. The man would kill her. The men of her family would kill him, and I said, Very well. When the women are found and trained, and they work well, I will employ one man for each, and he said, What will the men have to do? And I said, They will break the rocks for a road, and he said, I will find the women. No man would be such a fool.

On the morning after Shabbath, thirty girls squatted in front of my office before six in the morning, so they must have started walking before four o'clock. I spoke to them all through Salah, schooled in Beirut, and well aware of herself. I put her in charge, and Malka, one of the top operators, became their instructor.

At a few minutes before noon, the *Mukhtar* came to see how I was treating his girls, and I took him into the classroom, clean floor and whitewash, air-conditioned, with a blackboard, and on the walls, one-hundred-times larger scale models of what they were to make, and he listened to Malka explaining how to stretch a wire from point A to point C without touching B, and shook his head, and turned the mournful eyes, and nodded outside, and we went.

How will these girls marry? he asked. They will know more than their husbands, and I said, the men shall learn the machines. What you saw is the work of women. They have small hands. Used to a tenderness with children.

But only men work the machines. The machines are the camels. They need strength.

I showed him the main machine shop, each lathe with a man, and the co-ordinators at their desks, and the computerists taking notes at the banks down at the far end.

Send your young men to me, I said. Not those who plant tobacco in stones and wait for harvest. Not the others who sell what was born of the year. Send me those wishing to save for their own house and vineyard, and dream of sitting under the cool airs of their own fig tree when the shadows grow long, and wine has no taste.

Even I have no wish for this, he said. It comes too soon. Let them race their camels. *Saalam a'leichum,* and I said, *Shalom.*

TWELVE

In pauses between paper work and supervising classrooms and the work area, I thought of the *Mukhtar* and his responsibilities.

If the Arabs came back to rule, either by victory in war, or by political error, and it was proved he worked with us, he would die with his family, and so would all my girls, and anybody else employed in any work connected with us. I knew how he felt. But I had no idea how he thought. I had to strengthen our position. Shoshi found another nurse and started a crèche for Druse and Arab mothers, and the doctor came in twice a week to look at them and their babies. More girls came for employment, and more married women. A bus dropped them at their homes along the road, and in the morning collected them, and we started a school for the older Arab children.

Meantime I became a work hermit.

I began before six in the morning, I ate lunch in the office, and had coffee through the afternoon till we closed at four o'clock, and then started on the paper, finishing often after ten at night and going home, thankful to Whoever, to crawl in bed. Shoshi sent a girl to look after the house, though I never saw her. But flowers were always in the vases, and the rooms were too tidy.

Meanwhile, our packers piled the crates, and trucks took them away to Tel Aviv, and the files got fatter and the office grew more desks, and more girls worked, teams and classes were larger, the graph in the main office climbed, and I was still a hermit.

I knew it in certain moments. Salah, promoted to the office, got on a chair to open the window and shone the long leg, and saw me, and pulled the overall down, and the button broke, parting on a white mini-bikini.

I walked out with flame shooting in all my world. But why? She was to be married. Why should another man's woman excite me? This was exemplary thinking, and a code had to be maintained. This was my training. But it was far from my feeling. I had to grope for the verities, and tussle, knowing all the time I was being the righteous fathead. I knew what I wanted to do. But duty was paramount, and I asked, kept on asking, Why?

Kar, secretary of the commune above us, came in with three of his senior members, and stood in the doorway, workclothes, whiskers, sandals, air of parched will.

We like to know what we have to do to get in this workshop game, he said, and I said, Game?

Well, you know, he said. We been told things are shaping here, and Arye promised us he'd do what he could. We'd like to diversify. It's the new word. We don't have the members to work any more land. They're getting old all the time. Want quiet jobs. Use the brains. Instead of all these Arabs, you could use our people. They might do better.

121

Do you have the capital? I asked, and he said, For the right kind of scheme, we have all we'd want, and I said, I believe I have the idea. I'll get on to the Merom Co-operation and see what they have to say.

What's the Merom Co-operation? Groz, one of the seniors asked. We don't want to get swallowed, and I said, They sell the product, and they pay us. Outside that packing complex, we have no problems. Expect to hear within the week.

Merom and Olim were out, and I spoke to Roch, the treasurer, and he said, I'll call you back. By the way. You don't draw on your bank account, I notice, and I said, I didn't know I had one, and he said, Ah, look, don't you ever read your mail? and I said, Not if it's in Hebrew.

I heard a silence, like thunder, rumbling, rumbling away.

You're no businessman, he said, almost laughing, and I said, I don't pretend to be. I'm an engineer. There, I have competence, and he said, All right, now I see what's been going wrong. I'm sending a treasurer down there. The man you've got never wanted the job. His wife didn't. Too lonely. Look, I'm going to call him right after this, and tell him to report here tomorrow morning. All right with you? and I said, Fine. I never even talked to him, and he said, So for heaven's sake, how are things going so good, you don't see the figures? And I said, I have my own, and they're not in books. They're in boxes.

I see what you mean, he said. The new treasurer's going to be there day after tomorrow. Give you time to fix an apartment, and all like that?

Plenty, I said. I'll see he's comfortable, and he said, What do you mean, *he?* This is distinctly *she.* Top. Best head for a set of books I ever ran into. Incidentally, one of the old man's apples, and I said, What kind of apple? and he laughed and said. Not *that* kind. He put her through school. Almost like family. Her daddy died. Friend of his. So? He's interested the past fifteen years. Like his own daughter. I wouldn't say she's smarter. She just has the head. Call you back.

Why did I see the long line of Salah's leg? Why, the shine of the silk stocking, the sheen of pale flesh? I fumbled at the dial to call the accountant I had never spoken to. He was out. His assistant said he was in the café, and she would call him, and I said, Don't bother. I could still see that leg, the white, crumpled, inverted linen triangle, imagining what dark silken wonder lay behind.

And the moral artillery crashed *Nonsense!* A girl, like any other, and why waste time? But something wept, someone sobbed, somewhere a joy was lost, a hymn blunted, and I went in fury down to the machine shop to find peace, another rhythm.

Lodging for the new treasurer was difficult, and I thought of leaving my place, and putting a bed in the room next to the office, but again Shoshi found a billet behind the small-stores, where stock had been kept until the main storeroom was ready. That little suite had been meant for a guest, but everybody forgot it, except Shoshi. When I saw it that evening, it was scrubbed, painted white, furnished with a bed, lamp table, wardrobe, a rug, and heater, and the living room had an armchair, table, small chairs, a rug, a few prints on the walls and a big divan with a goat-hair cover.

Did my best, Shoshi said. She knows anything, just take a couple of days, she'll be home. All she got to do is ask, and I said, I think you did wonders, Shoshi, and she said, Abba fixed it. He painted out. Did it for you. Hope this new kid rates.

It must have been a month since I had seen Aliya, and I went in the café almost fearful, why? *Why?* Asking myself why, I saw her by the *espresso*, and the shock of her beauty stopped thought.

What word is beauty? What other word is beautiful? What, exactly, the meaning? Is it the mask? Is it light from the eyes? A smile? A luminous warmth in an aura of greeting? Something released in the self? A heat between her wonder and my hunger? Her hunger and my greed? Her self, my self? I saw from the instant dark of her eyes, the deeper smile, that she felt. I know that innocently I showed what I felt for those idiot moments of shame, though why shame? I felt what I felt, and then pretended. But I knew I was caught by Shoshi's eye. I felt her hand on my back when she passed to go behind the counter.

Stranger, Aliya said. Don't you like me any more?

Not much, I said. I have to work over there. Why don't you come over? You're shut when I finish, and she said, Now, listen. Days, I have enough to do. All *you* have to do is tap on the door when *you* finish. Everything here's yours. *You* know that? and I said, How *could* I know? and she said, Listen, any of that don't-know stuff after this, we aren't on speaking terms.

But, I said, it could be late at night, and she said, Don't you think I'd love that? A late talk? Anything better? I read before I sleep. I read and read. I *must*. But I'd so much more love to *talk*. After all, if you can't say what's *in* you, if you can't give *out*, you're a mental basket case before you know. Oh, I can talk here. Sure, But I mean, *talk*. Why won't you *please* come over? Even just for a few minutes? I'd *love* it.

I'll be over tonight, I said. Sometime after ten.

Be waiting, she said. Zuz'll bring your coffee over.

The cognac's on me, and I said, Why not make it two, on me? and in the straight stare, half a smile, alight in some way, at, or near me, she said, Nothing before ten at night. So come on over.

Zuz answered the telephone before he brought the tray, and said, Four of the Army waiting, the office. I tell to the girl, give him a chance, the coffee, it's hot.

I drank the coffee and the cognac, and I smoked a cigaret, and all the time I was thinking of ten o'clock, and that vicious seethe of feeling, or what else was it? What *is* passion? What *is* that rod-muscle in the crotch? Something medical, or psycho, or a joke? I had to ask the questions, but I had no answers. I knew a great deal about how to put together wire and this and that, and I had a certain control in higher mathematics, though why higher I was unsure.

But I had no knowledge of myself. I knew far more about a machine. About myself, less than nothing. I was even unaware of how I thought, or what process permitted me to think. I was producing a small item, which once I had imagined, and now was being packed by the gross, and I was about to produce a larger unit which it would profit the commune to make. But although both could be transferred from the ideas-world to the practical, I had no conception how the ideas occurred, or how I knew how to bring them into being, and even less how the sight of a girl's leg could disturb me, or any reason for the completely foreign—though how could it be?—invasion of what had been a sober mind—though not if I thought of afternoons—if only of them—with Plus A—what *is* sober?—and the moments-long searing heat for Aliya.

But searing, where? Heat, what? Passion, which?

All I had was words. But the words represented nothing. There were no words to explain or describe any small part of what I felt. I was well aware of what I was feeling. But there were no words. I went all round, I mazed, and labyrinthed, but nothing gave answer, no phrase or sentence, no single word meant anything to compare with how I felt, and I began to fear I was trapped, without light or outlet, or any surcease except, and instinctively I knew it, with a woman, to explode all sense within her, and lose a birthright, gain a blessed cleansing, a freeing, a solace, a relief from words in joyous romp far from the mouths of men.

Back to the office, the lawn, the honeysuckle, roses, jasmine, still with an echo of ten o'clock, and four Army men, none with badges of rank, waited for me.

What can I do for you? I said, and one of them said something in Hebrew, and I said, I speak English.

Right, he said. You've got a lot of Arabs working here. We've been over them. They're all right. But just for the record, how many people here know how to put this unit together? Could anybody steal one, complete, let's say, and whip it over the border?

The only team putting these components together are all in one room, I said. They're all ex-Army girls married to serving soldiers, except two, and they'll be married next month. Even they don't know exactly what they're putting together, because the inspection team is four girls, in another room, and *they*'re married to Army men. I doubt they know what the units are for. They've never been told. All they have to do is test. If the unit works, it passes. Then it's packed. The others including the Arabs, simply make components.

Would it be possible to smuggle parts out? one of them asked, and I said, All parts are numbered and counted. If a part were missing, all the bells would start ringing up and down. The entire work pattern would come to a halt. That part would not be on the assembly line. We'd look for it.

Nobody could steal bits, or a complete unit? the officer said. After the plant closed?

Bits wouldn't be any use, I said. Units, by parts, are counted by the computer. The girls do the rest. And they're pretty good. When the line shuts down, there's nothing to steal.

Could we put a couple of our own girls in here? The senior officer said. We'd like to be sure, and I said, Bring them in. Place them where you please, and he said, Do you have Israelis working with the Arabs? and I said, Of course. They all have to go through training, and he said, All right. Put them in with the Arabs. They'll be here tomorrow. Treat them like the rest. We'll be in touch. *Shalom.*

A truck backed into the space between the office building and the next, and Traul jumped out of the cab, putting a couple of the officers out of stride, foxgrin and fingers telling me he had the garden ready to plant, and I waved him on. All the cuttings, most in cans, were unloaded, lined by the dozens in shade, and Traul stood under the tail, catching the trays of plants his mate threw out, stocking them in half dozens, and piling the small sacks of bulbs.

He, and four Arabs from the village worked into dusk to plant two spaces between three buildings, going back now and again to check by Abu's sketch. I looked at it, but I saw nothing so much as a rune, though when I put on the flood lights, all that was planted lay in odd and oblique patterns, and Wilma, the collective's gardener, came to look, and said, You'd never do better, and I agreed, and went back to work.

But my mind was on ten o'clock. Deliberately I took out the blueprints for the new commune venture, and made adjustments to conform with what we were making. It would give our product far more value because the two together made a unit of micro-size which could displace an entire floor of present day, that is to say, five-year-old machinery. Thinking about it, the telephone almost electrocuted me.

Merom, the voice said, Thou shalt have none other God, and I said, Good evening, and he said, Still working, uh? Listen, I like this new proposition. Sounds about what they could do. You like the people up there? Kar, and them? and I said, They're first class. One of the top communes in the country. They know what they're doing. Mean what they say.

Glad you feel that way, he said. I have the record in front of me. Listen, Roch told you I'm sending down a gal I trust? Means you can put all the weight you want on her. She's trained. Taking her own secretary. Also trained. I've given her instructions to translate all the contracts, all the correspondence and accounts, and read them to you. I'll say it again. I told her to sit you down, and read every last word, in English, right up to date. She will also instruct you in the matter of your bank account. There's a lot of money. You could invest.

No interest, I said, and he said, Let her handle it. See you soon. *Shalom.*

The clock chimed ten-fifteen. I ran down to the rose garden, through the arbor, across the lawn. The café was shut, dark. But light to the shipwrecked never raised a heart to such palpit as mine to see her window, an orange square, ribbed by the venetian. I tapped at the door, and instantly the light above flashed white, and Zuz opened, and stood aside for me, and Aliya, in the

128

armchair, took her spectacles off and put down a magazine.

At last, she said, sounding happy enough. Zuz, just leave the buffet where we can reach it, and you may go. *Laila Tov.*

I heard the pause of his bow, and the door closed, and Aliya waved to the trolley.

Help yourself, she said. Seems you've had a tough day. The commune people were in tonight. Real excited about the new job. Look, let me ask you something, first. I'd like to study math. I used to be good. Could you look at this, and tell me? I'm told you're a whiz.

She gave me a copybook. In a few pages of her tiny script and figures, I saw her reasoning held up, but her method was ancient, of the old school.

Find a tutor, I said. Go back a little, reformulate, and start again. You should do very well, and she said, I thought of getting someone in Haifa, two or three times a week. I could air taxi in for the morning. Be back here by four, or so, and I said, That's a good idea. Plenty of mathematicians there, between the University and Technion. They could probably use the extra cash, too.

That does it, for me, she said. You don't want the job?

Did I hear an nth tremor in the voice?

No, I said. First, I haven't the extra time, and second I'm not a tutor, especially for what you want. My field's, let's say, space, distance, force. The rest, I'm not interested. Poor little me, she said. Straight amateur. Wasting everybody's time, and I said, I disagree. Nothing like it for keeping the mind sharp. Matter of fact, I'm surprised. I didn't know you had the ability. Why waste it? and she said, But what use would it be? Let's suppose I take a six-month's course. What's at the end? Wouldn't it be better to buy a knitting machine? At least I might make

129

a useful buck. You see, I find living so object*less*. What *am* I living for? What do I *do*? Make life just a little more comfortable for people who don't know how? Keep dear Zuz in a good humor? Shoshi grand-daming back there? But *me*?

You were born to other things, I said. If you'd kept on, wouldn't you have had a happier time? More useful? and she said, I did a lot of hard work. I suppose it paid off here and there. But the end result wasn't what I wanted, and I said, Do we ever get what we want? Are we *here* to get what we want?

She sat back, staring at me, and beyond.

Well, all right, she said, What's your idea about all this? and I said, I don't have much of an idea about anything. I certainly think that so far as we've gone, or just as far as *I've* gone, in a few years' time, an electronics specialist will be able to put a pregnant woman on the Logo, and tell her what her child's going to be, what it's going to be useful for, and that'll be fed into the national computer for acceptance or rejection. I'm pretty sure of *that*.

Horrible idea, she said, and I said, Why, horrible? You want today's waste? Prisons full of misfits? They're not criminals. They broke a law? It's a crime? Ergo, they're criminals? No. Millions of unemployed? Unemployable? Why? They're not part of the machine. Any more than you are. Except that you control the *espresso*.

Wait a minute, now, she said. That little machine's pretty important in this community, and I said, I wholeheartedly agree. It's a type of amenity that satisfies most of the senses at one time. Outside of that, anybody can operate it. Why *you*? The conductor of an orchestra, matron of a hospital, headmistress of a school, a biologist, a pathologist, years of training, experience, are they going to come here to operate a machine to make coffee? And find any taste in living? What's your *idea* of living? To be what? To *do* what? and she said, All right. Now tell me *your* idea, and I said, I don't have one.

We stared, or simply looked. She wore a long Arab mummery showing the points of embroidered shoes, and the plaits were coiled about her head. The rest was a colored sack, vibrant. Traul had filled the room with flowers in earthenware bowls on the floor, tables, shelves. Books racked, infantry of the mind. Near my chair, ants carried a fly in on-shoulder procession across the tiles towards the door.

Aliya looked at her hands.

Personal question, she said, and I said, Say on, and she said, That nice girl. Mind if I ask what happened? and I said, Not at all. She just went. She wanted to go. Nothing I could say. That's as much as I know, and she said, But you were wonderful together, and I said, That's what I thought. But you can make a mistake, and she said, Boy, *can* you. Listen, don't you *really* know what happened? Did you have a fight? and I said, Nothing like it. No fight. Ever. She said just that. Let me go.

You didn't put your arms around her? Aliya said, You didn't even try? You didn't wear, and tear, and argue? You just let her *go?* Don't you know that's when you ought to be fighting her own *self?* After she's lost out? Why *don't* men put their arms around? Why do they *have* to be the lonely kings? and I said, Goddammit, sometimes we don't get a chance, and she said, Ah, *shit,* and I said, Chinese friend of yours? and she lay back, eyes closed in a slow, subtle eruption of giggles.

I went across, and put my hands on the arms of the chair, leaning over her, looking into her eyes.

You know why I came here? I said, and she said, Why

do you think I invited you? Bathroom's where I'm going. Bedroom's next door. I shan't be long. But, *don't* be here in the morning, will you? And don't recognize me tomorrow. Just look the way you're looking. It'll tell everybody. Cognac's over there. You can pour me one. Give me a kiss.

THIRTEEN

I ran a tongue-tip over the shoulder's cool silk and left, in darkness, crêpe-foot over stone, down to my place, and in, to a stun of quiet. I felt hollow, giddy even in the knees. Those moments stay. The alarm buzzed while I was certain I was still awake, and I shaved almost sure I was asleep.

But no dreams were allowed in the day. Before coffee time, Kar and his three disciples were in the office, and I had to show the bucolic what the sophisticate accepts as rote. The bucolic ploughs, plants and wants to see growth for harvest. The sophisticate works. What else happens is for others, working. Work's work. Finish work, get paid. No more work, no pay.

Kar looked at me, and I saw the generations.

You mean, you don't know what this is *for?* he asked, and I said, No. It's none of anybody's business what it's used *for*. Just happens they want it. We don't ask why. We make it, we sell it, That's the be-all and end-all.

That's *your* end of it, he said. Suppose we come in.

How *about* that? and I said, About what? The unit we make is going to be far more useful if it's conjoint with your product. Later, I can see we'd make it in one, and start a much bigger job.

No, Kar said, stamping roll-mop toes in run-down sandals. Listen. We don't know what the hell we talking about, see? You have to be patient.

I could have put my arms around him. I could have kissed the four faces, so troubled in heart.

Look, I said. Suppose I come to work up at your place, and you tell me what to do. Are you going to make a fool out of me? You *know* I don't know the first thing. So are you going to show me wrong? Lose money? Waste working time? Do you *have* that sort of time to throw away? If you saw it happening, would you permit it to go on? So, all right. You don't think anybody here's going to try fooling *you?* and Kar said, Yes, but they all say we don't know what we getting into, we can lose our socks, and I said, Don't be dull. In the time the plant gets built, all of you get trained. When the doors are open, you know just what you have to do. What you have to produce. How many of these people working here knew what they were doing when they started? How many know *now* just what they *are* working on, or what it's for? Listen, I've ploughed that number five plot of yours twice since I've been here. Did I know what was going in it? Did I ask the question? My job was tractor, plough. So that's what I did. Same as you. You'll be trained. You'll produce. What you produce will be sold. What more?

You going to take care of things? Groz asked. We got the other people. I mean, the unions, and the society, and all that. I rather trust in one practical man, and the others nodded, and Kar said, We have to see the bank, and the committee, and all. But we rather know you

134

had charge of this. Rest's easy. All right. See you, and I said, Come over and let's see if we can get some coffee, and Kar said, No. We took time out. We have to put it back in.

I watched them go in the twenty-year-old power wagon, and I was saddened with responsibility for good, simple men.

In the office, I put a book on the floor, and lay down with my head on it, flat, pressing my spine against the rug, pushing my eyes into the top of my head, and I slept, a few moments, or minutes, of absolute nothing, and got up when knuckles rapped the door.

Salah came in, stood, hand on the latch, and said, Somebody from the Merom office, and I said, Send her in, and she looked surprised, and said, It's a man, and I said. Send *him* in. I believe I knew he must be Roch before I saw him, shorter than me, a bush of grey hair at the back of his head, and a face like Punch, always ready for a laugh, but with sorrow just beyond.

Listen, he said, when we had the handshakes over, Tâl Ben-Hillel won't be here for a couple of days. Your new secretary. Well, call her accountant. *Her* secretary, Paula, she's getting used to not being in the Army. Adjusting. Kind of. Wearing longer skirts. Me, I take the minis. I'm here to see the commune people. Get *them* started right. See, Merom's idea, get all the communes busy in advanced industry. What's coming the next twenty-five years. That means the children. Start a factory for the older people? Fine. But start a plant for the children. Let *them* make a product. Like their daddies make. Couple of hours a day. A game. Five days a week. Twenty-five days a month. Twelve months. Five, six, seven years. You're training the finest work team in this world. See the idea? For children, it's a game,

Nothing to do with work. *And* they get paid. Later on, somebody else takes over. Objection?

Seems like a breach of confidence, I said. It's our job to protect them, and he said, from what? Breach of *what?* Listen, they been getting boxes of toys, plastics, how long? Girls get dolls. Breach of?

Well, I said. That's toys. A factory's a factory, and he said, Get your mind back. Find out what you're talking about. A toy's a symbol. What's a symbol? In make-believe, it's real. Tractor's a tractor. The doll's a baby. And the factory? It's real. It's where Daddy works. So now the children work there. I said *work*. They produce. They get paid enough to put them through school. But it's not *work*. It's a game. It's fun. But far beyond that, it's the training of the future. How else it going to be done? Don't you see that? Always you'll have people in the fields. But people, brains, in the future industries, like this? Listen, consider this. What you have here, in twenty-five years' time? Who is in charge? Who is working? What sort of things you turning out? Who's doing it, they don't get to be trained *now?*

What's Mr. Merom think about this? I asked, and Roch put the files on the desk, and said, It's his baby. He don't think of nothing else. Before he dies, he wants to see one in work. He says the industrial revolution started with a lot of English child labor. To bring money back to the family. He says the new revolution isn't child labor, but child *train*ing. Train them for the future. So they always got the job in their mitts. Always needed. You go for this?

Beginning to like it, I said, but I could see, so clearly, Aliya, feel the marvel, and passion's underthought of the morning burst, and I wanted him gone so that I could think of her.

Yes, he said. But listen. Where do *you* fit in, here? and I said, Give me a chance to think.

But when he left, I couldn't think. Ideas were all on top, flittering clouds, any color.

What gloried below was thought of Aliya. To run palms along shoulders, waist, hips, thighs, was wondrous essay in other beauty, a new alcohol, further drunkenness. I listened to what people said, and I could tap what they meant, as a seal bounces a ball over its whiskers. But I thought of Aliya, and wondered when I could go to her again. She had to be careful. So had I, for her sake.

But something, a feeling, a sense, undefined, a shadow, worried me, nagged, gnawed, gave no rest. The secret feeling of sorrow I had always known in any thought of her became, suddenly, urgent, as though she were target of attack. I tried to approach the notion in so many ways, and realized I was giving excuses, pretending, evading.

From those few hours, I thought I knew why. She was utterly a woman, but with a man's instinct in heat of meat, the greedy, wanting, taker, brute where necessary, or gentlest robber at moments, rough, for the rest, giving, reaching, murderous and selfish, and then blasted, suppliant, careless.

Plus A again, but so much more. And that was how I knew, guessed, pretended, worried, and wanted, needed to go back to her. Plus A had never wholeheartedly given. There was always a hesitance, which might have been shyness, or a harking to a more modest day, though for some reason I seemed to love her the more, and used strength to impel, persuade.

Not with Aliya. I knew she had far more than Plus A's physical experience. But mentally she had a man's approach, and that was something I had never met before, or, for that matter, imagined. How that physical state, and the at-odds mentality existed in apparent harmony, became a small miracle, because her normal self-control, that distant and yet warm attitude towards everyone, never seemed to falter. The more I thought, the more respect I felt, and even more the yearn to be with her again.

I heard fear, felt the gut congeal, knew the katyusha bomb's scream-whine, half-saw pink light flash beyond the wall, moonblur glittering wicked white in splintering glass.

FOURTEEN

In the bare room at the hospital's top floor, greenish blinds down, Merom came to see me every day for a few minutes, and towards the end, Roch brought in the accounts and production figures. Nothing had prevented our constant growth.

If anything, as Merom said, the bombs really sent our peoples' backs to the wall. Two of the Arab gardeners working on the path had been killed, which brought the *Mukhtar* and his chief men to scream rage, assuring everyone the young men were out helping Army trackers, and if the bombers were found they would suffer, slowly, and depart this life without joy. There were more than a hundred village women working in the next building, and the men looked for justice.

It was Monday afternoon, and time for tea.

An enormous bunch of pink roses appeared in the doorway. The blossoms sank, and Aliya's raised-eyebrow stare seemed to beatify me. A nurse came in behind with the tea trolley. She took the roses out. Aliya sat on the bed.

I have five minutes, she said. Does all that hurt?

I put up a finger to the strips of plaster, and said, No. What *has* hurt is not seeing you, and she said, They wouldn't allow visitors till today. I telephoned all hours every day. They must be sick of me. They just said you were satisfactory. I could go mad.

I'll be out at the end of this week, I said, and she ran an index up the back of my hand, and all the voltage ever stored seemed to hum in my skull.

I've been thinking, she said, looking down at the hand. I could do with a few days off. I'm told Eilat's wonderful. You know, down there. The south. Sun. Beach. Fishing. Do you like fishing? and I said, It's about the only sport I'm any good at, and she said, Well, why don't I book two rooms somewhere, and let's go there, and. Well. Would *you* like that? Just be ourselves? and I said, I think *that*'s the best idea I'll ever hear, and she said, Fine. Leave it to me. I wish I could tell you how I want to kiss you. And where, and I said, Do I think of anything else?

The nurse came in with the teapot, and said, Just time for a cup. Matron's strict. Everybody out, couple of minutes. I'll call you, and I said, Thanks. Make us the last, and Aliya said, How many lumps? and I said, Three, please, and she said, *Silver* tea service? In *hos*pital? and I said, That's Merom. He saw the chamber china, and said, Let's get a little civilisation in here, and he sent everything up. Notice the porcelain, please. Joy to drink out of. I believe it's a good thing others before us found out what's good. We don't make much of it any more. We get the blessing. Or what would we *have*?

The mouth above the cup's rim *o*'d to drink, and the nurse tapped on the open door.

140

Come along, please, she called. All right, finish your tea. But it's time.

Aliya sat straight, with the cup and saucer in her lap, and looked at me down her nose, and said, Darling, never mind. I'm enjoying it. Just to look at you. And remember. And tear off those calendar dates. Just seven more? I'll go down there the day before you do. I'll find out when you're leaving. I'm not going to kiss you. If I did, I wouldn't go. Are you fond of me? and I said, Yes, and she said, That's all, and stood, and the nurse came to the door again, and said, It's taking you an awful long time to drink a cup of tea, and Aliya said, Please, I'll be out of here, and she looked down at me.

I'll be waiting for you, she whispered. At the airport. *With* a cab. Remember me. *Shalom,* and I said, *Shalom, Shalom,* and heard her heels along the corridor, silver hammer-beats between my eyes, and the sigh of the lift doors was mine.

The nurse came in to pull the trolley away.

Sorry I had to throw her out, she said. Don't like doing it, only they're getting strict. People coming in, staying all hours, won't go home. This African lot. Want to sleep here. Anything I can get you? and I said, No, thanks. Just a few leaves off the calendar, that's all. But she was outside, and the door closed.

I had the white wall to look at, and so much to think about. I was too weak to get up, I knew that, but I also knew that the bomb had changed my way of thinking. Before, I lived in a country which a daily newspaper and radio bulletins told me was holding a line here and there, and politicians were saying this and that, and everything went on just the same.

Now, I knew by the nicks in my face, and the tremor in my hands and legs, and a thought of the bodies of

141

two innocents, that living only went on because we refused any idea of the realities. Only the Army took care. I should have known it before. I never thought of it. It never got through the bone. Bombs only fell on other people, like Arye and Dalia. To most, they were names in the paper, hard luck, memory of Plus A's broken sobbing, and grapefruit.

I was tired of thinking of it, where I could help, what I could do, and too restless to read.

Raps on the door were not the nurse, and before I could say, Come in, Merom stood at the foot of the bed.

Passing by, thought I'd call in, he said. How are you, young fellow? and I said, Pretty good, thanks. Just had a fine cup of tea from that service. It certainly tastes better, and he said, Why not? Ever try drinking a scotch and soda out of a cup and saucer? Same idea. Everything has to fit. Listen. They tell me you'll be out of here the end of the week. What are you thinking of doing? and I said, Well, a few days off ought to set me up. I thought of Eilat, and he said, Now, there's an idea. You'll want a boat. I'll have them ready one for you. Listen, do you feel up to talking about the commune business? and I said, Of course, and he said, Tell you why I ask. The patents you have in the works, the lawyer's got everything set, could you sign them over on the agreed terms so we can get the contract sworn? and I said, Any time, and he said, I'll send Roch in tomorrow. The new buildings ought to be up the end of next month. About when you'll be back. Your secretary is doing a fine job, by the way. Talking about Tâl Ben-Hillel. Great girl. Known her from a baby. Her daddy was a scholar. Very learned man. You got to look after them. They kept us together.

Kept who together? I asked him, and looked up from the papers.

Us, he said. Just us. See, I'm not Orthodox. I'm not religious. Oh, well, I have the candles and the wine Friday nights. Don't work Saturdays. Go down to the Wall if I feel like it. Y'know. 'Part from all that, I leave it to the others. They take over where I leave off. I think it's all right. It works. They do what *they* want to do, and study. I do what *I* want to do, and work. Between the two of us, we do all right.

How long before there's a head-on? I said, and he looked at me, and took off the spectacles, and his eyes were the color of sun-baked aquamarine, still bright, but hazed.

Don't know, he said. Wouldn't want to guess. Hope it's a long time. You're secular? and I said, Whatever that means. I'm nothing.

I used to be, he said. Now, I'm not so sure. There's room for everybody. You listen to them read that Torah, and I'm telling you, it's just like yesterday's paper. It's all going the way it says, and I said, That's pretty close to superstition, and he said, Look, it was written more than two thousand years ago. Before that, it was word of mouth, father to son, teacher to class. How's it so *right*? It *tells* you what's going to happen, and I said, I never expected to hear that from you, and he said, You read it lately? Ever picked up a Bible, and just read over the first five books? You're due quite a shock. Them old guys, they could be talking for now, and I said, When did the human ever change?

We won't argue, he said. Just sign in these two places. I'm going to be real happy when you and that secretary start working. She'll have everything straight by the time you get there. I never saw such a goddam mess in an office. Why you're sitting up here, I don't know. A yard

143

nearer, you'd have been like them Arabs. We gave their families enough to see them right, by the way.

I had to try twice to write a recognizable signature. My hand shook.

Eilat, Merom said, and took the pen from my fingers. Couple of weeks, at least. If you didn't lose the shakes in that time, couple more. No use forcing. Give the natural mould time to shake back in itself. That's all that's wrong with you. You got shook out. I hope they catch them bastards. They could do it again. That's what ruins me. Wonderful business wherever you look. People ready to work. Production all the way up there. But you got people throwing bombs. What kind of mentality *is* that?

Other end of the pole from the Orthodox? I said. One throws bombs. The other throws stones. Any difference?

Ah, now, look, he said. Between a bomb and a stone, there's a hell of a difference, and I said, Given the higher ratio of intelligence in the Orthodox, well, anyway, let's be kind and presume they *are* more intelligent, what *is* the difference?

We can go on like this, he said, clipping papers. If being alive's taught me anything, it's don't argue. Just put the case, and the hell with it. But I can't tell you how happy I am you're round the corner. I didn't expect it when I saw you wheeled in here. And look at you *now*. Glad I'm not a Rabbi. Run a three-ring circus round me.

I've met some fine Rabbis, I said. They have a pretty rough time. It's the hard-liners that worry me. They cause the trouble. The ones they call the goats.

Happy about that, too, he said, carefully patting papers. Awful lot of sheep in this world. Somebody has to take care of them. Ever see a flock of Bedouin sheep? You must have. All around you, down there. Not white, like you think of sheep. Sort of goldy. See who's out front? Always on call? Goats. Big, black *goats*. That's who. And the sheep get there. O.K.? I'll be in tomorrow afternoon, young fella. Start losing them shakes. See you.

He turned back from opening the door.

Ah, one other thing, he said. The boys looking into this, the Army, they been to see you? and I said, No, and he said, They'll be around. Just to get your bit of the story. Complete the report, that's all. Don't let it give you more of the shakes, see? *Shalom* again.

I went through the magazines he brought, French, Italian, English, German, American, and with all the pictures and letter-press racing in mind, I looked at the blank white wall, seeing a college, and in any part, Aliya, the long legs, the taste of breasts, thighs, memory of whispers, and shut my eyes, trying not to think, striving for peace of mind, pretending to be stronger than the old Adam, confessing defeat in abject rout.

The nurse came in with the lemon water, and I asked for a sleeping pill.

It's too early, she said. Couple of aspirin do you? and I said, I'd like to get knocked out, and she laughed pity, and said, That's the worst of visitors. And being in bed. Alone. I'll see what I can do.

FIFTEEN

I was just awake, and it smelled early, and the Army team of three came in, all young, but looking as if they could do with a sleep, a shave, and a clean rig.

We don't want to bother you, the senior said, in English of a good school. Just wanted to check. We have the rest. What happened, in your own words?

I was sitting there, I said, I heard the screech, and knew what it was, and I saw the light, and that's all, and he said, How *did* you know what it was? and I said, I heard too many like it. I worked in timing mechanisms, and the major said, What's that got to do with this? and I said, Plenty. We tested everything.

They nodded down at their para-boots. They all seemed to think and do alike. None of them looked *at* me. I tried to imagine how many times those thick soles had squelched flat under weight of a jump landing.

We found the site, the major said. Just over eight kilometers east. Near the border. Any idea why they'd pick you? I mean, the area? You haven't been open long.

146

That kind of job takes planning. Takes time, and I said, The only thing I can think of is the Arab work force. Women. I haven't heard if any of them stayed away?

The major shook his head.

Didn't miss a day, he said. Right.

The other two seemed to take it as a signal, picked up their automatics, stood, and went to the door.

You just happened to be unlucky, the major said, and held out his hand. If we learn any more, we'll let you know. Get well.

I had the distinct notion they had something further to say. I followed the entire business, from the moment the glass slivers shone in the white blur coming towards me, but nothing steadied. As ever, the Army had its own business, and viewpoint, and it was useless trying to guess.

The nurse came in with the telephone, plugged it, and passed the handset to me.

I heard Aliya's voice, and immediately the world had other shape and light. Aliya, I said. Good morning, and the small voice said, I'm flying down today, and I'll be waiting for the two-thirty flight from Lod. Don't worry about anything else. Just go to the desk and pick up your ticket. You don't need much luggage. Are you sure they'll let you go tomorrow? and I said, I'm marked out. Just keep thinking of me, and she said, What else *can* I do? and I said, What else do you think *I* do? and she said, I can see there's going to be some real soul-food cooking tomorrow. Look, the car's here. I have to go. Keep thinking *right,* and the line buzzed.

I was thinking more than right, and the nurse came in with an armful of clothes, and threw a pair of slippers down.

Put these on, she said. There's a big library down on

147

the ground floor. Cafeteria's next door. Take some money. Nothing free. I don't want to see you till lunch. *Be* here.

I dressed, feeling the tremors of a couple of weeks flat, and floated to the door, and out. I remembered somebody's telling me how to walk downstairs after a long time in bed. I found it was right. One step at a time, at first, hanging onto the rail, but after a couple of flights I was walking down without help, and on the ground floor I felt fine.

The library stays with me as a mausoleum of years'-old dogears, a heap of dead newsprint, and racks of paperbacks showering pages in German and Hebrew, that I had to pick up. But the one table had a pad of paper, and I had a pen, and I sat to schematise an idea I often thought about, but might have dreamt, and wanted to see proven or not. I was surprised to find it might work, and I was still thinking of Aliya. I went next door to the cafeteria, took a bottle of mineral water and a cup of coffee to a table, and sat down at the same time as Merom, this time in a blue suit, tie, the businessman, no jokes.

Dolled up, he said. Bank directors' meeting. You're out tomorrow? I can't get here. I'll be in Athens. The car'll pick you up, take you to the airport. Know where you'll be in Eilat? and I said, I believe it's called the Red Rock, and he said, You couldn't do better. They even got good coffee there, and I said, See that somebody picks up that silver service. I'm going to miss a real cup of tea. I'm grateful, and he said, Forget it.

How are things at the plant? I said.

He nodded.

Wish everything was going as good, he said, but I was suddenly sure there was something behind that nod, a defence, a warning.

Anything wrong? I said, and he said, Wrong? Only thing's wrong, you're here. Ought to be down there, and I said, Blame Al Fatah, and he said, I can blame plenty of people. What's Al Fatah? Collection of bums. Listen, you never converted? and I said, No. Never saw any reason, and he said, You're not a citizen? You never applied? and I said, No. I like the way I am, and he said, They cut the visa, they could turn you out, and I said, All right. I take the brain with me.

But what made you come here? he said. I mean, to this country?

I belong here, I said. I'm happy here, and he said, Any idea why? and I said, The same reason you get in bed at night. Seems the sensible thing to do.

You thought of getting married here? he said, and I said, I had it all planned. But she went away. Not a word since.

Listen, he said. I have to square with you. I believe this is the time. We going to work together, we have to square. See, I like the way you work. Else I wouldn't do business. I believe you have a great future. Financially you don't have to worry. But you have to be right. I mean, both feet on the floor. You said you planned to marry. That's a step for a lifetime. Did you ever ask *who* you planned to marry? I don't mean *her*. I mean, who she *was*. Ever know anything about her family? No, I said. What's that got to do with it? She never asked about mine? Who else's business is it?

White bristles nodded down at the file. I felt anger in the throat, hot.

Look, he said. Family's family. That's one thing. Everybody got one. But a bloodline, that's another. Race horse, cab horse? Lots in between? When that girl and me were talking, she happened to mention a name. Friend of mine.

149

One of the great families. This is history. She said he was her daddy's older brother. Then it came out she was the youngest daughter. Her daddy's a Rabbi. At the top. I mean, the *top*. Great scholar.

What's so great about the scholar? I said. Lot of people are scholars. In other ways, and he said, This I don't expect to hear from you. Scholars have to stay with scholars. Rest of us, we keep things going our way. But scholars we have to have. Only reason we here, it's them, and I said, Plenty of people don't believe it, and he said, A whole lot of them never opened a book. The rest, they don't want to. Afraid they going to learn. Look, so anyway, I'm talking to this gal, see, and I said, You mean your daddy's so and so? and she says Yes, what of it? and I says, You mean you're going to marry and he don't know? And she says, What's it to do with him? And I says, You know him a whole lot better than me. You going to wreck him, the end of his life? What did he do, such a thing should happen? How's he going to feel? What's he going to say to people, my daughter got married, she never said a word to me or her mommy? Marrying who? A duke, it should matter? Who *is* a duke? Who *is* this guy she married? Israeli? No. Hebrew? No. Convert? No. So? Mixed marriage? With her father's name, his position, it's possible? It's what I tell her. Not against *you*. But listen, she has no respect for her father's name, how much she going to have for yours?

I saw it, I heard it, and I knew.

The hesitancy, the hold back, the pull here, the tug there, the give-only-sometimes, all wrapped up in a sense of duty, guilt, wanting to be herself, knowing she had other call, claim, but indulging, and careless because distant, heedless until faced with the cold fact. And then excuse, lies, flight. I thought I saw why the medico at

Beersheba had taken those carefully selected moments. He must have known.

Suddenly I was sorry. Sorry is a lonely word.

You probably did me a favor, I said, and he said, Glad you see it that way. I have a letter from her daddy. Like to see it? And I said, No, thanks. Enough she's gone.

See what I mean? he said. Suppose she was still here. Think you be happy, you feel this way, now?

I don't know a thing about anything, I said. What the hell's it to do with you?

Like I'm telling you, he said. I didn't say a thing against *you*. I just talked about *her*, and what she was doing to her daddy. Sure you don't want to see his letter?

Hell with it, I said. I'm all through.

I had to tell you, he said. For the best or not, I just had to get that gal out of here. Bloodline's a bloodline. What the hell, I said. How about *my* bloodline? and he said, Not even a convert, hell kind of a bloodline's *that*? I tell you, even dukes don't count. Anyway, that's that. Listen, would you ever want to convert? Consider it?

No, I said. I thought about it, I don't see any reason.

Know something? he said. Just like me. My dad came from Poland. Bookkeeper. Very brainy guy. Got jobs everywhere. Berlin, Paris, all over. Couldn't settle down, see? Spoke eight, nine languages, keep books in any of them. My mother and him met in the office in New York. She was smart, too. They both had the new idea. No more ghetto. No more synagogue. Just be like everybody else. Way I was brought up. Study, sure. School, nothing like it. I was top every time. He took me through accountancy. Ten, eleven, I was helping him. So, London, Brussels, Vienna. Best friend I ever had. The only real teacher. Just happens to be I never had a Bar Mitzvah.

151

Nobody, least not many, know this. I'm telling you because you're just like me. Only other one I ever met. You're in, but you're out. You got it, but you don't. You feel it, but you can't prove it. Way I been all my life.

Putting a lot of trust in me, I said, and he said, Trust, nothing. I'm telling you so you don't get to feeling nothing's any good. When I found out about me, I thought the world's finished. Everybody washed-up. No use. Gone crazy. I married a gal. I'm going to cut this real short. She's the pick of any season. Forty-some years ago. Couple of days after, we suppose to be honeymooning, she says, Listen, you're no Jew. You're not circumcised. You know I never thought about it? I heard about it, like you hear about, oh, scarlet fever, but it's got nothing to do with *you*. Know what I mean? So I said, What, circumcised? She said, Look, *you* know. You don't have to be told. I'm going to see my father. Well, he come and see *me*. Anyway, we arranged things. A divorce. Nobody knew anything. I got fixed up financially. No talk. That protected her. I went to Europe. She married again, God should be kind to her. Now, what I'm trying to say is this. Marry who you want, and good luck. But stay out the bloodlines, see?

But what do you call a bloodline? I said. Everybody's the same, and he said, No. They're not. Anybody in the race horse business tell you that. Look, there's some women born to carry the line. Them you have to protect. So can *you* help? No child of yours means a thing, and I said, That's just the nonsense I don't want to hear about. Tribal fallacy, and he said, Listen. Why are we back in Jerusalem?

No, I said. I'm not listening.

Listen or not, he said. Reason is, they stuck to bloodlines, in the body, in the soul. Gave the spirit. Kept us

152

going. Well, that's what I think. It's how I live. Tâl's not
my own daughter, I got to tell you. So I love her more.
Neither are the others.

What *is* this about bloodlines? I said, and he looked at
me, a kind of Final Judgement sum-up, and he said, Because only the women produce the sons and daughters
of Israel. Long as he's not married, and she's not committing adultery, don't matter *who* the father is, long's the
mother's Hebrew. That's the law. So the better the woman,
the better the child. Better the child, better the nation.
People like us, half and half, we can help. And I'm helping. But marry, no. Just producing a cast-off.

He got up and snapped the brief case shut.

Glad I got it off my chest, he said. I didn't know how
you'd take it. I mean, me talking to her and. Well. Sending
her off. As good as. But she listened. So she must have
been real worried. Don't want to read her daddy's letter?
Nothing in it about you? and I said, No.

Listen, he said. This isn't going to louse things up? I
mean, between us?

Didn't do much good, I said.

I had to get square, that's all, he said. *You* know that.
I couldn't go on working with you if I knew I'd stuck a
knife in your back and you still didn't know. I stuck the
knife in. Now you know *why*. Know something? Way you
act, I believe it was the best.

He looked at me from the side, if I might throw something, and a comic note made me laugh.

He stared deadpan for moments, and then he bent in
half. I never heard such a funny cackle, as if it hurt, as
though he kept it in for years and suddenly let it break
out, breaking him, and it went on, head down.

Dam'est thing, he said, in chokes. Got me sewed up,
there. I'm glad. I'm awful glad it turned out this way.

153

I don't often get into personalities. Know something? People, I don't like. I mean, just people. I stick to business. But this I couldn't help. Happy we got something out of it. Anything else I can do?

Better not try, I said. Could be disaster.

He honked, a mule, all teeth, shut-eyed at the ceiling. So right, he said. I'll be in touch. Eilat. O.K. See you. And listen, lose the shakes. Want anything, I'm on call. *Shalom.*

I stared at the blank white wall. I tried to think of time with Plus A. She was alive in my mind. Thought of her still hurt. The tenderness of a girl has thorns. Thinking of her, they tear, bring blood. So many memories of her, all wonderful, in the green dusk of citrus groves, in apple-scent, down where the oranges hung many lights. Her warmth, the tight clutch of her arms, the cry in orgasm, the long shudder, and abandon in repletion, all in the rich honey of the mind, part of her. That she could forget, fail, lie, and go without a word daunted me. But there could have been no love.

On either side, none. On my side, no love? How believe it? What, exactly, *was* love? Staring at the wall, I found no answer. I thought us in love. Was it a climb into bed, an exhaustion, and pax, until the next time, dictated by energy and mental prodding?

Or was there a desire to fend, assuage, promote? To rise beyond, above the ruck, away from the ordinary, to share the sheerest joy of being simply ourselves between two? How often can anyone be, simply, her, him, themselves? To strip the social clothes, the everything every day, the outside entire, all the rubbish, the spirit-polluting musk of the day's brunt, the argument of muscle over will, all, merely to give desire its carrot? But is this love? Getting together, scrubbing backs, washing dishes, making beds, taking a small warm hand to walk down in early dawn, feeling a grip of fingers not for anyone else, a look in eyes for none other, the pressure of a body felt by two alone, a promise given, kept, sometimes anywhere, oftener and always in the bed's own wondrous battleground, but *is* this love? Or what else is it? Which voice speaks? Thinking, feeling, what? For what reason?

But I remembered her voice in a sudden bad-tempered moan over Romeo and Juliet on radio, Oh, turn it off. Find some rock. I don't *have* to suffer.

The white wall seemed to say, Right. That's it.

SIXTEEN

Evening was blue, and the duty nurse came in to say three men wanted to see me. I thought of the Army team, and said, Let them in.

But instead, Groz came first, Yeke behind, and Shmuel. Three more different, impossible. Groz, biggest, blue work-shirt, head of curls like a grey ram, Yeke, up to his shoulder, but wider, white shirt, brown face, deep blue eyes, and Shmuel, tallish, bent-over, watery-eyed, blond hair to the collar of a frayed jersey, shy.

We interrupt you? Yeke said, and I said, Come on in. Sit down. What's going on?

We came in to pick up a couple of tractors and a truck, Yeke said. Like to see if we could have a word, and I said, Let's hear it.

Well, Yeke said. It's this guy, Neb, see? He's supposed to be religious? Thinks people on earth to help each other? Love? Y'know?

I barely had a word with him, I said. So? and he said, Let him tell it, and nodded at Groz.

156

Well, Groz said, I'm standing up there, middle of that number seven stretch of fallow. You can see down to the fish ponds. I saw Neb going down there. But not by the path. I watched him. What's he going to do? Catch fish? He knows better. Law's dead against. No. He's going over that patch of trees, there. Next thing you know, here comes a gal down the other way. Way she's dressed, Arab.

Yeke put hands to his head.

Imagine? he said. Bedouin? Sorry. Go on.

Well, I stood there, Groz said. None of my business? Sure as hell is. Neither of them got the right to be there. This is commune property. Not collective. She's working at the plant? Not even that much right to go off the path to and from the bus stop. So I stand there. I see them meet, run in the dry patch down there. Don't tell me they never went in there before. So I thought, now what? If I go down there, catch them doing-what, what do I say? I went up and found Yeke, here, and told him.

Right, Yeke said. So we went to his place, and we waited for him. He come in, and we said, Where you been? Well, he tried the what's-all-this-about, and Groz slammed him against the wall, and he says, You dirty-soul bastard, you going to put us in trouble with the Arabs? What is she, Druse or Bedouin? Both as bad, see? And he says, I don't know. She's in the office, there. So I said, Get your stuff together and get your goddam self out. And he says, Listen, I can't, I have to translate for the plant. It's why I'm back here. Counting on me.

Trans*lat*ing? I said. When was this?

Last night, Yeke said. He don't have nothing to translate? He sure had some paper, and I said, Not that I know of. What happened to the girl? and Groz said, We coming to that. See, we thought, he's a scholar, if he's got this stuff to translate we can't do much. It's important. So we said, All right, get the job done, you go in the morning. Then we go back to the park. It's dark. We see Achmed, the patrol, ask him if a girl passed there, see?

So he says, Yes. She got a ride out of here. So I said, Who she get the ride with? And he says, Aliya. I said, How *she* get into it?, and he said, She was working on the car, and the girl come in. So she took her down.

Let's hear the rest, I said.

Well, we waited up the café for her to come back, and it's a long time, Yeke said, looking at the floor. Then it turns out she's in her room. Won't see nobody.

Groz stuck the big hands out between his knees, looking down at stretched fingers.

This is where Shmuel comes in, he said, and Shmuel said, Like, I went down there to play chess with Suleiman. *Mukhtar*'s eldest son. We're in the coffee shop, there, and one of them runs in yelling, and the whole shoot piles out in the street and I said, What's going on? and Sul, he says, You better go on back. Going to be trouble. So I get out, and just down there, on the highway turn-off, there's Aliya's car and the crowd around, yelling. So I went down there, and shoved through with Sul, and boy, they going to get her out and smash up the car. She's real frightened. Well, the *Mukhtar* got down there, and talked, and Aliya opened the door for me. She's plain lucky. Just the look of them.

She did the girl a big favour, I said.

Groz shook his head.

You think the other kids didn't catch on? he said. You know how they talk? Minute she didn't show up on the bus, the family wants to know where she is. Her dad, brothers, uncles, they go around the houses of the others. Where she go? They pretty soon get the story. Aliya shows up. The gal gets out. They grab her.

Aliya was smart, Shmuel said. She had the doors locked, windows up. We hadn't been on hand, they burn the car, her in it. Another minute, that's all.

What happened to the girl? I said. What's her name?

Don't know, Shmuel said. Time we left, she wasn't in no state to ask. She got beat with camel shackles. Chains.

They look after their women, Yeke said.

Aliya get back safely? I asked.

I drove, Shmuel said. She pretty near went mad. I had to fight with her to keep her in the car. Gal was getting beat. Everybody putting it in. Didn't take long.

Who got you out of there? I asked, and Shmuel said, The *Mukhtar*. Else, like I say, they burn the car, us inside. Lot to be thankful for.

Look, we come in to tell you what the *Mukhtar* come up to say, Yeke said. Rest of his gals, no trouble the next twenty years. But they got to have their own place to eat, up there. No dealing with us. Else you don't have nobody working. What's the word?

Where is Aliya? I said, and Groz said, She won't be back for a couple of weeks. She had enough.

Right, I said. Yeke, you ask the secretary to fix up the north end of the machine building for a dining room for the girls. Nobody else allowed in. Have a Druse count heads at the bus stop. No more mixing. Girls with girls, O.K.? No men. What happened to Neb?

Slept in a construction truck, Groz said. I talked to the boss, there. Went out before sun up. Luckiest guy around. He knew. How do people get like that?

Adam did, I said. Same reason. Goes on and on.

Just thought you ought to know you lost a top girl, your office, Yeke said, and stood. Everybody turned up today. Seemed like it was peaceful. But just one more like that. Know what happen to us? and I said, We need more guards, and Groz said, Do no good. They the same people. Touch a woman, that's *it*. Have to be lots more careful.

What happened to the body?

Shmuel scratched his shoulder under the jersey.

Well, he said. We went down there this morning. Like, ants, rats, dogs, all had a share. Just bones. Kids, they kicking the skull around. We put her in the box. Lot of Traul's flowers in there. Took her up the plant, buried her behind the office building. Traul got the idea, like, a garden, she rest easy. All right with you?

I'm glad, I said. Sweet girl.

Sweet, the word, Groz said. This one, Neb, I lay the hand, his bones break worse than hers. Them down the village, they going to be jumpy the next ten years, maybe more. No talk. They work, they like the money. That's all.

So how do we get any sort of co-operation going? I said. It's what we need. Dialogue, and Yeke said, No. Two generations, maybe. And listen. Don't let a lot of people hear you say even so much. Don't even think it too loud, and I said, Why not? I'm allowed an opinion? and he said. No. No opinion. Us, it's O.K. I mean, outside. For lots of people, there's the law. Not the law of the land, but the Book. Only one there is. Break that, you get stoned. They using that word another way. Like, for drunk. A stone they ought to have in the head. Remind them. Stones kill. I like to keep you alive. Brains, we need. You know you got yourself a new secretary?

No, I said. At least, yes. I knew she was on her way. Shoshi seeing to her? and Yeke said, Everybody is. Got yourself a good deal. When you going to be back? and I said, Depends how I feel, and Yeke said, Take your time. Mayerkopf, he's pretty good. Listen, we miss you. Get better, and Groz said, Get well, and Shmuel said, See you.

I looked at the white wall. I was sure I knew the girl. I saw the sheen of a thigh.

I thought I knew what papers Neb was "translating," and why he slept in the truck's cab instead of in his own place. I reached for the telephone and called Merom. No reply. I remembered he was in Athens. I had no notion how to reach the Army team. I knew I must.

I called the nurse and sent a message to the chief medico on duty, and when he came, I said I wanted to talk to the Chief of Police. Not more than ten minutes later, an Inspector came in with a couple of sergeants. I said I had to talk to the Army. He got the nurse to bring a telephone, and called a number.

Here, I was lost.

Hebrew is hell on the mouth and ears, at least, for me, and after a few words, I got not exactly lost, but certainly bereaved. I called myself an ass for not being smart enough to catch the words and sounds as they flew. But they evaded. Ancient language turned modern held a mental oil defying clumsy grip. Anger, frustration, impatience, all that, but for nothing.

Be here in a few minutes, the Inspector said, sounding very English. Been here long? Last year, I said. Beersheba area, and he said, How do you like it down there? and I said, I wouldn't swap it for anywhere I've been. Peaceful. Lot going on, and he said, Hard luck about the attack. Creep in like rats. Rough business. For them *and* us. The ordinary Arabs are afraid their own people are coming back. Egypt, Jordan, so forth. If they work with us, they know they're going to die. Painfully. If they have relatives on the other side, *they* suffer. You have to be sorry for them. Nutcracker job. Both jaws. So they help the rats. Then we catch them. What can they say?

Why can't we offer citizenship? I said, and he said, It's offered. We encourage it. But how many apply? A photograph and a rubber stamp, what's it mean? Identity? And anyway, most of them wouldn't want to. I tell you. They're afraid. They can't believe we're going to win again.

Two of the Army came in, neither of the first lot.

I told them I thought Neb had some explaining to do, and I had an idea the dead girl was a filing clerk with daily access to most paper.

Just a moment, the senior said. A filing clerk? How many do you have? and I said, the office has been re-organised since I came in here. She was in charge of technical papers, journals, reviews, and the officer said, In what language? and I said, English, French, and Hebrew, and he said, But she was Arab? Druse? and I said, Druse, I think. She was educated in Beirut. Got her bachelor's at the University. Smart girl. Her father's well off. Came to the office dressed like the others. Well, modified. Smarter. More fashionable. If that's it?

Know nothing about this man, Neb? The senior said, and I said, Beyond what I've told you, nothing. He was religious. Or appeared to be, and he said, What could this girl give him beyond the obvious? and I said, the blueprints and graphs were constantly going out to the workshops. Engineers can't carry details like that in their heads. Apart from that, most of the correspondence was in Hebrew, but there was quite a lot in English, French, and Italian. Some of it could be useful.

Unusual sort to find in a village, the junior said and he was *very* English. Any more like that on the staff? and

162

I said, Several. Three or four of the girls from that village study in Cairo. But the rest of the office, all Army girls. She seemed to get along with everybody. I never had the smallest excuse to worry.

Get this off, the senior said, and ripped a page, and the junior went out, trotting.

Three items here are strange, the senior said, putting the ballpoint in a hip pocket. I'm wondering if anybody's cottoned down there. If she was giving him classified stuff, she was useful. Why would he let her risk not getting home on time? Why would *she* risk it? She'd know what was going to happen. This woman who gave her a lift, wouldn't she know what she was getting into? and I said, She isn't the kind to worry too much. The girl wanted a lift home, she had the car, let's go. But she almost lost her life.

If she was useful, why would he let her walk into trouble? the senior said. He'd know he was washed up from the moment. Did he ever *do* any translating for you? and I said, None. He never had any reason to come near the place, and the senior said, You see, I'm throwing questions around to see if I can touch a nerve somewhere. Something you could have seen, or heard, and forgotten, and I said, He never had the smallest thing to do with us. I never for a moment imagined the two knew each other, much less met. If I had, I'd have put a stop to it. One thing, it can't happen again, and he said, I heard that once too often too many times. Anyway, now it's in the works. You certainly did well to let us know. *Shalom*, and the policemen saluted.

Problems, the Inspector said. Wherever you look, creep, creep, creep. Fifteen, twenty years if they're caught. What's the attraction? and I said, But he was Israeli, and they all laughed, and a sergeant said, If we lay hands on him, we'll find out what type Israeli. He speak English? and I said, None of us speak anything else. It's why we're there. We can't work it in Hebrew, and the Inspector said, Took me twenty years, and I'm still not what I'd like it to be. Anyway, you did the right thing tonight. There'll be a report about the girl's death in Beersheba, and this'll tie in. Wouldn't surprise me if the man didn't do it deliberately. One less witness. It happens. If you need us again, just say the word. *Shalom.*

I saw the salutes and the closing door from the side, but I was staring at the blank wall.

To think of that beauty flogged with chains brought an arid sense of despair. Pain, death came as merest whim of any brute. Cold aversion lay in thought that even in an age of electronic marvels and moonwalks, we still lived in a mental sewer with no better company than the killer rat.

But true cold lay in memory of Aliya's voice, only that morning. She saw what had happened. She lived through it, told me nothing. I still heard the froth of seeming love-talk, a sickly attempt to deceive for what reason?

Because she connived in a brutal murder?

I saw the sheen dulling in that thigh, blood flooding in bruises, heard chains in beat on gentle flesh, and felt the wickedness of that death, in broken bones, and pulp.

Salah, of the long, beautiful legs?

Why?

SEVENTEEN

The last time I flew had been with Plus A, and I was reminded of her smile, strapping myself in, feeling alone,
weak knees and hands, trembly, and when the engines
howled to their gods, I could have called with them.

We were rising, and Israel's green body passed under,
and I remembered sweat glistening on muscle in the
long grove down below, seemingly the size of a baby's
palm, and yet a mile square, and I saw myself carrying
saplings in rusted cans, one in each arm, all day, back
and fore, loading the truck, and with only a nap under
the dark trees, walking through dry leaves in a silent
yellow sunrise that warmed my face, bundling rose cuttings, seedlings, and over to the garden for plants, and
back, that night, to Beersheba, a pulsing ache in every
muscle of a splendour I had never known, and yet the
others sang.

To the West, hotels and apartments toothed against the
sands of Ashkelon in purest yellow strip along the Mediterranean's blue, and Plus A swam beside me again, cold

as alabaster, a goddess in those moments, and now a hurt in thought, remembering the small room up the stone stair from the patio filled with mauve begonia, the palm—she said—caressing us through the window shutters, the doves on the roof that spoke to her, and the wonderful wake-up aroma when they opened the oven in the bakery downstairs, and the call of coffee roasting next door. I wondered if she thought of any time of ours, and tried to think myself in her place.

I felt I should have been angry with Merom, and yet I saw his truth, and if she agreed, she must have been thinking so all along, and only needed a push. Again I thought of the holding-back, the reluctance, and saw them as so many grave-marks of scruples overcome, buried in a moment's want of the body, wanton, and myself, a willing provider.

We tipped, swaying over the Plain of Sharon, and the beet fields, and the spreading wealth of wheat, a green glow of orchards, pale squares of lettuce, and stands of maize where so often I had sweated at the truck, doubting if the job would end before my spine broke. And yet none of us had stopped working until Yeke gave the sign. Looking inward, I thought that a greater part of the national secret.

People worked from early morning on, and never stopped, except for the Shabbath, at least where I had been. Never had I seen men and women work in sweat for hours on end, no grumble; or any need to exhort. Others I heard complain of laxity, a slowing down, perhaps as Shoshana said, making themselves a lamp you should strike a match.

But people worked together, purposefully, of a single mind which gave results far beyond any norm in most countries. Plus A had often come home too tired to drag herself to the bath, which was always a pleasure for me, and might have been a desire of hers to be babied, since I bathed her.

But in the early days before we met, I had often turned in unwashed, without even the energy to make a sandwich. As muscle hardened, we became equal to the demand of the day, but I doubt we were ever anywhere near the Sabra for effort through the hours and the heat, whether they were our age or older, though Yeke, Sam, Avram and the rest, all European, were a law to themselves, an example to all of us, part of the rule that proved the exception. In them we felt the rock-hewn will of the pioneers, the single mind of self-denial, a devotion to an ideal, a faith in themselves and all they believed they were born to do.

Among the hills of Judea, where generations of their heart had lived and battled, I wondered if that faith would die with them. Looking at the terraces rolling in curving rock-wall stairways, from the crests, down to the river beds, grey-green in the olive groves, deep green patches of orchards, paler spreads of vineyards, houses splashed with the purple of bougainvillea, I tried to imagine exactly what that faith might be.

My family and all my relatives, so far as I knew, had been assimilated into the common peoples of Europe and North America for more then four generations.

Only once, my uncle had spoken to me about it, on the night before going back to school for the final term.

Look here, he said, It's necessary for me to say a few words. You won't repeat this, especially to your mother. She knows. But it might upset her. Follow closely what I say. On the death of your Grandaunt Sophia, in Paris, you will inherit. I don't know how much. But under the terms of your great-grandfather's will, a certain portion came to your father. He refused, and put it in your name. That was before you were born. You may also refuse, and put it in your son's name. But whether you accept or reject, you will have to sign papers. You will find that this family is Hebrew in origin. Your father and I became Hebrew because our mother was. *Your* mother is not. Therefore, according to present Rabbinical law, that's the law of the priests—for want of a better word—you are not a Hebrew. You can be American, English, or French. You may claim the nationality you wish. On your father's side or your mother's. The fact of being Hebrew has nothing to do with nationality. It's religious. That is why, in this house, religion has been reduced to a minimum formality as in the houses of both your grandfathers. We wanted nothing to do with it, your father and I. Have you anything to say?

I don't think so, I said. I don't feel any different.

He put his hand on my head, and said, My son, be very careful. You attend a school of the Church of Rome. Your mother did that deliberately. She felt you would know more discipline, more scholarship. She's proved correct. Your reports are a comfort. We are also told that you have little interest in religious activity. Very well. For us, we have less. But never tell anyone what I have told you. Never. To be known as a Roman Catholic is one thing. To be known as a Jew is quite another. It is like being branded. For some reason, the word is like a poison. Some people, the least Catholic, and even the most irreligious, the barbarians, seem to go mad with the sound of this English word, Jew. It is in no other language. A pejorative term always. It is reason for the pogrom, the gas oven, the concentration camp, the horror. Be careful how you speak. We understand each other? and I said, I think so. But what's the difference? I mean, between us and the rest? and he laughed, and straightened the newspaper with a slap. Well, he said, If you read the first five books of the same Christian Bible, that's what the Hebrews believe. One, and only one God, no family, nothing to diminish His importance. The Christians believe that, too. But they add on a new testament, about Christ and the Holy Ghost. Well, the Hebrews say it's unnecessary. Everything that this man Christ taught is in the first five books. The belief of the Christians is that he was the Messiah. That belief isn't shared by the Hebrews. And that's the crux of the matter. Plus, of course, the early Christians tried to make our people responsible for the crucifixion of Christ. It's demonstrably untrue. But that's perhaps not important in these days. If another six million are carted off to be rendered for their fat, and the gold in their teeth, I'd far rather know you weren't one of them, d'you see? I dislike the thought of you under the knife without anaesthetic. Or cattle-trucked. Or cooped. By the way, when did you last see a dentist?

I remembered the question when I sat in that chair and the surgeon started picking about, and I asked him how humans could be rendered for fat, and the gold in their teeth.

He took his spectacles off, and stopped the machine.

Very simple, he said. You fry them for the fat. Then you break the teeth, and there's the gold. What made you think of that? and I said, I heard it the other day, and he nodded and said, I'm glad people are still talking about it. At least, it's not en*tire*ly forgotten. I often try to imagine how many of you youngsters know *any*thing about it. In future, no doubt, it'll pair with the sacking of Rome, and let's say, the burning of the books at Alexandria. Nice, comfortable little lumps of historical toffee. Those of us, we lost our families, it's no honor.

I heard his voice in the engines' hum.

Below, the road I knew so well curled across the pale gold plainlands of Simeon, and I saw tents, dots of shadow speckling the high ground, and I knew we were over the Negev, near to the wilderness of Zin, and I waited for the wastes before Beersheba, and as the shadowed sprawl of buildings passed, I tried to see the life down there, the café tables on the pavements, Army girls, bathed and combed in hot streets, the little stall where we drank long glasses of almonds distilled to a pale milk, and the shop of the tinsmith, ready to make any shape, and between hammerings, drink a beer and make a champion's move at chess, and the Bedouin saddlers sewing camel furniture for kings, and their women, weaving rugs fit to hang in palaces.

Far on the left, to the East, beyond the *khamsin*'s red cloud, the Dead Sea went down to Sodom, that place of desolation, though many a man kept a family in the salt pans, or in the bitter white dust of phosphate plants, and in the road gangs along the one black ribbon sliding down the mountainside, over the plain of Arava, down to Eilat and on, to Sharm-el-Sheikh.

Sheba, Solomon's love, how many times did she camp down there, between the landing of her papyrus barge at Eilat, and the trumpets' welcome to Jerusalem? I tried to see her camel-litter swaying over the track, and the details of her daily toilette, the troop of milch-asses, the water in how many jars, the kitchen, her servants, bodyguard, an onward march in the night's cool, torches flaming for miles along the way, she asleep, perhaps, or wakeful, listening to Solomon's musicians, or story tellers, or dealing with matters of State relayed by couriers, all within the fortune of perhaps thirty miles between sundown and dawn, camp sites ready in front, and beside the Dead Sea—*and did she, too, find her breasts floating above water, and look down, unbelieving?*—and a turn to the west, and Jerusalem, and where would Solomon meet her?

Or did he go to Eilat, and board the barge? But why would she go to Eilat? Why not sail from Alexandria to Jaffa, or any coastal port on the Mediterranean, and make a far shorter journey by land? Or were Solomon's enemies between the coast and Jerusalem? Philistines?

She, in all conscience, was precious cargo in herself, and if, perhaps, both were almost in love by report of each other's ambassadors, then Solomon might have taken extra, most tender, precaution.

I wondered how Plus A might have looked in that litter. But she seemed clumsy, not in place, removed, and not by time alone, woman though she might be. Curiously, I thought any of Sheba's handmaidens might have been more in style. What was the confusion? How mix Plus A with unknowns of a couple of thousand years ago? Why not? Why should the women of this day be less than those all the way back in time, even unto Eve? I had to think of Aliya.

She was not in that litter. That surprised me. I could think of it, but something in me refused. Beautiful—who is beautiful?—tall, princess-like? Yes. But in place of Sheba? No.

Snobbery? Perhaps. Spawned in the petit salons of bourgeoisie Europe? Richesse of the Diaspora? Those islands of psuedo-civilisation? Where my mother, and how many thousand others, poured the tea, and their men sat in the other room, talking business?

But where *was* this, and which Sheba camel-jogged her way to Jerusalem? We were flying direct south, above the Arava Desert, and evening shadow mauve-washed

171

Jordan's red mountains as Sheba must have seen them, though in her time they were in the land of Moab, and Moabites and Edomites probably bowed down at the port, that splash of lights below.

We were over the Red Sea, across the cusp of the bay, and we tipped in a turn, and the town's lights passed over the wing, and that small black dot on the world map, a full stop between Asia and Europe, glimmed, alight, and alive.

Oven-heat smote on the stairway, even hotter than the Negev, making me glad I had nothing to carry. We walked over to the baggage stall, and in shadow I saw Aliya, apart, long legs in white trousers, resting on a hip, arms folded. She saw me and might have run, but the Druse guard shouted her back, and then I was with her, an arm around her waist, her arms about my neck, her perfume in all my world, her strength part of me.

Welcome to Eilat, she whispered. It's been the world's loneliest place till a minute ago. When I saw those lights up there, I don't know what kept me on the ground. How do you feel? and I said, About a thousand percent much better. How soon is it to a drink? and she said, Here comes the baggage trolley. That taxi better be waiting. Then it's two minutes to the best scotch-and-soda in this entire neck o'nothing, and I said, Is that all? and she kissed my cheek, a pout of lips, and whispered, And *me*.

The taxi waited, we had a life-saver in the hotel bar among a tour from Brooklyn, and she told me that Zvi and Moshe were back from the University and the secret was out. They were setting up a pottery, and they had the Museum's permission to copy the designs of three thousand years ago in the original clay with details of glaze and color.

I said, The best people are leaving the land, and Aliya

said, No. Yeke told them they were better off doing something they wanted to. The land doesn't need work. It asks love. It was love it or leave it, but don't fool with it, and I said, You often talk to him? and she looked away, nodding.

I suddenly felt bed-weak, tired. Trembling showed when I lifted the glass, and Aliya said, I'll get you an aspirin. Meet you upstairs. I nodded, and the porter came to show me the room, on the top floor, in greens, with a big window looking out to sea, and the mountains of Saudi Arabia far off.

The knocks on the door I thought were Aliya. Instead, a tall man came in, and said, I'm the doctor. Mr. Merom called me, and I said, I left hospital this morning and I'm still a little shaky.

Ah, yes, he said, putting the stethoscope's cold disc on my chest. Let me have the name of the hospital and I'll phone your physician.

I might have gone to sleep, and I heard a voice saying, Nothing much wrong here. A little tired, that's all. Let's have the address, will you?

He watched me print capitals, and nodded.

If you're not hungry, don't eat anything tonight, he said, Stay in bed tomorrow. I'll be here at eight. Take these two, now. If you wake up, take these two. With this air and a little treatment, you'll be galloping in a couple of days.

I almost laughed, thinking of Aliya, but I must have slept before he left.

EIGHTEEN

Aliya stood in the doorway, tall, impossibly beautiful—I had to ask myself what I meant, and the answer was before me—in a red bikini that looked like satin because it shone, hair flairing and said, Darling, you're awake? in *that* voice, almost like singing, and I said, Yes, how about some breakfast? and she said, At four o'clock in the after*noon*? But I don't see why you shouldn't have eggs for tea, do you? How about coffee instead? Then we stand the day up-side down. Won't that be lovely? and I said, It'll improve when I've had a shave.

I'll order, she said, and raised her arms, out, to the sea's clear blue.

The streets are full of white chicken feathers, she said, in triumph. I thought it was snow. Every house in this wonderful place has two or three chickens for the pot. White. Nothing but white chickens. I never heard of it, did you? and I said, Dimly. When I was a boy. This must be a big day, and she said, It is. It's the Day of Atonement tomorrow. Everything's jammed shut, nobody

174

around. All repenting. Most of them don't have an idea why. And they all go hungry. One day fast. Won't harm anybody.

Not religious? I said, and she shook the fall of hair. Forgot the whole nonsense, she said, with what seemed a studied defiance. I think we're held back by this desert worship. That's what my father called it. We kept Shabbath, but not strictly. I mean, we didn't work. I did. I had to. He didn't mind. Get on with your career, he said. So I sort of gradually forgot everything. I don't see anything here to remind me, much. But this Day of Atonement, I believe it might be sort of important. Fasting now and again's good for you, and I said, That reminds me. I've been on a fast pretty near two days. How about that tray? and she said, Oh darl'. Watch me go.

I saw her, the long back, the legs, the hair, and the door shut. But I was still too shaky to do much more than hold on to the wall. I had one of the best baths of my life —why does a bath stand out?—and I had one side of my face shaved, and the telephone rang. I felt like letting it ring but it could be Aliya, and I wandered—I understood the term—into the bedroom and picked it up. Yes? I said, and the voice said, That you, young fella? Merom, Tel Aviv. How's everything? and I said, Just fine. Woke up ten minutes ago, and he said, I was on to that doctor down there. You're in great shape, he says. I can't tell you how happy that makes me. Listen. Day after tomorrow, think you feel like having lunch with four of us? Tell you why. Ship of mine, she's due in tomorrow night. I want to fly Roch down there, and your new secretary, see? There's a lot of paper. The four of them, couple of hours' work, job's done, and she's ready for the turnaround. Nobody down there, take those guys a couple of weeks. Could I count on you? And I said, I'll be happy to see you. Could Roch bring down the latest figures? and he said, Don't think he won't. Your secretary's got everything set. Anything you want? and I said, I believe I have everything I ever wanted, and he said, I think I know how you feel. I had it, once. Don't suppose I'm ever going to feel like that again. Champagne's what you wash the floor with. Get shook back in, will you? *Shalom.*

I had to lather again. Merom called *me?* I should have called *him.* Why was it never in mind? *Why?* No answer.

I looked in the glass. Twenty-odd years looked back. Since a year ago, alone. Greataunt Sophia saved me, blessed be she, and the lawyer found me via Poste Restante, Paris. Why? I had to ask myself. Flight? Could be. But I refused to think. The padded door shut. My uncle's study had a door like that. It shut everything out. But unlike my father, I left nothing to my son, and I thought of the considerable balance in Switzerland as eskimos think of thick furs. Anything could happen, but I was safe for life. Yet I preferred to leave it there, and make my own way. So far, I was able. But it was recent, in the past few months, since meeting Plus A and the end of the footloose period, through Europe, and the Greek Islands, and almost by fatal attraction, to Israel.

I felt I was home. I could lie down anywhere in the land and sense I was in my own domain, sleep as one belonging, northern Galilee to Sinai, from the sea to the Golan and down to the Red Sea, I was part. Nothing was foreign to me, except the language. I had the whisper of it from childhood, listening to grandparents and their friends, being almost frightened by their foreignness. My mother once told me, Be still. It's their way. Yours will be different.

The days passed, and here I stood.

But the days *do* pass. My mother and my uncle died,

and millions of others, and I was standing there, shaving, and chicken feathers whitened the streets, and people starved themselves to atone for their own sins, and their fathers'. I had no surety that my father and mother ever sinned, or, for that matter my grandfathers and grandmothers. Kinder people I never knew. In many ways, I wondered if I were as good a man as my uncle or either of my grandfathers. I doubted it. But how *do* people sin? What *is* sin? Murder? Theft? Adultery? False witness? Only a very few. Worshipping false gods? Who was to say which was false? What proof? Not enough to wave a book, Bible, Talmud, Midrash, whatever. Mao Tse-tung's hundreds of millions could also wave a little red one. But the truth was in no book, never mind how many waved it. The truth was not in words. Truest words, ever, were Pilate's *What is truth?* If only on that, he had a place in history.

I got tired of it. The razor taught me I was still shaky.

The knocks again, and I wrapped a towel to answer the door. A waiter brought in a tray, eggs, toast, coffee, and I signed, and dried on the terrace, but then I saw the tray was for one. I rang downstairs, and suddenly I was shocked that I knew Aliya as that, but no surname. I never heard it.

I put the telephone down.

Toast, butter, eggs, coffee, all good, and then the pills. Then I was tired. I put a knee on the bed, face down. The bell beside me, *rrrr*. I felt for the thing.

Darling? Got everything? and I said, Wonderful breakfast, and the sun's going down, and she said, I'm staying in my room till tomorrow, this time. It's *the* day. Only one I take any notice of. Well, maybe Passover. But that's a party. This is different. You agree? and I said, Any day's different. And important. Might be the last.

Oh, my, she said. You sound terribly doomful, and I said, I'd love to know where you found that word, and she said, Well, I bought a paperback down at the airport, and I've been dipping in all day. Listen, are you sure you had enough to eat? and I said, One crumb, and I urp.

Wonderful, she said. Fasting won't hurt *you*. We'll have the best dinner ever tomorrow night. But *no* cheating. They have *Shabbath goys* working here. They'll bring you anything you want, and I said, Hold on, Shabbath *what?* and she said, They do the work on the day of rest. Light fires, attend to this and that. Anything we're not allowed to do. Come on, *you* know that? and I said, I never ran into it. Do you have any spare reading, there? All I have is a Hebrew Bible. For me, it stays in the drawer, and she said, Oh, poor you. I'll get somebody to take a couple down. Call you this time tomorrow? Think of me. It's really rough, just this couple of days. But afterwards we'll set the record straight. I don't even want to *think*. Tomorrow? Bye.

And still no word about Salah?

But again, in those moments I felt repelled by a strange do-as-I-say tone. I could understand why a husband would quarrel, never mind what his instincts might be. Dealing with her from day to day, with the distance of the café counter a no-man's-land, she seemed feminine in a way that Shoshana, for example, was not. Closer tie made clear a drive that could have been male. I hardly knew what I meant. I knew what I felt, and I was warned. But I was happier in thinking I had at least twenty-four hours to myself. She was still good to think about. I wondered if I could tempt her out of the Day of Atonement quarantine, but it seemed unfair, even though I judged it to be no more than lip service, a word to the "desert-worshippers," a sop to some hidden quirk of conscience.

I had no feeling about it. We had never kept any day of any sort, except Christmas and New Year, and Easter meant eggs, and holidays, and Whitsun was more holidays, and generally a family reunion in Paris. For the first time I realised my uncle must have had a word with the priests at school. I went to morning chapel with the rest. A fifteen-minute gabble was all I remembered. But on Sundays, with others, I sat in thirty-minute Old Testament classes, and later, while the rest of the school was at Church, I studied for examinations, again with others, and at last I understood we had all been of some other sect, Islamic or whatever, and set apart. That, it seemed to me now, was good sense.

Taps brought in a waiter, a hippy from the hair. He threw the books on the other bed, and went out, leaving the door open. I got up to close it, picked up the books, read the titles, *White Bread,* a gripping novel of the forbidden trade in women, and Flaubert's *Salammbô*.

The first I thought unappetising, and the other too far from my mood.

I took a couple of pills, pulled the curtains, and lay on the bed, and seemed neither to sleep nor wake, and yet the clock showed ten to nine, and I opened curtains I might have closed a moment before, and saw the appeal of Eilat.

Bright sun, calm blue water, red mountains, and complete silence.

Opposite, the beach turned up to a yacht harbor, and right to the port. It seemed a small city of hotels, new, or building. Nothing moved.

I remembered the day, felt hungry and thirsty, and lifted the telephone. A girl answered. I'd like some coffee

179

and toast, please, I said. Grapefruit juice, if you have any, and she said, No toast. Bread and butter. Coffee, yes. Instant. No juice. You will have to wait some minutes, please.

I bathed and shaved and put on shorts and shirt, and picked up *Salammbô,* skimming, but Flaubert was out of reach. A paragraph of the other was enough. I tried to imagine what could make Aliya choose them. Most bookshops were racked with every sort of paperback. Plus A bought them by the half dozen. Then it was my turn, and the choice was amazing, and we soon had a library. I tried to think what it was about *Salammbô* that had no appeal, and I remembered we read Herodotus at school that year, and beside it, the fiction which enthralled the salons of Flaubert's time wilted, if, now, I saw the power of many a page not always happily translated. Yet I found I had read a couple of chapters before the door shook from a couple of light kicks. I opened it, another waiter put the tray on the dressing table, and held out a slip. I signed, found some change, and he, too, no word of thanks, left the door open.

The bread, stale. The butter, half-melted. The coffee, a spoonful of powder in a cup, water barely hot.

A day of atonement was all very fine for those believing they had a duty. Others, unbelieving, paying for service, had a right to be treated as guests in the normal way. I went for the telephone. The same girl answered. French? I told her what I thought.

It is an important day, she said, as if she had answered more than one complaint. We have nobody on duty. The kitchen is closed until after four o'clock. There is also no room service. It is only temporary. I am sorry. It is all I can do, and I said, Are you a Christian? and she laughed and said, No. I am nothing. It is why I am here.

That made two of us. I chewed some bread and butter, and drank some instant water, and went out, down the stairs. The lobby and foyer were silent.

Outside the sun blinded. I walked towards the town. But the silence, the emptiness, wore me down. I turned back for the beach, took my shoes off, paddled along the shoreline, wondering how many in all Israel were keeping this day, and how many not. I knew that nobody would fast at Uriel except perhaps Lod and his friends, and they were not many. Yeke and the others would eat twice as much in contempt of all ritual.

It seemed to me, in the silence, in a place unchanged since Israel passed through coming up out of Egypt, that in all conscience I was stranger in a strange land.

I sympathised with any attempt to preserve tradition, but without any desire to take part, though I knew that if I were a father, I would insist that my children were taught the rite and the reason. That lack was my defeat, and it was too late to learn. The will was, if not against, then absent. But at the same time I asked myself what right I had to burden a child with mental lumber. I found it difficult to answer, except that it seemed in reason that a people held together by tradition of feast and fast, rejoicing and penitence, spread across the year, and every year, would be stronger in national spirit, more robust in outlook, the more determined to preserve what they held in all faith as their inheritance. Those qualities, throughout the country wherever I had been, were demonstrably present. There were certainly the Yekes and the others, all excellent people of their kind, holding all religion as a plague. But they were first to defend any word against the State of Israel, and most wore the medal ribbons of three wars of Independence.

I found within me a will, almost a written scroll of

dedication, to preserve the land and its people, as they were, and as they wanted to be, and this small town of concrete blocks, raised in hope between the sea's edge and the desert, made a fitting seal.

I wondered if a Yeke, or a Groz or an Avram, in their secret hearts thought as I did, or if I was simply victim of an excess of sentimentality, emotionalism, whatever. Both were human qualities, too often diffuse, and wonderful targets for the cynic. I tried to imagine how far, how deep, those feelings ran in me. I was not cynical. I, in simple terms, did not believe, though certainly I had no wish to mock religion, or any form of worship, still less the believers. All held the sacral fire of faith and the hallow of time, and about me was evidence of profit.

But I put a Yeke and his kind, and a Lod, with those even more strict, in the balance, trying to imagine which of the two factions had most to do with conquest, whether of the land, the economy, or a place in world affairs, and I had to come down on Yeke's side, if only because he was guided by the Meroms, that generally unseen corps of captains and kings, neither one thing nor the other, but steadfastly their own men, believers to a point, ignoring the rest, protectors, never destroyers, another Wall in themselves, at truest core, Israeli.

Zuz's figure-of-eight flick of the napkin took my eye midway on the hotel's top floor.

Aliya held the towel in strong breeze, touched where the wrist watch would be, and held up six fingers, pointing to her room.

I waved, nodded, and she blew a kiss and went in, sliding the window shut.

I felt I had been given an order, resented it, wanted to countermand, but memory of her in bed brought pause.

It seemed worth a little curbing of bad temper.

NINETEEN

I tapped at almost a quarter past six, and when she opened the door, in an orange bath towel tucked under her arms, her barefoot lounge in front of me was more pout then walk.

I didn't think you'd keep me waiting, she said, shaking the hair over her shoulder, and starting to plait three tresses. What were you doing? and I said, Shaving, and she said, Ah, now, look. How long's it take you to shave? and I said, How about a drink? and she said, Just a moment. I've had no food. I don't need one. A drink's the last thing, and I said, It's number one for me. When you're ready, join me, and she said, Hell with it. *Wait* a minute. You mean you're leaving me? and I said, Yes, and shut the door.

I almost got to my room and her door crashed against the wall and she stood in the corridor, fists at her sides, staring eyes reminding me of the Gorgon, and I remembered Plus A, *She's a horror*, and I waited.

I take the trouble to come down here, and you do this

to *me*? she said, in a stage whisper like a scream. How can you treat me like this? and I said, I told you. I want a drink, and she said, What are you, an alco*holic*? and I said, No. I want a drink. Come join me, and I turned the key and went in, leaving the door open, but hers slammed. I called the bar and asked for a bottle of scotch, and soda water.

I found I was shaking again, and badly. I took a couple of the pills, and sat on the bed, wanting to take the next plane out. But there was Merom and the party tomorrow, and anyway, I felt if I walked outside the door it would have to be hands and knees.

For the first time, now that dreams had worn off, I realised I was no use to Aliya, or, for that matter, anyone else. All I wanted to do was sleep. But the taps on the door pulled me up. The waiter came in, a real one, short-haired, clean white jacket, slid the tray on the table, held the slip, I signed, gave him some coins and he went out and shut the door. He had the idea.

I poured a shorty, filled up with soda, drank a mouthful, put down the glass, and lay back.

I dragged, heavy, still in a dream of looking down from a railroad carriage into a deep gorge, and a river pale green, and knowing we were tipping in, and a red and white fighter plane took off and shot water over everybody except me, and two guards said I was allowed in, but the voice I was sure must be Sheba's, languorous, deep, in a hymn of words I knew and never heard, and I was in a green room, a light behind, face to the pillow, a hand on my ankle running up, behind the knee, and down, and a voice?

Wasn't anybody's fault, Aliya said, softly. Just happens. Sick, y'sick. So? Way it goes. All the time. Well.

In a hiccough.

I lay, cold. Her weight left the bed, and I heard the pace, a pressure, perhaps a hand on the mattress, and she fell across the next bed in a half-scream, groan.

And silence.

I stayed for moments, still, opened an eye. She slept, arms overhead, lower legs off the bed, breathing with no sound. I turned over, toward the light. My glass was almost full. I drank a tepid mouthful, stood, went to the bathroom without a waver, poured the drink down the pedestal, pressed the button, and went back in the noise. Aliya slept. I poured another drink, and lit a cigaret, but these were acts of bravura. I expected her to waken. Instead, she might have been a corpse. I went to the other side of the next bed, put both hands under her far side, and pulled her towards me, rolling the counterpane under, turning her the other way, lifting her shoulders, thighs, getting the padded silk free to cover her, and the towel fell away.

But her beauty was no longer all of desire, or whatever desire means, and I had no wish to get into her, or for that matter, be anywhere near her. But there she was, warm for the night, and my part was done, and I poured another drink.

I was about to put out the light, and I thought of her room, a night watchman, perhaps an open door, and an alarm.

I got out of bed, put on shirt and trouser, and went out, and there, her door was partly open. I looked for the key, not in the lock, and went in. The room was a shock. Clothes were thrown everywhere, most torn, rags, floor, beds, even in the bathroom. Combed, bathed, always well-dressed Aliya, and this?

I gathered all the rags, heaped them on the unused bed. The sheets of the bed she used were flung aside. The pillow was dented. There were no bottles. But in the bathroom I saw, down in the open bag, a long, tooled-leather box, perhaps a manicure set. But inside, the syringe, and ampoules shouted. Two glass shatters in the wastebasket were enough.

I was utterly sorry, determined to take care of her.

I tidied the room, took the key from the table, turned out the lights, and shut the door. My room seemed curiously warm, and homey. She was on her left side, away from me, I sat on my bed, had another drink, thought about her, found little enough to be thoughtful about, flipped the light off, and got under the sheets. I tried to solve the riddle, why, at one moment I was willing to sell Atlas and his world to know a woman, and now, in arm's reach, she meant less than a drink.

I woke with the thought, and turned over. She was gone.

I reached, and felt the cold. She must have left well over an hour. Her key had been taken from the table. My dressing gown should have been over the armchair. I breathed relief, pulling the curtains to white sunshine, blue sea and red mountains. The board told me, Your breakfast, sir? *Immédiatement,* and I asked for a paper in English, and for Aliya's number, eight doors from mine. She lifted the receiver with the first ring.

This is me, I said. How are you this morning?

Oh, I had the worst spell yesterday, she said, listless, cold. I have diabetes. Not all that serious. Just hits when I don't expect it. I shouldn't be here. Thinking of flying back today. See the doctor. Won't be any use. I think I'm getting worse. You had to be nuisanced with it. Listen, was it you cleaned up in here? and I said, Well, I just pushed a lot of stuff in one place, and shut the door, that's all, and she said, That was real boy-scouty of you.

I remembered when I woke up. I must have been crazy. I have nothing to wear. Gal downstairs is buying me a dress. Just to get back in. Look, I don't think we ought to see each other before I go, and I said, You met me, so I see you off, and she said, Uh-huh. Glad to see me go, that it? and I said, Depends on the time. My finance people are here today. I'm lunching with them.

And you didn't tell me? she said. We could have slept up a storm, better than the other time, and you'd still be lunching with somebody else? Not a word to me? and I said, I didn't know till last night. Why do I have to tell you? and she said, Well, just a little question of loyalty, that's all.

Listen, I said. You were in no condition, and she said, Hell's that got to do with it? I knew what I was doing. I was sharp. I remember every word you said. What are you trying to *do*? and I said, I don't want to get in any argument, and she said, We didn't get that far. I'm only putting the facts where they belong, and I said, All right. I had enough. You hear me? Enough. Goodbye, and put the receiver down.

Only a moment later, her fists hammered.

Open this door, she screamed. You can't treat me like this, goddammit to hell, you can't. I won't let you, and I picked up the receiver, and asked for the manager, and told him a woman was annoying me, and please have her removed, and he said, A woman? and I said, Yes, in this hotel. She's right outside this door, and screaming. Now. Mean you can't hear her? and he said, Right away.

But she was still hammering, though her voice was a mumble, almost a monotone groan, and I listened, moments long, certain she was not coming in, though I felt I should go out there, the soft heart, if only to get her back to her own room.

But then other voices echoed, and the beating stopped, and a quiet came, and I lay back on the bed, and something told me I was near the breaking point. My hands shook so much, I put the cup on the table, knelt to drink, and had to pull myself up.

The telephone rang, and for a second or two I looked at it, ringing, and finally took it off the holder. Yes, I said, and the operator said, The doctor's on his way up, and I said, Fine, and looked at the watch. Dead on eight o'clock.

A key was in the door, and taps, and I said, Yes, and the doctor came in, fresh as a Shoshi pancake, and said, I hear you had a little trouble? and I said, Nothing. There's a girl down there, she's diabetic. Had a spell of some sort.

He went through the pulse, the heart, mouth, throat, and said, Perfectly good. You can still do with plenty of rest. Sit in the sun for an hour. Not longer. Lie down when you feel like it. Sleep's your best friend. I'll send some medicine down later. This woman. I'd advise no further meeting, and I said, Please tell the manager that, and he said, I will, indeed, and snapped the bag. I'll call in about six this evening. *Shalom.*

He had just shut the door, and the telephone rang, and again I lifted it, ready to put it down.

Merom, the voice said, and how could a voice, a name, suggest Thou Shalt Have None Other God? and I said, Well, and how are *you?* and he said, We got here early. Everybody's working down at the port. Going to be ready for lunch? and I said, Yes. Where? and he said, Downstairs. One thirty. You want the figures up there? and I said, Certainly, and he said, I'll send them up. How you feeling? and I said, This place is setting me up, and he said, For what? I been hearing things, and I said, Don't worry, I'm fine, and he said, See you.

I asked the board to call me at noon, and went out in the sun, to the deck chair, and sudden sleep.

The bell got me up in deep-blue sun shadow, dry-mouthed, and the voice said, Midday, sir. There is a package for you, and I said, Send it up, and went under the shower's thousand-needle freeze.

Taps, of a different sort, almost timid, brought me out, wrapping a towel, and I opened the door, one hand out for the package.

I was asked to bring you this by Mr. Merom, the girl in shadow said. We're downstairs, but he told me to say there's no hurry. We're early.

I nodded drips, and took the envelope, and said, Sorry, I'm not dressed. Are you Miss Ben Hillel? and she, a lovely, big, plump lolly of a girl said, Oh, no. I'm *her* secretary. I'm Paula Van Tjin, Mr. Leslie, and I said, Fine way to meet anybody, soaking wet. I'll be right down, and she said, The sticking plaster's hanging off your forehead. Could I put it on for you?

Glad if you would, I said. I can't seem to make it stick, and she said, It won't on wet skin. We dry it, first.

She took charge like a pro nurse, and I said, When did you pick up the medical stuff? and she said, I just finished in the Army, and I said, Go slow on that fluid. It stings like hell, and she said, Tough. It's necessary. Stitches aren't out too long, and you've been sweating, and I said, Is that my fault? and she said, Mr. Leslie, either you stand still, or I'll have to sit on you, and I said, Not my idea of punishment, and she said, One more dab, and that's it, and I said, Where did you learn English? and she said, I went to school in Holland and England. My father was Dutch. He and my mother died when I was a baby. Hold still. Mr. Merom took care of me. And Tâl. And others. He has a large family. I'm certainly the largest. There. Let it dry.

She swept the debris in the wastebasket, and said, We'll be in the bar downstairs when you're ready, sir, and I said, Please. No *sir*, and she said, Sorry, it slipped out. Training, and I said, Nobody says sir in this country, and she said, That's phoney democracy. Egalitarianism. Won't do. Discipline, or chaos, and I said, They seem to thrive. And she said, Seem. That's all. Try that nonsense in the Army. That's the *real* basis in *this* country. May I be of further help? and I said, You've been an angel. I'm a lot more comfortable. Now it only aches, and I saw her face change, and the flash when she turned away. I'm sorry, she said, in a high voice. We feel very much for people who suffer for us. You will be well, thank God, and she shut the door.

I looked in the glass. She had indeed done a pro-job. All the plaster ran the same way, and parallel, an improvement, I thought, if only aesthetic.

The file surprised me. We were well over estimated production, but not keeping up with orders, even though we were on a two-shift basis. It was clear we needed to triple our staff even without thought for the future. I began to pencil, and then remembered the party downstairs, got into shorts and a shirt, took the file with me, and ran for the lift.

Merom sat facing me, with Paula and Roch. The bar was full of a bus-load tour. Most spoke German.

Well, young fella, Merom said. Sit down. You don't know Tâl? Your new secretary. If *you* say so?

I shook hands with Roch, and turned.

Shalom, she said.

From the Other World.

190

Grey eyes, brilliant, spoke loud that the hand of her father was still upon her. Violet sunglasses over a Thracian nose, mouth, beautiful, skin shining, hair below the waist, coiling on the chair. I felt a dry hand, minimal pressure. Discreet? The glow of her stunned me.

We're in a mess, I said, and sat. We have at least a hundred more to train just to keep up. How about the commune? and Merom said, You're the boss. You tell *us*, and I said, I don't think I'll be much use for a week or so. Couldn't you ask Mayerkopf to double the intake? and Merom said, I'll do that. How about lunch? and I said, Look, I'm not a plate man. I'd like a plain sandwich and a glass of beer. If they don't want to serve us here, we can go up to my place. But I don't even want to *see* a knife and fork, and Merom looked at Tâl, and around at Roch, and said, Didn't I tell you? Like me. Dry lunch, glass of beer, we're in. What sort of sandwich? and I waited for Tâl.

Cheese, tomato, glass of milk, she said, and Paula said, The same please, and Roch said, I like chicken, a glass of beer, and Merom said, That's two, and I nodded, and he said, Three, and nodded at Paula, and she got up and stopped a waiter.

Looking fine, Merom said. Doctor thinks you have a few days. He wants the plaster off. How's the shakes? and I said, I seem to have them under control. Till I think about it. Then I shake, and Merom said, Tâl, take a note. No shakes. It's a company order. We have to straighten this guy out, and she said, Oh, don't *say* that. Even to joke.

She turned to me. Mr. Leslie, I'm on your payroll so I'm on your side, she said, so gently I wanted to purr. I'm also supposed to be your secretary. You didn't have an awful lot to say about it. But I really *am* on your side.

I've seen what you've done. Do you want to talk business? and I said, Certainly. I hate to think everything's going on without me, and she said, Let me give you the add-up. Everything's going magnificently. That's the word. It's true the orders are swamping us, for the moment. Mr. Mayerkopf's done what you did. Doubled the trainee classes. He was worried you wouldn't agree, and I said, You tell him from me, double, and redouble. We still won't be up to it. Tell him to scrap the present training program. Twenty operators every two weeks doesn't do it. Minimum, twenty a week. See the *Mukhtar*. Use younger girls. How about the commune project?

They're doing well, considering, Tâl said. They don't like using Arabs, and I said, Why not? and she said, Well. There was a bomb, and I said, That's a different sort of Arab, and she said, They don't think so. They already had three wars in the past twenty years. All they're waiting for is number four.

That's fine with me, I said. But I'm worried about work. Either they have the hands, or they don't. I say, bring in the Arabs. They've done a lot for us.

I'm with you, Merom said. Sooner we get together, sooner we get everybody living right. Listen, we're all part of everything. Who's this mental case been staying here? She got the café up there. I mean, at Uriel? You know she was here? What's her name? Aliya?

I saw her in those moments, knew her sweet, felt her womanliness, refused all interference even in flashing thought of Salah.

Aliya's a friend of mine, I said. She's sick at the moment. Gone back to Tel Aviv. She's done a lot for us. I don't want to talk about her. Don't want her talked *about*. All right?, and Merom said, That's fine with me.

Talking among ourselves. You all have to work up there. I'd just as soon get it straight. Look. She isn't in Tel Aviv. She's right there at the desk.

I had no wish to turn round. But I did.

She leaned on outstretched arms, hair in long fall against the edge of the reception desk.

I got up, and went there, put an arm around the small waist, and said, Aliya, this is me. Come on, I'll take you up, and she put her arms around me, standing, and it felt like a world-wide wrap around, and she put her head on my shoulder and I remembered Arye, and the heavy head, and I said, Which room? and the clerk said, She checked out, and I said, Give me my key, and I helped her, stumbling, to the lift.

We had to wait, and she was heavy, almost asleep. The cage came, two got out, and I pressed the button. She leaned, I loved the head. We got out on the fourth floor, and I carried her to my room, opened the door, and half-walked her to my unmade bed, and let her lie down. She seemed a little child, and I covered her, pulled the curtains to darkness, and went downstairs.

Merom stood in the foyer with the doctor, two men in white coats, and a policeman.

Listen, he said. You could be in trouble. That girl broke out of hospital. She in your room? and I held up the key, and the doctor took it, and said, Thanks. She'll be on the next flight out, and I said, She's asleep. She shouldn't be disturbed, and he said, That's for me to decide, and the cage shut.

Merom held out his hands.

Look, he said. You got too much to lose to get in any mess. You know it? This dame could murder you, and I said, Wait, now. She's been kind to me and a lot of others. She's sick, and he said, You better watch it, else *you*'ll be sick. These people don't fool, let me tell you, and I said, Why should they have to? She needs treatment. Nobody's trying to fool anybody, and he said, Listen, that doctor's official. That means he's Army. And *that* means he's real *power*. He don't want her here, so she's out. Don't run his shadow, see? A word from him, it goes in your file. For the sort of job you're doing, you're finished. You get no clearance, and I said, What do you mean? Just for helping her? and he said, Start *using* it, can't you? Get smart. They *have* to have something on her. Probably this isn't the first time. She's making it certain it's going to be the last, and I said, Somebody's sick, so you make an example? and he said, Sick, nothing. She's playing her own game. You don't think a doctor's fooled that easy? Specially not *this* one, and I said, But does he think she's got an act going? I know her. Known her months. And I say she's *sick. Looks* sick, *thinks* sick. And she's no actress, and Merom said, Listen, son. Don't say another word. Please. You'll find out. Come on. Sandwiches.

I watched the foyer while the others talked. I had little appetite. I remembered the heavy head. Memory of being with her in those hours behind the café tantalised. She *was* beautiful, at times a little mad, or something near it. But part of her, not perhaps her body. She had nothing to compare with Plus A, not the honey, not the womansweet, but a groping, claws and teeth desire for orgasm that eluded, yes, but part of her sought, almost in fear, and there seemed two selves battling each other, one wanting to give, the other denying. Unlike the nature of Plus A. Once in, she gave and wanted. But not Aliya. She wanted, but without having to give, and so

194

gave little, except a memory of tortured struggle, teeth marks, scratches, exhaustion, pliant limbs, silence.

Merom leaned to look at me, pointing to the half sandwich on my plate.

Eat, he said. Don't worry so much, and I said, I'm thinking of a friend. I'd think of you the same, and he clasped his hands, and said, Why do I always have to get stuck with people I like? Why can't I have a run-in with somebody I *don't* like? and Paula said, Because you know he's right, and he said, I don't want no back-up from you, and she said, No back-up. A friend's a friend. Either you stand-up, or else you point that finger at your-*self*, and he said, Kid's talk, and she said, How often we saw you. Yes, Tâl? and Tâl said, Yes. I wish I had as many pennies, and he said to me, You know something? Worst place for friends is your own family, and Roch said, Best place for most friends. Listen, if we're going to get the two-thirty flight, I have to talk a little nuts-and-bolts, and Merom said, No. I have a better idea. The two girls stay here. House just up the hill. About time it got used a little, and Tâl laughed at Paula, and said, We were going to ask you if we couldn't have a day or two. It's a beautiful little place. Is Nelda still there? and Merom said, Sure. But you'll still make your own beds. Nothing got changed. Now, did you bring all the stuff like I told you? and Tâl said, Every tiny little piece of paper. Just happened to have them with us, and Merom said, Fine. You can sit in the sun and read it to him. Won't be wasting any time. All right, Marcel, what's your problem? and Roch said, Not mine. *His*. Who's in charge of the plant while he's here? They squawk. They don't take orders, and I said, Mayerkopf in charge overall. Arendts, chief engineer. Rugzin, chief of stores.

Jaroslov, in charge of staff. Malka what's-her-name, in charge of girls' training. Bonessi, men's. Any questions, refer to me, here and Merom said, Great. Anything else? and Tâl raised a hand, and said, How long do we stay?

Mermo nodded at me.

There's your boss, he said. Ask him. The boat's going to be ready for you this afternoon. Forty horse. Down in the yacht harbour. Fishing tackle, all set. Catch anything good, fly it up to me. One thing I love, it's good, thick, white, juicy fish. Dry stuff you can have. Hey, there's the doctor.

I saw the group walking down the stairs. Aliya seemed entirely at ease, talking to him. His attitude was any man's talking to a beauty. All the men laughed, the glass doors shut, a car came in, the doctor spoke, and the others walked toward the highway.

Merom looked at his watch, and said, Probably catching that two-thirty. Well, that's that. Boy, am I glad. That kind, they ruin the earth, and I said, She did no harm to anybody, and he said, Listen, I don't agree. I'm getting my bag. Tâl, I want the car at Lod. Paula, suppose you get me a cab. Young fella, you didn't eat a damn' thing. I wish you stop worrying, and I said, I feel like a heel. I ought to see what's happening to her, and he said, You saw what I saw. Couldn't be in better hands. Leave it alone. She don't seem too worried about *you*, and Roch said, So right, and Merom said, Nobody asked the opinion, and Roch looked like the sorrowful Punch.

But suddenly, the vision.

I stood in a daze of blue sun shadow, and I saw the litter swing between teams of camels nightbound in torch lanes along the Arava, and I heard wild music and the clattering jingle of guarding cavalry, and I knew who lay beyond the silken curtains, naked, beneath the nodding peacock fans.

I knew, and in all certainty, I saw.

Tâl.

Sheba!

TWENTY

Who is this that cometh out of the wilderness like pillars of smoke, perfumed with myrrh and frankincense? Thou hast ravished my heart, my sister, my spouse, with one of thine eyes, with one chain of thy neck, The choir sang, soft, and pipes played antiphon, and gentle fingers rippled across drums against a counterthrash of timbrels, and harps plucked the deep, roaming chords.

Sheba lay in the golden bath, and handmaidens poured milch warm from the teat, and laved her, and lifted her to the oiling slab's marble, and glossed her with spikenard, and caressed her dry, and carried her in slow pace to the robing tent.

Her nightly city along the Arava glowed in a mile of silk-curtained pavilions, joined by alleys of tall plants in flower, on the East and West open to the evening breeze, all lit in the white flame of a thousand wicks in purest oil of enemies, and only shadows moved across the lights.

But the sentries of King Solomon were quick to see two Edomites, far away, where the camp of Sheba seemed a long golden bar against the night, and fell upon them, and brought them to the Captain of the Guard.

It is the hour of the Queen's bath, he said. By order of the King, no man shall enter within a distance of fifteen minutes' gallop by the royal chariot troop lest they see the Queen's nakedness, or so much as a shadow. She is guest, inviolate. You have seen what was forbidden. Take out their eyes.

Thumbs pressed, and eyes bulged, were torn by the root, and screams infected the night, and the Captain of the Guard said, They disturb the Queen's peace, and the King's order. Fill their mouths, and wick bowls were lifted, and hot oil poured, and screams choked. Tie them to your horses, and take them back whence they came, the Captain of the Guard said. They shall be companions of their thoughts. Let them have their knees to crawl. The rest, cleave. Pass word what happens to the curious. Peace, and all blessing, be here.

Tâl stopped talking in a turn-down of paper, and looked up at the sky, lips drawn in over her teeth, sighed, and said, I don't believe you heard a word of it. Tell me what it was about, and I said, When do secretaries give their bosses orders? Cut me a little more shrimp. I believe that big one's gobbled what I had. I'll have to learn to fish all over again.

Paula opened the basket, chopped a prawn, and I swung the hook towards her, outboard.

Look, I said. Paper's fine. I think I have a fair general idea. But I don't want to fill my head with it. I have things to do. I'm working out a few ideas. And Tâl said, I have the pieces of paper you scribble on. Doodles? and I said, Not. I have a thumper I'm not satisfied with. But I'm glad you saved them, and she said, Paula did. Most, anyway. Paula, a little bouquet, and Paula bowed, sitting at the back of the boat, and said, What I'm here for.

In bikinis, they were a pair. Paula looked overweight most times, but in a bikini she gave the lie. She was a big girl, that was all, a woman any man would be proud to be with.

Tâl? Delicate, graceful, slender, the long, perfectly shaped legs, and yet, close to, no giantess. A waist any elbow ached to grace. Breasts of Aphrodite, sharp-tipped, and the long plait swung between, about, over, and sometimes she shook it loose, and the glowing mantle flowed, a wonder.

Sheba, beyond the camel-litter, and the thousands of slaves flattening the path in front, sitting with me in the rubber boat, Paula putting the papers away, and the three of us floating over the Red Sea's coral, a dream in practical overtones.

Tâl, I said. I think I heaved the shakes, and she said, I noticed. The past couple of days. Thank God, and I said, I didn't hear from Mr. Merom for quite some time, and she said, He's in Europe. I hear from him every day. Sometimes, twice, and I said, What's this? A conspiracy? and she said, No. He likes to be in touch. So do I. When would you care to go back?

Well, sounds to me like the day after tomorrow, I said. One more day of sun and a fishing rod. Just to make sure. How's that suit you? and she said, Oh, so much. I could just come out and watch you fish every day. But it's *such* a wonderful business. They have problems.

Right. I said, That's it. Book us day after tomorrow. Get us there in the late afternoon before everybody goes home. I want to talk to them. Look, what happened about the girl in the café? She all right? and Paula, chopping a prawn, said, She's fine. Goes to school every day. Haifa. Private tutor. Mathematics, and I said, For heaven's sakes. How do you know? and she said, Well, it gets around.

Sheba's foot rested in front of me, perfection in toe and nail. She was from the South, a Yemenite? Shulamith? Shunnamit?

How fair, and how pleasant art thou, O love, for delights. This thy stature is like to a palm tree, and thy breasts to clusters of grapes. We will be glad and rejoice in thee. We will remember thy love more than wine. The upright love thee.

I believe, if you'll let me suggest it, Tâl said, tentatively—what?—asking a favor? Please don't think I'm taking advantage of a prawn and a basket of beautiful fishes, but couldn't we please have an office system? The plant has computers and all that. But in the office, we're dealing with more than two thousand parts, and hundreds of companies. We have cardboard files. We'll never catch up, and I said, I'm sold. Get the best there is. Carte blanche, and she clapped her hands, and turned to Paula, and they both laughed as though I made a gift, and I saw that Tâl was marvellously sun-burned.

That couple-of-fingers-width of flesh showed white where the bikini stretched.

I am black, but comely, O ye daughters of Jerusalem, like the tents of Kedar, like the curtains of Solomon. Look not upon me because I am black, because the sun hath looked upon me.

What sort of stuff do you put on yourself to get that colour? I asked her, and she said, That gal in the pharmacy up there. I believe she brewed it. Real witch, and Paula said, Birnam Wood's not far. Only thing they don't have is toads. Got enough of them in the café across the road. Long hair and dirty underpants, and Tâl said, Oh, don't say that. They're young. Going around. I often wish I could break free. I don't know, though. I can't. Simply can *not*. Wish I could. Even just for a few days. Or weeks. Just float. A hippie. Free, and I said, Aren't you free now? and she said, No. Not really. There are some things I *have* to do. Some things I *must*. I can't go dirty. Or ragged, I can't just sit and drink beer and listen to somebody playing a guitar. I can't listen. Can't just sit. Can't feel dirt. Smells. Can't keep out contempt. That's what really brings out the rash. Why must I feel contempt? I sympathize. But I'm a traitor. I'd love not to bathe for days, and wear any kind of rags, and stroll over there and sit down among them. *Be* one of them. Sleep on the beach. I *wish* I could. I wish I knew why I can't, and Paula said, I'll tell you why, *duchka*. You're not the kind. They're born sloppy. Weak. Any kind of life'll do. If they can eat, and sleep, and sit, that's it. It's music, what they listen to? It's words? It's half-assed tunes. For punks. I'll tell you why you can't sit down over there. You couldn't be a punk if you tried. You weren't *born* one. You can't learn to *be* one. Everything in you says No. That's the breed, and I said, Bloodline, and Paula looked surprise at me, and nodded.

That's exactly it, she said. Bloodline. You can't go against the blood. It's in you, or it's not. It's not in you, go ahead, sit with the punks. It's in you, you can't.

I looked over blue, blue water, and what did I see?

Jordan's mountains, seen by Israel three thousand or more years ago, unchanged since then, scarlet in that sun, pale blue shadow in the rifts and clefts, not quite the tender blue of shadow between the breasts of Tâl.

A bite almost took me out of the boat, and Tâl clutched me about the waist, and held.

I pretended I needed her grip, and weighed upon her. I wanted her near me. I reeled, and lifted, reeled, lifted, and all the time myself, the one apart, was with her, and from her grasp, I exulted in knowing that the same part of her, the Other part, was with me.

Slowly, without thinking, feeling too much, I brought in the fish, until Paula could use the gaff and net, and we shouted to see the size, but still Tâl's hands held me, and still I stayed, to keep her hands there, on my hip bones, and I wished my hands were on hers, and I never wanted to be further away.

Right, I said, in return to sanity. We won't top that. Pack him in ice, and up he goes to Mr. Merom, and Tâl said, Marvellous idea. He'll be there tonight, and I said to Paula, Let's have the engine on. Back to the harbour. Dock the boat. Tomorrow we're normal, and Tâl said— I thought with passion—Oh, I *hope* we can come here again. It's the nearest I ever was, and I said, To what? and she said, To being my*self*, and I said, What *is* your-self? and she said, I don't know.

She turned away, and hair fell, a lit mantle, and I heard the sound break from her throat, and Paula knelt and put her arms about shaken shoulders, and looked at me and frowned in a half-shrug, and clasped close.

Sometimes we all feel the same, she said. Not always. That's why we can help each other. You know the song? Sometimes I feel like a motherless child? Times I felt like that.

Tâl shook the hair away, and sat, not looking at me.

I'm at the wrong time, she said. Don't take any notice. I'm glad you caught that marvellous fish. I'll tell you who's going to be pleased. Two counts. One, a plate of fish for dinner. Which he'll love. And he'd better. And two, we'll be be back at work the day after tomorrow. Anybody ever know such a wonderful day? Paula, drive that engine. Salt's in my hair. I need a bath.

TWENTY-ONE

The huge black shape slid in again, closer, and I knew it
was a shark. Tâl swam just in front of me and I took her
heels, pulled gently, bringing her back alongside, pointing
up, to the shadow of the boat above and behind us. The
coral glowed in a mass of crimsons, yellows, blues, and the
small fishes swam, marvels of design, fins, tails in sworls
delicate as a girl's hair, coming towards us, turning off, but
I wanted to keep an eye on that brute, and loaded another
flash bulb, treading water, up, behind Tâl, and the shadow
came in again, faster, and the little fishes broke in flashing
colors, and I saw Tâl's legs dangling, and she, half out of
the water hanging on to the side of the boat.

Paula, thank God, waited and helped her in, and looking down, I saw the shark turn and come up, open maw
red, teeth white, and I pressed the button.

The flash seemed to set the water on white fire for
moments, and the shark turned off, the same shadow,
enormous, down, away, and I got out in the air, and

both girls grabbed, and I went over the side, head first, and lay on the drainboards, trying to get a breath.

You saved my life, Tål said, and I said, No. Paula did, and Paula said, I only pulled her in, and I said, We're lucky we had this type of boat. If it had been the ordinary sort, we'd never have got aboard quick enough, and Tål said, But I thought the sharks here didn't attack, and Paula said, Probably only trying to show off.

I think this winds up the stay, I said. I'm hurting to get back. How do you two feel? and Tål said, Couldn't we have another day? Just one more, and go to Taba? That's a steak you don't get every day, and Paula said, I'll support the motion, and I said, Carried. I believe I have the shakes again, and they both said O!, and sat near, putting their arms around me, anxious, protective, and I said, This doesn't have the smack of the office, and Tål said, Office is the day after tomorrow. Today, we're ourselves. We don't like shakes and Paula said, We have them all the time, and Tål said, You speak for yourself. I'm a little nervous, yes, but that fish frightened me. Always been afraid of teeth taking a collop out of me. Perhaps that's why I'm not especially fond of fish, and Paula said, Me, too. I hate the idea of a net. Or a hook, and Tål said, So how do *you* catch a fish-ie? Sing? and Paula said, With my voice? You'd be stuck on porridge. That's a thousand calories a whack. Once round you, twice round Zion Square, and Tål said, Listen to the sylph, and Paula said, There's nothing wrong with me. I'm pure, and Tål said, Doll, sylph means a slender almost-nothing, a tiny blow of thistledown, but the right shape, know what I mean? and Paula said, Leave my family out of this. Talking about fish, and me. What's the boss, here, think? and I said, I'm enjoying this. First time I hear gal-talk. And you're keeping me warm. Any closer, it's a case of sympathetic combustion.

Both moved closer, hip-bones pressed, and Tâl said, We have a wonderful office, and Paula said, We better have swivel chairs, and I said, Don't judge the office by this. This is pleasure. I love it. But up there, it's work, and Paula rolled over, and groaned, and said, At such a time we have to use the word? *Work?* Here, it's an obscenity, and I said, Look, all these days you and Tâl have read documents, accounts, journals, figures, letters. It's not work? and Tâl, still warm against me, said, But it didn't seem like it. I've loved every moment. I just want one more day. Sort of dessert, and Paula rolled back, and said, The kind you have to say No to, the one with the cream on top. Give your right arm. But it's four thousand calories, and there goes three months' suffering. For the tum. The flattie. I have one, now. But I'm tempted, and Tâl said, Don't be. I'm with you. Sisters in distress. Don't let me down. If only we could get a steak, sometimes. A *real* steak. The steak you get here, well, it just *isn't*.

I did a little thinking. Girls have to be fed. I remembered Plus A.

Look, I said, Did you ever talk to Shoshi about this? and Tâl said, *Did* we? We used to go home with her. But she couldn't get the sort of meat she wanted. Nothing going in to Beersheba, and Paula said, That's our girl. Believe me. Abba, that's a man. Been so kind. We love him, and Tâl said, Both of them.

How about Aliya? I said, and neither of them moved.

I looked at red mountains, blue shadows, dabs of gold where sun broke through clouds, smears of violet in deep crevices, bright beige patches in places the sun got his shirt palled by white cirrhus, and despite the heat, the air around me was frigid.

Come *on*, I said. What's the answer?

I know I'm talking to the boss, Tâl said, colder than I had known her—and I was glad, because then I knew her strength, and I exulted in her strict control, even in such a place—I hope you'll forgive me, but I have no wish to say anything.

Goes for me, twice. Paula said.

Listen, I said. Both of you. I asked the question. I have the right to know. We have to work there. Shoshi's an employee of hers. Come on. Let's have it.

I don't like her, Tâl said.

I don't, Paula said.

Why? I said, to blue water, with white froth bubbling behind us.

She is dishonest, Tâl said shockingly, and I said, How can you *say* that?, and Paula said, She doesn't pay proper wages. Months behind, and then only a little part, and I said, That *can't* be, and Tâl said, Ask our wonderful Shoshi.

You're pulling my leg, I said. She's just not the type, and Tâl said, We only had a few days there. Just enough to love it. Except her. We only went in the café about half a dozen times. Shoshi's our mother, and aunt, *and* baby sister. We love *her*, and Paula said, Say it again, a couple of times. But the other's for the vultures, and I said, But you can't *say* that, and Paula said, You're the boss, but I'll say it, and I said, But, please, why? and Tâl nodded at Paula, and said, Look, we grew up together. What she doesn't think, I think. What I don't think, she thinks. What we *both* think has to be right. We don't *like* her, and I said, All right. But why? and Paula said, She's not what she pretends to be, and I said, You can't say that, and Paula said, Why not?

Neither looked as though they intended to say another word. The warmth between us in some strange way cooled, and I had a feeling at the back of my neck.

Come on, I said, I want an answer. A reason. Just a negative won't do, and Tâl said, Look, boss. You're making it an order? and I said, Exactly that. You're senior. You start.

Right, she said, clear, sudden, and sat up. First, she relies on money. What she's spent. What she's done. The collective's in debt to her? She plays on it, and I said, How? and Tâl said, She doesn't pay for water or electric light, and I said, Small stuff, and Tâl said, Small, all right. But everybody else pays. They *must*. She says it counts against what the Collective owes her, and I said, But the collective *does* owe her, and Paula said, It doesn't, and I said, It does. Many thousands, and Paula said. No.

I said, Look, what are we getting into?

Tâl sat straight.

I'll tell you, she said, She *uses* people. They think she's wonderful. Zuz, that little waiter, he thinks she's the mother of God. Why? She gives him the run of the café. Traul, that deaf-mute, the gardener, he can do what he likes. The rest, they do what they want. But not Shoshi. She's not there any more, and I said, Why?

Because of that girl, Tâl said. The one they killed. We got there a couple of days after. She wasn't there. I mean, the woman *you're* talking about. Shoshi was. We *love* her. She's *real*, and Paula said, She's really for real. The other you may have, and I said, But why? I insist. Why?

She's not a *woman*. Tâl said. She's anything else. And

209

Paula said, Let's put it on the line. She's got a hole between her legs. That doesn't make her a *woman*. She's a usable item, and I said, You girls are rough, and Tâl said, You know, we're not, really. We don't like to be.

All right, I said, Now, what's this about the Collective doesn't owe her money? and Tâl said, The Merom Corporation has its own credit unit. Doesn't take a couple of days to find out all about *any*one. That's how *I* know. But you wouldn't expect details, and I said. Correct. I'll ask Mr. Merom.

Paula sat up, rubbing sun lotion on her shoulders.

She won't last long, she said. Shoshi'll take over. *Then* it'll be good, and I said, Just one thing I don't get. I always thought Aliya one of the friendliest people I ever met. How did she manage to fall out with you?

She never had the chance, Tâl said. She's all right dealing with the members. That's Collective or Commune. They're average people. They think she's doing them a big favor. So? They look up to her. But the moment she runs into somebody with perhaps a little more of the city, or school, or whatever, she's jealous, and I said, Ah, now, this can't be, and Paula said, What other reason? Why's she rude? Why scream at people? Us, for example. I never was so surprised. But she made an enemy of Merom because of it. That's why she's on her way out. Beside him, Moshe Dayan's a fluffy poodle.

Especially because it was us, Tâl said.

But what did you *do?* I said, and Paula said, I went in to order coffee for the office. I'd been told it was usual?

It is, certainly, I said. Always was, and Paula said, She told Zuz he was employed to serve in the café, not run errands, and when Shoshi said something, she screamed. So I left. Tâl went over to try to do something, and *she* got screamed at. I believe that's when Shoshi left.

Why she did, I don't know. We've made our own coffee ever since.

Mystery to me, I said.

But truly, it was not. It fitted with what I knew, though I had no intention of retailing it. That sense of sorrow perched, black. But I was unsure how to help, I wanted to. I thought of those hours behind the café. A man has a plain duty towards his love, however momently. I put the thought away, swinging in to the harbour's rocks, steering for our place on the quay, and Yosef's ready boathook.

Except that I felt it stuck in me, and the hurt was Aliya.

TWENTY-TWO

The car met us at Lod, and Paula went off to wait for the baggage, and Tâl said, Mind if I make a suggestion? and I said, Say on, and she said, The office system. Do you suppose we might go back via Haifa? They've got a branch there. It's out of our way, but the wife of the man running it was in the Army with me. He can do with the commission. Two children, and I said, I never asked. How *was* the Army? and she said. Great. Sometimes a real sweat. But *great*. Best in this world, and I said, How is it you never married? and she turned away, and said, Marrying's wonderful. But it has to be right. Right man. Not yet, and I said, Nobody tried? and she smiled the wondrous hidden-eyes smile, and said, Yes. They tried. But they had Merom for short-stop, and I said, He seems to run everything and everybody.

No, she said. They live as they want. They just have to be right, that's all, and I said, But it's *his* concept of what's right.

No, Tâl said. If you don't agree, you can do something

else. He won't insist. You just don't get any more help, and I said, Sounds like blackmail?, and she said, Fall in the water, you get wet. Blackmail?

Paula came back with a porter and the bags, and a cellophane sack with sandwiches, a package with bottles of beer, and plastic cups.

I know what goes on here, she said. I don't intend to suffer like the last time. Hours, hungry, thirsty. Not *this* time, and Tâl said, I'm with you. But listen, I said, No roadside cafés? and Paula said, You tried them?

We went up the wide road to Haifa, dunes on both sides most of the way, and I thought of the new idea, and tried to see the schematic diagram, but I had to get out the paper, and Tâl gave me a pen. The idea seemed to hold up, but I knew I had to put a model together before I could be sure. Too many ideas look right on paper, seem correct mathematically, should be workable, but on the bench, duds.

The new road passed along miles of virgin beach, with dunes stretching back inland, a new village here and there, sometimes an ancient sprawl of rock-built ruin among green-grey olives and pink-flowered oleander, festoons of Arab washing, and dozens of children, but rarely an adult, except perhaps a woman carrying a can of water headload, baby in arms, and once, a crone leading a troop of donkeys.

Women do the work, Paula said, Men just lay around. A lot of ours'd do the same, give them half a chance, and Tâl said, Depends where they were brought up. Europe, America, Russia, generally they work, and Paula said, North Africa, Syria, Iraq, that's where they breed the idler, and Tâl said, Some. Not all. I'm terribly sorry for them. Especially the children. They're taught one thing in school, something else at home, and the street's not the best playground. Remember when I came over all damp and altruistic and announced I was going to work with the underprivileged? I never saw Merom in such a rage. He was white. A little whisper. No shouts, and Paula said, That's when you break for cover.

He didn't like the idea? I said.

He loved the idea, Tâl said. He didn't like the words. Underprivileged. He said they all had the privilege of being alive, first, and second, living in their own country, and third, proving by work they deserved it, just to show the rest they were getting value for their taxes. But I didn't go on with it, and I said, Why? and she clasped hands and sat back.

If the men Merom sent to keep an eye on me hadn't been near, I'd have been gang-banged, she said. Charming expression? and Paula said, You were lucky. Those swine don't have a moment of mercy, and Tâl said, Up till that point I'd thought it was going so well. I found out it wasn't for me. So I went to London for more study, and joined the Corporation last year. Then Paula finished her time in the Army, and here we are, and I said, Are both of you confident about things? What you're doing, and the place?

Never been more satisfied wth everything, Tâl said, and Paula nodded. I'm doing what I've always wanted. Watching something grow, and helping, head and heart. In a beautiful place. Can't want more than that. Couldn't ask for as much. Yes. I'm very happy, and Paula said, Goes for me. Could I ask what you're drawing, there?

Merom's idea, I said. Did he ever tell you about the idea of training children to produce? Like their daddies? and Tâl said, He's a child-nut. Everything begins with them. Are you pulled in, too?

Let me explain, I said. They can't just make a piece of

214

junk. It's got to be small, and pretty, and useful. Small, because they're children. Pretty, because colours attract. Useful, because you can't fool a child for long. They catch you out, you're finished, and Tâl said, So right. Suppose some of them aren't interested? and I said, Fine. Like adults. Plenty of other things to do, and Paula said, What age is this going to start off? and I said, Who knows? Let them see what's doing. We'll soon find out.

I went on drawing, page after page, part by part, and suddenly I knew it would work, if not with children, then with adults in a more complicated version, possibly at some other commune.

Wait a minute, Tâl said, For heaven's sake. It's a little TV, isn't it?

That's exactly it, I said. For children. Made by children, for children, and Paula said, But that's terribly difficult, and I said, The TV box you know's been foisted on us. We know a lot more today than thirty years ago. We'll take advantage to make a simple version, new style.

Have a sandwich, Paula said, and unpacked. Brains you have to feed. You ought to have a housekeeper looking out for you. Good cook. That kitchen's terrible when Shoshi isn't there, and Tâl said, That's the one thing isn't right. Food, and I said, An up-to-the minute office system and a no-good kitchen? That's absurd. See we get a dining room, and advertise for a first-class cook, and Tâl said, If we pay her, we already have the best, and Paula said, Shoshi.

But *did* she leave the café, I asked, and Tâl said, I already told you. Wasn't paid for months, and then only a fraction. But that wasn't the reason she left. I didn't get into it. But she's available, and I said, How about the laundry? and Paula said, Stop gap.

See her, I said. Fix her wages. She's needed.

We reached Haifa, and I dropped the girls at the office equipment depôt, and went up the heights to the University, in wonder at what had been built in the few months since I was last there. With, of course, Plus A. But time takes some of the sting out. Not all. Some.

I was thinking of Tâl. I was well aware I had to be careful. I knew Merom, and I was warned. But she was constant temptation of a sort I had never known. A first-class mind, a couple of degrees, complete control of her job, a certain type of rare beauty, a natural grace, elegance, all had appeal of their own, though together, on two beautiful legs, they were Eden's own temptation, a Tree of Knowledge waiting for the Pluck.

But I apprehended the consequence, remembering the bloodline warning, and anyway, I had the factory to think about. She, and it, were part, though the thought had elements of incongruity I had no wish to separate, or to examine. I had enough to do.

I knew I had an extra fondness for Paula, maid of all work everlasting, pillar of the civilised, Mama Immortal, Beloved Ever, Matron Eternal, Milch Cow of the World. I knew I could take her to bed. But I knew with horrid instinct I would be wrong, quasi-criminal. She was one true man's simple, and single, love.

I had no place.

Suddenly, a pleasant shock, I saw a blue car in the University car park, knew the number.

Aliya's.

I looked at the time. She would, I thought, be at a lecture, but even as I leaned to speak to the driver, a man pushed through the space between her car and the next, put a key in the door, and squeezed behind the wheel. Smartly dressed, white shirt, tie, no beard or moustache, razor-cut hair, no lack of confidence, and no doubt about his identity.

I touched the driver on the shoulder, motioned him to stop on the spot, and he braked in a screech.

I got out, swung the door shut, walked the few steps, and Aliya's car backed, slowly, and within a yard I looked at the driver, and he looked at me.

I saw the flash of recognition, and darkness.

No sign.

Why?

How could Abu fail to recognize me?

Why should he be driving Aliya's car?

I remembered that cut, stubby tongue, and looked away, at the sea.

Wondering.

TWENTY-THREE

Days seemed to caress and pass between quiet nights and the only difference I found was on Saturday, because that was Shabbath, and I missed Tâl's reading of the morning post, the peachbloom of her presence, the lull of her voice.

I knew if I walked down the garden, out to the arbour, I would see her in the lilac bikini, sunning on the lawn among all the others. Whether she watched for me I never asked, but I always got the slow wave of an arm, saw the shining smile, and I knew that in a few minutes she would be in the office with a coffee tray.

That morning the telephone wrenched me from the drawing board.

Merom, the voice said, And the Lord God spoke unto Moses, saying, How's things, young fella?, and I said, Just finishing the drawings. How are you? and he said, Pretty good. I see you did another beautiful month down there, and I said, Do better next. I believe we're going to have the children starting in about ten days, and he said, You better let me know just when. I want to be *there*. Don't forget it, and I said, With the office staff I've got, it's likely? and he said, How are they doing? and I said, If they did any better I'd have a couple of angels in here, and he said, That's nice. You know something? Your letters are a real pleasure to read. Even the reports. I can read them a half dozen times, and I said, Blame Tâl, and he said, But you dictate in English. She puts it in Hebrew, and I said, Probably better, and he said, Don't you believe it. Wasn't the way she was trained. Word for word's the only way. Listen. Them guys in the Army been to see you? and I said, No. Why would they want to? and he said, Ah, you know the Army. Can't tell 'em nothing. Got their own way. So? Best to work in. What they want to know, tell 'em, and I said, Tell what? and he said, What they want to know.

Tâl rattled her nails on the door, a sound I loved, and came in with the silver coffee service, and I said, All right. I'll tell them what they want to know. Incidentally, your magnificent coffee set just arrived. Coffee has another taste. I know it's no use trying to thank you, and he said, Listen, it's a dust collector in this place. Thank me for nothing. Just enough sense to see it gets used, that's all. Least I know it's going to get cleaned now and again. Think I could talk to Tâl? and I said, She's here, hold on.

She took the receiver and spoke Hebrew, and I went back to the board. Merom seemed to say a lot, but she simply said, *Ken*, now and again, and held out the handset to me.

Look, he said, You going to Technion tomorrow? Why don't you use Tâl as a translator? and I said, I didn't think it was right, and he said, What do you mean? She's your secretary, and I said, That's right. That's one thing. But asking her to translate a lot of technical stuff, that's tiring for a girl, and he said, Listen. Will you do me a big favour? Take her with you. Then she'll know what's going on, see? Case of slip-ups, she's the best witness you'll ever have, and I said, I'm talking technical matters. What slip-ups? Why do I need a witness? and he said, You know who you're talking to? You don't speak Hebrew. Take her with you, and I said, It's no burden, and he said, What's wrong? You don't like her? and I said, The other side of the coin, and he said, O.K. So that's fine. Listen. Don't play footsie with them Army guys. They want to know, they want to *know*, see? Let me know what happens. You want anything, something go wrong, call me. *Shalom*.

Tâl poured coffee from the silver pot. A small vase on the tray held a single white rose. The éclairs were little-finger size. I knew Shoshi had a hand.

You're coming with me to Technion tomorrow, I said. I'll want the drawings and data in D.26, and she said, It's ready. I tried a new coffee. Tell me how you like it.

I did, and I said, A real improvement. Could be straight Brazilian, and she said, It is. The coffee we were getting from the café, wasn't. Everybody complained. I found out it's Turkish, cheapest. For the *espresso*, all right if you don't know coffee. This is the bean, ground in our machine. I gave the *Mukhtar* a cup. You should have seen his face, and I said, What's he doing up here?, and Tâl said, He came with the doctor. Some of the mothers are leaving the children overnight. It's a compliment, don't you think? and I said, Glad if all of them did. Did you find out if any of the Arab or Druse children are go-ing to join the Studio Pueris? and she said, So far, not much interest. Perhaps later. Our own people aren't too gone on the idea of having them. I mean, mixing with our children. Touchy.

We have to deal with *that* as-soon-as, I said. If necessary, we'll have a special room for them. I'll think about
it, and she said, Why don't you come for a walk? You're
always stuck in this office, and I said, Those drawings
have to be finished for tomorrow. Tell you what I'll do.
After the Technion hassle, we'll walk down the hill to
Haifa and get some fish for lunch. How's that? and she
said, Sounds great. Look, if you don't eat just one of these
éclairs, you're in trouble with Shoshi. You want that?

I took an éclair, wonderful, and went for another, about
two bits of paradise, and enough.

Shoshi doing all right? I asked, and Tâl said, Happier
than anybody. She only complains you never come to see
her in the new kitchen. Always wanted an American
kitchen. She's the queen there, believe me, and I said,
With a lot of them leaving her cold, what's going on at
the other café? and Tâl turned away, and said, I don't
think too good. She's losing friends. Lot of people are
coming to our place. For the films. And the coffee. Even
poor Zuz isn't so happy, and I said, Why? and she said,
I don't want to gossip. It's the Collective's business, and
I said, Telling me isn't gossip. What's the trouble? and
she said, I don't think Aliya's so well. Or she isn't mentally
stable. Or both. She sent an account last week for the
coffees and teas we had before our place opened. It's out-
rageous. I showed her our book, everything itemized.
Zuz initialled every order. She wouldn't accept it.

Why didn't you tell me? I said, angry, and she said,
Why should *you* be bothered with it?

I said, Let me see that account please. I'll talk to
Avram.

Tâl turned the double-lock on the filing cabinet,
brought out a small book, and opened to a page.

The figures are hers, she said. The notes are either Zuz's, or hers. Zuz writes in blue. She's in red.

I saw figures crossed out, totals substituted, notes, *"This has to stop!!! Ask them to pay this immediately or face legal action!!!"* and on the last page *"Who do these people think they are?"*

But whatever small shock there might have been was drowned in far larger surprise.

Is this Aliya's handwriting? I asked, and Tâl said, Yes. Zuz tried to argue, but she screamed at him, and I said, But what's wrong, exactly? and Tâl said, I don't know. She has fits. She's bad-tempered. It's not what it was, and I said, That's a shame.

But I was looking at pages in that little book, obviously "doctored" by a ruffian pen, and I was sure, judging from memory of an exercise book with pages of neat script and minutely draughted numerals, that all these illiterate tottings could not have come under the same hand. This scrawl was backhand, i's dotted with a lopsided circle, all the upper strokes ballooning, g's trailing a preposterous loop reaching to the line below, and b's the shape of a seven-month foetus. Not the hand of a mathematician, and certainly not from the pen which wrote the pages I had seen.

I gulped another cup of coffee, thankfully, and went back to work.

You seemed worried, Tâl said, putting the tray together, and I said, Yes. She started that place from nothing. I don't know what's happened. But I feel I should go over and see her, and Tâl said, Please don't, and I said, Why not? and Tâl said, All right. You force me. She speaks horribly about you. We've all tried to stop it. I hope you won't get into it. Not necessary.

I'm going across now, I said, and racked the pen. Nobody speaks "horribly" about me. Or there's an explanation, and Tâl said, I wish I hadn't opened my mouth, and I said, It's a beautiful mouth. Not another word.

I went over the same old way, that I hadn't seen since I went to the hospital, and all the blossom welcomed, and I caught the scent of honeysuckle along the rock stair to the café.

Zuz, on the terrace, saw me with the instant figure-of-eight flick of the napkin, and held out a chair, but I nodded, and went inside.

Someone I had never seen stood behind the bar.

Where's Aliya? I said, and she, poor soul, said, She's in Haifa. Won't be back till tonight. Or tomorrow, and I said, Any idea where, in Haifa? Any telephone number? And she said, No. She's studying.

I went out to a strangely changed Zuz, still in starch, polished shoes, but he seemed bowed, no longer the *maître*, and his burnish was not at brightest. A light was in quench, and suddenly I sorrowed. Everything went on without him, and he seemed to know it. But he should have been solid part.

What's wrong, Zuz? I asked, and he shook his head, waved at empty tables, rattled chairs in place, walked to the door, and turned.

Signor, I tell to you once, you remember?, he said. Soon, someday, yes? She meet somebody, do something, *psst!* she go? No? Now we are near. She go. Finish, and I said, How do you know? and he said, I live enough. I know the woman. It is time she go, and I said, When? and he shrugged, and said, When she want.

We have a café over there, I said. If you finish here, see me. We shall welcome you. Where's Traul? and he said, I don't see him two, three days. He find the plants, the small tree, perhaps. Always plenty, the work, and I said, How about Abu? and he said, I don't see.

The cloud of dust coming across the unploughed land was the Army, in an open truck with a heavy machine gun, and another under a green canvas cover, and they wore steel hats. The truck stopped in dust, and the officer beside the driver got down. He shouted in Hebrew, and Zuz shouted back, and pointed to me.

Right, the officer said, and he had two metal stars, or something, on his shoulder tabs. I want to talk to you. You don't speak Hebrew? and I said, Don't let it worry you. I've got the best translators in the business, and he said, We don't need them. You have a factory here? and I said, Yes, and he said, Lead on. That's where we talk.

TWENTY-FOUR

I looked at the five pieces of scratch-pad in front of me, and half-saw the Colonel take a sixth from his file case and carefully place it in line.

Recognise them? he said, and I nodded.

They're all originals, he said. You always as careless as this? It's classified AA material, and I said, Nobody could make anything of it, and he said, All right. Take a look at these. Our own techs based them on these sketches.

He took a roll of prints out of an elastic bind, and I had only to glance at them.

About a thousand miles off, I said. These schemas are my own way of realising an idea. When I've gone far enough I give them in next door. They're mastermen at the draughting-board. But these bits of paper can't mean much to anyone except me, and he said, How do they get into other hands? and I said, No idea.

He and the other three looked down.

Any idea where you were when you drew them? he said, and I picked out the first.

This one I drew in the hospital at Tel Aviv, I said, and put it above the line. This one in Eilat. And this. This, I started in Eilat, and finished in Haifa, This one, and this, here. In this room.

Who comes in here? the Colonel said, and I said, My secretaries, the visitors, and the cleaners, and the Colonel said, All right. Now. Were you ever friendly with the woman in charge of the café? and I said, Yes.

She ever come in here? and I said, No, and he said, Was she ever in that place where you sleep, down there? and I said, No, and he said, Never?, and I said, Never.

All right, he said, But you were in her place, back of the café? and I said, Yes, and he said, Often? and I said, Once.

They all looked down.

Nobody looked at me.

I thought I knew how it felt to be a leper.

Tâl's nails rippled, and I loved life again, and she came in, a clean breath from another world.

I wondered if you'd like some coffee, she said, airy as only she could be. There are also doughnuts. Hot.

You know *us*, the Colonel said, human for the first time. Be glad of a cup, and thank you, and Tâl said, Won't be long, and walked out, and the eyes followed her, including mine, and worth it.

Back to this woman in the café, the Colonel said. You never gave her any of these sketches? and I said, No. Why should I? and he said, *I* ask the questions. Did you know somebody called Neb? and I said, When I was Collective labour. I never worked with him, and the Colonel said, He was never close to you? and I said, I don't remember talking to him.

One of your secretarial staff got killed by her own people, the Colonel said. Any idea what was behind it? and

I said, I know as much about it as that ashtray. She was a splendid girl, and he said, You didn't know she had anything to do with this Neb? and I said, He had no business anywhere here. I don't know how he could meet her, and the Colonel said, Except at the café? And she was taken back to her village by the woman running it? and I said, That has to be a coincidence, and the Colonel said, Matter of opinion. Do you know anybody called Abu?

I said, Yes. He used to carry our water jars. Then he joined an architect's company. So I was told. He seems to have become some sort of success as a landscape gardener. I should tell you that not long ago, I saw him driving her car in the car park of Haifa University.

They were all looking down.

Her? the Colonel said, at his boots, You mean the woman running the café? and I said, Yes.

Glad you happened to mention that, the Colonel said. It's in a report we have. How do you suppose anybody could have got hold of these sketches? They cover quite a stretch. Tel Aviv, Haifa, Eilat, here. Who'd have the *in*? and I said, It's a lot worse than I thought. Never penetrated. I don't begin to know.

Tâl rippled the finger nails, and brought me back to her own beautiful world.

Anybody ever come over here? the Colonel asked, watching Tâl at the tray. When you weren't here, anybody come in here? and I said, You'd have to ask Tâl, and he said, We don't have to. She's strictly *us*, and Tâl nodded, and served me, first.

I don't have the keys to this place, I said. When I go, it's locked. Automatically.

So how do these pieces of paper appear somewhere else? the Colonel said. We got them from somebody.

227

They took them from you. How? and I said, I'd like to know.

Good coffee, the Colonel said, and clamped into a doughnut. You people certainly live, and he chewed. You never talked to Abu? and I said, How? He's a mute, and the Colonel said, *Mute?* With a throat-mike? He's, let's say, informative. He can talk. To anybody. Any time, and I said, Not to me. I gave him the job of planting the garden here. But when I passed him he didn't recognise me. He did, but he pretended not.

Why would that be? the Colonel asked, and I said, Because he was driving her car, perhaps? and the Colonel looked down, and said, The woman in the café? and I said, Yes.

Everybody champed, spreading sugar on the floor.

I still want to know how these sketches come into other hands, the Colonel said, through doughnut. This man, Neb. Who else could he be in touch with in this office? Look. Let's say this Druse girl stole a few pieces. She couldn't steal *all* of them. When you were in the hospital, she was dead. Did she steal *any* of them?

I don't believe she was the kind, I said.

They all looked down.

More coffee? Tál said, behind me, my lovely Wall.

All the cups went up.

Somehow, somebody got hold of these sketches, the Colonel said. They can't fly. They had to be physically picked up and handed over. Who? Look. It has to be after you came back from Eilat. Didn't you miss them? and I said, No. I draw them to see where I am. Then I draw a better one, or two or three. In those six sketches there are a dozen different ideas. The lads next door simplify them. I don't know what use they'd be to anyone else.

They all looked down.

Tâl poured coffee, soft dribble, almost a hand on my shoulder.

People we're fighting, they have a lot of money, the Colonel said. Pay anything for even half an idea. Look, these sketches, they're all military ideas? and I said, Two are. The others are a child's TV set.

Hnf, the Colonel said, through doughnut. Our people thought it was a missile spotter, and I said, It says a good deal for their intelligence. A couple of moves, and that's exactly what it *could* be, and the Colonel said, I believe. I have to arrange a meeting. Between you and our tops. Seems to me you have plenty to say to each other. But what I want to know is, how did somebody get hold of these drawings? and I said, I can't help you. I certainly didn't give them away. I believe you'll find the rest, I mean, the progressions, in the file, here, and he said, That's correct. It's been examined.

He saw my surprise.

We make sure, first, he said. Who looks after your living quarters? and I said, I believe Shoshi has that in charge. Shoshana. The cook, here, and the Colonel said, She worked in the café? and I said, For some months, and he said, Could I talk to her? and I said, Tâl, would you please call Shoshi? and she said, Immediately, *sir*, and went out.

Everything's a whole lot easier because of her and Paula, the Colonel said. We know them. Where *they* are, nothing goes wrong, and I said, I believe you, and he said, Look, don't get sad. Don't lose heart. We know the kind of job you're doing here. What we want to do is protect. Defend. I told you. The other side pays a fortune for what we think's a joke. But this Neb, for instance. He had a radio under the floor in his place. Looked at the map? This is halfway between the Gaza Strip and the border. In the desert. So when they want to move people across, he gives them a signal when the patrol's down the other end. I mean, that's just child's play. I don't need to tell you there's a lot of our troop and air movement around here, and I said, Never thought of it, and he said, Lot of others did.

Tâl's nails rippled, and my world was suddenly warm.

Shoshana came in, broad as the door, kitchen whites shining, chef's cap we bought for her tipped down on her eyebrows, and Tâl put a hand on her arm, that said almost aloud, Don't hurt her, please.

Look, the Colonel said quietly, leaning towards her. This is no terrible business. We're just trying to find the answers to a few questions. I understand you found the girl to look after the living quarters of Mr. Leslie, here? and Shoshi said, That's right, and the Colonel said, She still the same girl? You trust her? and Shoshi said, Hold on, here. See, I worked over at the café. We had a good cleaner there. I asked her if she had anybody wanted a job. She said she did. Her daughter. She's married, couple of kids, she can use the money. So, fine. She goes to work. The cleaning, laundry, sandwiches and leaving the night tray, he works nights, see? Every day I go down, rub the finger, no dust. All of a sudden, it's a shock, this gal, daughter of the café cleaner, she tells her ma she won't work any more. So I say, why? And she says Aliya, y'know, the one I'm working for in the café? She goes in there, and she pokes around, see?

They all looked down.

I didn't know that, I said, feeling utterly left out, lost.

Who did? Shoshi said. Who is going to think? She had a key. She said you give it to her, and I said, That isn't true, and Shoshi said, Didn't I say so? I *told* her. Every house in this collective got two keys. One stays in the secretary's office. Other's in your pocket. How she get a key? I *asked* her. The cleaner gal, she got *your* key. She give it back to me when she finished. I give it back to you. Right? and I said, That's correct.

Just a moment, the Colonel said. Let's have this in proper order. You mean, the cleaner got the key from *you,* and you got it from *him?* and Shoshi said, Right, and the Colonel said, And you gave it back at night? and Shoshi said, It always come back to this office, and the Colonel said, Who took it? and Shoshi said, Well, I'm not sure. One of the girls here.

May I say something? Tâl said, and the Colonel said, Say on, and Tâl said, Since I've been here, the key's come to me. Before, I believe the girl who was killed took it, and the Colonel said, You mean the Druse girl, Salah el-Medgid? and Tâl said, Yes. I never met her.

Look, the Colonel said to me. These sketches. Could they have been stolen from your place down there? and I said, Probably. Perhaps it's the only place. I always put them in this pocket. Here, and he said, You never looked for them? and I said, Didn't worry me. I must have drawn hundreds. I never saved them.

Going to be more careful in future? the Colonel said, and I said, I have a secretarial staff looking after things, now, and he said, Glad about that. Any more of this kind of leak, you could be in trouble, and I said, Why? and he said, This plant is top security. Any paper is under wraps. *Your* paper's a State secret. You never know. Somebody on the other side might make a good guess. Or give somebody a new idea. You have to be careful. More than the ordinary.

Listen, Shoshi said, Lot of things cooking out there. Could I go? and the Colonel said, Why, certainly. Listen, what happened when you told this woman you didn't like what was going on? and Shoshi said, She give me the dirty mouth, and the Colonel said, So what did you do? and Shoshi said, Well, I figured she was, you know, sort of not-quite. Know what I mean? That kind of state, you can say pretty well anything. Feel sorry after. So I wasn't going to take any notice. But she screamed. I mean, *screamed*. So I said, Wait a minute. The dirty mouth you should keep. Made her screech louder. So I took off the apron. I don't want to say it, you should tell me I was never the friend. I was. The one I *knew*, I *was* the friend. Not any more, believe me. This new one, I make a present.

How do you mean, *new*? I said, and Shoshi said, Not like she was. She got the devil in her.

They all got up with the Colonel, though I saw no sign.

Believe that puts us about right, he said. Sorry to take your time, and I said, Puts you right, *how*? and he said, I already told you. *We* ask the questions. Nobody here talks. Understand what I say? Don't *talk*. Even between you. Other people can listen. Make something out of it. *No* talk. Even a word. This is an order.

Believe you can rely on us, I said. We prefer the clear.

Thanks for the coffee, he said. And the doughnuts are really super-special, and Shoshi said, There's a parcel out there in the truck, and the Colonel said, Ah, now, we can't accept that, and Shoshi said, A dozen you already waltzing around with, you can't waltz some more? and the Colonel said, Strictly, it shouldn't be, and Shoshi said, I should have wrote the book. Soldiers fighting for me, I get the right to fight with doughnuts. Fair? Only one thing. Bring back the plate.

No holding them, the Colonel said, and held out his

hand. Forget this. If I want more, I'll be back. I believe
I have everything. Thanks for the hospitality. *Shalom*.

We watched them rubber-march along the garden
path.

Know something? Shoshi said. I really believe she's in
trouble. Wish I knew how to help, and I said, Remember
what the Colonel told us? Don't talk, and Tâl said,
Know something else? I believe I can smell burning from
here, and Shoshi held her face, and whispered, *Oi-veh*,
the goddam oven, and ran, slopfoot.

Tâl looked at me, and started piling saucers, twinning
the cups, rattling spoons in a glass, pretending a lot of
work.

What's all this noise? I said, and she said, That girl over
there. That *wo*man. Does she still worry you? and I said,
Any friend of mine in trouble's a worry. I don't know
what got into her, and she said, I wish you'd take your
mind *off* her, and I said, It's not even *on*. It's only she's
in trouble, and Tâl said, Listen, she went after it, and I
said, Even so, and Tâl said, Sometimes I could just *shake*
you, and I said, I'm sitting here, waiting, and she turned
the beautiful head, a moment, and lifted the tray, and
went out.

With the *snap* of a closed door, no argument.

TWENTY-FIVE

Studio Pueris opened on the last night of *Hannuka*,
Festival of Lights, reminder of a moment when Judah
the Maccabean lit the sacred lamp in the rebuilt Temple
of Herod, and Israel rejoiced in new light, other hope.

Merom was not the one to stint in a matter touching
the Spirit. Crates came day by day from Tel Aviv and
Jerusalem, and Tâl, Paula, Shoshi, Zuz, and anyone in
between lent a hand to unpack and decorate.

The children's building had been started and finished
in virtual secrecy. Everybody helped. The tool desks
were miniature copies of the adults' in the main plant.
The charging boards, the cutters and lathes were all
scaled down, made by our own people in spare time. The
idea caught, and Merom's decorations, the candles, electrics, and the buffet, the stage for the puppets, and all the
scurry of getting things in order seemed to take fire, and
suddenly, without a word, no appeal, no asking, everybody was down there, doing something, anything, for
the children.

Roch came in on the four o'clock bus, and gave me a couple of hours with the accounts, which I listened to, and he said, Nothing here got the interest? and I said, No. I like to see another kind of brain take what I'm doing and make something else out of it. Accounts, for example. It's needed. But for me, it's superfluous, and he said, So how do you know how you making money? and I said, Look, everytime a box goes out of here, I know it's money. We can't be losing and he said, So it's nobody the other end, you making money? and I said, We know who we're sending it to, and he said, So he's out on bail, maybe?

I looked at Punch. He had a smile around the corner. I loved him. I once had a setter looked at me like that.

Listen, I said. What *is* this sudden submersion in accounts? Something gone wrong? and he said, Nothing. Going too right. You're up there, the millions. But up there, you got to have a pen-hand. You don't have one. You have the brain. The Lord God smiled when you left your Mama. But a pen-hand, it's necessary. Tâl, she's wonderful. A light in the head. What it's needed, it's a man, control the in and the out. Such as you don't have. A woman won't do. She has to shout sometimes. Only a man got it. Look, Merom's got a boy coming out of the Army. Major. Pay and Accounts. Cut out for the job. You want him here? and I said, Why didn't Merom ask me? Why leave it to you?

Punch's own wicked smile bloomed, and I thought he might clout me with the bladder-and-bells, but he said, Merom don't ask no favours. He gives the *orders*. And he knew he couldn't give *you* none. Didn't want to. That way, he's always looking out for peoples' feelings, see? and I said, All right. I'll take the boy. *Boy?* and Roch said, Couple years older than you. I'm happy about it.

Now we got it right. I bet even you see the difference inside of a month, and I said, Why? Things not so right now? And he said, Ah, listen. You got the Collective, and the commune, and this here kids' *wirtschaft* all in together. You got to think two years, five years ahead. You got to have a chief-of-staff. Take over when you go someplace. You use the brain, the ideas. He's the pen-hand. Take the knots out. Like me. Merom only looks at books. Looks at this, looks at that. They better be right. You don't even do *that*. So how do you know what's right? How do you know who's stealing you blind? And listen, mind if I ask, What *is* this Poo-ris, this with the kids? and I said, Pew-*err*-iss. Latin. Means infant. Child, Studio Pueris, where children work. I don't like the term "kids". Kids are the young of goats. About time we started treating human offspring with a little respect.

I saw Punch crumple.

Sorry, he said. Get to say things sometimes. Know what I mean? The language I can use. Not always good. The others, French, German, Polish, Russian, Arabic, it's about the same. Hebrew, I know I'm safe. I'm right. Merom, even he says sometimes, Roch, you're a scholar. Every time I'm a foot higher, and I said, I believe we could do with a cup of Tâl's coffee, and he said, Now we talking.

But we met her along the corridor with the tray, and took her with us, back to the main room, decorated in tinted plastics and tinsel, all the candles alight, colored lamps, wicks in big brass bowls, all the children dressed in fancy get-ups, everybody wearing a paper cap, puppets jigging on the stage, and the young laughter another music, wonderful.

Merom's going to be here in ten minutes, Tâl said. Could we clear the car park? and I said, Tell Ahmed.

Why? Security? and she said, No. Helicopter. Coming from an Army base, and Roch said, Probably bring the boy. Good time for it. See the way you live.

I saw Shmuel walking around the coffee bar, and he looked over and held up an open palm in greeting, and put down the plate to meet me.

Wanted to see you, he said. Never get a chance. Big name these days, and I said, Come off it. You know all you have to do is ask, and he said, Well, we've been building the waterway the past couple of months. Never got much time. Listen, them Army guys ever talk to you? and I said, Why? and he said, About when Aliya came up here that first time? Down in the olive grove? and I said, No. Never mentioned it, and he said, I believe she's in bad trouble. I wouldn't talk. Only I think she's done a hell of a lot for us, and I said, I'm with you. What kind of trouble's she in? and he said, Well, listen, how do you make an enemy out of Shoshi? What do you have to do? and I said, Past me, and he said, Yeke talk to you? and I said, I haven't seen him in a thousand years, and he said, He's been with us. I don't know what goes on, and I said, Do I? What's the trouble?

He pulled in the deep breath of conflict, and looked at the puppets, and the backs of children's heads.

I'll put it on the line, he said, slipping his voice under laughter. I always thought there was something, y'know, phoney about the way she came in. I didn't say a word. Moche said to sew the mouth, so we did. But it's a hell of a way from Beersheba. Lonely road. What sort of Bedouin she going to meet? They don't have their tents anyways near the road. You ever see a Bedouin at night? Give you tea? How long it take you to *walk* from Beersheba? Where she say she was going? Kfar Sido? No such place, and I said, But don't you remember? Yeke said he'd send her over by truck next morning, and Shmuel said, Ah, now please. Yeke? Top intelligence officer, this area, and I said, I didn't know, and he said, Don't worry. Everybody else does. So he just plays her along. Which is why we don't say nothing. I know he's got something going. That's why nobody said no when she wanted to spend her own money on the café. Let her. Let's see the next move, and I said, What's that? and he said, I don't know. See, all through this, Yeke's stuck on her.

I said, That's hard luck.

Shmuel looked away, and said, for a *good* guy like Yeke, it's a lot worse. She's one son-of-a-bitch-tease, nett. He's going nuts. He'll kill her, and I said, Now, just let's take it a little easy, here, and he said, Take it easy, hell. I ought to be down at the ponds. I'm here to talk to you, and I said, Why me? and he said, Well, you can talk to her, and I said, What about? and he said, Yeke. He needs some help.

I looked at him, but he seemed not to want to meet me in the eye.

What help could I give him? and he said, You could see her, and I said, Look, if he's a man, *he* can see her. No help from me, and he said, She *won't* see him. No *how*, and I said, So what in hell am I supposed to do? Order her? Who am *I*? No. I have enough to do. And she's her own boss, incidentally.

He was hoping you could do something, Shmuel said. He's in a hell of a state, and I said, He's top intelligence and he's in a hell of a state? What sort of intelligence? What's the idea? and he said, You'll be sorry, and I said. *Me?* Why?

I heard the helicopter shake the roof, and all the children raced in shrill shriek for the door, leaving the puppets in a dangle.

Tâl brought me another cup of coffee, and I said Shmuel would like a cup, and he said, No. Listen. You got Merom behind you. Where can you go wrong? and I said, What's that to do with it? and he said, He's the boss. I mean, a word from him.

I faced him square, and he had to look at me, and I said, Shmuel, come on, now. I don't believe a word. What's this all about? Where *is* Yeke? and he said, At his place.

I took Tâl's hand when she put the coffee down.

Stay here, I said. I need you. Never mind anything else. Something I don't like seems to be going on, and Shmuel said, Look, all I'm trying to do is help, and I said, Help who? What?

Yeke loves her, he said. He's a case. He can't *see* anything. He don't want to work. Don't want to do nothing. Just *her*, counts. And she won't even answer the door. What can anybody do, this guy beating his fists on the wall? I mean, blood. It's blood there, the marks on the wall. Yeke. Why I'm here. Dan and me can't do nothing, and I said, So what am *I* supposed to do? and he said, *Talk*. Maybe he listens. In love, you don't know how it is? *Please*. I go with.

I looked over at Tâl, and I thought of her, and I knew. All right, I said. Won't be time later.

On the way I remembered Plus A, and the effect of her going. True, I had certainly known a sort of hungry misery, and food, sleep were little for many a day, but the pain had eased, until the morning I saw the Arab mason and his son.

But had that feeling been love? and I had no answer.

239

Certainly what I felt for Tâl was unutterably different in so many ways.

I was ravenous for her, yes, but unwilling to show it. When she was near, when she leaned to put paper in front of me and I caught the fragrance of her shining hair, the warmth of her vital scent, I had to stifle, crush, think away from a savage desire to put a hand on her, caress, and not gently.

But.

The office was not the place, first, and second, she, her beautiful self, was not my plaything, and third, though ever present, I heard Merom's bloodline warning and I knew what to expect. For the moment I was content to be with her, knowing she would be there, listening for the sound of her voice, the ripple of fingernails on the door, drinking the purest womansweet of her presence.

Yeke's house seemed neglected. Any time I went there, I knew a hand was at work in the garden. But it was overgrown. Weeds howled. The hand no longer worked.

Shmuel knocked, and opened the door. The book-shelves still stretched tall on the walls, but the room was smelly, heaped with clothing, paper, and I had instant thought of my own room, quiet in tidiness, flowers.

Yeke sat on the bed, elbows on knees, chin on fists, staring blear at space, unwashed, unshaven, horribly unlike the man I had known.

I brought him, Shmuel said, standing beside me. Tell him what you want. Talk, and Yeke turned his eyes up at me without moving his head, and looked away at the dead plants.

No use, he said, a croak, as if his throat was a lime pit.

Come on, Yeke, I said. I'm here to help. What's wrong? and he said, I wish you get her just to talk to me. So I can tell her, and I said, Go up to the café. Stay there till she *will* talk, and he shook his head. I tried that, he said. She screamed. The words. No place in her mouth. I don't want to hear it.

Is that a good excuse for living like this? I said. Any woman on earth want to talk to a man in this kind of a state? You stink from two hundred yards. You know what kind of a woman she is? Particular. How does she open her mouth, holding her nose? She has to suffer because you suppose the weight of this world's on you? Get up, get bathed, get shaved, tidy this pigpen. You wouldn't allow animals in here. Why are *you*? and he said, Fine, you talk, and I said, What the hell else am I supposed to do? Listen. Get shined up. Come and see me in the office. Then I'll go to her, and he said, Orders I don't take, and I said, You're not the man I knew. I'd never give you orders. I'm just telling you to get back where you belong. There's no woman on this earth can do this to you. Rejoicing in your own defeat, that's your character? Victory, they dress up, hang out the flags. You? You hang out the whiskers, the dirt, and Shmuel said, Ah, don't say that to him, and the anguish faltered in his voice, and I said, Why did I come here? Sing him a lullaby? I came here to talk to a man I respect. All I see's a heap of shit I don't even want to spit on, and Yeke said, No, O, no, and his head went down, and he fell sideways, and he wept the hard, snoring breaths of the male in woe, and Shmuel said, Ah, for God's sake, look what you done, and I said, Fine. I burst the boil. Now he can wash more than his face. Then I'll talk. *Shalom.*

I ran along the path of roses, carnations, through the jasmine and honeysuckle, under the arbour of scarlet rambler, and I was praying, because I knew that if Tâl turned her beautiful back on me, and I howled inside

241

me tearblind, Lord God, please don't let her, I knew, but I knew, I would fall in the same way, another of dead eyes, and dirt, and a throat too dry to want water.

Lord God, save me, I prayed, and ran.

TWENTY-SIX

Zuz shrugged and said, We don't see her three days. *Disastre.* It's what happens here. Nobody coming, and I said, When were you paid the last time? and he said, I don't think the money. Not important, and I said, Look, when you're ready, come over to us. Take complete charge. You get along with Shoshi? and he said, The Shoshi, we friends. Nobody better, and I said, She's in charge of the kitchen. Here, you serve the ghosts of better times. What's the use? How can you stay in a place, no customers? You *know* why nobody comes here? Look. We have a lot of children there. Why not leave? Now. We need you.

I saw the way he looked at the room, and the shining *espresso* machine, the racks of glasses, chairs, tables, friends of months, though the mump-face of the woman behind the bar watching us seemed to force decision.

He folded the napkin, calm, sure, and said, *Basta.* It's enough here. I go.

I went over to the plant, seeing with pleasure the

243

gardens, flowers blooming, making a note to reward Traul, by heaven's blessing not one of the bomb's victims.

Tâl waited at the door, throwing up her hands to see me, putting them behind, walking towards me.

Merom's here, she said, in the hidden-eyes way I loved. I said you'd gone to see a friend, and he asked who, and I had to tell him, and he said, *That* low-life? Why's he waste his time?

What's it to do with him? I said, and Tâl almost took my arm, and said, Don't be angry, He only wants the best for you. He thinks Horowitz is trying to cover for that woman in the café, and I said, Who's Horowitz, and what's he covering? and Tâl said, *Please* don't get *angry*. Horowitz is the one you call Yeke. He's been trying to hide what she's doing, and I said, Wait a minute. What *is* this? What's she been doing? and Tâl said, Let Merom tell you. I'm out of it, and I said, Remember that. Stay out. I never want to have the thought. *You* are *so* far apart. You understand me? You'd better, and I saw half the beautiful smile, and she said, I'll stay out, and I said, Not because I'm giving any orders. I don't. Especially to you, and she said, But you're the boss. Why shouldn't you give the orders? and I said, I'm not that kind of a boss. I'm for work. I love to see it come off the line, and she said, But everything doesn't come off the line, and I said, Everything useful *does*. It starts with a little idea on paper. Then it grows. You start drawing. Now you have a whole idea. It works? Go ahead.

But that's just paper, she said. Not people. People live, and love. And kiss. Paper only tries. Doesn't it?

I stopped outside the door, in the cold of shadow, and looked at her, tall, bathed, combed, everything I loved, slim-trim in blue, with the grey eyes that sometimes

looked at me and oftener did not, and I said, If I ever
kiss *you*, you'll stay *kissed*.

But then Roch trod on the *OUT* mat, and the door slid
open, and I saw Tâl give him the Look, and I laughed,
and she said, What's funny? and I said, I don't see the
temper so often, and she laughed, but not much, and
Roch said, Here I find you? Merom's losing his mind, and
I said, What about? and he said, He don't want to miss
the opening of the Studio, and I said, He won't. Come
on.

How it happened—who knows?—but I found the hand
in mine, an accident?—and I looked at her, and she was
looking at me, and her mouth half-opened—to say something?—and I had to look away and think where I was,
regret talking about a kiss, and yet, I regretted nothing.
I had a wonderful feeling about it. I had to ask myself
what sort? And in that sudden moment I saw her in
voile, the thin linen, naked, *Sheba!* and I exulted, hearing
the creaking camel-litter, savage music, and a rumble of
guardian chariots.

How fair and how pleasant art thou, O love, for delights! The joints of Thy thighs are like jewels, the work
of the hands of a skilful workman. Thy navel is like a
round goblet which wanteth not liquor. Thy belly is like
an heap of wheat set about with lilies. As the lily among
thorns, so is my love among the daughters.

Merom sat among children in the back rows, and he
laughed more looking at them than at the show. He
seemed to change before my eyes, and become a child,
and I realised that a good part of him had never grown
up, held an innocence I wished were mine.

But looking about, seeing me, he changed to a tyrant
self, and stepped over benches, hands on children's heads,
support and blessing in one, and pointed to the office.

Listen, he said, A heart attack I'm supposed to have? It's what you want for me, I'm such a friend? What's the idea, going down there, talking to that bum? and I said, He's no bum, he's in love, and Merom held his head, thumb-and-middle-finger, the little finger held away, and said, This is the 'pocalypse? He's in love, so *you* got to ruin yourself? How many times I have to tell you the *Army*'s in this? and I said, What's *that* got to do with it? I told you, he's a friend of mine. He's in trouble. *Trouble?* I didn't know a man could get in that state because of a woman.

Merom held out his hands, looking at the roof.

What did I do? he whispered, and I remembered Tâl's warning and heard Paula's voice saying Break for Cover. So I talk to the brain, nobody home? Two and two, it's five? Listen, anybody gets in a mess for *that* type *shikse*, you know something? A poleaxe, it's too good.

But *is* she a *shikse?* I asked, and I was surprised. She ran that place *kosher*, and Merom shut his eyes, bunching his fingers.

Listen, he said. Will you please listen? You listening? Could I explain something? No interruptions? What she is, it's an inter*nat*ional pain in the *crack*. Nothing local. Certainly she's a *shikse*. Mother's a grook unorthodock. Lets *her* out. Father, he should know better, there's plenty cheaper, no risk, medical supervision. So that's where *we* stand, and I said, It's not good enough for me. *Shikse*, all right. But she's in trouble, and I turn my back? No.

Again he looked at the roof and weighed both hands.

If I did something, you couldn't take the life? he whispered. I get the torture? It's a pleasure? I ask it a favour. Take the life, I shouldn't hear, and I said, Don't you stand by *your* friends? and he said, My friends, they build the country, help the people. Nobody got a friend better. They wreck the country, cheat the people, it's a friend? You like a rattlesnake for breakfast, maybe? Listen, this *prutzah* tell you something about herself? and I said, No, and he said, What kind of passport she got? and I said, I don't know, and he said, So where's she born? Where she go to school? What's her father do, he should give her a two-dollar wedding and drop dead? and I said, I don't know. It's none of my business, and he bunched his fingers, and said, What kind of friend, you don't even know where she's from, it should get a nuke?

Look, I said, If she's done wrong, she's going to suffer. I won't add to it. That's all.

Keep out of it, he said. A false passport? The wrong name? The money, not hers? A dancing team comes here, pretend they know her? They don't. Just paid to. They leave tapes, her voice singing? We know who belongs the voice. Not her. So where's the money come from? These days, you just trace the paper. That money come from Beirut. To Rome. London. Toronto. Miami. New York. Different accounts, not her name. Couple more I didn't mention. Finally, here. Tel Aviv. Why the runaround? Nothing to hide?

Doesn't sound good, I said. Whose money is it?

From Beirut, you asking *whose?* Merom whispered. Beirut? Lebanon? They don't have Arbas there? Terrorists, they don't have a head office the main street? Right next door, the bank, they should all blow up? Listen, you got kids just out of school coming here, suitcases full of bombs. You read about it? People older than me, suitcases of plastic and detonators. Why they do it? Who paid?

But listen, I said. If all this is true, why hasn't she been

arrested? And how long's it been known? and he said,
Long enough time to be sure. When they have everybody
she deals with, they all go in the wire together. You could
be one. You're happy?

Time to open the Studio, I said.

Merom rubbed his hands, and laughed the baby side of
him, and said, Now we got the oven on. I been praying at
the Wall, lately. About a lot of things. This is one. I have
a feeling. It's going to go. It goes here, it goes any place.
Country gets the benefit. You know how grateful I feel?
and I said, What for? It's your idea, and he smiled wide,
shaking his head, and whispered, Look, son. One thing,
it's wanting to *do* something. Get something *going*. That's
the smallest part. *What* to do, and *how*, and what *with*,
that's the meat in the *kreplech*, and the shape, and the
cook-up, and the whole *zehu ze*. That's you. The Lord
God, blessed be He, sent you. Know something? I take
care of you.

I put my arm about his shoulders and turned for the
door, but it opened on a knock, and Roch ducked a head
in, Punch alight in his smile, and he said, Just thought
you ought to know. They got that guy. That bastard, Neb.
Up in Safed, and Merom said, Safed, where all the
scholars are? and Roch said, Scholars nothing. The guys
with him were running a hardware store. Army got him
with a truckload. Grenades, Bananas. Everything. Going
after the rest, and Merom said, What do you know? They
got 'm? I tell you. And that's just the start. We know him?
and Roch said, O, why sure. Done a lot of business. Pip-
ing. Boilers. Water tanks. Cover-up. Name's Shitrit.

Merom, stoneface, looked at stoneface Roch, and I was
there, but I saw no light in the eyes, no more.

Stone, both, for seconds.

Merom looked down at his shoes, and said. The name,

it should fit. It's a lesson? and Roch said, Shows you, and Merom said, Me, it don't show a thing. I could smell it down the phone. Let's get some hope, see the new talent.

We went out, to the main room, dark, passing the tool desks, and went in the lit door, all colored electrics, to Studio Pueris.

Every small desk had its group of children, and a couple of adults showing them how to use tools.

Merom stopped, looked up at me, and whispered, See what you done? Look. Just look there. Don't tell me. I *know*. They're working. It's how it's done. It's going to work. *Work*. Ah, son, I done a lot of praying.

The handkerchief came out in flutter of white, and the noble head went in, as a rock washed by a wave, and Roch stood closer, the guardian, yearning Punch, and I looked away, at Tâl, alone, watching the children at the first desk. She turned, saw the handkerchief, and seemed feather-light, flying to wrap her arms, whispering. Sometimes, somebody spoke, oftener silence.

I heard an owl outside, and remembered my mother, An owl, it's lucky. It's the wise one. He looks at you, don't blink. Throwing out the luck.

I went over, and stood close, and Tâl took Merom to watch the little girl handling tools at the desk. A fixed light of wonder shone in the grey eyes, and I watched Sheba, entranced by some marvel, and loved the shadow-seen shape of her breasts and the jut of hipbones, a voluptuous line of thigh, a knee I longed to kiss, the hand on Merom's shoulder, and I said, Who said something about a cup of coffee? and she seemed to waken, and said, Oh, yes. Paula's bringing it. Did you know Zuz is out in the café? and she looked again, and said, with a motion of the hips, That shirt's simply *ter*rible. Would you mind if I throw it away? Somebody has to start taking care of you.

Merom looks like a tailor's wax beside you, and I said, Do as you want. Do I look such a mess? and she said, You couldn't look a mess even *trying*. You just don't have the kit. You have to buy some clothes. *Look* at you.

I looked from her to Merom, and said, You really *mean* that? and she said, Why else would I say it? *My* boss has to look like a *boss*. You look as if you just came out of. Well. Chokey, and I said, What's that? and she said, That's good old English for jail. You never heard it? and I said, I never mixed in that society, and she said, I read it in something. Chokey says such a lot, and I said, That's how I look? and she said, Just the outside part. The threads. That's all there is. Threads. *Bare* threads. You don't look like the boss of this place. Don't begin to, and I said, Nobody dresses up here. They're all open-necked. Cabinet, on down, and she said, They're just pretending to be democratic. You know. Be on the same level as the people? People taxed over their heads? Can't afford *any-thing*? Except their wives wash and iron, and use a little starch? That saves it. At least, they're clean. Small good. What else? and I said, What do you mean, what else? and she said, They think clean's all they have to be. Dressing up they can't afford, and I said, So what's my problem? I'm clean, anyway. Who *wants* to dress up? and she said, There's a level. Under that you don't go. So would you *please* throw away that shirt, clean or not? And I said, You want me to do it now? And she said, Let's say you wore it for the last time. Tomorrow we buy new? The others are just as horrible, and I said, You never told me. Are you going to buy them? and she said, Give me the car, and just one of everything for size, you're another man.

It's a deal, I said, and she said, Aren't you going to look at what the children are doing? and I said, No. It's *their* job. Leave them alone. Only *they* know what they want to do. Don't let's be a nuisance, and Sheba smiled the little wrinkle of mouth and nose, and said, Zuz is waiting for us.

TWENTY-SEVEN

I had a call after midnight from someone I never heard of, telling me to be ready at six the next morning for a helicopter ride to an Army complex in Sinai, and to bring blueprints of all I had in the experimental stage, and any special tools I might need, and he hung up, no please, nokissmeass, nothing.

That's the Army.

At six, almost on the second hand, the bird came over the hill behind us, and settled in the car park. The pilot signalled me in, the door shut, and we were in the air for the bumpiest ride ever. Nobody spoke. My side had been blacked out. All I could see were two heads, and the clouds in front.

Why did I know Tâl was thinking of me?

ESP, yes, I believe, and I *know*. I knew when she felt miz, or when she climbed on a sunray. How many times did we think together while she read the morning mail? At first I thought it of no importance, a simple exercise in secretarial efficiency.

But a morning came when we said it together—whatever it was—and I looked at her, and her eyes seemed huge, paler grey, lit with the half-laugh and amazement, staring at me, in a moment filled with glitter, and she looked down at the pad, and said something, and went out.

I knew, then, that we were one.

Except for Merom, and that warning.

Bloodline.

I wondered if she would listen to me if I told her I was willing to throw it all up to marry her and go elsewhere, and live beyond the trammels of religion. Knowing the strength of her character, I doubted it. I had no financial problem. I could settle in any country of her choice, live better, but incomparably better, than at the moment.

But I felt Merom looking at me. There was no question of fear. I was certainly not afraid of him. I was, though, worried about what he might be able to do to her, spiritually, mentally.

I was aware of her affection for him, her gratitude for his constant care, the education, travel, the expense of a well-born girl which he accepted, not in one case, but several. Batsheba, Paula, were two more, and there were five others, and three boys. That type of patriarch is not easily thwarted, and I knew beyond any doubt that if—*if*—I could persuade her to marry, there could be no life for us in Israel.

That thought, alone, chilled me.

I had no desire to live anywhere else. I knew, beyond all doubt, that she *would* not.

I tried to understand why I could feel in such an absolute way about a people and a country completely alien to me. Perhaps because of marvels created in the land, changing a desert into a mighty garden, planting forests in rocky hills, each tree a memory of someone loved, green flames ever burning, reminder for everyone that men and women care.

Or because of Groz and Abba, and Orfa, and Shoshi, and the tens of thousands like them, or Merom and Roch, and Mayerkopf and Arendts, or Zuz and Traul.

A thought of Aliya brought that twinge of sorrow, or remorse, I was unsure. Equally, I was unsure why I felt sorrow. Remorse, perhaps, because of Tâl.

Any thought of another woman was disgust by comparison. But why the sorrow? And yet, I *knew*, knew so well, I sorrowed for her. I had that failing in the heart. Why? And I had no answer. In words, nothing. In feeling, everything. In the heart? In the gut? That was where it was strongest. Because I had shared that—denied—orgasm? Knew her agony, sorrowed in her desire?

I had no time to sort it out. We fell like a lead plumb, and I felt the wheels bump, and I was never happier than to put one foot solid on the hard tarmac of the airfield, and follow a girl soldier to a car, get in, and go.

Somewhere.

I never had any notion where I was.

We got there, and I was taken into a dining room, shown the toilet, sat at a table, all, guided by unknowns, sitting with unknowns, the khaki anonymous, bearded, whiskered, bemutton-chopped, and they talked to each other, but not to me, and the girls were mini-skirted, beautiful, over-all cleaner, smarter than the men, and still distant, arm's length, and I felt Nobody.

I was still Nobody in a tour of what they—the anonymous khaki ones—let me see.

It was little enough, but what I saw gave confidence by its quality and last-minute now-ness, ahead of a great deal I had thought.

But I set them up in a couple of talks, and showed them where they could improve what they had. I worked on a couple of ideas, explained, went over blueprints, drawings, drew on blackboards, answered questions, saw only khaki, never remembered a face or a voice, though the beauty of the girls—except that not any one of them knew I existed or gave any sign—well, yes, it was compensation of a kind.

These were the eighteen-to-twenties, gentlest flower of the Nation, the daughters from immemorial, guarded and cherished as future mothers of Israel, here, freeing a man of a job, giving at least one more warrior to the field, oftener two or three. In my department, at least fifty worked by day and night, always and at any hour bathed, combed, crisp from the laundry, and so Tâl was always with me.

I saw her, and Paula, wherever I looked.

But I was purposefully distant. They were not less with me. I felt I was being tested.

I object to tests.

The days passed, busily enough. I made models, gave lectures, showed how existing types could be improved, projected ideas for the future, refused after-hours meetings, any entertainment, all—however hesitant—offers of hospitality.

I had Merom in mind.

But, riding over-all, Tâl enwrapped mind and heart.

She, the womansweet of her, was about me, reminding me, moment by moment.

There was no opportunity to telephone. When I asked, I was told by faceless khaki that lines went only to Army Headquarters, and that in any case, talk must be in Hebrew.

Which annulled me.

Most of what I heard, apart from the interpreter's few

breaks, went over the fence. It was all right with me. I had Tâl to dream about, and I knew, beyond argument, that she dreamed of me. Thinking of her dreaming was a marvellous concept, dream in a dream, anaesthetically a glory. But I ached for the touch of her. I felt the grip on my hip bones, wanted it always there.

Between that, and twisting a lot of wire, and cutting copper plates, and drawing diagrams, schemas, sketches, and blackboard sessions, talking, talking, eating what I never tasted, always facing and challenging the faceless, and sleeping in what seemed a hospital bed, bathing, shaving, what the hell, time passed, and a girl soldier put flat hands at volupt thighs, and bent slightly, and told me to be ready in fifteen minutes, and I got my pathetic bits together, and I was on the helicopter, en route to our place.

And the dream of Tâl.

But she had gone to Tel Aviv.

It had the impact of a bomb.

I felt the world fall down.

I wanted so much to see her, look at her, *know* she was there.

And while I bit cheekleather, the phone rang.

Merom, the Lord God said, I hear you got back, son. How's things?

Pretty good, I said. Except Tâl's not here, and he said, So? You want to start dictating this time of day? and I said, No. I just want to hear what's been going on, and he said, Nothing but good. The best. Only beautiful, and I said, She should be here to tell me, and he said, Son, I agree with you. A slip-up. But didn't you tell her to buy some shirts? and I said, Look, does it take all this time to buy a shirt, for God's sake? and he said, It's not for God's sake. It's for *you*. You think she's the kind walks in some store and says, Give me a shirt? Hell kind of play's that? No. She's a *real* secretary. *In*cidentally, likes her job. So she had them made. By hand. Got your initials. On the heart. And I said, How do you know? and he said, I seen a couple. He makes for me. Not angry with her? Don't be. She wanted them ready. You know *her,* and I said, When's she going to be back? and he said, Well, I'd say inside of an hour. Helicopter. Better clear the car park. Going to stand behind the door and say boo? and I said, Bosses can't do that, and he said, You be surprised. Even bosses got feelings. Listen, that studio. The children? They produced the first job. Complete. I got Tâl to give it to me. Don't blame her. It's on my desk. I can see you talking to me. Roch went nuts. Listen, son. You look kind of awful tired. Would you please go to bed? Rest a couple of days? Be getting them goddam shakes again. Do me a favor. Go to bed, will you? and I said, I'll wait for her. For Tâl, and he said, That's all I wanted to hear. I'm down at the Wall in the morning. Good night, son. Listen. Remember. I'm looking out for you. *Shalom.*

I heard the blessing in the voice, and I remembered the noble head, and I knew Paula's rap on the door, and I said, Come in.

She stood there, with Zuz behind, tray at shoulder.

Thought you might like something to ease the aches, she said. I know that flight. You don't have a stomach for days after. How about chicken with Shoshi's pastry round it? and I said, About all I'd want, and she said, You see? I knew.

Zuz laid the cloth, put out plates, cutlery, set down the coffee service, and took off the hot-plate's silver cover with the flourish of a conjuror, showing a choir of golden rolls all seeming to sing *SHOSHI* together.

Would you go out there and give that gal a big hug

for me? I told Paula. When I'm more pulled together I'll go out and do it myself, and Zuz said, She wait for the signor. She wait so much. Tomorrow, the lunch it's something *speciale della casa*. Spaghetti alla Zuzoni. Make with the spinach. After, lamb in champagne jelly.

He put finger and thumb together and wiggled the hand.

For the best, only the best, he said and pointed the finger to heaven, hung the napkin over his cuff, bowed, and went out.

The difference *he* made here, Paula said. Shoshi's another woman.

I don't understand it, I said. Why did they stay there if life was so unbearable? and Paula said, They were loyal. She did so much for them. *If* a coffee shop is so much? and I said, You should have seen that place before. I think I know how they felt. Even so, I don't understand. How *does* somebody like that suddenly go berserk? By the way, where is she? and Paula looked out of the window and said, She's not here any more.

From the way she said it, I knew something was wrong, and I said, Why? and Paula said, There was a terrible scene at last Saturday's Collective meeting. They called the Police to throw her out. Nobody talks about it. She called them everything. I wasn't there. I thank my mother.

Don't understand it, I said. She always seemed the gentlest. Got along with everybody. What do *you* suppose could have happened?

Paula shook her head.

I quit after what she told me, she said. I only heard men use that sort of language. Nothing gentle about it, believe me. She might be sick. I can feel sorrier to think so. But she came over here to find you. Wouldn't believe it when we told her you were away. She went mad. Tried to attack Tâl. So I had to deal with her. She swore she'd do her some harm. I believe the Police let her go in Beersheba. But she won't be free long, and I said, But what's she done? and Paula shook her head, and passed the chicken rolls.

It's something to do with security, she said. I don't know enough about it. I shouldn't have said as much, and I said, Ah, now, look. You're talking to *me,* and she said, I know, and smiled, and I knew, then, I could have put her on the floor. So easily. Or asked her down to my room.

But I was held by thought of Tâl.

I'm going out to see Shoshi, I said. Those rolls are the best I ever tasted. She should open a restaurant somewhere. She'd kill the competition. She and Zuz. Partnership. I wish Tâl was here.

Paula quietly put the cups and saucers on the tray.

Back to me, she put the coffeepot in place. But that prismatic drop fell against the light, flashed, made its small plaint on the saucer.

Any idea that I could have hurt her made me ill. I went over and put a hand on her back, but her instant half-turn and almost-defensive raising of the right arm told me.

I was wrong. From the beginning.

I looked at her for moments, and her eyes changed from fright to wary, to a small smile far away, and nearer, to her own smile, warm, confident.

What's the trouble? I said, and she breathed deep, and said, I was just thinking. You've done so much for everybody, and yet you're surrounded by the *un*happiest people. You know the saying, it hit me on the funnybone? Well, it hit *me* on the tragibone. That's all, and I said, But *who's* unhappy? and she said, Well, we can start with me, and I said, What's wrong with you? and she said, I've been in love for years. He doesn't know I'm alive, and I said, Want to bet?

She shrugged, and said, Doesn't even *look* at me, and I said, He's probably shy. It happens. And perhaps he thinks you might laugh at him. After all, you're part of the Merom family. People have to take a little care. I'm not an Israeli. But I think I know what goes on. Is he a Hebrew? and she said, Yes. Not strict. Not ultra. Not idiotic. Just. Well. Sort of like I am, and I said, Who is he?

Suddenly she turned, and put her arms about me, and said, I trust you. You'd never tell? and I said, Ah, beauty. What am I? *The* bastard? Who is he? and she said, Bax. We were in the Army together. I was his left hand. Or left foot. Now he's here. But he still takes as much notice. One day—I swear—I'll strip naked and walk in on him, and I said, *That* ought to do it. You'll let me know, won't you? If there's one thing I ever wanted to see, it's you. Stark-o.

She turned away, and I pulled her back.

Is there a more wonderful feeling than both arms full of a *big* girl, close-held, warm, leaning, breathing the natural scent of her? Yet, I thought of Tâl.

Tell him I want to see him, I said. In the kitchen. Shoshi'll make a wonderful interlocutor, and she stood closer, and said, You promise not to say anything? *Please?* and I said, You mind your business, and I'll fool around with mine, and she said, You'd never tell Tâl? and I said, How do *you* know she doesn't know?

She stood away, clasped hands under her chin and looked up, at the hills, *Whence Cometh My Help?* and said, That's the fortunate one. Brains, everything. Nothing denied her. Merom's favourite. Probably marry a Cabinet minister. Or somebody up there, Simply lucky. Born.

I looked at her, feeling I'd been flung in a corner, trampled underfoot.

Any talk of marriage? I asked, in what I hoped was a normal voice, though it sounded to me like escaping gas. She leaving us? and Paula said, Up to her. She's not happy, either, and I said, Why not?

Paula held out her arms, a hopeless, beautiful gesture. We need *marriage*, she said. *Need* it. A job's fine. I love it, here. But to have to go home at night? And nobody? Sleep? Day after day? Nothing's got colour. Where's the music?

Are you the only one? I said. Who else is unhappy? and she said, that poor man Horowitz. Yeke. They just stopped him from suicide. He's in hospital in Beersheba.

I took time to think of a heap of smelly rags, remnant of a man we all loved.

Right, I said. Order a car. I'm going there now, and she said, They won't let you in. He's in the Army wing, and I said, Why? and she lifted a shoulder, and said, You know the Army. After all, he's an officer.

Get on to it, first thing, I said. I want to see him. Tell Bax I'll meet him in the kitchen. When Tâl comes in, tell her where I am. And listen. Don't be unhappy. Or if you are, it won't be for very long, and I saw her cheeks fatten in a smile, and she said, How do *you* know? and I said, I have a feeling.

Voice and words echoed in the corridor and over them I heard the helicopter land on the other side.

Suddenly, just the idea I was going to see Tâl's smile filled the world, and I was happier in those moments than I suppose I have ever been.

I waited the wondrous aeons, hearing the door slide open, the swift rap of her step.

My dove, my undefiled, is but one. She is the only one

261

of her mother. She is the choice one of her who bore her. The daughters saw her and blessed her, yea, the queens and the concubines, they praised her.

But instead of coming to the office, the step turned left, towards the café.

And yet not. They went out, through the south door, towards her own place.

Which yet my soul seeketh, but I find not. One man among a thousand have I found, but a woman among all those have I not found. How beautiful are thy feet with shoes, O prince's daughter!

The telephone rang, and Paula turned back with the tray, but I said, I'll get it, expecting Merom, but somebody said, Look, I'm sorry, but this is C.O.B One-One. Israel Defence Force. *Zahal.* We want you back here. Tonight. If I send a kite in about ten minutes, will you be ready? And I said, For how long, this time? and he said, Well, till we get this soaked out, and I said, When does private business get done, here? and he said, Listen, if it wasn't for what you and a lot more of us are doing here, there wouldn't be any, and I said, you got me. I'll be ready.

I trotted down to my place to get some clean changes, and soap, and books, and saw the lights on, and Shoshi's girl carrying in boxes. She spoke little English, and always seemed for some reason afraid of me, and I let her go, a waddling goose in over-the-shoulder cackle.

Boxes piled on the bed.

I opened one, and found white shirts, and in another, some pale blue and others dark blue, and socks, handkerchiefs, underwear, and I had a thought, and I was right. My wardrobe and the chest of drawers were empty. Everything I had was not there. I saw Tâl in the hidden-eyes smile. She probably made a bonfire.

I never felt taken care of before.

New shoes glossed on the rack. A blue jacket and grey flannels hung from the top of the door. I tore off what I had on, and got into her choice, with a shirt and one of her ties, and put on her socks, and the shoes, and felt new. I got what I wanted, put a couple of new shirts and handkerchiefs in with the books, and ran, hearing the helicopter, wishing I could meet her, but Avram met me at the car park, and there was no time to speak.

It's everything going marvellous, he shouted, under the blades. We got to thank you. The children, I can't tell you. Listen, everything under control here. Take your mind off, and I shouted, Thanks, Avram. Keep an eye on Shoshi, and everybody. Especially Tâl, and he yelled, You think we don't? and I waved, and the door shut, and I was off in the bumps.

But if I wished I had seen Tâl, at least I had her shirt on.

TWENTY-EIGHT

We worked each day and most nights until the eyelids imposed small will.

Blanket rolls spread along the corridor seemed cocoons of royal comfort. We soaped in a hot shower, and slept. Food came when appetite called, or any sort of drink at all times, but no alcohol, and I had constant sense of being part of a divine mission.

I was the only member not wearing a skullcap. The rest were covered in the Presence. I found a remotely comical pathos in so many *yarmulkas* held in place by a woman's hairpin.

I shut my eyes to hear their prayers, understanding no word, but I knew, I felt what they meant, the faceless, nameless, men and girl soldiers, khaki anonyms, working to the glory of God, and the survival of The People Who Crossed The River.

We were linking a series of ideas, some of them mine. We were not told what the end job was to be, but I saw enough to guess, and when the Colonel asked what I thought, I said we had a good tool for a massage parlour, and he smiled and said, You have the correct idea. Keep it so.

Except for the haunt of Tâl, I was happy enough. But the world awoke and laughed in gold when I found her letter on my bed in the coffee break.

She began with figures and percentages, and I skimmed, agreeably surprised at output and sales, but amazed at the figures for the Studio Pueris, and happy enough to see what the commune was turning out, almost seeing Groz's grey ram-curls and the smile-lines carven deep in the jaw.

As you see, we work well without you and we all hope you never come back, she wrote. Paula asks me to say that when you are not here there is nothing to do and she prefers that. The hardest work we do is answer the telephone, generally Merom, hoping you are not back yet, and so glad at no news. Even he cannot speak to you where you are, and you have no idea how he appreciates not talking to you. If we knew when to expect you, we would not be here, Shoshi and Zuz as well. Dear Boss, we wait so impatiently for you not to come back. Please give us plenty of time so that we may run to the hills. We know the Army tells you a month ahead when you may go. Two weeks will do it for us. I was disappointed you saw the shirts and things and took some with you. I hope they don't fit. If the shoes pinch, then I am happy to think you suffer. They can be changed, but I have no patience. Paula thinks this is a horrible letter and I must type it myself and so I shall. I have just spoken to Merom and he says please will you get back before they have to put the barrel irons on him. This is the longest you have been away. Dear Boss, where are you, how are you, and how long more? As if we care. Report ends. T.

It set me up. I knew what she meant, or I thought I did,

and I asked the Colonel and he said, When the pilot models work, you can go right the next minute, so run it your way.

I went in, knowing where the hold-up was, and I took the men off, and showed the girl-soldiers what to do. No question about it. They were smarter, and they had the hands. The men took it as work, but the girls thought of it as duty. There *is* a difference, and those girls, combed, bathed, crisp, were dedicated.

The Mothers of future Israel had a further, finer, idea. I saw it working when we went in the map room. All Israel spread in bloom of glory, and I stood in wonder, looking from the north on down, sea coast to the Jordan, remembering that each small flag was a place where people lived, each little black full-stop a collect of streets and houses, schools, shops, kindergartens, women and children, breadwinners taxed beyond endurance, but all of them faithful, hopeful, or in other ways determined not to be less, or die.

In that time, while we waited to see if the models worked, I understood far more about the country and the brave remnant of twelve heroic tribes, once again fighting to avoid destruction, dispersion, massacre. The calm of the room underlined the efficiency of men and girls, every move deliberate, all work cued by lights, each cue answered and passed, or where it failed, we went over, found the cause and set it in order, and the second time, I knew my guess was correct.

But I said nothing, and I felt the Colonel's eye.

Late that night all the models worked without fault, both for the outgoing, and for the incoming shift, but nobody danced or sang because none of them knew what they had done. I heard guesses among my team, most nonsense, and still I said nothing.

Thanks, the Colonel said. And thanks again for not discussing the project. What reason you going to give for being here? and I said, Making an automatic drive for rocking horses, and he nodded, and said, Do fine. Thanks again. Work all the units odd times in the night till tomorrow morning, and make sure. Then you go back. *Shalom.*

Kiss me ass. That's the Army.

We were pulled out of the blankets time and again, but the models worked without a blotch, and in the morning, bulgy-eyed, we were happy to see them work again.

We went in for coffee, and my favourite sergeant-major put her hands flat to a sweet of hams, and said, You have no time to change, sir. You are on travel orders. Follow me, and I made a dive for my bag, waved goodbye to a roaring *SHALOM!* and followed beauty out, to blue, cloudless hot desert air, and whirring blades, a black-out cabin, and off.

I put my feet up, wishing I could have gone back bathed, shaved, dressed in the new clothes, still in their plastic envelopes, but I opened my eyes when the pilot said, This is Tel Aviv. You have a car meeting you. Stand by.

Cold breeze met me, rain was near, grey cloud lazed, and Merom opened his arms on the edge of the tarmac.

Get over here, he shouted. Want some lung trouble, standing there? They *have* to turn this on, goddammit. How are you, son? Don't look a day older than eighty. Doctor has to give you a go-over. Don't want you going back down there knocked-out. You know what a business you got? and I said, Couldn't have been done without a lot of help. Got along fine without me, and he looked sideways at me, and said, It's the idea does it. You got

267

that, rest's a follow-on. Listen, you got some more ideas? Places in the country, just crying. See what you did up that commune? Never saw such a bunch of happy people. Don't have to plough and fool around any more. Earning real nice. Better than they ever did, and I said, I'm sorry they're coming off the land, and he said, Don't be. Plenty youngsters take their places. The older ones, it's like they just go to the office every day. Taking a vacation. What they do, it's work? Pleasure. And getting paid for it? Hear what they say, even *I* got to like you.

How's everything in the office? I asked, and he said, Your office? They went on strike till you get back. Gone down to Eilat, and I said, Any doctor wants to see me, it's the one in Eilat, and he said, Son, I'm ahead of you. So you're booked on the two-thirty flight. Roch, Bax, they're down there already. Bring you up-to-date, And I said, looking out of the window, What are you getting here, *snow?* and he said, They tell us its unseasonal weather. They always got some goddam excuse. So the heat don't come on this morning? I own thirty blocks, the building, my own office, I like to get my ass froze off? I tell you, son. I don't look after my*self*, who's offended? and I said, Well. There's Tâl. Paula. Batsheba. Some more. And me, and he said, Be glad to think you *mean* that, and I said, Be sure, and he said I feel lots better about everything, and I said, What was there to feel bad about? I thought everything was going fine?

He nodded.

Listen, son, he said. This *prutzah*, the one in the café, she mean so much to you? And I said, She's a friend of mine, yes, and he said, Friend? All right, we got different ideas, see? Now, she says you had a pretty cosy time together. And them sketches must have got in her stuff when she stayed with you, and I said, She never did. I

268

was in her place once. I'm pretty sure I had no sketches with me. Why is this important?

He looked at me.

You ever hear of an Army Court of Inquiry? he said, and my neck-hair froze. It's pretty tough. Them guys don't know nothing and nobody, you included. They don't *care*. Nobody got enough money to buy 'em. They don't even know what money *is*. So it has to come out. Her word's good as yours. You know you had some pretty smart people spotted around the plant these past months? Well, they don't have a lot to say about you. Except good. But they got *her* moves, time she's out of bed in the morning, she should drown the bath. Going to Haifa? Times she never went further than Beersheba, Dimona. Haifa, sure. Meet this Arab guy. Other times, a café down there, about midway between Eilat and Beersheba. Jerusalem a couple of times. What she do? They *know*, and I said, What are they waiting for? and he said, Pick up the rest. I believe they lost the idea you had a hand in it, and I said, *Me*? Hand in *what*? What's she supposed to be part *of*, anyway? I can't believe it, and he said, Get the head to it, son. Where these people get the grenades? The explosives? Listen. Know something? The two bombs hit your place, you draw a line direct from where they found the tube, passing through them craters, just a couple hundred yards further on, it hits the café. That time in the morning, full of people. Get it?

And she was travelling that day, I said.

He patted my knee.

Talk to a brain, you get the answer, he said, and I said, Well, what the hell, wouldn't you want to protect her? Instead of throwing her to the dogs? and he said, The dogs, they got the right to expect better, and I said, Ah, now, look, and he said, *You* look. She's part of a whole gang here. We want the lot. We got patience. Everyday coming closer. That's why *you* stay out. Else? and I said, Else what? and he said, Else they *let* you out. You want that? and I said. No. I want to stay here, and he said, So? Only one way. Stay out the soup.

But that secret sorrow burned, and I was unsure why.

To know a woman in love must be for the rest of life to have a sealed bond with the memory of her. But to feel sorrow?

I had no answer.

We were slowing in to the airport.

Lod, Merom said. Fourteen minutes, you're up there. I have to get back to Tel Aviv. You're staying at my house. Hotels, you don't get the rest. Full of tourists. There, you get a cook. Take care of you. Girls be waiting for you. Son, would you please take care yourself? Or let some of us? You just spread yourself around. Wasting the sympathy. Listen, Bax I sent there. Give you some of those figures you don't like. But they tell it. What you did. What you started. Think we let go of you? Get some rest. Lots of fishing. Lose ten years, anyway. Bye, son. I might be down there. *Shalom.*

I was out on the breezy paving and the car turned out. The bag weighed nothing, but I was tired. I went in and put it on the search counter, and the officer went through every item. I signed a form declaring I carried nothing for anybody, and I had no weapons. I booked in, went in the search room, took a landing card, and boarded, and my seat companion became human when the stewardess handed us the plate of sweets.

He nodded, and I recognised the young major on the first interrogation team. My stomach became part of an automatic mixer. There and then I made up my mind that Eilat was not for me. Neither of us spoke. In the entire forty-five minutes I read, or shut my eyes.

But all the time my mind hammered. It was difficult to swallow that the meeting had been either accident or coincidental.

When we unfastened belts, the major, looking like a workman in a wind-cutter jacket and blue canvas, nodded again, and stood aside for me to go out, and followed me, not a word.

I saw the girls over at the baggage stand—where once I had seen Aliya!—though both seemed charged with a simplicity she lacked, some cheerful cleanly quality, essence of womanliness, and for my tired eyes, a blessing that made me open my arms and run, and they were ready, but the Druse *haga* shouted them back, and Tâl stamped her foot at him, and Paula put her fists on her hips, but then I was up to them, and never mind the *haga*, they ran to put their arms round me, and at last I felt I was home.

Enough of this, I said. I want the three of us on the next flight back. Tâl, telephone Merom. We want the car at Lod. Paula, see if they have three seats. The officer on the interrogation unit sat next to me. How do I rest here? Need to say any more?

Both frowned as roused lionesses, but neither said a word.

Both ran, and I saw that Tâl's moon, if smaller than Paula's, held the deeper dimples I longed to kiss.

TWENTY-NINE

Suddenly I was sick of the grimy wastes of want and denial. I could do so many things, start others, but I seemed unable to do anything right for myself. It was no bout of self-pity. I knew it must be that accepting facts as they were, Tâl was denied, and part of me lay grey, and because by nature I was pragmatist, I expected no miracles. As for any thought she might be fond of me, apart from her concern as secretary, I had smarting memory of my state of mind about Paula. I had been wrong. It had been a mental thrashing. A lesson that still jeered.

I took the only seat back to Tel Aviv. The girls had seats on later flights, but Roch and Bax had to wait till morning. I rebelled at any notion of going back and inflicting misery on everybody. Instead I took a cab outside Tel Aviv airport, and said the first word in mind, Haifa, and the cabman turned out as though two-hour cab rides were normal.

Rain and darkness suited me. I could even laugh at myself as spectacle of the inane, the lugubrious in ascent.

I thought that probably some of my ancestral traits were flowering late-bloomer sprays in unlit corners of a mind barely mature, or that perhaps had not altogether absorbed the benefits of assimilation.

I felt cursed in feeling as I did. I was young, healthy, at any rate, in body. I had a growing business, many loyal colleagues, friends everywhere, money enough. Yet, I had a curious fear it could all be taken from me. Dachau and Belsen were in the air, and the gas ovens' stench blew murderously foul, and I dreamed myself in a night of dying children, naked, beyond help.

The cabman spoke, somewhere, in lights. Rain still spotted the windshield, and I said, out of the dream, Not here. Drive on till there's no rain. I want a quiet hotel, and he said, Look, north of Nahariya there's a commune. They got a hotel. New. Sea's right outside the window. Quiet, a mile away you drop a straw, it's a bomb, and I said, That's for me.

In darkness the lights were comfort, and they had a room, and I ate an omelet and walked through the garden to a modern block, and held patience till the woman drew the curtains, had a hot bath, and went into a springy bed, and anodyne.

The days are not in memory except for the misery on waking, resentment in having to dress to go over to the restaurant, and relief in getting back, a turn-away thought of Tål, and instant sleep.

But that early morning, a pair of doves bickering outside the window woke me, and I looked out, at clear blue, a glorious sun, and the Mediterranean glittering not far away. It was surprise to find I was unshaven for so many days, but I seemed dry inside, as though ducts were emptied, any doubt resolved.

Back from breakfast, I waited for eight o'clock and put

273

in a call, and the voice that spoke unto Isaac said, Ah, son, you want to bring the grey hairs down to Gehinnon? Where the hell you been? and I said, I took a little time out. Feel a whole lot better, and he said, That's great. About how I figured. You know you give them gals pretty near a nervous breakdown? Didn't you even want to *call* them? and I said, What for? Give them more misery than they have? No. I just holed up. I'm taking a cab now, and going back, and he said, Hold on, here. That's six-seven hours any way you look at it. I have a better idea. I'll send a 'copter up there, and I said, I'm not all that important, and he said, Portantshmortant. Time, that's what. Listen, you get in that thing. Call in here. I get you flew direct back home. Right? And I said, Right, and he said, You know what I like? You called *me*. *Shalom*.

I paid the bill, and wandered round the grounds, and went in for another cup of instant boil, aware of a certain tranquil quality shining in the place and the people working there. A man behind the desk told me they were from South Africa, some from the United States, many survivors of the concentration camps.

Now we just live, he said. As *we* want. It's good? No apartheid. No colour here. Nobody more than anybody else. No discord. Vote for, or against. Better? and I said, The result says so.

The kite dropped in the parking space, and I ran, got in, and we took off towards the sea, and swung over the coast line, and I had a view of an Israel I might never have known, of new housing blocks for the incoming, and gardens, orchards, plastic greenhouses for roses going to export, and the pilot pointed to new villages, and roads ending in heaps of rocks with the yellow bulldozers, mites, in dust to clear them.

Every time I come up here, something new, he said, and

274

we were bumping. But the way it's growing, it's like somebody got a wand. You know, Moses? The waters of
Meribah? Look there. Akko. Acre. Different place every
time I come here. Same as Haifa. Digging out the ruins.
When I was this high, mess of stones. Now look at it, and
I said, Where did you learn English? and he said, First in
London. Afterwards, Baltimore. Then here. Not too
good? and I said, Wish I spoke Hebrew as well, and he
said, See down there? Industrial. The smoke, they com-
plaining. Who? The ones got jobs? Or them got property?
I tell you, we got problems. What's that? Problems? What
you live with? So? *Live.*

I thought that said most of it, and we were over the
streets of Tel Aviv, and the pilot said, Coming down over
there, all right?

But I was lost, and I said, Fine, and I believe that's
just the way a lot of things happen. We bumped on a
roof, and the door opened, and the pilot said, See you,
and I ducked under the blades and went for the door
and the arrows pointing down.

Merom stood there, held out an arm to me, waved to
the pilot, and turned for the lift.

Good to see you, he said. Looking better. But I wish
you told me, and I said, Sometimes you have to be by
yourself, and he said, Them times, you need a gal, and I
said, I don't have one. Wish I did, and he said, There's
plenty, and I said, Not that *I* want, and he said, You're
a difficult customer. I got to know how to handle you.
Come in. What do you say, a cup of *real* coffee? and I
said, I pretty nearly forgot there was any such thing,
and he said, You don't know Blum. She's the queen. Coffee,
that's her blood. So what's the big worry, son? Come on,
now.

As out of a cloud, I told him.

He nodded, listening, and walked to the window, looking down at the streets.

Look, he said, Come on over here. See all them people? They all got the tears in their eyes. Everybody the same. Sometimes they get this feeling. Let's give it all up. Going to be taken off you. Throw it in. Then they get another feeling. We don't let go. All of us between the two. Give up, we sick of it. Fight, we hold what we got. So? That way, you live. You doing all right? Fine. Things not so good? Make the social disorder. Go slow. Strike. All the sharp union stuff. Histadrut. Don't have an idea among the bunch, and I said, What's this Histadrut? and he said, All the unions. Unions of what? Put all the crap in one pail, what do you have? We're stuck in European crap. American crap. What's the difference? All them people in the streets know goddam well they under sentence of death from four sides *and* up above. So? They got an Army. All depends the Army. They *pay* for an Army. Army's the boss. The rest? They talk. But the people, they crying what happened. Or what they afraid's going to happen. You any different?

I'm not Israeli, I said, and he said, It matters? Israeli, that's paper, stamp, photo. What's inside of you, they can get *that* on paper? Same as all of us. I'm born American. So all of a sudden I'm Israeli? We all come from somewhere. We all come back here. Why? We want to hear the Rabbis? *Nuts.* We come back to live like *we* want to. Nobody tell us how to live. We do the living, we do it the way we want. And I said, That's just about my way of thinking, and he said, So what's wrong with it? You got to go in details? All you got to know is, tears you got in the eyes, everybody else the same. You feel bad? Me, too. You going to dance, sing maybe? I'm in. It's so important you got the misery? Everybody got it. Melancholy, you call it? Nobody got more than me. Go down the street. Find somebody got more, I give the prize, cash. Why else we here? To be *us*. That's all. Who looks after us? Who got the arm around us? *Us*. That's who.

I'll get back, I said, and he said, I'll call Tâl. Tell her you're on your way. You don't like her? and I looked at him, and he was giving me the pale, pale-blue sideways power glare, and I said, Too much. *Shalom*.

I went up on the roof, and got blind in the kite, and the door shut, and we went up, and I pretended interest in the streets, looking away from the pilot, trying to get rid of water.

It's the smog, he said. They got to *do* something about it. Take years. Minute we get some peace, we start some *real* building. No use spending, a bomb knocks the lot down. Looks a mess? When I was in school, just a village. Wait, we get us some peace, get the bulldozers in there. Couple of years, come see us. Be a real city, and I said, You an Army pilot? and he said, Why else I'm sitting here?

We went over the hills, but *we* danced, not they, and the mist came in, and the pilot said, Snow. You going to have a cold time down there.

It seemed the sky swung us about in rolls of steam, but then, we were in clear air over the plain, white in snow, and the Bedouin tents and sheet-tin shacks were just underneath, with camels all facing one way, and lines of donkeys, and goats in black knots among sheep, and dogs running. Beersheba poked far to the left, chimneys and cisterns, blocks of buildings, but then we were over the Collective, coming from the other side in white mist, and I saw Ahmed down there, and we were over the car park, and on the floor, easy as that.

I got out, and Ahmed threw a blanket over me, and the

pilot waved, and swayed away. I ran down to the plant's side door, and in, to warmth, and Bax, waiting for me.

Real happy to see you, he said. Sorry about this, but that woman in the café, she's been here with stocktakers and accountants, and a couple of lawyers. Wants a lot of money for the furniture and goodwill. The collective's voted against it, and I said, Listen, we need the place, so get a deal. Pay her. Finish, and he said, Fine. How about running it? and I said, Let Shoshi and Zuz. I'll put up the capital. Move everything here over there. Use this only for Arab women. We need a lot more, and he said, Great, and I said, Merom know about this? and he said, Yes. Told me to leave it for you. The girls went into Beersheba with some of the wives. Shopping, and I said, How do you get in touch with that woman? and he said, Her lawyer's in Beersheba. I can fix it on the phone, and I said, Ask how about some sandwiches, will you?

I liked him. Grey eyes, trimmed beard, moustache, direct manner, almost cold except for the smile, sudden, gone. I saw him with Paula, a fine pair. But it made me think of Tâl, and that twinge jabbed again, and I was happier I had time to adjust to the idea of never having a chance to slip an arm about her, and saying, Come on. The rest can go to hell.

Bax came in with a company check book, and put a paper on the desk, and I looked at the total, and said, Pay it. Worth it.

The taps were Zuz's, and his smile was light. He prattled, laying a place with Merom's silver, how happy Shoshi was to go home.

How about Aliya? I asked, and he shrugged.

Un' disastre, catastrophico, he said, putting a chair to the place. Something like this, I don't see. Smile, now, *bellissimma,* in one second, scream. The mouth. Is sick.

In the heart the *misereria*. Shoshi, she like to see you, and I said, When she wants, and he bowed short, and went.

Bax came to the door, and held up a file while I was inspecting work on the tables in the drawing office.

All over, he called. Everything in order, and I said, What's going to happen to her? and he shrugged, and said, She'll go on if the Army wants it. Find the first, you might find the second. Have any luck, you got the lot. Takes time, that's all, and I said, But what's a girl like her doing in a mess like this? and he said, I know enough *not* to want to know. Ever see a fishing lure? All prettied up? That's her. Let the boys up top do the fishing. By the way, Moshe wants you to see the pottery exhibition here, and I said, How is it? and he shrugged, and said, I probably don't have the eye. Just down the passage, here, and I said, Let's see it.

As soon as he opened the door I had a strange feeling of something hidden coming clear. I looked at exact copies of ancient sculpture, and loved the lines, and funny faces, almost as if the old ones had joked. But the new shapes, matt, glazed, or tinted in raw colour were all annealed and spewed whole into the world of *kitsch*.

Immediately, perhaps because I had been thinking just below conscious level, I knew the source of that sorrow for Aliya.

She had some quality of *kitsch*, in her clothing, in the way she dressed her hair, her manner, the way she spoke. She wanted to impress, but her natural beauty was not enough, the process of her mind never reached the dictate of ambition, and that gap held the dead root of her sickness, part petrified in resentment, envy, erupting in screams, insults, at once defiance, and sole, pitiful defence.

I felt even more that urgent desire to help, but I heard Merom's voice, Stay out the soup.

Moshe came in running, threw his arms round me, and said, You see? What do you think? and I said, I like the copies. We can use a lot for decoration. But the others, no, and he nodded, like a young, beaten rooster, and said, It's true. The old ones, they had the idea. We thought *we* had. Till we saw them finished. We think we know so much, and Bax said, They were the first artists, and Moshe said, We thought we had a moneymaker. You get to know how to do things. Clay, and stuff. You can bring what you like out of that oven. Or off the wheel. But how do you get to think like an artist? Where's it come from? We been beating our heads. Don't do a thing. All you get's this.

Anyone know what happened to Yeke? I asked, and Moshe nodded, looking away.

Some of them go with the drink, he said. Some of them, drugs. Women's worst. Nothing you can do. You take a woman. You leave her? There's another. Anywhere you go. But some, they *don't* go. Just fix on one. Die if they can't have her. Yeke got it. Third try. The wrists.

Moments, moments, in the calm fields, in orchard shadow, a scent of apples, and peaches, and the Psalmist chanted *I removed his shoulder from the burden, his hands were delivered from the basket* and a gravemound grew beyond the green he loved, where sand blew, and so swiftly made night, and nothing.

Wherever they buried him, get Traul out there, make a garden, I said, and Bax said, One of the reasons the girls went in today. See what's been done. Groz and a lot more went in, and Moshe threw up his hands, and said, What happens to some guys? You can't have a woman, you kill yourself? and Bax said, No. The woman's rotten, and you know it. You have a disease? So kill yourself. It's easier, and I said, Easier than what? and he said, If you can't cure yourself of thinking of her. Some men don't want to think they're wrong, and Moshe said, That's Yeke. He could make dead trees grow. But he couldn't do a thing with her.

Let's get a little health, I said, I'm going to see Shoshi.

We went in the big, warm room, with about fifty people just finishing the break, sitting at tables, and they stood up, shouting welcome, and I waved to them. Radio played a tango, and the big windows showed the hills, clear of snow, flaring the green of little trees that each seemed a friend of mine and everyone else.

Shoshi saw me, threw a copper pan aside, and came arms out, head up, and grabbed me, and we waltzed.

You didn't get here soon, they all going down there and get you, me too, she said. Listen. Tomorrow, six o'clock, we change over. Zuz and me. Back home. But I take this whole kitchen. Right? and I said, Everything here's ours. Bought, paid for. Where's Aliya? and she turned her back.

But listen, Shoshi, I said. Why the big change? All so wonderful. She's beautiful, generous. What happened? and Shoshi said, Look. What makes the friend? You can answer me? *Who* can? I told her, get out of here.

Shoshi, listen, I said. What's the reason? She started it. She *was* wonderful. You *know* she was. Why the break? Bad temper? It's a reason? and she shook her head.

No, she said. What she got, she got tied up. Somebody she didn't want, the first place. She knew it was wrong. If you know it's wrong, you keep on? You don't know the feeling? You know it's *wrong*. So what do you do? You *got* to love somebody you don't want to? So? You *have* to hate yourself? You can live with it? Turn the hate on me, or Zuz, or anybody else? and I said, You never talked to her? and she said, Talk to what? A dirty mouth? She take the advantage? Not with me. Abba, he likes to screw the neck, a chicken. Sit down. I got a honey, rum, and cream blintz going. Three minutes. So happy you got back, I dance the *harrah*, I bust the ankle. *Oi-veh*.

The radio cut, and the voice spoke rapidly, coldly.

In a sudden movement, all the girls and women got up to crowd the Out doors. A band played the slow chords of the National Anthem, and everyone stood still.

What was that? I asked Bax, at the end, when everyone went out, and Shoshi, head down, back to us, leaned on the table, and I knew she wept.

They found one of us up on the Golan, he said, to the window. They cut off his genitals. Took his head with them. With such people you sign a treaty? The paper, it means something? You trust?

THIRTY

I saw the blue car turn in, and the driver got down to open the door.

A big woman got out, black coat, black hat with a feather in full flight in front, as I remembered both my grandmothers wearing, and sometimes prettier, all black flowers, and little black things sticking out.

Miss Blum, Bax said, behind me. Power behind the throne. Real brain. Only mother the girls ever had. Touch them, nothing save you, and I said, Couldn't they make up their own minds? and he said, They'd have to be right, and I said, They have no choice? and he said, Choice of what? and I said, Well, the man they want to marry, for example.

Look, he said. There's *no* choice. He has to be *right*, and I said, What's right? and he said, He has to add up, that's all. But what's the use of marrying? What's the *use* of it? If you know one day you have to kill them?

I had to look at him to see if he was serious.

He laughed at me, but not the best laugh.

Still you don't know? he said, and I said, Don't know what? and he said, We have to fight for it. Us, *and* the children. You never heard of Massada? It's why I don't want to get married, and I said, You don't want to take the chance? and he said, The chance, yes. But the thought of having to kill them? You can live with it? and I said, I can live with a lot of things if I can have today, *now,* what's denied me tomorrow. To*day, Now.* Give us *this* day our daily bread. Says nothing about tomorrow. When did we ever live for the future? Who can see it?

He sat down. No man ever had a more brilliant, or fearful light in his eyes, as if he saw other worlds.

You believe that? he said, and I said, Why do I say it? And he looked away, and said, Never had that much hope, and I said, Then why work here? and he said, You have to be yourself. We know we can fight. But you can't help thinking. And there's history. Massada. They had to kill themselves. Couldn't happen again? and I said, Certainly. Anytime. But between then and now? Take care of a girl? She takes care of you? Anything better? If it's only from now till tomorrow?

He punched the table, soft butts of the fist.

Never thought of it like that, he said. Here's Blummy.

Miss Blum came in with a look here, a look there, a smile for Bax, and one for me, pulled out a chair and sat down, no help.

I'm so cold I can cry, she said. I'd like some coffee.

I never saw a more perfect complexion, a little more camellia-petal creamy than ivorine, with barely a wrinkle, no make-up, a perfectly shaped crinkly pink mouth with a small line each side deepening when she spoke, and eyes the colour of moonstones, made rivets by thick lenses, hair like Groz's rams' curls hidden under the hat, and extraordinarily small, white hands without rings, natural nails, and an air of the monolith about her, more than a hint of immovability, and despite friendly eyes, almost threatening.

Satisfied? she asked, and I almost blushed.

Sorry, I said. Glad to see you here. Anything I can do? and she said, I'm on my way to Sde Boker. Library of David Ben-Gurion. You can lend me Paula? She always comes with me, and I said, She'll be back any moment, and she said, No hurry. I'll take Bax. He drives better. This man rates a buggy, no horse. You feeling better? and I said, A lot, thanks, and she said, Merom was worried. When he is, the world is. We searched all over. Found you couple of days ago. Nobody fools Merom, and I said, You think a lot of him, and in the middle of lighting a cigaret I saw her eyes in matchflame, wild as a cat's, and she puffed, lifting an arm, pulling back the sleeve, and I saw the number tattoed below the elbow.

He got me out, she said. That's why, and I said, You didn't have a family? and she said, All went. I got done something to. In that butcher's shop. So I studied instead. Take the mind off. Help Merom look after the girls.

Zuz came with the coffee, and blintzes, mincemeat rolls, éclairs.

You got the best place in the country, she said. Like Merom says. Depends the people. I never saw Tâl happier. That's strange. Always the broody one, Merom called her, and I said, There's some idea going round she'll marry a Cabinet minister. Or somebody high up.

She tapped away cigaret ash with some of the delicacy Merom used in handling paper, and took off the spectacles to look out, at the hills. Her eyes were enormous, pale, vaporous.

I didn't hear it, she said. Pretty certain Merom didn't.

Way this country is, she couldn't, and I said, Why? and she put the spectacles on, and took an éclair on a fork.

Well, first place she's like all of us, she said. Her daddy's right. Her mama's not. She's gentile. So? Tâl's in, and not. So's Paula. And all of us. Éclair's the best I had in years. You could send Merom some. Anything he loves, it's éclairs. Can't get, and I said, Say that again about Tâl.

She smiled at me, chewing.

Had a feeling, she said. Tâl's daddy was some kind of new type engineer. Wouldn't work in with the Hitler gang, so they put him in Gelsenkirchen. Always a problem, Tâl, and I said, Do I understand you? Her mother was gentile? and she said, That's right, and I said, What's this about bloodline? and she laughed, and said, Merom's pet. Keep it all in the family. Takes a Book down to the Wall. Pray for strength. The coming days, and I said, You don't?

She shook her head.

I had my share in Belsen, she said. That's all the wall I want the rest of my life. Anybody up there, he forget me and lots of others those years, I can forget him the rest.

This mean Tâl's not bloodline? I asked, and I heard the whisper.

Any more than I am, she said. Could I have some more of this coffee?

Zuz hurried at a nod.

I could just breathe. Some kind of wild storm blew torments.

Would you mind if I left you for a few minutes? I said, I have to change. Just realised how I look.

Miss Blum smiled, and poured coffee.

It should be your only problem, she said.

Bax called me before I left the office, holding up a key. You've been moved, he said, That place belonged to the Collective. Your new place is through the garden. White gate, and your name. Girls been working.

I was glad of Ahmed's blanket, trotting the path through the rose garden. My name in English and Hebrew gave me a curious feeling of being rooted, and the house, a new place, white, with green doors and shutters, made me feel at home in the moment I looked at it. I saw Traul's hand in the garden, and Tâl's hidden smile taunted everywhere.

I went in to a small foyer, opening to a long, broad room, tiled white and orange in big squares, Bedouin rugs, orange and white bases and bookshelves, black leather furniture, posters on the walls, a big kitchen at the end, a dining alcove looking out on the garden, a bathroom in blue and white, a bedroom and on the biggest bed I ever saw, an orange cover, then a dressing room, and a studio, of bookshelves, desks, filing cabinets, and a safe.

Suddenly I felt rich, my lungs were almost too full to take a breath, and my legs trembled.

I went back to the dressing room, and found suits I had never seen in the wardrobe, but my mind was on Beersheba, and I changed the shirt and tie, took the sheepskin, coat, and ran out, through my friends, the jasmine and honeysuckle, and tendrils swept my face in kisses, reminding me.

Tâl's place had been planted, ramblers spread around the walls, everything painted white, grey, and pink. I rang the bell. The door opened, and a Druse girl looked at me with all the appeal of a goat, said something, shook her head, and shut the door.

I looked up at grey snowclouds. They seemed to say it for me.

THIRTY-ONE

I walked back to the plant, for the first time seeing it from another direction, surprised at its size, and new construction under way on the left. I knew I slackened grasp, and made hard resolve to put things right, and went in the first door, out of a kniving wind, grateful for warmth.

Studio Pueris had moved. The size surprised me, but the number of children working, singing to the radio, was far beyond anything I might have imagined. I watched the assembly line working, steadily as any in the adult bays, happy to see the expert way those infant hands used tools, snapped switches, and out in the inspection room, I stood wordless at a line of finished models, each with a Final Inspection tag, waiting for packing.

This, you have to open the mouth, Arendts said, smiling, at the senior inspection desk. You got something, and I said, Blame Mr. Merom, and he shook the spectacles.

Sorry *adonnai,* he said. I laid out the drawings. I *know.*

What next do you have? Children, they like a change, and I said, See me tomorrow.

I thought only of Tâl. I walked through the plant, passed by the café, along the garden, hid behind walls out of snow-wind, to the rock ramp of the old café, a far better place than ours, in size or appointments, and even in winter the gardens were splendid. But the shutters added a drab note of disuse, and I thought of other days, and an unbearable memory of Plus A, and that little hand. She could still hurt. I wondered if any thought of me might make her stop a breath, and turn away.

I heard a shout. Bax waved from the rose arbour.

Tâl, he shouted. Phone, and I ran for my office.

Yes, I said, and her voice came as a ray of light.

Aliya's with us, she said. We met her coming from her lawyer's. She says you've bought the café. She wants to see you. Urgently. And I said, Why not come here? and Tâl said, She doesn't want to meet anybody. She's so different. Apologized for all she did. We're in the café on the right of Yael Daroma. She just heard about Yeke. She's terribly upset. But this is nothing to do with him.

Look, I said. I'll talk to her only if Paula and yourself are there. *Not* unless, and Tâl said, I'll ask her.

In those moments I thought of Yeke, and Arye and Dalia, and Salah, and the two gardeners.

What was it *for?*

She says all right, Tâl said. May I offer a word? Bring Bax. He was based here. Knows everybody, and I said, Good idea. About twenty minutes? and she said, I'm going to be impatient. *Shalom.*

I went in the canteen at the moment Miss Blum started on a third coffee, and I said, Any chance of borrowing the car? Paula can come back in it, and Miss Blum said,

Sure. How far? and I said, Beersheba. That girl Merom doesn't like ran into Tâl. She wants to see me.

I caught the full light, the wild cat light, in Miss Blum's eyes.

Listen, she said, Think again. She can be jailed any time. A whole ring of them. Lucky if she gets ten years, and I said, But for what? and she said, Look, that café was only ever a cover-up. People turned in for a coffee, something to eat, what's easier? Meet, talk, you got it. She ran the place, they used it. There was an Arab here. No more gardener than I am. Architect. Cairo University. One of the top brains. Liberation Front. He's on the Army's most wanted list. Why get into it? and I said, If Tâl and Paula are witnesses, where's the harm?

Miss Blum stubbed the cigaret in hard jabs.

My dead body, she said. Merom has to know this. Give me the phone, and I said, Meantime, I'm gone.

I went out and found Bax.

Come with me, I said. Beersheba. Meeting the two girls, and he said, Great. That town's mine.

The run in that car was a long sweet hum, and Bax drove Army-style, fast but steady, no talk, both hands on the wheel, eyes on the road, and I was trying to think what Aliya could say to me, and what Merom might do, but first I thought of Tâl. Just the idea of being near her was joy from Paradise, and suddenly I was thinking of Yeke, and I knew how he must have felt.

It was no heartener.

We passed the camel market and turned in the one-way, and the girls were sitting in the arcade. Bax stopped and I sat there, looking, and I saw only Tâl.

Aliya, Paula, were part of the housefront.

I followed Bax, and sat down.

Right, I said. What's the trouble?

Aliya took time to drink and look in the cup.

I want to marry a Palestinian, she said.

What's in your way? I asked, and Tâl's knee warmed mine, and flame was in my head.

I'm *agunot*, Aliya said. Divorced. But while my ex- is still alive I can't marry again. At least, in this country. Anywhere else, yes, and I said, So why don't you go? and she said, They took my passport. I'd like to get him away. He doesn't have a passport, either. Once we're somewhere else, we'll be fine. We'd make out. He's bright.

I knew Tâl was looking at me. Her knee was still against mine. I found it strange, but Aliya had lost colour. She seemed in some way shrivelled.

But what can *I* do? I said, and she said, You have influence, and I said, Now, look, Aliya. Do you realize I'm only here on a temporary visa? What influence? and she whispered, You're the only one I know to turn to. Couldn't you help us get out? and I said, Out of where? and she said, Israel. We'd swear never to come back. We'd go to Canada. Look, he's Palestinian. My mother was Saudi. Make things any clearer to you? I believe they're on to him, and I said, What for?

I told you he's Palestinian, she said, and her eyes bled tears shining down to the corners of a mouth I once had kissed.

But listen, I said. What am I supposed to *do?* Tell me. Who'd take any notice of *me?*

Nobody, she said. There's nobody. When you're in trouble, who *is* there? and Paula put a hand on her shoulder.

The idea scorched as lightning.

I took Tâl's hand.

Come with me, I said. I have something to say.

We walked a little way into the arcade.

What's this business about bloodline? I asked her. Anything to do with you?

She stared as if coming awake, and shook her head.

Nothing, she said. My mother was Latvian one side, American the other. My father's mother was Swedish but his father was French. Hebrew. I also have Czech and English here and there. Mixture, pure Diaspora. Ashkenazi cocktail. One shake, who am I?

This is the news I've waited for, I said. Would you want to come to Cyprus with me tonight? Couple of days there, and on to Paris?

She pulled the coat collar tighter at the neck, and looked down.

I saw the scarlet in her face.

The hair shook light.

No, she barely whispered. I can't. I want to. So much. So, so much. But I couldn't hurt Merom. I *couldn't. Couldn't.*

But what's going to hurt? I said. We'd be married, wouldn't we? Or don't you want to be? Or is this the wrong way to ask? Aren't I saying it right? Some kind of law I don't know?

I had to hold her shoulders.

She swayed, and slowly put her arms about my neck, nodding.

I have to call Merom, I said. Could you get him for me? and she nodded again, and said, I *so* want to kiss you, but not here, and I said, You won't. Too good to waste on kibbitzers.

She almost ran in a TV shop, and I shouted to Paula, but she pointed to the road, and Bax came hurrying to meet her, waving a paper at me, and I was on my way down, and Tâl called, waving frantically from the door.

He was whispering *mad,* she said, laughing, but still a

little frightened. I mean, about Aliya. But then I told him about us. He's better now, and she seemed to glow with rarer beauty, newer light.

She stood against me, and held my arm between her breasts.

Hullo, I said, and the voice that spake unto the Prophets said, That you, son? and for the first time I heard the Lord God sound as if he might have been laughing on the hilltops. I just have to tell you. I don't know when I had this kind of a day. I got the *schechinnah*. It's just beautiful. Shining all around. This one was *meant*. How soon can you two get here?

Now, look, I said. So far, I did the thinking and *you* did the talking. Now *I'm* doing the talking, and *you* do the thinking. Don't say *any*thing. Just listen. I want to take Tâl to Cyprus *now*, and marry her. Would you make us a *real* wedding present? That girl at the café. Aliya. She wants to marry that Arab. They don't have passports. They both know they're in trouble. Now, look. You're the one told me we have to work in with the Arabs. Help them all we can. Here're two. If they get taken in, stand trial, go to prison, what good's it going to *do*? One day, there's peace, they're let loose? Look, how can Tâl marry me, and we both know two like us are separated? For years? How could we forget? How do we wake up in the morning? How do we kiss? How do we live a day? It's *us* in there. *Us.* Couldn't you, *can't* you help? Isn't there *any*thing *any*body can *do*? Give us just this. We'll love you. Or else the whole deal's off. I'm looking Tâl in the eyes. I even love the ground she stands on. The air round about her's the same sweet. If they can't marry, we can't. She agrees. Do you?

Silence, the minus—fulminant rumble of the Lord God's mind turning over.

293

You got 'em all *beat*, he whispered. *All* of 'em. The *bunch. Flat.* But I follow the line of reasoning. All right. Put Bax on. You don't have the Hebrew. But stick around.

I called Bax, and strolled down to the café with Tâl, for the first time hand-in-hand, and never felt so near the clouds.

But I was shocked at Aliya's face, fear-lines deep from nose to mouth and beside those staring eyes, pouched, bluish.

Come on, now, I said. Don't lose heart. Where *is* Abu? and she said, Working on the biggest job he ever had at the University. If I can once get him out of the country, we'll have no more trouble. I swear on my mother's heart. It's not patriotism any more. That's why he wants to quit. Killing women and children isn't his way, and I said, What do these Palestinians want, exactly? They're better off now than under the Egyptians?

That's the point, she said. They don't want to be "under" anybody. Any more than you do. They want their own government in their own country. They want to travel on their own passport. Asking too much? and Tâl said, It'll come. But not with bombs, and Aliya nodded, wearily, and said, For that, we want *out*.

Bax came at a trot, wrapped Tâl and kissed her cheek, almost shouting in Hebrew, and then wrapped me, and held up notes.

We don't have much time, he said, and looked at Aliya. Do you know where this man is? he asked, and she said, Yes, and he said, Right. There's a car coming. You tell the driver where. Then you leave the rest to him. No baggage. Just the two of you, and make it fast. No talk. No questions. Follow?

Aliya nodded, and got up, put a hand on Tâl's shoulder, and bent over me, and whispered, I'll never have the words. But lately I prayed a lot. You only pray when you're in trouble. This could be the answer? and Bax said to me, Call Merom in five minutes. He has things to do. Where did Paula go? and Tâl said, Probably in there, looking at the shops. Let's get that number.

Aliya looked at us, and shook her head, and walked away, behind Bax, and we saw her get in the car, fall back, and Tâl said, I know just how she feels.

We went along hand-in-hand to the TV shop, and Tâl dialled and got Merom on the dot, and started laughing, leaned to kiss my cheek, spoke not a word I understood, and gave the receiver to me.

That you, son? The Lord God said, from the mountain top. Now, look. You did *your* talking. Now listen to this. Let Bax handle everything. I have an oil tanker in Ashdod, not far from you. That takes care the other two. The four of *you*, five-thirty, you fly to Cyprus. Two girls one hotel, you two another. Got that?

I don't care where we are as long as she's Mrs. me tomorrow, I said. Then I have everything.

I felt her arms tight about me, and the weight of a head resting heavy against my spine, and put a hand behind, on her thigh, and she pressed towards me, and I knew then that the idea of two becoming one was real, no longer wish, or dream, but solid in the bone and trust of a woman, and she was Tâl, and she was mine.

She took the receiver, and I put my arms around a waist about the substance of a doll's, exquisite in promise.

Her voice ran music in my hands, and she leaned to me, and said, Merom thinks you have a case, and I said, I've got my arms around it and I'm not about to let go, and she said, You hear? and the voice that spoke unto Jacob said, Sounds like he means it. What counts with me. The both of you, couple the saddest cats I ever saw, only this little time, you even *sound* different, and Tâl said, We turned sad into glad.

They spoke Hebrew, and she was laughing again, and gave me the receiver.

That you, son? the Lord God said. I just had the notice. Those two going to be aboard the tanker inside the hour. Get in Larissa tonight. Free as the birds. Free as you two. No problems, and I said, Thank God, and Tâl's arms squeezed my waist.

The four of you going to be met at the airport, Merom said. Tomorrow, eleven o'clock, Tâl and Paula get picked up for the civil marriage office, and I said, Who by? and he said, Me. You think I stay out of this? Listen, you got any money? and I had to think, and I said, No, and he said, Ah, son, what the hell. So you going to get married, another country, no money? Listen, that gal has to take care of you. Put her back, will you? and I gave Tâl the receiver.

I sat down, and saw her laughing and talking, and she bent to kiss, and her hand warmed the back of my head, and she gave me the receiver, and the voice said, Did you have any idea about a wedding breakfast? and I said, No. What for? and he said, What the hell kind of wedding you think you going to have? Listen, the two of you, for life? It's nothing? Children, nothing? So a wedding, everybody rumbling the belly, the place caves in? Tâl's daddy, the Lord God love him, keep him the books, he's alive, you think he go for it? I'm the stand-in, think I do? Listen, a plane-load of Tâl's relations going to be there. Paula's. Bax's. These are big families. Influential, and I said, I thought we were going to have a quiet wedding, and he said, You want it quiet? So, we cancel the band. Listen. Let Tâl handle the money side. She knows where to go. Miss Blum's going to be there with the rings, and I

said, She's going to Sde Boker, and he said, She's hell.
Weddings, the family, who do you think's doing the work?
Listen. You didn't think about flowers, or anything stupid
like that? and I said, No.

Jehovan silence.

Son, just what *is* your idea of a goddam wedding? the
Lord God said, from a long way off, and I said, Take a
girl, sign the papers, she's yours. You're hers. That's *it*.
No argument. She *is* the flowers. She's *every*thing. Without her, *no*thing. There isn't a world without her. That's
all. The world's another place, and he said, I like the
way you talk. Let me ask you a question. What are you
going to call number one? and I said, If he's a boy,
Merom. A girl, Tâl. What else? and he *whispered!* Have
Paula call me, and the line *clicked!*

You broke him up, Tâl said, and I said, So? Let him
mind his own business. Do you realise we have about a
million years to wait till tomorrow? and she said, Wonderful. I'm going to treasure every moment. Sad cats,
achey cats, not any more. Glad ones. The gladdest.
Darling, *ahuvi*. I love you. Life *does* have small, sweet,
moments. This is one. Why do you love me? and I said,
Take five thousand years to answer the question. Feel like
waiting? and she put both those beautiful hands soft to
my face, and said, I already waited too long. *Yakiri!*

And in those moments, once again I stood on a ladder,
reaching out, above the road from Beersheba to Gaza,
and I knew what I had reached for, and her hands were
warm on my face, and I thanked the Lord God, Blessed
be He, for my bride, of Israel.

My love.